I0699144

# ALSO BY FAE QUIN

### SPOOKY BOYS

*Bite Me! (You Know I Like It)*

*Possess Me! (I Want You To)*

*Hunt Me! (I Crave the Chase)*

*There's a Monster in the Woods*

### PNR/OMEGAVERSE

*The Devil Takes*

*King of Hollywood*

### CHRISTMAS DADDIES

*Let Your Hearts Be Light*

*You Can Count On Me*

*If Only In Our Dreams*

# I'M NOT YOUR PET!

## FAE QUIN

# I'M NOT YOUR PET!

Copyright © 2024 by Fae Quin



Cover Art and Interior Artwork by Fae Quin
INSTAGRAM.COM/FAE.LOVES.ART

Typography and Interior Formatting by Molly Phipps
WWW.WEGOTYOUCOVEREDBOOKDESIGN.COM

Edited by Angelo O'Connell

Dedicated to my husband,
**MY PERSONAL PROTECTOR.**


For anyone who wants to be rescued
**BY A SQUISHY PINK SHARK.**

# CONTENT WARNING

A full list of content warnings/tropes are on my website:

## WWW.FAELOVESART.COM

# ONE

## HUGO

**I GOTTA BE HONEST, WHEN** I was accepted into Harvard at the end of my senior year of high school I never once expected I'd end up here, a galaxy away, contemplating sucking a squishy pink alien's dick.

I was open to the idea for a plethora of reasons. I knew I'd get a raise, for one, and that was supremely motivating.

Raises for slaves on F'ukYuu—the pleasure planet—came in the form of jelly-filled donuts, and these weird burrito things full of spongey stuff I didn't recognize but tasted kinda like Mexican food, and sometimes—if we were *really* lucky—an entire night off.

It was the positive side of things I focused on, because if not, the fear of the punishment I would receive for not serving my purpose would consume me.

Punishments were…yeah. I don't even want to go into that.

I'd seen other captives disappear behind the red, red doors that led to the room of "retribution"—as I'd dramatically nicknamed it in my head—and I was fairly certain sucking cock would be far more palatable than anything that happened back there.

*"Make him happy"*, that's what The Manager had commanded. He hadn't given me a step-by-step guide, even though I would've *preferred* that. He'd just pointed at me while I put my translator on, narrowed his four yellow eyes, and directed me toward my "office" of the day to wait.

I'd been assigned this room on a few occasions over the three years since I'd been abducted, and every time, it had been to entertain politicians or the rich.

Though the space was visibly the same as the other pod-like rooms—a round exterior, color-changing lighting, and a pole in the center to dance with—this "entertainment room" was different from the others because of what lay *beneath* the white walls. Somewhere inside it, this pod in particular was outfitted with a non-transmitter device.

This was only necessary because the "elite" who came to visit from other planets didn't want details of their nights here spread around. I'd asked once, and one of the other slaves had explained how it all worked. Which was…endlessly fascinating. What was less fascinating, was the grimace on the other slave's face as they'd wiped their mouth and chugged a glass of water to get rid of the "taste" left behind from their turn in the room.

The translator headset I wore over my ear felt impossibly heavy as I readjusted it for the hundredth time, heart thrumming. The fact I'd been picked for tonight was unsurprising. Just another event to add to the long list of things that'd fucked with me in the past. For example, the reason I had to wear a headset at all.

If I'd been anything but inherently unlucky I would've had one of the permanent translation disks that A&R installed for all humans before "relocation." A&R, short for "Abduction" and "Rehabilitation" was a Space Facility that used advanced technology to abduct and prepare "talented" humans for distribution across the galaxy. The shipment of translators for my group had been stolen by pirates. And after failing the test—rather than bring me back home like I'd hoped they would—they'd dropped me off here, sans translator implant.

The idea that there was a device that could not only translate all the languages in the galaxy but *also* neuro-transmit them directly into the wearer's ear was just—wow. *That* was the kinda shit I'd always dreamed existed. Unfortunately for me, The Manager hadn't thought I was important enough to order a replacement from A&R which meant from that point onward I'd been stuck with temporary headsets only when upper management deemed it necessary.

During my time as a captive on F'ukYuu I'd done my best not to be too crushed by what was happening to me—projecting wonder at the world rather than the fear that simmered deep inside me.

Always pushing forward and looking ahead.

Now that I didn't have power over my life, the only thing I still controlled was my mind, after all. And I'd decided early on that there was nothing I could do but remain positive. Laugh in the face of danger! And enjoy this, in whatever ways I could, otherwise I'd break.

My temporary translator sat centered over my ear like it always was on the occasions that I was blessed to be given one. It offered a little comfort, though there was still a nervous energy buzzing beneath my skin that I couldn't seem to turn off.

*Normally*…no one was supposed to touch us.

Unless we were given extra direction from the higher-ups.

At least…that's what they'd said during orientation.

This was the first time I'd been pulled into The Manager's office and received said "extra instruction." He wasn't a good man, and I'd been unsurprised by his request. In fact, I was shocked it'd taken this long.

It had only been a matter of time, right?

I'd gone three entire years without any "special requests". I figured I should be grateful. It wasn't like I hadn't thought about sucking dicks before. Because I had. Plenty of times. A thousand. Maybe more? I'd just…never really had the opportunity or guts to do it.

Besides, who would want their dick sucked by me of all people?

*Stay positive, Hugo.*

*Who cares if this is your job?*

*You get to touch a real-life person!*

*An alien!*

That's what I told myself as I prepped for the customer and hyped myself up about my first *ever* sexual encounter. To be honest, I'd been a little disappointed when I'd finished orientation and realized that "pleasure slave" was synonymous with "space stripper." Which meant instead of hooking up with a butt-load—literally, ha!—of interesting organisms, I more than likely would die a sad, lonely little virgin.

So really, this was a *good* thing.

*It was.*

I'd ace it.

I totally would.

The room felt smaller than ever as I squirmed in my uniform—a pair of black shorts that left literally nothing to the imagination. They'd chafed at first, but now I barely noticed, even when they rode up my butt when I danced. Pulling at the metal collar The Manager had quite literally welded around my neck on my first day, I did some jumping jacks to warm up while I waited to see what kinda creature I'd meet this time.

Hopefully, it was someone vaguely humanoid.

As I stretched, my thoughts wandered.

Don't get me wrong, the work didn't bother me.

Honestly, seeing the different species was fun as hell. For a guy who'd never left his hometown but was obsessed with strange, fascinating species, working with clients from across the galaxy was kind of a dream come true.

I mean, our clients came from planets scattered all over the galaxy, which made this an occupation that never grew boring. Once, I even gave a lap dance to a dude with three heads and *four* thumbs. You got that right. Four *thumbs*.

Fuckin' wild.

He worked as an "accountant" for a firm three planets away and had been attending a bachelor party for his wealthy friend. Whatever the galactic equivalent for a bachelor party was, anyway. As far as I could tell, the accountant-guy was the only one in his group who had four thumbs, so I wasn't really interested in the others.

What was the purpose of that, anyway?

Four thumbs?

He'd be a whizz at opening bottles.

*Anyway*, he'd enjoyed his night in "Space Vegas" and I'd enjoyed asking him questions, because it had been one of the rare occasions—before now—that I'd used this room and was given a translator to wear.

Distracting myself by interrogating him had made the night go by swiftly. Now, however, even the prospect of talking to someone new was not enough to divert my attention from what I was expected to do. Even without the translator, I knew that this customer was important. I mean, *obviously*. Because of the whole "SUCK HIS DICK OR DIE" thing. The translator only further solidified that.

I hoped I'd eventually climb up the ranks high enough The Manager would let me get a replacement implant from A&R. I knew they were expensive. But it would be nice to have something that would lend me more permanent understanding. I had about a thousand questions, and I wished I could ask them whenever I wanted.

The GPS-locked translators were okay, though.

Even if I only got to use them for really important clients.

Like this guy.

My current customer who had just opened through the door.

Who was…apparently pink.

And squishy.

Like Jell-O.

I'd gaped, maybe a bit rudely, when he'd stepped inside the room. With a quiet *click*, the door had shut behind him and he'd paused directly in front of it, ogling me for a beat as I ogled him right back. In my defense, he'd closed the door by shooting out a thousand tiny prehensile tentacles. Though…I wasn't sure if that was an accurate name for them, as they reminded me more of ropey bubblegum than something an octopus would have. "Tendril" was more fitting.

The guest seemed to shapeshift effortlessly—his tendrils disappearing just as quickly as they had formed, leaving his upper limbs arm and hand-like once again.

Just pink.

And—did I mention *pink*?

Which was just…so fucking cool.

Aside from being able to transform, his appendages looked fairly "normal". Five fingers. Even fingernails, though those were more like claws. Other than the fact they were partially see-through, and clearly made of the same mystery organic substance as the rest of his body, they weren't all that odd.

Which was…a relief, to say the least—considering where the night was sure to end.

Pink-guy was humanoid, like I'd hoped. Bipedal, with a man-shaped frame—giant pillowy pecs and a musculature that if I *squinted,* wasn't all that different from a human male. His belly was thick, as was everything about him. And luckily for me, he even had an "acceptable" number of thumbs and heads.

Which apparently was a standard of mine now.

That was where the similarities to my species ended, however.

As he stood there, right in front of the door, observing me, I shivered.

Just how goddamn *tall* was he?

At least seven feet. No—fuck, maybe eight? Nine. *Definitely* nine.

Easily one of the largest aliens I'd encountered.

And the teeth. He had to have a *thousand* of them. Which made sense, considering his head was the size and shape of a shark's. Maybe a great white? That was the closest comparison I could think of.

*Hello, Bruce. Humans are friends, not food.*

When he finally moved it was at a glacial pace.

Like, painfully slow.

If I didn't know any better, I'd think he was worried he would frighten me if he moved too fast. Which…if that was true…I genuinely appreciated it, because holy *fuck*. This was just—wow. Giant shark-man. Giant muscle-y pink shark-man.

And I was going to touch his dick.

Oh my god.

I stumbled back a little, trying not to look as nervous as I felt as my cock perked up and my bare back touched the outer shell of the room.

Slowly, carefully, he took his seat on the bench that ran along the edge of the circular room.

The lights were flickering, pink, blue, and yellow. His spots, because he had *spots*, were gray at first. Which meant because they had no color of their own, they took on whatever shade the lights shifted to as he sat still, big thighs spread, and waited.

I wasn't sure if I was supposed to just…you know, dive in? Or if I was expected to dance like usual. Erring on the side of caution, I began to move. The shark-man's pale blue eyes flickered over me as I swiveled my hips to the beat. I couldn't make sense of the expression on his face. He was hard to read. But his spots were changing color on their own now— so that had to be a good thing right?

Pink, red, pink, gray. Pink, gray, red.

After three years of doing this for hours every day, it was safe to say that I'd gotten so used to dancing that it was second nature now. I hardly had to think about it as I bent over and shook my ass, other than to make sure my hips were tilted at the right angle to flash him the full curve of my scrawny butt.

Curiously, I tried to peek at the bulge between his legs to see if my display was working. And also because I figured if I was going to be sucking him off, I should get an idea of what I'd be touching, right?

One glance was all it took to confirm that shark-man was packing *for sure.* A thick bulge sat between his massive thighs cupped tight by his trousers. I wasn't sure if that was a good or bad thing. But I tried not to get nervous—even though that was a moot point. I couldn't fail at this. I couldn't. I was actually kinda excited, dammit. I mean…he was hot, right? If you were open to that sorta thing.

When I reached back to frame my ass he *growled.*

That was a good thing, right?

*Growling?*

I don't know.

He was harder to read than my other clients. And he was staring, not necessarily like he wanted to shove me onto his dick—but more like…he found me as fascinating as I found him. When our eyes met, something in his gaze called to the darkest, loneliest parts of me. It was odd. I'd done this hundreds of times but never…never like *this.*

Never for someone who looked at me like he was actually *seeing* me.

Like I was a person, not a body.

I hadn't felt this raw since the day A&R had dropped me off in this godforsaken place.

It was strange.

So fucking strange.

Because I'd spent the first portion of my life invisible—and now I was here, front and center. I'd been the object of desire for so many aliens I'd lost count. I'd been ogled, lusted after, and longed for.

But until this moment I'd never been *seen.*

*I'm scared.*

It wasn't a thought I'd allowed myself to have, especially not while working. It didn't help. Just like mourning my old life didn't. Just like being sad didn't. I'd shoved those feelings down as far as they could go until they were buried beneath my observations, my notes, my excitement. But…unbidden, they rose to the surface.

*I'm scared.*

*I'm scared.*

Not of him. But of this place. Of these people. Of the fact that one day—if not today—those red, red doors would push open for me. It was only a matter of time before I made a mistake. Before it was my turn to face punishment. With *that* reminder and newfound determination, I tried to focus.

*Shake your ass, Hugo. That's what he's here for.*

*Make him happy or today will be that day.*

I peeked over my shoulder again—because I couldn't help myself—to see that his attention hadn't wavered. His cock was thickening up. At least…I thought it was? I hoped I hadn't messed this up already. We'd kinda had a moment, but again, I wasn't sure if that was a *good* thing.

I felt naked, in more than one way.

Trying to find confidence again, I stopped jerking my ass like a red-capped manakin performing a mating dance and grabbed on to the pole. *This would be better.* If I was spinning, I couldn't keep looking at his face—couldn't see the way he watched me. I could build up the mood again. *I could salvage this.* For both of us.

*Make him happy.*

*Don't fuck this up.*

*Put on a good show.*

The cold metal of the pole was familiar enough to be comforting as I latched on tight. The sweat on my hands made me slip more than usual, but I still somehow managed to climb higher anyway. Up, I went, swinging round and round.

The walls and floor blur, blur, blurred as I swung in arching loops. The music reached a crescendo. The pole stuck to my bare, sticky skin, clinging to the back of my knee and the inside of my elbow as I swooped down. Breathless, my toes dragged across the floor before I swung my legs high all over again.

I'd never conversed with a shark-man before. Four-thumbed aliens, yes. Creatures with dozens of eyes, fur, and oddly shaped limbs. Beasts in every color of the rainbow (mostly.) But *never* a shark-man. Which was why I'd gotten so distracted by him earlier—not because of the way he looked at me. Nope. Totally not.

Spinning helped a little, but not enough. Every time I swooped around and he came into focus, it was like something magnetic pulled me in.

The floor was chilly against my bare feet when I dismounted. As I paused to catch my breath, my chest heaved. Inhaling greedily, I forced my hips to move to the beat again, dragging a hand down my torso and watching enraptured as the shark-man's animalistic eyes followed the movement.

The spots that decorated the top of his head, down his back, and across the backs of his massive biceps shifted colors again, slower this time. *Was it like…a chameleon thing?* Only that didn't make sense, because the booth was white—and his spots very much were not. I tilted my head curiously to the side, as they shifted pink, pink, gray, gray, gray.

Huh.

*Maybe it's a mood thing?*

And if so, what the hell did red, pink, and gray mean?

Hopefully at least one of them meant horny.

*I'm scared.*

The thought came back, and I hated that it did.

I hoped he wouldn't notice. Because again, it wasn't him I was scared of. It was what awaited me outside this room. What awaited me if I failed.

When he spoke I was *not* prepared. He'd been totally silent the entire time we'd been in here. Which wasn't unusual. Some aliens didn't speak, even with translators. I hadn't really thought anything of it, because— again, he was a fucking shark. Sharks didn't talk. Except that he apparently did, and could.

I had just bent over again, legs spreading wider as I slid my hands up the backs of my thighs, my tiny black shorts doing nothing to hide the wag of my ass.

"Enough," he said simply, the crackly low rumble of his voice shifting through the air as the device I had over my ear transformed the words.

Enough?

What did he *mean* "enough"?

Wasn't this why he was here?

For a second, I was offended. It had taken me almost six entire months to get my lap-dance skills down. These hips were not made for wagging. At least, they hadn't been before. I had never been physically gifted at anything. Not even video games—though one could argue those were far harder to master than most sports.

You could blame my dad, really.

We'd never played catch.

"Enough," that same growly, rumbly voice sounded.

He's probably tired of you stalling.

Not that *that* was what I was doing. Because it wasn't. I was *excited*, dammit. Even if I was admittedly kinda terrified too. But that was because of my inexperience and had nothing to do with whether or not I found him attractive.

Apparently shark-aliens did not like eye candy—or foreplay.

Nerves danced in my belly as I tried to figure out what to do next. How was I supposed to seduce him without *seducing* him? Should I just get on my knees?

Was that why he'd said he'd had enough?

Tall, pink, and sexy's translator blinked where it sat against the earless sides of his head. Did he have a tympanum like a lizard? Or three semicircular canals like the sharks on Earth? Either way, he could clearly hear—or he wouldn't be wearing a translator. He looked mildly uncomfortable, if the tension in his body was any indicator. Though that could have easily been arousal.

Maybe I should say something?

As Sharky shifted his muscular body, thighs spreading wide, I got the hint.

*It's time.*

*He wants you to get on your knees.*

Right.

Okay.

I could do this.

I could be sexy.

I totally could.

*Breathe, Hugo.*

*You can do this.*

I dropped to my knees, the cold metal floor leaching the heat from my bare skin. My collar felt like it weighed about a thousand pounds all of a sudden. Barely a second passed, and the shark-man made a noise that sounded suspiciously like a gasp. *That had to be a good thing.* I hoped so anyway. Back on Earth I'd been what most would consider nerdy enough to be undateable. The sexiest thing I'd ever done was win a chess competition.

Here though? I was considered hot shit for aliens. Like catnip. But nerd-nip. My scrawny ass could make their multitude of eyes practically pop out of their heads. And I didn't even have to try to do it.

Not that I didn't try. Because I did. Because I was a *perfectionist*—and even though this wasn't my choice—it was my lot in life. I'd never been able to stomach the thought of not doing my best, even for something like this.

*Keep going.*

I knee-walked forward till his calves framed my body and those big-ass thighs sandwiched my shoulders. The alien didn't move to push his pants down or anything, even with me between his thighs.

In fact, he was rigid—frozen still.

Kinda like he had no idea what was happening right now.

His legs were even *larger* up close. I didn't dare touch them, even though I kinda wanted to—not even because I'd been told to, but because they looked comfortable. However, they were the only part of his body that was clothed. Which made them less interesting than his barrel chest and muscular arms.

*Is he sticky like bubblegum?*

*I can't wait to find out.*

Was I supposed to undo his pants for him? Would they be difficult to get off if his skin was sticky?

It hadn't occurred to me that I hadn't spoken a word. Not until that moment, with his crotch in my face and his pale blue eyes staring down at me. I shivered, cold all over.

How hard could this really be?

Lick-lick, suck-suck, done-done.

It'd be fine.

I reached for the button on the alien's pants. His nostrils flared. His chest began *heaving*. When his sharp teeth flashed, my belly flipped. A flood of butterflies spun frantic circles inside me as I got the button on his pants open and attempted to pull down his zipper.

"No," he said, the deep rumbling growl making my hair stand on end. Immediately, I froze, hands beginning to shake. What had I done wrong? Hadn't he requested this? Did he not like me? Oh fuck. Oh fuck. I'd already fucked this up.

*"Make him happy,"* The Manager had said.

*This* was not happy.

This was annoyed.

"Please?" I offered, suddenly kinda terrified. "I need to. I mean. They said that I—"

He growled, this deep ominous sound, and my hands went icy. I removed them from his general vicinity, the limbs quaking as I settled them on my bare thighs and tried to understand where I'd gone so very wrong.

The sound he was making was almost…*distressed.*

"Please don't growl. I didn't—I mean, I didn't mean to upset you. I thought this was what you wanted." My heart was hammering. Red doors flashed in front of my eyes. "I'm—" My words cut off as I released a distressed sound of my own.

*I'm scared.*

My words had some sort of effect because the growl the shark-man had been emitting softened into what was almost a purr. Like he was trying to *soothe* me now, rather than warn me away. Tentatively, he reached down. For a moment his hand hovered above my head, like he was afraid to touch. When I nodded jerkily, giving him permission, his hand crossed the last of that distance, gently stroking over my hair. It felt wonderful to be touched. I wasn't sure why he was doing it—all things considered— but I couldn't help but melt into it despite that.

Peering at him through my lashes, confused and a little freaked out, I let the gentle scratch of his thick fingers soothe me. His hand was so large— *Christ.* He had to move so carefully not to hurt me. We were at an impasse as his chest heaved with each ragged inhalation, his spots gray, yellow, gray.

Fear made my hands shake.

"I'm sorry," I managed again, confused and more than a little terrified. "I thought you wanted me." I couldn't fail this. I *couldn't.* I couldn't- couldn't-couldn't. A distressed whine escaped before I could stop it.

"It is alright, little one," he rumbled, the quiet purr of his voice far more soothing than it should've been. The shape of the words did not match what I heard in my head, but it was still comforting. "You do not know what you ask of me." His chest was still shuddering, those big thighs framing my face. But the bulge in his pants was soft. His earlier arousal had faded. *I hate failing. I can't-I can't-I can't.*

To my disgust, my lashes were wet with tears as I clenched my hands into fists.

*They're going to punish you for this.*

"*Please*," I begged again, not sure what I was asking for. "Tell me what I did wrong. I'll fix it." Clearly I'd gotten something incorrect. Maybe if I showed my sincerity he'd take pity on me and tell The Manager that I'd done a good job, even though I quite obviously hadn't?

Shark-guy shushed me. It was a sweet sound, despite being different than something a human would make. He didn't have the lips to make a proper *shhhh* noise. The effect was the same though. Still soothing. Still soft. The scratching continued, and though I was shaking—it did help.

I should've been scared when he lifted his hand from my hair, moving to gently stroke one thick finger over the wetness that clung to my cheek, but I wasn't. When he cupped my jaw, the warm stickiness of his skin pressing to mine only amplified the magnetic force crackling between us.

I wasn't sure what he saw in my eyes.

It felt like he was looking through me. Like he could see where I was brittle and lost, his pale blue eyes searching, searching, searching mine.

*I'm scared,* I thought again, a pit in my belly.

The shark's spots turned blue, a tranquil sort of color. Like the ocean painting my mom had put above the toilet in the guest bathroom.

His skin was warm and solid. Maybe not the same kind of solid that mine was—but certainly pleasant. I'd take the time to analyze that later. He'd be the newest entry in my journal. I'd compare him to other organisms I'd studied and see if I could find a creature with a similar texture, just for fun. But for now, I trembled, another tear slipping down my cheek.

*Men don't cry, Hugo.*

My father's voice accompanied me all the way across the galaxy.

It was the only thing he'd taught me.

"Calm," shark-man urged, using the grip he had on my head to nudge me to settle against the inside of his knee. At first, I thought that this meant blow jobs were back on the table, but I was quickly proven wrong. No. Apparently, *calm* meant literally that. It meant *breathe.* It meant slow the fuck down and enjoy the squishy softness of the big-ass thigh against my face.

The alien's hand returned to my hair, gently petting me. Now that he was touching me it was even more apparent how aware of his overwhelming size he was, careful of his claws and how easily I could be crushed. He smelled like *apples,* and I inhaled the scent greedily. When my eyes slipped shut, it became clear the only thing alien-man wanted from this interaction was to soothe me.

Until that moment, no one had ever done that for me. Not even before—when I'd been a real person, and not…whatever it was that I was now.

It was comfort in the purest sense.

A strong creature lending his strength to someone who was smaller.

A lion and a mouse.

This was care and *concern.* An emotion that felt suspiciously like affection—though I knew that couldn't be what it was. Not after only knowing each other for fifteen fucking minutes.

Affection was hard-earned.

You fought for it, tooth and nail. And even then, usually you didn't get it. Sometimes it felt like a myth. A fairy tale for children who came from happy homes. Children who grew up with bedtime stories, cookies on the table, and party hats for their birthdays.

I was embarrassed to admit the few tears I'd spilled turned into a torrent. With every gentle scratch of his claws and every soothing rumble, I cracked a little more. I hadn't expected this. And while I'd tried to tell myself that I was ready for what the night entailed, I hadn't been. I realized that now, as alien-guy gave me the first human decency it felt like I'd ever had.

I rolled with the punches, sure. When I'd gotten abducted I'd been upset, *obviously*. But I'd accepted my new role in life quickly. However, at twenty-one now, I knew how rare a touch this sweet could be. Like a unicorn, even in space.

While I quaked and sobbed, the alien continued to rumble. The sound buzzed through his body, vibrating my cheek as I pressed hard against his knee. Tucked between his hand and his leg, I had never felt safer.

Ridiculous.

I was fucking ridiculous.

He was about to leave. I'd never see him again. I was going to face the consequences of my actions. And the empathy he'd shown me surely wouldn't extend to telling The Manager I'd done a good job when I hadn't. My weakness would be my downfall. This embrace would fester and mold till it became just another snapshot of all the times I'd had my heart torn out.

For now though…I was content to pretend. To be comforted and loved, even if it was only for a few moments, by a stranger I had disappointed.

This alien was a goddamn saint, apparently.

Because I didn't stop crying for a long, long time.

And when I finally did, he urged my chin up with one thick finger. His chest shuddered as he inhaled. If I didn't know any better, I'd think he looked just as overwhelmed as I felt. He bent his head low and those terrifyingly sharp teeth crept closer and closer to where I crouched.

"Pretty one, do not cry," his voice was soft and sweet. Awkward. Nervous. Like he'd never comforted someone before and he had no idea what he was doing. "It will be okay."

It wouldn't, but hearing that meant more to me than he probably realized.

"I will *make* it okay," he added, a promise I knew would be broken the second those doors swung shut behind him.

My head spun and spun.

*Pretty one, pretty one, pretty one.*

*I will make it okay.*

No one had ever called me *pretty* before. I'd been called plenty of things. Smart, stubborn, sweet. Gullible, forgiving, blind. But *never* pretty.

Pretty was a word reserved for girls, action stars, and botanical gardens. It was a delicate word. Soft. It smelled like fresh cut fruit and springtime blossoms. If it had a sound, it'd ring like bells. *Pretty* was the shade of my mother's lipstick.

It wasn't for me.

Or at least…I hadn't thought it was.

Until now.

My pulse thrummed.

*Pretty one, pretty one, pretty one.*

*I will make it okay. I will make it okay. I will make it okay.*

My shaking hands stilled. The big pink beast stroked the path my tears had taken. His gaze was heavy but soft. As unreadable as it'd been since he'd entered the room. And…just like that, I knew my time was up.

That the petting was over.

And that his promise was about to be broken.

Even still, when he helped me to my feet, his hands were warm, warm, warm. His grip was commanding as he guided me through the door ahead of him out of my pod. Normally I'd wait in here on my own, but

I didn't have it in me to tell him that. We'd been inside for long past when we were supposed to. If my lack of blow job-giving wasn't cause for punishment, that surely was.

One of his massive palms stayed on the small of my back the entire time we walked, traveling down the hallway toward the front desk together to face my doom.

*He's going to complain.*

The thought made me feel sick all over again. Rather than argue, or try to run—a stupid idea—I simply accepted my fate. Slumping, I stared at the chilly floor and my bare feet, and tried not to break right in half.

As kind as he was—as gentle—I had no doubt there would be nothing but complaints about my service. I didn't know what that would mean for me, but it certainly wouldn't end in jelly-filled donuts.

But that didn't matter.

It didn't matter, because no matter *what* it was, I would take my punishment like a champ.

Because for the first time in my life, I was pretty, pretty, *pretty*.

Even if I was also pretty screwed.

# TWO

## ROARK

## THE PREVIOUS NIGHT

**F'UKYUU WAS MY LEAST FAVORITE** planet on our route. I was not the kind of beast that partook in what the godforsaken place had to offer. I found it unpalatable. Downright wrong. Especially when most of the people who were employed—at least in the pleasure venues—had been wrongfully abducted and relocated against their will.

Which was why I couldn't believe the fact that I was standing outside one of those same facilities.

Mala—my first in command—was beside me. A group of the younger recruits had wanted to visit one of the larger venues to look at the merchandise on offer. That's what The Managers that ran such establishments called the people there. *Merchandise.* As though they were property.

On our home planet such things were illegal.

Mala told me to loosen up, but it was difficult to look past my own morality. Even for the recruits who I loved as though they were my own blood.

"It's been a stressful trip," Mala had said earlier that day over breakfast. And I knew…I *knew* he was right. "We're here for three days. Let them blow off some steam."

Despite the fact that our species was one of the largest and most physically powerful on this side of the galaxy, I still hadn't been able to stomach the idea of letting the cadets travel alone. They were young and inexperienced. And most looked at our species and wanted to take advantage of the money we were often associated with. So Mala and I had offered to escort them to one of the more reputable pleasure houses, and wait to accompany them home.

It was that offer that had gotten me into this mess in the first place.

Because while I'd told myself countless times that I had no business at this end of the planet, I couldn't seem to help but look. Pity and shame curled cold and hard in the pit of my stomach as I watched the windows on the building light up one by one. I knew that they only did this when there were shift changes. New entertainers would swap with the old, the darkened glass flooded bright as they took their positions to act as living advertisements.

Like mannequins, they'd stay impossibly still, often posed provocatively to entice more visitors.

Species of all kinds flickered into focus as the lights in the windows turned on and Mala and I settled in for a long wait. I tried not to openly observe. It seemed rude to do so. Part of me was tempted to break the glass and free them all, but I knew that would cause more problems than it would solve.

Pirates ran amuck here—the very pirates that had caused our trip through space to be as stressful as it had been. Freeing the slaves would only result in them getting stolen again—and placed in establishments far less safe than these. Additionally, it would put a target on our backs. And as the largest cargo ship that traveled to and from our home planet, it was imperative I got the supplies home safely.

It still felt wrong though.

Even though I knew all of this.

Maybe it was my childhood that caused me to feel this way. But I'd always had a hard time stomaching the idea of leaving the weak to fend for themselves.

"Not everyone operates under the same strict moral code that you do," Mala reminded me, as if he was reading my mind. "I agree with you, for the record." The other Sahrk jerked his head toward the windows, still steadily lighting up as dancers took their shifts in the tiny booths. "But you and I both know we have no power here. If you empty the windows they'll simply fill again. And you'll put all of us in danger." Mala sighed, and I nodded, though I hated that he was right.

"I don't understand why they want to go inside in the first place," I grumbled, even though I *did* understand. This was their first voyage. They hadn't seen what I had during my years in space. They were curious. And in our culture, there was nothing to prohibit them from looking. It was only touching that was taboo.

"Yes, you do," Mala called me out. His blue skin caught the flickering street lights as he shifted his weight, arms crossed over his bare chest. "You were young and curious once."

"Not like that."

"Yeah," Mala snorted, head tossing back, his pearly white teeth flashing.

"I suppose that's giving you too much credit. You're right. Not like that." He slanted me a coy smirk, and I head-butted him playfully.

We hadn't met until my fifth voyage. But even then, I'd been the way I was now. Jaded. Traumatized. Unable to let go.

Another window flicked on, and I swiveled to look at it without thinking. Mala didn't speak again as he straightened. Which was good. Because the second my eyes caught on the newest dancer my thoughts fizzled out entirely.

He was different from the others.

Bipedal, like I was. With downy orange fur on his head. Spots all over. *Thousands* of them. Like the constellations I'd coveted as a child. Like space. Unlike the other dancers, he sported no tentacles, no suckers, no claws or sharp teeth. Harmless, he stood stock-still, dressed in nothing but a tiny pair of black shorts that left absolutely nothing to the imagination.

He glanced behind himself at the now-shut door he'd entered through. When it was obvious he was alone and whoever had urged him into his booth was gone, he relaxed. And then…he did something entirely unexpected. Rather than take his position, he…simply sat down.

With his back to the wall in the tiny booth, he pressed his peachy face to the glass till it fogged. I watched, enraptured, as he traced designs inside the condensation. Constellations, just like the ones I'd been thinking about, formed beneath his clever fingers.

It was such an odd display considering where and what he was.

My hearts thumped erratically, a ringing in my ears that only grew louder the longer I stared. It felt like the ground beneath my feet was shifting, even though I knew it wasn't.

"Roark?" Mala's voice startled me, but I couldn't look away from the tiny dancer.

*I couldn't.*

"I…" My breath caught, my hands clenching into fists as the small creature puffed along the glass some more to keep himself distracted. The other performers had taken their poses by that point. All were more provocative than he was. And yet…none of them caught my attention the way he did.

He looked…

*God.*

He was beautiful.

So different and yet—

"That's a huu-man," Mala explained, leaning into my side, observing what I was. We'd been friends for long enough I'd lost count of the years. He knew me better than anyone, aside from my childhood caregiver from the orphanage, or Ushuu, the man who had taken me under his wing when I was a cadet.

"A huu-man?"

"They're from a planet called Earth," Mala added. Because again, he knew me. So he understood that something was happening here—even if he didn't know what it was. "I've been seeing them pop up more and more around the galaxy lately. A&R's newest hot ticket item."

*Had I truly been so focused on my duties that I hadn't paid attention?*

The answer was right in front of me.

"He's…"

"Gorgeous?" Mala supplied. "Yeah, he is."

Mala was married, and should therefore not be commenting about anyone else's gorgeousness.

I growled at him, and he laughed.

"He looks so…" I managed, still staring at the peach-colored creature. He'd stopped drawing now and was instead peering down the street, fingers cupping the glass like he was trying to see through it. That only confirmed what I'd suspected, that it was difficult for the dancers to see out. In a horrible way it made sense. Less distractions.

After a moment, he settled, arms curled around his knees, his head resting against them while he waited.

Knowing he couldn't see me made me relax a little.

I wasn't at my best, after all.

And I was sure my spots were an ugly shade.

"He looks so…?" Mala wheedled.

"He looks so *lonely*," I managed, because he *did*.

He looked lonely.

So fucking lonely.

The only one of his kind.

No doubt frightened out here—in a world that wasn't his own. Surrounded by creatures that didn't understand him.

I could relate. Though I was on a crew full of Sahrks, I had never met someone who understood the bone-deep loneliness I often felt. Like because I looked and sounded like the others, I was supposed to fit in, even though I never had.

"Maybe you should go keep him company," Mala suggested.

And though I hated the thought—I hated the idea of leaving without speaking to the huu-man even more.

The small creature was even more interesting up close. At first, I hadn't been sure I'd made the right choice in requesting him. It'd been something I'd mulled over all night, only to come to the conclusion that I could not live with myself if I did not.

I was now glad I'd trusted my gut, as meeting him in person had led me to realize that my feelings the night before had not been a fluke. He interested me in a way no other creature ever had. So many things about him were curious, like the fact he leaked when he was sad. *Tears.* That's what they were called. I'd heard of them, yes, but Sahrks did not leak—so the term wasn't something I'd often thought about.

There were other interesting things too. Like how soft his fur was. How lovely his spots looked in person. How small and frail he appeared and yet was able to move so sensually and with such strength. Or how watching the curve of his back, and the shape of his ass had made my blood heat in a way it never had before.

Most interesting of all, however, had been his proposal.

Only minutes into our first meeting and he'd asked to *mate* with me.

My denial of his proposition had obviously upset him. I figured he didn't know what he was asking me. Physical intimacy was something that was saved for one's mate. And though, at the time, I'd felt like I was doing the right thing, I wasn't so sure now.

I did not like the way he leaked because of me.

After I'd asked to speak with The Manager to sing his praises, the small creature had been sent away. Because if there was one thing I was certain of after our encounter, it was the fact that I could not leave him without making sure The Manager knew what a wonderful job he'd done. At the moment, it was all I could do to ensure his safety.

I'd promised.

My reputation proceeded me.

The Manager's gaze was assessing the moment we were alone, yellow eyes narrowed. Creatures like him were common in my line of work. Give them an inch and they'd take a mile. Unfortunately for me, he had a rather lovely bargaining chip.

"You like him much," The Manager cooed, money signs practically dancing in his beady gaze. I was used to this reaction to my species. Sarhks were known for their generosity and abundant wealth. We rarely left our planet, which meant when we did, we often encountered greed. "He is for sale if you are interested."

The idea of purchasing a person was abhorrent, but I said nothing, aware that my words would only end in tragedy for the huu-man. Other slaves walked by the glass window of the office I'd been led to, all scantily clad, flushed and sweaty from a long day's work dancing.

The door was shut, so the room was quiet.

Still, my ears roared.

The huu-man did not have fangs, the way I did. He did not have claws. He was defenseless. Weak. There was no way for him to fight back against this man or anyone here. Luckily for him, I had all of those things. And while I knew that I couldn't free all of the aliens here, perhaps I could…free one?

"How much?" I asked, the translator beeping in my ear as The Manager debated with himself. I already knew he was about to state a price far higher than he would give a man of any other species.

"One million," he replied, then grimaced. "Actually, two million," he corrected himself, his eyes narrowed. "*That* particular specimen was considered intelligent on his planet."

I found his comment interesting. It was common knowledge that A&R were notoriously picky with the creatures they abducted. Anyone who did not meet the cut was dropped off here, or the more rural planet, U'Suhk. He must be quite clever to have been abducted in the first place. I felt immense empathy for him—knowing that he could've ended up somewhere far better than here if only he'd passed the test.

Poor little one.

He had probably been so frightened when it happened.

He was probably *still* frightened.

At least if the looks he'd been giving me all night were to be believed. Like he was begging me to save him. Like he trusted me to do so—despite not knowing me at all.

I wasn't sure what I should do.

Ethically speaking, the idea of buying someone disgusted me. I was attracted to him, yes. He'd make a perfect, although unorthodox, mate. Truly, I'd never been interested in taking one until the moment he'd sunk to his knees and his proposal had made my hearts race.

"Two million," I repeated as my thoughts swam in circles. "Two million and he can come with me?"

"Correct."

I'd promised the huu-man I would make things okay.

I just…wasn't sure the best way to go about that.

In a daze, I went back to the ship for the night to figure out what to do.

I did my best to act casual as I prepared dinner, but Mala saw through me. He'd been the only person who knew I was heading back to the pleasure houses. And before I could even sit down on the bench beside him, his spots were green with curiosity. He paused, a bite of bambuu halfway to his mouth, eyes searching mine. I took my seat, preparing for the worst as my plate clinked against the table.

"Something is wrong," he accused.

"Nothing is wrong," I reassured, far too quickly to be telling the truth.

"It is." His eyes narrowed and his sharp teeth snapped with amusement. He glanced around the room to make sure we were alone, confirmed the coast was clear, then cocked his head at me. "Tell me what happened."

It was not my way to overshare with my crew, even Mala, who I considered to be my closest friend. However…the huu-man's dark eyes haunted me even now. I swallowed, embarrassed that my own spots were sure to betray me.

"*Roark*," Mala softened his tone, moving closer. "It is unlike you to act so uncertain. Tell me what's wrong so that we can fix it."

"I…" I pushed my plate away, suddenly no longer hungry.

How could I eat when I knew my huu-man even now was sitting inside that godawful place wondering why I would reject him? I swallowed the lump in my throat again, lowered my head, and explained.

"I don't see why you can't just buy him," Mala said when I was finished. He crossed his arms over his chest, his pale blue biceps bulging. "It is not as though any of us would mind. There are no rules against interspecies mating."

"He may not even want a mate," I said softly. "He does not know our ways. His proposal was more than likely a misunderstanding."

"Still." Mala paused for a moment as he mulled over what he was going to say next. "You said you could smell his arousal?"

"Yes."

"So he was attracted to you."

"He could've been confused," I countered. "He was frightened of the situation."

"But not of you."

That…I wasn't certain of. I didn't think so. But the whole thing had been confusing for the both of us. When I'd stroked his hair he'd melted, and his eyes had…well… His eyes had spoken what his words did not.

My gut told me that he wanted me as badly as I wanted him.

But all of this was new and foreign, and I wasn't sure my instincts knew what was real—or if it was wishful thinking on my part.

"I want to save him," I said softly. Admitting that *hurt.* "But…I don't want him to think he's trading one cage for another."

"You said yourself that you don't think he knows what he offered you," Mala countered. "Why not let him make the first move?"

"Bring him aboard…" I murmured, thoughts spinning. "And see if he tries to initiate something after he is free?"

"Right." Mala bobbed his head. "Then you'll know for certain that it wasn't just the situation. And that he's as serious as you are about mating." Sahrk's mate for life. It is simply our way. It wasn't something I wanted to get wrong.

"Right," I agreed. "He is intelligent. The Manager said so. But even without his confirmation, it is obvious. He would fit in here."

"He'd fit in with *you,*" Mala snorted. "You've always been odd."

I rolled my eyes.

"An odd mate would perfectly suit you."

I couldn't help but think he was right.

"Do you *want* a mate?" Mala asked, eyes searching mine.

That was the question, wasn't it?

I hadn't before.

But maybe…maybe that had been because I had never met my huu-man before.

"I do not even know his name."

"That's easy enough to fix," Mala shrugged and gave my shoulder a slap, his tendrils sneaking out to squeeze around the muscle affectionately. "I say you go back and get him. We can spare another day before we head to our next stop."

I couldn't stop thinking of those haunted eyes. The way he'd *trembled*. The way he'd leaned his weight against me. The way he'd trusted me—a total stranger—not to hurt him despite the fact I was easily twice his size.

"Alright," I decided, my hearts thumping. "I think you're right. Tomorrow."

"Yes!" Mala pumped his pale blue fist, grinning at me, his eyes squinting happily. "Tomorrow. I'll go with you. We can get the paperwork figured out. You'll need a second set of limbs to carry his belongings when you pick him up."

This could be a mistake, but it didn't feel like it.

Maybe I could make him happy.

At the very least I could free him and give him a choice. His proposal didn't have to mean anything unless he wanted it to. The ball could be in his court.

Hope fluttered inside my belly as I pictured what my life could become. A small warm body to curl around. Those dull flat teeth twisted into a happy smile as I pampered and spoiled my huu-man to the point he forgot all about the injustices that had been inflicted upon him. The way he'd feel in my arms as I sunk inside his body, soaking up his pleasure like a sponge.

Tomorrow I would make good on my promise to him.

I would make things okay.

It was the right thing to do.

At least…I hoped it was.

# THREE

## HUGO

**IN CASE YOU'RE WONDERING, I** did not get the donuts I'd wanted. I *did* somehow manage to gain a new owner, though. Not that I knew that right away, as I woke up the next morning expecting the worst. I'd slept fitfully, tossing and turning as my inevitable fate taunted me even when I was unconscious.

The world had a funny way of flipping itself upside down when I least expected it.

I kept waiting for the other shoe to drop.

I didn't know where I stood. Didn't know what the shark-dude had said, or what was going to happen to me. And I dreaded the meeting I'd no doubt have with The Manager later, and the red, red doors that even now taunted me from the safety of my sleep pod.

I expected the worst.

So imagine my surprise when my alarm went off like usual long after I'd been awake—and nothing seemed amiss.

As I walked down the hallway toward breakfast with the others, everyone kept congratulating me. That should've clued me into the fact that something was off. But I was too relieved not to see The Manager to think anything of it.

When I returned to my room after I'd finished eating, it had been emptied of all the belongings I'd managed to collect over my three years on F'ukYuu. Staring at the barren space, my heart began to race.

This is it.

You shouldn't have let your guard down.

You expected this.

"6934," The Manager's nasally voice crackled from behind as he addressed me by the number I'd been assigned. I whipped around, the pit in my stomach growing heavier by the second.

*Just breathe.*

*Just breathe, Hugo.*

*You can survive anything if you just breathe.*

The Manager was waiting in the doorway, his robes dragging on the floor. He held a tentacle out, the slick appendage brushing my bare chest as his eyes narrowed, and I immediately began to tremble.

Maybe they'd taken all my stuff because they were going to give my pod to someone else? Maybe I'd fucked up so bad last night, blubbering all over the VIP guest that they'd decided I wasn't worth the trouble of keeping?

Before I could further spiral, clothes were shoved into my arms and I stared down at them in shock, confused and more than a little worried. The Manager's tentacles retreated as quickly as they'd come, but the slick substance they'd left behind made my skin crawl.

"Get dressed," The Manager said in garbled English. He pointed behind him toward the communal bathroom that those of us in our shared wing used. I stumbled a little when he poked me with his tentacle again to get me moving, but promptly did as I was told.

If I was *already* in trouble, I refused to get into *more* trouble just because I wasn't fast enough.

Twenty minutes later, dressed in more clothing than I'd worn in years, I was escorted by a handful of enforcers into the elevator and down the hundred or so floors to The Manager's office. I felt more naked in the thigh-length tunic and black leggings than I had when I was in my usual uniform.

This was unfamiliar.

Terrifying, really.

As I pushed through the doors to the office, hope trembled deep, deep inside me. Because of all the times I'd seen slaves taken through the red doors, they'd never been clothed. Already this was an anomaly.

The room was as sterile as it always was, the desk at the back corner full of knick-knacks I didn't understand, and a handful of tablets that were currently turned off. Even the wallpaper was bland. An odd greenish color that reminded me of being sick. Or maybe—that was because I felt sick right now. Either way, it was unappealing.

I could count on one hand the number of times I'd been in here.

The first had been when I was sold by A&R to the pleasure planet. The second had been the time I got a glowing commendation from four-thumb guy. And most recently, last night—when The Manager had told me to make the shark-alien guy happy.

Hope continued to blossom as I kept my head down and toward my slippers, not wanting to anger the man as he brushed past me to grab one of the abandoned tablets.

I wasn't sure what I expected when one of the enforcers pushed the door open behind us, but it certainly wasn't what I got. A sound rumbled from behind me, and against my better judgment, I twisted to see where the sound came from.

Bubblegum-dick dude was back—standing in the open doorway, his eyes on mine. It felt just like it had the night before. That same magnetic pull as pale blue irises swirled in the overhead light and The Manager made a curious sound from his place beside his desk.

Shark-man said something in a low guttural tone. His own language, probably. I'd never heard anything like it. Like gargling rocks, it was rough and primal—though very obviously words. The Manager seemed to understand well enough because he made another sound, more annoyed this time, and made his way toward us. I pressed back against the wall to get out of the way as he pushed something into shark-dude's hands, before side-stepping his massive body and heading back out into the lobby.

When the door shut again, the room was quiet.

Shark-guy cupped the things he held gingerly, before turning his palms toward me so that I could see what was inside them. Translator headsets. Two of them.

I was confused, to say the least.

But curious too, as I gingerly reached out to take one. In sync, we pulled them on, the soft whir of the overhead fan the only sound in the room. For such a big dude, he sure was quiet.

Why the hell did he come back?

Why didn't he tell on me?

He should've.

Pink-dude moved deeper into the room, far away from me. I wasn't sure if I was grateful or sad about the distance as he stood stock-still, his arms behind his back. It gave me a moment to admire him as I decided if I wanted to be the first to break the silence.

He was wearing the same pants he'd had on the night before and a sash that looked weirdly…formal? Like he'd gotten dressed up for this. Though, that didn't make sense. Why the hell would he dress fancy to come here of all places? To see *me* of all people?

More than likely I was simply an errand on his very important list.

Maybe he was here to admonish me in person?

Though…the longer we stood in silence the less likely that seemed.

Shark-guy's broad back filled up what felt like half the room as he turned around to face me fully, those slate-blue eyes flashing with emotion I couldn't understand. His spots turned pink again. Then gray. Then pink.

I swallowed the lump in my throat, oddly naked beneath his gaze despite the clothing I wore.

"Hi?" I tried, annoyed when my body began to shake all on its own.

He cocked his head at me, what looked to be a smile gracing his not-lips. It was kinda menacing-looking, if I'm being honest. Which was… genuinely unavoidable considering how many fucking teeth he had. I'd seen *Jaws*. I couldn't help but replay that scene with the shark chomping its way through the ship over and over again as he spoke.

"Ro-aarhk." The sound was guttural and deep as he patted his chest, waiting patiently for me to reply.

Was that?…oh. That was his name.

"Oh." I blinked. "We're doing the *Tarzan* thing." I shook my head to clear it and slapped a hand against my own chest, because I didn't want to get chomped if I was accidentally rude. Maybe the chest-tap thing was customary?

"Hugo."

"Huu-goh?" Roark tried my name out carefully. He spoke…weird. In the light of day it was even more obvious. He was cultured, despite sounding like he was gargling nails. Kinda like a posh lord or something. Which…tracked, considering what I'd been expected to do for him, and the room I'd been given to service him in the night before.

"Hugo," I annunciated, softening the vowels. I pointed at him. "And you're Roar-k?"

"Ro-aarhk," he corrected me.

"Roark," I repeated. He beamed, if you could call a long line of razor-sharp teeth flashing at me, beaming. This smile was no less intimidating than any of his other expressions.

"Cool." I beamed right back at him. I was pretty much an alien expert now. Which was awesome. I would've shit my pants back home if I'd found someone like Roark while I was studying biology at Harvard. That was just a pipe dream though. As it was, his little smile and our *Disney* moment were pretty cool, regardless.

"Kewl," Roark repeated, sounding out the word carefully. "Huu-goh Kewl."

Oh shit.

Now he thought that was my last name.

*Where had we gotten this twisted?*

I laughed, shaking my head. "No, no. Cool means good—" His smile shifted into a frown, making it obvious I'd confused him. "It's just something humans say when we—you know what? Never mind." Wasn't like I had a huge attachment to my real last name anyway. "Hugo Cool. Yep. That's me. What about you?"

Great. This was super great. The greatest.

"Roark, Captain of The Dreamer."

A captain.

Huh.

So not a lord then.

That explained the way he stood all military seriousness. And how he was kinda…uptight? Not that I thought all captains were. I just…figured you had to be kinda a serious guy to have that job and travel all the way here. F'ukYuu was kinda far off the grid, as far as I understood.

"Do you want to stay here, Huu-goh?" Roark asked. I didn't have to think to reply, my head shaking automatically before my mouth had time to form words.

Roark studied me for a beat before nodding.

The door pushed open behind us and suddenly—everything changed. The warm mood that had begun to build turned icy cold. I kept my back to the wall as The Manager's eyes gleamed. He eyed both of us before he crossed the space and took a seat at the desk.

"Have you made your choice?" The Manager asked, his voice rough as usual.

Roark nodded.

And just like that, they both went into business mode. I was left reeling as the tablet was exchanged between the two of them, murmurs of payments and relocation bouncing around inside my head.

It felt like a fever dream.

To be sold and exchanged like cattle.

By my new alien buddy.

But there was no denying that was exactly what had just happened.

I wasn't sure if I'd just traded in one evil for another—but...I got the feeling I hadn't. Roark was gentle with me. He had been since last night. And there was something about the way he looked at me that made me feel...

It made me feel...

God, I didn't even have words.

It seemed stupid and silly to think that someone who wasn't even my own species could make me feel anything real at all. But he did. I was in a daze as we gave our translators back and were escorted out of the building. All of my things were packed into a single solitary suitcase, already waiting by the door.

It looked tiny and sad as Roark grabbed it, carrying it easily down the steps. He didn't touch me again, but his gaze was always on my face as we stepped into the street. Like he was trying to get a read on my feelings, even though my expressions had to be as foreign to him as his were to me.

It was weird to be out here.

This was the same street I'd squinted at through foggy glass for three years, but never actually *seen*.

I wish I could say that it was a magical moment—that F'ukYuu was wonderful and bright and amazing. But...it wasn't.

The street wasn't...very pretty.

Dirty and littered with trash.

But it was new, and that was enough to excite me despite the haze I'd fallen into since Roark had purchased me.

I ogled the weirdly rounded buildings and the glass windows I'd occupied for years, a sick curl in my gut when I realized that dancers already populated the booths. They couldn't see me. Not really, but I gaped anyway as we paused at the base of the steps and I tried to wrap my head around what had just happened.

I was still shocked enough that I barely noticed that we weren't alone. A large baby-blue shark alien—similar in looks to Roark—took my suitcase from him. Without the translators on I couldn't understand what they said to each other. Just more growly-growling-growl sounds. Blue dude held my things gingerly in one of his massive hands.

I felt like a kindergartner getting escorted home from school.

It sucked honestly, but I understood why we couldn't bring the translators with us. They were tied to this location—and even if they hadn't been, the headsets didn't work in space, only the permanent implants worked while space-borne.

Touching me for the first time since last night, Roark laid one impossibly large hand on the small of my back. It stuck a little, but it was warm, and I was grateful for how gently he urged me forward. Without that touch, I wasn't sure I would've been able to get my feet to move.

My world had just become a whole lot larger.

And while that was endlessly exciting—and I couldn't wait to see new things, and explore a universe I hadn't even known existed—the part of me that had always been small and frightened was grateful that I wasn't alone.

That I was with someone bigger than I was.

Someone with more claws and teeth.

Someone who no one would dare mess with.

Roark continued to gingerly push me forward as we headed down the busy street. He lent me strength as my eyes wandered, the sky above vast and inky black despite it being daytime. Transport shuttles—at least, that's what I assumed they were, zoomed back and forth, barely blips on the horizon.

Shops and stalls selling goods and food lined the street that led from the pleasure district toward the port. I could see the spaceships from here. Some large enough they should've been planets of their own.

The scent of fried food—even if it was different than the food back home—made my stomach gurgle.

Roark frowned, eyes narrowing down at me at the same time I spotted a fucking donut shop. Donuts. Just like I'd wanted! I jerked toward it automatically, curious to see if they were the same kind I'd received for good behavior at work.

For a single terrifying moment Roark's hand left the surface of my back. I'd moved too fast. And the tether I felt fell away. Quickly, I wiggled back into place, fully expecting punishment. What if he thought I'd been trying to run?

I hadn't.

Fuck.

What had I just—

"Hungr-ee?" Roark asked before I could spiral. I startled, surprised by the butchered English on his tongue. I hadn't noticed before but he had a tablet in his hand. I squinted at it, trying to read the unfamiliar squiggles.

He was obviously reading from it.

Was it an English guide? That thing had to have cost a fortune if that was the case. From what I could tell huu-mans were new to this side of the galaxy. I was surprised something like that could exist at all—if that's what it was.

"Hungry," I echoed. My stomach growled again like it wanted to emphasize my point, and I eyed the donuts hopefully. I knew there was no way he was going to buy me one. They were *precious*. Rewards for good behavior. Not for guys who got excited and leapt into the stree—oh.

My back felt cold as Roark moved around me toward the booth, leaving me in the capable hands of his friend. The blue shark smiled down at me, but it didn't help soothe my unease now that Roark wasn't near. Nor did it explain what he was doing—

Aaaaand he was buying one.

Shit. No way.

I blinked in disbelief as Roark exchanged credits with the vendor, his back as ramrod straight as ever. He looked massive, even next to the other alien—who was easily a foot or two taller than I was. The vendor was a type of alien I'd seen before. They were common here. Green and slightly bulbous, similar to the "little green men" earthlings liked to populate stores with near Area 51. Only these guys had small beady eyes, and jowls that looked oddly like ballsacks hanging from their chins.

Ball chin or not, this dude's booth smelled like paradise.

And it wasn't like I was about to discriminate against a good donut.

Blue-shark-friend stood behind my back, guarding me dutifully as I watched Roark purchase not just one, but a whole goddamn box of donuts. A *whole* box. For a single, uncharitable second I worried that he was about to eat them in front of me. That this would be a power play to show me my place right after I'd made it clear how badly I wanted one.

But that evil little voice faded quickly enough.

Roark had given me no reason to think so uncharitably of him. So I would do my best not to poison this before it had even begun. No one had ever really given me a reason to give them the benefit of the doubt before—but I was the kinda guy who did that anyway. Or at least…tried.

I might've drooled a bit when Roark walked back over. Because of the donuts, obviously. Not because of those huge-ass thighs *flexing*. Okay, yeah. Maybe both. He was hot? I couldn't help it. When Roark very carefully offered the entire donut box to me, I wavered.

He opened the lid and I eyed the jelly-filled treats like they were traps. It felt too good to be true that he would purchase them for me, simply because I wanted them.

My stomach growled again and Roark gently wiggled the box to entice me.

"Huu-goh hungr-ee," he repeated in his growly voice.

I reached for a donut, warily, waiting to be admonished.

But I never was.

Not even when I ate the whole box.

The *whole* entire box.

All on my own.

And Roark watched me the whole time. His expression never wavered but his spots were pink as we stood in the street and I stuffed my face like it'd been years since I'd last eaten. If I didn't know any better, I'd think he was proud of himself. When I finished, Roark disposed of the box in the trash receptacle, and his warm hand found its place on the small of my back again.

Nervously, I licked sugar from my fingers. Roark's hand didn't move as we continued down the street toward the docks. He'd asked me if I wanted to stay here. I'd said no. But it hadn't occurred to me till the last of the sweets were cleansed from my fingers, and a giant spaceship— the biggest that was parked—proved to be our end destination, that by choosing not to stay I was choosing to leave.

To leave the only place that was somewhat familiar, even if it was a prison.

I didn't understand him. Didn't understand why he'd take me in when we were so different. Why he'd taken the time to research my language enough to feed me. Why he was doing his best not to scare me. Why he had come back for me at all.

Today was…weird.

So fucking weird.

But I figured going with Roark couldn't be worse than staying here. So, even though I was frightened and confused, I did my best to push those feelings aside. Excitement buzzed beneath the surface of my skin. A promise for newer, brighter things. To learn this world I'd been dropped inside of. To encounter more creatures to fill my journal with, and to explore places I never in my wildest dreams would've thought I could visit.

Hope was a tremulous, weak thing.

But it was still hope.

And that wasn't something I'd had for a long, long time.

# FOUR

## ROARK

**THE TRANSITION WAS NOT AS** easy as I'd hoped it would be.

Part of it was my fault, I could admit that.

I'd been alone for years so I hadn't been prepared for how odd it would feel to have another creature in my personal space—even one as frankly adorable as Huu-goh. It had been a long time since I'd been a cadet and shared a dorm with the others, and my time at the orphanage when I was a youth was nothing but a faded memory.

Which meant that I had some adjusting to do, just like he did.

Huu-goh was strange.

He gawked at everything, for one thing. He'd cataloged all the tech, all the hallways, all the crew that he met as we made our way through The Dreamer toward the barracks for the first time. I moved slowly so that he would have time to take it all in, though I was remiss, because it would've been nice to be able to explain what everything was.

As captain, I had a set of private rooms near the back of the ship. It was the largest lodgings on board, and I had hoped that the sheer size of it would be enough to make the space not feel overcrowded now that I had someone else inside it.

I'd debated giving Huu-goh his own room entirely, but that seemed cruel. He knew no one but me on board. And though I was a stranger to him, we had at least shared a few conversations and a moment that meant more to me than I was equipped to admit at present.

Mala and Ushuu assured me that they could take care of my duties for a week as Huu-goh settled in. I appreciated their assistance, though the thought of anyone else manning the ship rankled, because I knew we only had a few short hours before take off.

The Dreamer was *my* responsibility. With the ever-present threat of pirates hanging over our heads, it was hard to relax. I tried, but it was difficult. Even when Huu-goh was bouncing around my rooms.

He poked everything, opened all the cupboards, exclaimed in amazement when he figured out how the sinks and toilets worked. He thought my bed was fascinating—as evidenced by the widening of his eyes and the way his gaze kept lingering on it. And though I kept steering him toward the corner where I'd set up a bed for him too, he kept making his way back toward mine.

His single, solitary suitcase sat next to the door.

When I moved to retrieve it, Huu-goh was quick to dive in front of me. He glared up at me, hunkered over the damn thing like he was terrified I was going to steal it from him.

So instead of helping him unpack his things, I maintained distance between us, and let him continue his explorations.

I made myself busy at my desk, reading through articles about huu-mans on my HoverPad, the care guide I'd downloaded directly from A&R's website both enlightening and abhorrent. The fact they had one at all was disgusting to me, but I tried to push through that emotion as I made note of the things Huu-goh could be allergic to, and the requirements necessary for caring for one's huu-man.

I was so engrossed in my reading, I hardly noticed when the ship rumbled, preparing to take off. Huu-goh made a sound, however, and my gaze snapped from the screen to him, surprised to find him huddled in the middle of the floor cross-legged, his head tipped toward the ceiling like he could see the stars behind it.

Ah.

This was his first voyage.

At least—his first conscious one.

I flipped a few buttons on my HoverPad, pleased when the panels on the ceiling shifted colors, and the night sky spread out above us. It was a live feed, and would shift when our engines had warmed enough to take flight. I hoped he'd find it more fascinating this way. He was a curious creature, and I was more than a little excited at the prospect of making him smile again—like he had when I'd bought him pastries earlier.

Huu-goh made a shocked little sound that in turn caused me to grin.

Pride made my chest puff up as I enjoyed his reaction, pleased to have a captivating view of my own. His expressions were so easy to read. Though his features were foreign, I'd dealt with enough species over the years that I could recognize what most of the faces he made meant. At least…so far.

This face looked pleased.

More than pleased.

It was odd hearing him breathe and move around in my space. Difficult to tune out. But *this* wasn't so bad. The expression of wonder on his face, however, was short-lived.

When the sky blurred and we officially took off, something horrible happened.

Huu-goh's dark eyes went wide. He gawked at the shifting ceiling, the floor rumbling beneath him, and for a single solitary second all was well.

And then it wasn't.

It'd been a long time since my first voyage so I'd forgotten how odd that shift could feel. As we picked up speed, the ship finding its equilibrium was often turbulent. I hardly noticed it now, but Huu-goh certainly did. It only took ten seconds for his excitement to fade and his skin to turn an awful shade of green.

He'd been sick all night after that.

Sick enough we'd spent a good hour in the bathroom. Him, with his head in the toilet, and me, stroking over his back while I flipped through pages on my HoverPad and tried to figure out if I'd made a horrible mistake or not.

Nowhere did it mention turbulence or huu-man's weakness to it. And eventually, thank god, when Huu-goh stopped being sick I came to the conclusion that it was the space-legs that he didn't have yet that had caused his violent reaction.

I'd hosed him off in the shower, keeping the spray warm, and he'd been too miserable to protest.

"Mai dohn-uts," he'd said sadly in human-speak, his sweet, sick little head tucked against my shoulder. After he was dried off and I'd bundled him in blankets, I made a mental note to get more clothing for him.

After his reaction to me approaching his suitcase, I didn't dare try to open it again—and it didn't feel right having him naked in his bed without having confirmed his intentions toward me. I knew my own desire, but he was still a mystery.

Huu-goh cried that night.

After the lights had gone off, I'd headed toward my own bed. I'd thought he was asleep. If I'd known he was awake, I wouldn't have left him alone over there. Hovering, however, had only seemed to piss him off after he'd been stripped down and the worst of the sickness had passed.

When he'd fallen asleep it had felt like a blessing.

A rough first day finally over.

At least until I heard the quiet little sniffle sound he made—twenty minutes later—and realized that things could get worse before they ever got better. I rose from bed, my own body sluggish and exhausted as I settled beside him on the floor. He didn't shake my hand off when I stroked over his back, but he didn't say anything either.

He held himself in a tiny ball, quaking, as more of those curious tears leaked down his cheeks.

I fell asleep beside him, and when I woke it felt like I'd aged a thousand years.

Surely things will get better. That's what I told myself as I stretched out my sore body, my tentacles expanding to breathe after remaining cramped on the floor for so damn long.

For a week, I did my best to acclimatize Huu-goh to my rooms and space itself. I learned about him as best I could. Feeding him different treats and snacks, it was easy enough to get a feel for what he liked and disliked. He didn't enjoy bambuu, but I didn't budge, always making sure that he finished his plate for breakfast, lunch, and dinner.

He was underfed, and after the first initial frown he'd leveled me with, he hadn't complained. He was clever enough to understand that there was a reason I was feeding him the same thing every day.

Huu-goh and I developed a strange sort of sign language over the first few days. When my huu-man liked something he'd fold all his fingers into his palm aside from his thumb. Said thumb would point toward the ceiling as he wagged his hand at me. This odd gesture was seemingly a *good* thing.

It, however, had a negative counterpart.

When he *didn't* like something he made the same motion with the thumb pointed down. Sometimes, when he was feeling particularly excited about something—more pastries—or unhappy about something—me following him into the bathroom—he'd even double the "up thumb" or "down thumb" with both hands.

He didn't like his bed.

It didn't take a genius to figure that out.

But he didn't seem to understand when I told him he could join me in mine. Part of me was grateful for that—as I was also still getting used to his presence. Having him in my personal space was already an adjustment. To have him in my bed felt like crossing a line I wasn't sure we should.

At least…not until I knew where he stood.

My hope that we would become mates was beginning to dwindle as the days passed and Huu-goh did not make another move like he had at the pleasure house. Maybe his desire to touch me truly had been fueled by his occupation?

It wasn't as though I could ask him.

A&R's pamphlet included a few basic words and their pronunciations. But there wasn't a single thing written inside it that talked about sex, or had words that pertained to it. There was no way to confirm whether or not he was interested in me so I would have to wait to see if his actions dictated he was.

So far, nothing pointed toward Huu-goh feeling anything toward me aside from camaraderie. Which was…disappointing, to say the least.

Sometimes I'd catch him staring at my chest—and the scent of arousal would fill the air—but then the nanobots would come out to clean, or the ceiling would shift colors as we neared planets that blurred by on our route—and the scent would drift away.

By the time the week had passed and I needed to return to my duties, I felt no more secure than I had on that first day.

I tried to warn Huu-goh that the ship was going to land—but again, the language barrier got in the way. Pointing at the floor and giving him a double down thumb did not help. It made him frown down at the ground like he was expecting it to open up or something—which I supposed, was fair.

When the ship began to rumble however, he deduced what was happening. His dark eyes went wide and he scrambled toward the bathroom, hopping as fast as a Fruhg during mating season as he slammed his way toward the toilet in preparation.

Luckily for the both of us, he wasn't sick the second time.

Mala landed the ship gently. Not as gently as I would have—but gently enough.

When the rumbling stopped, and the steady swoosh that could be felt at any time when we were space-borne had settled, I stopped rubbing Huu-goh's back. He twisted to look at me, eyes just as wide as they'd been when the ship began to descend.

"Laa-hnd-ehd?" he asked, voice shaky.

I could only assume that meant something about the ship having docked. I nodded, hoping I'd gotten that right. Huu-goh relaxed, slumping into me, his face sticking to my chest as tiny tendrils that had a mind of their own reached out to cling.

I pulled them back as swiftly as I could—once again, terrified of crossing that line between us.

At least, before he did.

Though I was due back as captain, it didn't feel right leaving Huu-goh alone in my rooms. I wanted to. I really, really did. Though I didn't know where we stood in our relationship, I was still terrified of him becoming frightened or hurt if he left them.

The planet we'd landed on was a safe one, as far as planets go. It had a temperate climate. No fauna that was necessarily harmful—at least en-route to the pick-up station. Its yellow skies and red dirt were familiar as I held tightly to Huu-goh's leash, terrified he'd wander off the path even though I knew there wasn't anything out there likely to hurt him.

"Is that really necessary?" Mala asked from beside me, nodding toward the leash.

My spots turned fuschia in embarrassment as I glanced toward Huu-goh and made a sound in affirmation. He had his notepad out. He'd had it out a lot lately, scribbling away with a writing device that was worn to the quick. Page after page was full of the strange scratch-scratch of his people, along with illustrations of the many things we'd encountered on our trek from the ship.

Behind us, a progression of crewmates were driving the empty carriers that we'd be using when we reached our destination. By the time we returned to the ship the following day, they'd be full to the brim with gemstones—the very same gemstones that powered the fertility pods back home.

This was arguably one of the most important stops on our journey. It felt…wrong to leave Huu-goh behind when I couldn't explain to him that I'd be gone for several days, even if things went well.

"He could get injured," I argued, though admittedly even I knew I'd waited too long to respond.

"By what?" Mala asked, sounding more amused than he should.

"Shut up." I glared at him, and he shrugged, unbothered.

Huu-goh didn't seem to mind the leash. At least, at first. I was careful to keep my steps slow so that he could keep up—and even slower still when we encountered a new plant for him to sketch. His eyes were glued to the papers in his grip, a look of wonder on his face every time he saw something new.

The exchange went without a hitch when we arrived to our destination. Mala took over setting up camp inside the mine, and Huu-goh sat obediently beside me as I exchanged credits with the manager of the location. He eyed the huu-man with hunger, and it took everything I had not to lean over and bite his head right off.

That emotion left me feeling drained and a little shocked at myself.

I liked to think I was clear-headed, but apparently Huu-goh brought out a different side to me.

When everything was done, I kept a tight hold on his leash as we exited the main office and headed toward the front of the mine where the guest accommodations were. If you could call them that. This planet was less developed than Osheania, and I knew that the comfort we'd be offered here would be rudimentary at best.

Most of the crew was already settled in for the night, Mala included.

Beside him, a few feet away to offer some semblance of privacy, was a pile of furs for Huu-goh and I to share. I glared at Mala's back as he snored—he didn't fucking snore, so I knew he was pretending. It wasn't as though I didn't want to sleep with Huu-goh. But again…I was doing my best not to cross that line until he did.

He hadn't been given much autonomy, if any. He deserved to make this choice—even if it ached to know that this was out of my hands. I hated when I wasn't in control. Especially when I wanted something. But for once in my life, I kept that feeling to myself.

I didn't act.

Not even when we settled down for the night, the cavern of colorful rock climbing high above us, and Huu-goh sleepily snuffled beside me.

I ached to reach out, to nuzzle into the fur on his head, to taste the salt on his skin that I could smell after a day spent hiking through the wilderness. But I didn't.

When I woke up the next morning, however, Huu-goh was tucked against my chest. And he was trembling. It wasn't like the crying he'd exhibited that first night—but something else. Something that smelled musky-sweet—his lovely little hips rub, rub, rubbing against mine. I'd smelled this once before. *This* was the scent of Huu-goh's arousal.

Euphoria burst through my body as I pulled back to look at him, a grin on my face—only for that grin to quickly fall when I realized that he was asleep.

He hadn't chosen me.

For all I knew he was imagining someone else entirely.

Disgusted with myself and the situation, I held still till Huu-goh awoke, doing my best to ignore the panicked little sound he made—like he was embarrassed. His face was flushed, nearly as fuschia as my spots became when I was embarrassed. We had so many differences that the simple similarity settled me, even though I felt untethered.

Huu-goh liked the crystals. His eyes were wide and bright, constantly catching on the glittering surfaces as the crew filled the carriers, each box piled high. Iridescent, the jagged surfaces caught and refracted the light from the hanging lanterns above, casting rainbows on the walls.

"Pre-tty," Huu-goh said, mumbled under his breath as he furiously scribbled on his notepad beside me. I tightened my grip on his leash, my head swimming as the familiar word came back to me.

It was odd, remembering the sound of it through the haze of the translator. But yes. I could recall using that exact word to describe him.

"Pre-tty," I agreed in his tongue, voice rough. It was a gamble, but one that paid off when Huu-goh's attention snapped from the boxes to me, his eyes wide. A lovely flush spread across his cheeks, just like the one he'd exhibited that morning when he'd been rubbing against me like a beast in heat.

"Pre-tty!" he agreed, very obviously excited that we had found another shared word. I gave him an up thumb and he cackled, eyes crinkling with what I hoped was affection. "Thehy ahre ahrn-t thehy?" Huu-goh babbled, hopping on the balls of his feet. "Aye-v nehvahr seen eneethingh lyke iht!"

"*Huu-goh* pretty," I countered, because it was true. Huu-goh's blush grew darker. Nearly red enough to look like arousal. I licked my lips and he squirmed, eyeing my tongue like he'd never seen anything like it before. "Huu-goh pretty," I repeated again.

He made a high-pitched sound, like he wasn't sure what to say, and then—because Mala was the worst, he promptly came to interrupt us.

I didn't forget that Huu-goh liked the shiny rocks, however.

I logged that information away for later along with all the other little things I'd discovered about him.

We went to six other planets over the course of the next month. There weren't many stops on our route before we'd drop by planet Sha'hPihn. Though there would be a decent chunk of space travel we'd have to do before we reached it.

U'suhk was one of my least favorite stops, but it was as necessary as the rest of them. This time, however, I found something rather delightful when we made a detour through one of the villages. There were huu-mans mated to the Ly'zrd that made up the majority of the population. Seeing them did not come as a surprise to me, but it certainly did to Huu-goh as he ogled them from where he sat safely beside me in our transport vehicle.

There was a sadness to him then, because he was intelligent enough to understand that these people had been taken and discarded just like he had.

I'd stayed extra close to him that day, and he hadn't minded. He'd never pulled the leash taut, not even once, his little body warm at my elbow at all times. His journal remained in his pocket, and I felt the loss of his scribblings keenly.

When we returned to the ship he had a thousand questions. Questions I couldn't answer. I did, however, buy him one of the odd head coverings that the other huu-mans had created. Huu-goh grinned when I plopped it on his head, his sweet cheeks pinking up all over again. He repeated the words "Thank yew."

It was something he'd said many times throughout our travels, and considering how polite he came across, I figured the words were gratitude of some sort.

He stuck close to me for the rest of the night—and I waited…god, did I wait—for him to cross that distance again. For the day we'd slept together in that cave to not have been a fluke.

Planet two was more dangerous than the others. I kept Huu-goh close then, and every time he tugged on his leash I'd yank him back into place. Mala made a few comments about it, but I snapped at him every time he did.

I knew that it wasn't fair—that Huu-goh was merely curious.

But he was going to get himself killed.

And I refused to let that happen, whether he wanted to be my mate or not.

Ushuu, my mentor and the ship's chief technology officer, had questioned me about Huu-goh a few times since he'd come aboard, but I'd been too busy to sit down with him like I usually did. Part of me was ashamed. Ashamed that I'd bought a person—that I was…that I was still hoping that the magnetism I could feel between us was not one-sided.

If I talked to Ushuu it would mean acknowledging that Huu-goh did not want me. He would ask. I knew he would. And then I'd have to start planning how to let him go. Where I could set him up on Osheania when we returned home, with a house of his own—and me a galaxy away, chasing the stars alone without him.

By the sixth planet, Huu-goh had gotten fed up with me.

At least…I assumed so.

He'd been ornery all day, snapping at me over breakfast, and yanking on his leash every five seconds. I'd made sure he had enough to eat and drink, pausing periodically throughout the day to feed or pet him—and that had only seemed to set him off even more.

I could admit that I was on edge too.

Tension had been building between us for weeks—and while I'd tried to stay calm and cool-headed, I wasn't. Between the constant fear of attack from pirates after our cargo and my lack of solid standing with Huu-goh, I felt unmoored in a way I never had before.

I should've known things were about to change.

It was inevitable.

I only wish I'd known it was for the better.

# FIVE

## ROARK

**_"AYE-M NAH-T YER PEHT!"_ HUU-GOH** gasped out, his face an angry red, his whole body quaking. I willed myself to comprehend his words even though I had literally no idea what he was saying. We'd had a pleasant dinner in our rooms after returning to the ship so I thought his grumpy mood had passed. I'd been wrong. Because when I entered the bedroom after showering and brushing my teeth—I had been met with…with *this*.

Dinner had made me naively think I'd been imagining the tension between us.

Huu-goh had seemed happy.

That had been the calm before the storm.

"Yew muhthehrfuhker," he hissed out, stomping around the room, his tiny body stiff. I could not for the life of me understand what he was so upset about. I'd done everything the "How to care for an Earthling" pamphlet had told me to do today.

He was fed, watered, clothed.

I'd been gentle with him. Fed him treats. *Petted* him.

*What else could he possibly need?*

*You're not enough for him,* a traitorous voice whispered.

That sudden sense of inadequacy threatened to bring me to my knees.

*No, no. I could do this.*

*I could.*

I needed to stop fantasizing about mating with him and move on. That was the problem. Maybe he could sense how ill at ease I'd been. Maybe he was more astute than I'd given him credit for. Maybe he'd been learning me as I'd been learning him.

I held my hands up in surrender, purring low in the back of my throat to soothe him. The sound rumbled as I edged my way toward him so I could fix the mess I'd made of this.

*Slow and easy. Don't frighten him.*

"Treeteeng mee lyke uh dawg." Huu-goh stomped around some more, his ire turning to sadness that tasted salty-sweet in the air as his eyes began to leak again. "Tuh-gg-eeng mee awround ahll dae. Aye thot yew wehr dihffehrehnt—" He pointed at me again, in accusation. His eyes were red-rimmed. Tears leaked down his cheeks. My hearts ached. "Buht aye ahm juhst un ahnimahl to yew—naht uh purrsahn—and aye—" he hiccuped. I froze, floored by his beauty and the fact that for the first time in my life I had no way of fixing this.

I'd always been a fixer.

It was in my blood.

But I didn't know what he was saying. Didn't know how to solve a problem I couldn't understand.

I gazed at those stormy brown eyes as they filled to the brim over and over again. My hands shook, still raised placatingly—because I didn't know what to do. Huu-goh rubbed his palms against his eyes, the shirt I'd procured for him hanging loose on his long, limber frame.

He looked gorgeous when he was sad. He always looked gorgeous, if I was being honest. There was something about him that was so colorful. Even without the ability to understand his words, I could see his emotions written plainly across his face.

The longer I'd spent with him, the more I'd grown to admire him. His tenacity. His intelligence. His resilience. I respected him more than I'd respected anyone I'd ever met. So to see him hurt like this pained me. Especially when I knew it was my fault.

"Wah-ter?" I offered, because it was one of the only English words I knew.

"Noh. Noh wah-ter." Huu-goh put his hands on his hips. He stomped. Actually *stomped*. Then he froze, and frowned, realizing what he said. "I meen. Naht thihs sehcond. Buht yes, Aye-ll need wah-ter uh-gayen aat sum poihnt. Ore aye-ll dai."

I didn't understand what he was saying, but I nodded anyway. Slowly. "Fuh-d?"

"Noh fuh-d." To my horror Huu-goh's eyes filled with tears again, his frustration evident. I didn't understand. Maybe this had been a mistake. Maybe all of this had been a mistake. I was supposed to make his life better, not...not this—whatever this was.

"Aye juhst...aye juhst—" He deflated, looking lost and lonely as he crossed his arms over his chest and squeezed himself tight. "Aye-m lohn-lee."

His eyes spoke to me—the way they always had.

I simply had needed to listen.

*Oh.*

My hearts thudded unsteadily as I realized what he needed.

Relieved, I took a steadying breath and raised my arms out wide. Huu-goh's expression was wary, his brow furrowed in confusion as he bit his plush pink lip. "Wut…?" He wavered, and I held still as I waited for him to understand.

"Huu-goh," I said as patiently as I could. My pulse thundered. "*Huu-goh,*" I repeated, plaintively. Maybe he desired to be touched as much as I ached to touch him? Maybe…intimacy is what had been missing. Maybe…maybe we were more suited than I'd thought.

Maybe by waiting for him to make the first move I'd done him a disservice.

I couldn't be too angry at myself, even though I wanted to be. This was my first time in a relationship—if that was what we could call this. And I had…no idea what I was doing.

Huu-goh kept staring at me and his eyes were turbulent. Swirls of unease and exhaustion twisted inside their depths as he inspected me from head to toe—dressed in sleep pants as I'd been about to retire for the night—his lips wobbled and I ached for him, for his confusion, for his fear.

I wished I could soothe him.

I wished we were back on my home planet so that I could contact A&R about purchasing permanent translators. I had never had a reason to buy one in the past as I had always gotten along just fine speaking Common. However, I now had a fluffy-furred, clever reason named Huu-goh. Which meant I planned on procuring one for myself as well as for Huu-goh as soon as we arrived home. I would've bought them earlier, but it was copyrighted tech that wasn't readily available anywhere else, and unfortunately, at the moment, my hands were tied.

So this was…the next best thing.

A few more seconds passed.

My purr grew deeper, rougher, trying to entice him like he was a pup in need of comfort. In a lot of ways he was. Even if he hadn't looked so young, his behavior would make the age gap between us obvious. He was so full of *life*. Intrigued by anything and everything.

I had lost that spark long ago—if I'd ever had it at all.

It'd died the day my first captain had.

Until the moment I'd seen Huu-goh.

Huu-goh's face morphed through a series of expressions too quick for me to decipher. I was still learning him, though one day I hoped to have every one of his faces and their meanings memorized, just as I hoped he'd learn my colors.

My chest vibrated as my hearts lurched. Something in Huu-goh broke then. His eyes spoke to mine.

They said, *I need you.*

They said, *don't leave me.*

They said, *please understand.*

He swallowed, and I watched his throat bob, fascinated by him all over again as he took an unsteady step toward me. So brave. So goddamn brave. My hands shook, arms still outstretched as I waited for him to cross the space between us.

I could acknowledge that the distance had been there since the day he'd stepped foot on this ship. It was my fault. I knew that now. I'd done this to us. But I wanted to fix it. Wanted to hold him—even if holding him innocently was all I'd ever have. Even if he didn't want me the way I wanted him. Even if his proposal had been false, and his interest wandered.

I still wanted to be there for him.

Even if it broke my hearts.

"That is it, little one," I crooned in my own tongue. I ignored the ache in my groin that the sight of him obeying my command inspired. It was a new sensation. As uncomfortable as it was exciting. "Come to me. I will make it okay." It was the second time I'd made that promise, but it felt even truer now.

He took another step.

Pleasure, unlike anything I had never known tingled at my fingertips.

So obedient, so lovely, so beautiful.

His dark eyes glimmered with determination.

Five steps. Four steps.

Three.

I could smell him. Smell my own soap in his hair as his fluffy head appeared at my ribs, his head tipping up to study me warily. He was shaking just like I was. Like his body knew the trauma he had been through even when his mind did not. Brave as ever, Huu-goh stepped inside my embrace. I tentatively hovered my arms above his shoulders, terrified to touch should I scare him off.

I did not want to frighten him.

Even if I ached fiercely to embrace him.

I had never hated my teeth, my claws, my size. Until the moment I realized how easily they could be used to scare a person as defenseless as my mate. One day, a small part of me still hoped he would realize those same things were what would keep him safe. They would be a comfort to him.

The moment Huu-goh's cheek settled against my body I sighed. Something inside me shuddered into place as that soft skin rubbed against my own. My surface clung to him, tiny tendrils reaching out as desperately as I wanted to. Huu-goh giggled, pulling away from my torso to stare at it in wonder.

"Woah," he said, shocked—he did not look affronted, however. Instead, my endlessly curious companion tentatively pushed a finger against my bare skin. It parted, reaching for him, sucking him inside till part of him became part of me, the tip of his finger encased beneath my surface. "Woah," he said again. Huu-goh pulled his finger free. My arms remained aloft, but I lowered them around him the moment his cheek met my ribcage for the second time.

I was only a man, despite my inexperience and strict lifestyle.

What else was I meant to do?

He was so small, so sweet in my arms. Tiny. My cocks ached, twisting together in a way that made me weak-kneed. His close proximity did things to me that did not feel fair in the slightest. Like I was a teen just learning how his dicks worked—not living in my fourth decade.

Huu-goh had responded like this before, at the club, when he'd been frightened and I'd soothed him. He'd trusted me then as he trusted me now, curling his arms around me just as tightly as I held him.

I rumbled against his orange fur, petting down his back in slow, gentle swipes to soothe. Back and forth, back and forth. Huu-goh's panic faded.

I scented salt in the air.

He was crying again. I did not interrupt. Beings both large and small needed time to process their emotions. Some hit things, like me and Mala. Some, like Ushuu, worked through them silently. And some…were like Huu-goh.

Their emotions fled from them on trails of salt.

It was a beautiful thing, a huu-man's tears.

I felt honored to behold them. I wished I'd appreciated them more the first time around. That I had asked him more questions. That I had been able to learn him through words as well as actions. That I had told him how brilliant I found him—how strong.

He was small.

So *small.*

Delicate.

And yet he had survived so *much.*

Huu-goh still found joy in things, despite the bad that had happened to him. Despite how defenseless he was. He never appeared frightened. Not like I was—frightened all the time, every day. Frightened of losing the people and things I loved most. Frightened of losing control, because without it I had nothing left.

I traced his spine from top to bottom, reveling in the way he trembled and quaked in response. His tears had stopped falling, the scent of salt growing stale. Tighter, his arms twisted around my middle. "That is it, sweet creature," I murmured in my own tongue against his fluffy head, rubbing my cheeks against it to scent him.

It was the first time I'd allowed myself to do so.

I ached.

Huu-goh—thank god—seemed to appreciate the touch. He made a pleased little sound. It was a noise that I'd only ever heard him make when I fed him something particularly sugary—or when he'd seen the gemstones at the cave on our first field trip from the ship. I purred my amusement, stroking down his spine again in the hopes of causing another sound.

It was lovely.

*He* was lovely.

My cocks ached.

God, did they ache.

"*Roark*—" Huu-goh whined my name. The sound of it on his tongue like that cut through me, trembling through my body as the sweet man in my arms grew even more pliant. I should stop this. Except that it was so close to what I wanted—I just…I couldn't bring myself to do it.

"Roark," Huu-goh repeated, breathless and confused but no less pleased. My hand slipped lower and he gasped, stilling completely as I smoothed my palm over his rump for the first time. "Yehs."

*Did he like that?*

My cocks writhed together.

I squeezed.

Huu-goh's breath hitched and his hips stuttered against my body. "Yehr tehn-tah-cles ahr—"

I didn't understand what he was saying, too enthralled by the swivel of his pelvis and the way his dick was pushing against my thigh. When I glanced down, I realized why exactly he had become so breathless.

My body apparently had a mind of its own.

I hadn't meant to but…

Hundreds of tiny tentacles had sprouted from my elbow, slinking down his arms, sucking and pulling at him as they slipped beneath his shirt. Everywhere we touched they tickled across his skin, toying with the nubs of his nipples. It was a tantalizing sight, all that pink twisting and writhing across pale supple flesh.

*Wasn't this the sign I'd been waiting for?*

Something awoke inside me as I stared and stared and stared, drunk on the sight of him.

Huu-goh's cock was hard, just as mine were.

I could *feel* it. So much smaller, but no less masculine. Singular, but just as greedy as mine put together. I groaned, suddenly hungry for more. Hungry to *see* him in an entirely new way. To taste him.

His length pushed against the fabric of his own sleep pants, thickening with every second. My tendrils grew bolder, pulling at his nipples till they pushed against the fabric. For a creature of his stature Huu-goh's dick was *impressive*. Longer than I would've expected, and listing to the left as it pulsed against the thin fabric.

There was a wet spot forming beneath the crown, see-through enough I could see the pink head pushing against it. I confess, I couldn't bring myself to stop even if I wanted to. This was everything I'd wanted—and I just…I *had* to see what he looked like when he gave in.

Had to see him come.

Had to touch him—the way I'd never wanted to touch another person.

Growling, I buried my face in Huu-goh's neck, ignoring the voice in my head that whispered what I was doing was wrong. That I should wait. That he had asked for comfort, not this—

But he didn't seem to mind as he pushed his hips against my leg and began to hump me in earnest. My eyes flooded black with lust and I released a groan of my own, consciously tugging harder at his nipples now as my hand gripped his rump tight. He rutted harder against me, fucking my thigh like the little beast he was.

Ah.

Yes.

That's what he was—

Yes, yes.

"That's it, little beast," I purred in my own language. I shuddered when I felt him clutch hard at my shoulders, his fingers sinking in as he fucked and fucked and fucked. Tight snaps of those tiny hips, hungry and primal.

I urged him on, drinking him in greedily. My fingers rubbed at his ass cheeks, then between them, and lower still. With every touch his hips grew needier, grinding harder and harder. When I could feel where his balls were pulled tight, I paused. Huu-goh, because he was perfect, spread his legs wider to give me room.

His breath came out in desperate little bursts, and with each puff against my body, I felt like I was soaring.

*You're doing this to him.*

*You're making him feel good.*

My cocks jerked, slip-sliding in the mess they were making in my own sleep pants.

"Oh fuck," Huu-goh mewled, snap, snap, snapping against my leg.

I glanced down at his face, away from the insistent little cock fucking my leg, only to immediately regret not looking at his expression sooner.

His eyes were as black with lust as mine were and he was flushed from head to toe. Huu-goh's tongue was out as he panted, those sweet useless flat teeth flashing as he bore them, and his nails dug into my forearms tight enough to sink inside my flesh. "Oh fuhk," he repeated. It must be a curse of some sort, or a deity, for how reverently he said it. "Gahd yew feel soh goohd."

I clutched his ass harder, and pulled at his balls, my cocks throbbing as I watched his eyes cross and drool dripped down his chin. The wet spot on his pants was growing bigger and *bigger* as Huu-goh rubbed against me, that thick long dick leaving a mess all over both of us.

"Fuck me, little beast," I cooed against his ear in my language. I did my best to ignore the voice in the back of my mind that whispered I was doing this wrong. "Give me your cum."

A few more stuttered thrusts later and I got what I wanted.

Huu-goh made the *prettiest*, most wonderful noise I'd ever heard as he spilled between us. Like a wounded animal his head tossed back, the cords in his throat bared as he rutted one last time against my leg. My tendrils pulled at his nipples again, milking every last drop of his pleasure from him before they slipped away and retreated inside my body.

His expression was dazed and foggy as he came down from his high, that pert little ass clenching beneath my fingers as I rubbed between his cheeks from top to bottom just to make him gasp again.

"Enuff," he whimpered in human-speak, pushing at my chest weakly, his face flushed and his hair sweaty. "Sensihtihve."

"I do not understand you," I purred against his ear, "but you are *delicious* all the same. What a gift you have given me."

"*Fuhk*," Huu-goh whined, "whai yew gahtta sownd like that? All growlee and shiht. Jee-suhs." He nuzzled against me, his earlier ire forgotten. His legs buckled a little when I released his ass. An easy enough fix. I picked him up off the ground. He barely protested as I carried him into the bathroom and helped him get clean.

He'd made a point to get angry when I tried to accompany him to the bathroom before, but there were no protests this time. At least at first. When I reached for his soiled clothing, Huu-goh pushed my hands away and pointed at the door with an angry furrow to his brow.

I took the hint and left.

Twenty minutes later Huu-goh rejoined me in the bedroom, looking fresh-faced and relaxed in a way he hadn't before. He sleepily wandered to his bed in the corner of the room, curling in a ball on top of it, and snuggling in before he turned to look at me, his blue eyes wicked with intelligence.

"I thihnk…" he swallowed, speaking to me even though he knew I had no way of understanding. "I dohn't mayend bee-eeng a peht if it meens yew tuch me like that ahll the tayem."

He smiled, a sweet grin that made him look prettier than ever. My hearts pounded as I offered him a smile of my own, my cocks still pulsing with need inside my sleep pants. They hadn't stopped aching the entire time I'd been waiting for his return. Now that I was whole again, the memories my tendrils had made while wrapping around him teased the back of my subconscious.

His nipples had been so soft but hard, desperate to be twisted and plucked.

His skin was so *warm*.

No wonder why everyone was so obsessed with sex.

When Huu-goh was asleep I waited all of thirty seconds before I made my way to the bathroom. My hands shook as I pulled my toy from beneath the sink. I hadn't done this in years, not since I'd been young and virile, and thought I owned the world. I slicked the opening of the mount with lube, listening toward our room to make sure Huu-goh was still asleep before I pulled my cocks out of my trousers and pushed them into the device.

It sucked and slurped around me and I growled, ducking my head toward my chest to hide the sound as I tore my claws into the toy and pounded into it. My cocks twitched and writhed, twisting together as they sought the friction they'd been aching for.

And when they came my eyes rolled back, memories of Huu-goh's blissed-out expression playing in the back of my mind as I scraped my fingers through the remnants of Huu-goh's cum on my thigh and brought them to my snout to sniff.

Hope was a trembling, newborn thing.

And when I climbed into bed, satisfied and aching to hold Huu-goh close, for the first time in months, I knew I wouldn't dream of death.

# SIX

## HUGO

**SO MUCH HAD HAPPENED IN** the last month that it was difficult to wrap my mind around all of it. I'd seen so many things, met so many creatures, that my journal was completely full. When I dreamed, it was of planets with red grass, lavender skies, and mines full of glittery gems so gorgeous they made diamonds on Earth pale in comparison.

I was living a life I never could have imagined—even in my wildest fantasies.

And yet...

Discontent stirred beneath the surface of my skin. It was a seed at first, something small and easily ignored. But as it took root and grew, the difficulty of each day grew with it. It wasn't Roark's fault. At least...not intentionally.

I could tell he cared and that was...puzzling.

I'd never really mattered to anyone before I'd met Roark. That should have made me happy—and it did. But it was complicated, navigating the transition from slave to pet as my world changed drastically again.

It wasn't that he didn't make me feel safe.

He did, actually.

Roark was protective to the point of frustration.

Especially when we visited actual-real-life-foreign-planets—in space!—and discovered things that I could never have dreamed of. Roark kept me within two feet of him at all times. Which in turn, made the scientist in me riot. Unfortunately, no matter how hard I tugged on my leash, no matter how much I tried to bargain, he refused to ever allow me to stray from his side.

So yeah, safety wasn't the issue.

I understood that he was looking out for my best interests. Roark had proven to be nothing but serious and kind since the day I met him. But as someone who had always been independent, I hated the way I had no say in my life at all.

Don't get me wrong, I'm not saying that being a pleasure slave was any more dignified than what I was now. But at least back on planet F'ukYuu I wasn't sleeping on what was essentially a "doggy" bed. I wasn't dragged around on a leash. I wasn't pampered like a pedigree Pomeranian and left alone on the ship in Roark's quarters for *hours* at a time while my "owner" went to work at his very important job.

I was lucky he didn't crate-train me, for god's sake.

I bet he'd view that as "protecting" me too.

Roark had to have experienced something really fucked up to be as paranoid and controlling as he was. And I hurt for him, I really did. But that didn't make this transition any easier.

I'd had a purpose before. An occupation. A Manager. There was structure in my life on F'ukYuu that was noticeably missing here. I had always known my place, and I'd always known what was expected of me.

Roark was, admittedly, a much better person than The Manager had been. He was kinder, for one. He was *gentle*. Sometimes too gentle. To the point it was almost cold. Like he was scared to touch me the way he had the day we met. I suppose I could understand that too, as it wasn't like I'd crossed that line either.

We were both trying to figure out how to navigate this new life together. And it wasn't his fault that he was having an easier time transitioning than I was. Like a robot, he woke up at exactly the same time every morning— no alarm clock necessary—and went about his day with ruthless efficiency.

I was a blip on his schedule.

Between brushing his teeth—which took forever—disappearing to what I assumed was a gym based on how sweaty he was after, showering, and accepting our breakfast at the door, "pet Hugo" was simply another task on Roark's to-do list.

It shouldn't have bothered me the way it did. I knew he made time for me in his life because he cared. Or so I assumed he did, considering he bought me for a shit-ton of money.

But still.

The truth was, I didn't want to be Roark's pet.

I wanted him to *want* me.

And instead, I was stuck in limbo, following him around, waiting for him when he was gone, thinking and dreaming about him—unable to fully enjoy the wonders that made up my new life on the days he brought me with him—because the little part of me that had hopes for the future was starting to die.

When we weren't out running errands on various planets the only view I was privy to was the stars on our ceiling and the smooth, cold walls of Roark's rooms. I'd memorized every astronomy poster that decorated their surface ten times over. Sitting alone in the quiet with no stimulation made my brain *itch*.

What was worse was knowing I currently lived inside an alien spacecraft and did not even know where our food came from. Or where Roark disappeared for most of the day when we were in space.

The monotony was enough to make me feel like I was going crazy.

Everything wasn't all bad though.

The highlight of my day was the time the nanobots would clean. I'd sit on Roark's bed—because he was more than often gone at that point—and watch them scurry around the floor like tiny electronic mice. I wasn't sure *how* exactly they cleaned, and I was still working up the nerve to snatch one so I could examine it more closely. I wished I had tools to do so. Screwdrivers. Anything that would help occupy my withering mind.

I was sure, if I could leave the room these feelings wouldn't be festering. And the seed of discontent that had been planted would grow at a slower pace.

Not that I could tell Roark that.

Or anything really.

Language barrier, remember?

We'd been working on that during the hours we spent together after Roark returned to his rooms for dinner every day. We'd started our own version of sign language. Gestures to indicate both good and bad. Hand motions to ask for the bathroom, or the bed. And on top of that, Roark had learned a handful of words in English.

"Bed," I repeated, for what felt like the hundredth time one night after we'd finished eating the weird cucumber-tasting bark stuff he kept force-feeding me. There were a few hours left before he'd retreat beneath the covers of his bed, the lights would turn off, and I'd be left on my "doggy" bed to rot in silence.

The distance between us felt vast then. Like he was a galaxy away. Like I was even more alone than I'd been when I was a kid, or in my pod on F'ukYuu.

It was hard to think about that though when he was being so goddamn cute and earnest. Sitting there with glasses perched on his nose, his big hands scribbling the word I spoke on his tablet—presumably so he wouldn't forget.

"Peh-d." Roark echoed, scribbling away. He had a hard time with Bs in general, but he was getting closer. Each stroke of his pen was deliberate and careful—just like everything he did.

"Bed," I repeated, slower this time. "B-B-B- eh duh."

Roark huffed in amusement—or annoyance. I still hadn't figured out which.

"Pb-ehd." He tapped the tip of the pen thoughtfully against the table. It was a nervous tick he had—the only one, as far as I'd gathered.

"Yes!" I gave him a double thumbs up and his eyes turned into pleased crescents. "Closer."

"Pbed." Roark waited patiently to see if he'd gotten it.

"So close!"

"Bed." His voice was rough, his teeth razor-sharp and flickering in the light as he sounded out the word again.

"Yes!" Another double thumbs up—and an embarrassing victory lap later—we could officially add another word to Roark's list.

I'd tried to learn his language too, but both of us had very quickly discovered that my vocal cords were not equipped for the guttural tones most of the words required.

When I'd tried to say the word for "bed" in Roark's language I'd made him make an adorable barking-laugh sound. There were a couple words I managed more easily, but all of them felt uncomfortable and a little painful. They twanged my vocal cords like my throat was an untuned piano.

Those were the highlights.

Those little shared moments when I felt…normal.

It'd been so long since I'd felt normal.

But unfortunately, as the weeks wore on and my thoughts continued to fester—even those happy little moments couldn't fix what felt inherently wrong between us. Earlier that day, when we'd been planet-side, Roark had tugged me close by my leash one too many times. Something inside me had finally snapped.

I liked to think that I was a patient person. I'd never had reason to be anything else. But even I had my limits. And if I was being honest, my "freak out" as I was privately calling it in my head, had been long overdue.

*Years* overdue.

Way before Roark had picked me up and rehomed me.

And way before I'd been abducted and sold.

*That* was why I'd panicked. Why I'd yelled at him. Why I'd raged. I'd done all the things I'd sworn I'd never do. All the things I thought were scary, and uncomfortable to witness. I'd been angry, loud, and unattractive. My behavior had been nothing but *ugly*, I knew that. And for that I deserved punishment—or at the very least, retaliation.

But…

Roark hadn't yelled back.

He hadn't punished me.

Instead, he'd *soothed* me.

Again.

Just like the day we met.

He'd given me exactly what I'd been missing, without even needing the words to understand what was wrong.

Only this time was better. Because he'd *hugged* me.

*Hugged* me.

Pulled me against his big, solid chest and blocked out my antsy thoughts with his bulk. My frustrations were forgotten the moment he touched me again. Like they'd never been there at all. And the part of me that had been lonely, lonely, lonely for longer than I could remember faded into nothingness.

It was embarrassing to realize that all my complaints were truly just excuses for the one thing I actually wanted from him. And with mortification, I could admit there was nothing I couldn't forgive if I knew Roark reciprocated my feelings.

It was funny, back home on Earth I'd been the *easy* kid—upbeat, goody-two-shoes, straight As. I'd gotten a B once and cried all weekend. My teacher had taken pity on me and let me do some extra credit after the semester was over—and that had been that. I'd never given my mom grief, even though she was rarely home. I'd never asked my dad for attention— at least, not after my sixteenth birthday.

I'd done what I was supposed to *when* I was supposed to.

But now…

Now, with my identity compromised, with everything I'd ever known lost—*now* was when I'd finally broken. I'd never acted worse than I had then, throwing a tantrum like a toddler. But I couldn't be angry that I had. Because the peace I felt the second Roark's muscular pink arms wrapped around me had made everything wrong in my heart bleed away.

Maybe *that's* why I'd reacted the way I did.

Why I'd given in.

Why I'd cried.

Why I'd relaxed.

Why I'd let go.

Why I'd rubbed against him, chasing pleasure—his thigh a hard thickness against my aching dick. God, he'd felt good. Those tentacles twisting, tugging, *pulling* at my nipples, his blue eyes flashing black with what I could only assume was lust. I'd never felt so seen before, like every ounce of his attention was on me.

Like I was *fascinating*.

Not some loser with no romantic prospects. Not a slave with no rights. Not a man with no future, no home, and no family. Not a pet, saved for entertainment.

Roark made me feel *beautiful*.

And when he touched me like that…I felt whole.

*Pretty, pretty, pretty*—the way he'd said I was.

I hadn't meant to make a mess all over him. I hadn't meant to come at all, but I had anyway.

And now, nearly an hour later, I was…avoiding him, because what else was I supposed to do? I had never been more confused in my entire life. It felt like we'd taken off again. Like the floor was rising beneath me. Like the stars were ready to swallow me whole. I didn't know how to face what I'd done, or how he'd react to it now that the moment was over.

So I hid away in my "doggy" bed like a goddamn coward.

I tried to ignore the creak of the bed across the room as Roark returned from his trip to the bathroom, but failed spectacularly. Peeking over the corner of my blanket, I watched his bulky shape settle in the center of the circular mattress on top of the covers.

It wasn't like the beds I was used to back home. It was round and had a raised lip around the edge that was made up of soft pillow-like cushions. The mattress was also *massive*. It kinda had to be to accommodate Roark's bulk. Judging by the weight of his steps, his size, and the heft of the matter he was formed from, he had to easily weigh at least six hundred pounds. Maybe more? It was hard to say. Back home I'd never studied anything made of the same substance he was formed from—so I had no idea what its density was.

I shifted to see better so I could peek at him for a few more seconds. *He's going to notice if you keep looking at him like that,* I warned myself. Quickly, I shut my eyes, lying ramrod straight with my head toward the ceiling so he wouldn't catch me in the act.

Only…I was nothing if not curious, so I peeked again.

Roark shifted on his bed, those thick thighs spreading, the lump of his dick obvious through his thin sleep pants. I licked my lips, my cock twitching sympathetically as I remembered what it felt like to push right against those things. Made me wonder if his surface would grab at my dick the same way it had grabbed my chest if we were naked together.

Roark huffed out a long, sleepy sigh.

My thoughts were far from innocent.

I could still remember the way he'd felt above me, and around me. Could perfectly picture the way he'd grabbed my ass and played with me like I was a toy for the taking. He'd had such a serious expression on his face. Like he had no idea what he was doing—but he was determined to do it anyway. At least…I thought so?

Again, it was hard to read him.

Was he a virgin?

Why was that kinda hot?

I shouldn't find that hot, should I?

Fuck, okay. Maybe it was best to just admit defeat. Clearly trying to sleep was not working. Not when Roark was like ten feet away and I had the opportunity to ogle his dick through his pants.

I squirmed.

Roark sighed again.

I froze, holding my breath. When he didn't move, I exhaled, relaxing again before the squirming started up with a vengeance. Flipping over onto my side, I faced him fully, staring him down—all my earlier embarrassment forgotten.

*Did he like what we'd done?*

That thought plagued me as my skin itched and itched.

Thinking about sex with Roark was the lesser of two evils. If I let my mind wander elsewhere I had no doubt I'd do the thing I'd been dreaming about doing for weeks. I'd break out of our rooms and explore the ship I'd been living inside.

The only thing standing between me and an entire ship of alien tech was a bubblegum-shark and his sleepy sighs. Oh. And the steel door. But I could get through that easily.

I'd memorized the code to the keypad the first day.

Flipping onto my back again, I debated what to do.

Sleep was a no go.

Should I keep staring at Roark's dick?

Should I break out?

It wasn't like I was going to actually run away. We were in space, *duh*. Buuuut maybe while Roark slept I could get a peek at the technology I'd never thought I'd get the chance to see? No leash involved. He wouldn't even know I'd done it. I could sneak out and back in before he woke and I—

"Huu-goh," Roark's deep growly voice echoed through the silent room. I shivered, all thoughts of leaving snuffed out. The lamp beside Roark's bed flicked on, illuminating the room in a soft blue light. Slowly, Roark sat up, his eyes all squinty like he was tired. Like I'd been squirming for far longer than I'd realized—keeping him awake.

I couldn't read the squiggles on the clock on the wall so I had no idea what time it actually was. But they were definitely a different sort of shape than they'd been when I'd first started planning espionage.

"Huu-goh," Roark murmured again, tsking softly in a disapproving sound. "Huu-goh, tired?"

That was one of the few emotions I'd been able to teach him. A yawning motion and a stretch had been enough to clearly communicate what the word meant when we'd been role-playing teacher and student.

"No," I threw the blanket off my chest. It pooled around my hips as I sat up to glare at him—irritated with myself all over again. He'd just gotten me off. He'd just hugged me. Why did I still feel so—so—off? And

I was taking it out on him. Which was fucking awful. I just…I couldn't help it. "Hugo is *not* tired." I was, actually. I was pretty tired. But…there was just something about him that brought out the inner toddler in me. The parts I usually kept buried. Like I didn't have to mask what I was feeling when he was around.

Damn, I hadn't realized I was such a secret brat.

Apparently, Roark could take it though because he remained unfazed by my dramatics. He met them head-on with patience as always. Huffing out a little breath, Roark stared me down from across the room. His teeth were so bright they almost glowed in the dark. His spots were yellow. Which was a color I'd very rarely seen.

Huh.

*I wonder what that meant?*

After what felt like a thousand years he finally found the words he wanted.

"Huu-goh come," Roark patted the bed, his eye ridges shifting in a way that almost looked indulgent, like he thought my little tantrum was endearing rather than annoying. Which kinda only made me want to fight back more.

Yeah, right.

I was *not* going over there.

He waited.

I glared at him.

He frowned. It was kind of a comical expression on his face—considering all the teeth. Almost made him look fucking terrifying—if I hadn't known he was a giant teddy bear.

"Huu-goh come," Roark repeated, slower this time. *Growlier.*

With a sigh, I gathered my blanket and trudged barefoot across the short distance that separated us. Inside me, the "something" that had itched celebrated. The floor was chilly against the pads of my feet. Icy cold. Like it leached the warmth away with every careful step. My heart beat erratically as I stood at the edge of the massive mattress, trying to figure out why I was as elated as I was.

Roark patted the bed again.

I hesitated, but only for a moment.

Apparently Roark had had enough of my shenanigans. Because the next thing I knew he'd wrapped his arm around me and yanked me effortlessly through the air. His body was solid and warm beneath mine, the mattress impossibly soft as my toes brushed against it.

I squawked, more than a little surprised by the manhandling as Roark grumbled to himself and arranged the blankets he hadn't put on earlier around the both of us. The bed was cushy. Squishy. Comfortable. A bit harder than the bed he'd given me, but nice all the same.

Roark's thick arm wrapped around my middle. He arranged my limbs using a few slithery little tentacles that erupted from his skin. When I was exactly as he wanted me to be, he pulled me in tight, his hot breath tickling the back of my neck as his half-chubby cock pressed against my ass cheek. It was fucking huge. So big it was hard to believe it was a single dick at all.

I'd been such an asshole today. And I knew he didn't deserve that—and that I should give him an apology. I wanted to beat myself up about it. Wanted to tear apart every little thing I'd done wrong. But I just…

Christ, he was comfortable. And safe. And—and—I felt…god. For the first time in weeks I felt seen again.

Too tired to care anymore, my eyelids began to droop.

This was the first time Roark had let me into his bed. And something loose within me settled. Like for the first time in my life I was exactly where I was meant to be—with who I was meant to be with.

The festering faded.

My ire melted away.

"Huu-goh," Roark murmured. It was just my name. I'd heard it a thousand times before. But…I'd never heard it spoken so softly. Like it was a full fucking sentence. Like it meant something to him—like he was…thanking me somehow.

Like Roark was as relieved as I was that things had shifted between us.

Maybe he'd been…lonely too?

Roark stroked that big warm palm down my spine, soothing me like he had earlier, that strange rumbling purr in his throat starting up again. Only this time we were pressed so close together it vibrated my whole body, made my lashes flutter, and my limbs go limp. Like a whole-body massage—damn.

I was asleep in seconds, despite the alien dick pressing against me. Roark didn't move to get himself off, seemingly content to lie stationary behind me as I rested easily for the first time in three long years.

He pulled me tighter.

He was warm, warm, warm.

I dreamed of galaxies, stars, and tentacles.

Roark never let me go.

# SEVEN

## ROARK

**HUU-GOH WAS…MORE THAN I** ever could've expected. And though I was delighted with the course of events that had transpired the night before, even I could recognize that I was out of my depth. Things had shifted between us. And I didn't know how to react to that.

This was what I'd been hoping for.

But it was also my first time having any sort of feelings for another person. And I was completely in over my head.

The feelings I had been having had only grown stronger after touching him. After the line that I'd drawn between us had been scuffed out entirely by his sweet little hips.

I found myself thinking about him even more now, as I extricated myself from bed and headed into the bathroom to begin my morning ritual—earlier than usual. That alone made me anxious. I rarely, if ever, deviated from my schedule.

But my mind was reeling, and I just—

I needed answers. Needed to speak to someone, get these feelings out—and figure out a battle plan moving forward.

As I brushed my teeth, a memory surfaced. It'd been one of Huu-goh's first days on board and I'd been giving him a tour of the rooms, the bathroom included.

After I'd seen his initial excitement I'd taken to showing him every single facet of the room all the way down to the way the nanobots cleaned up when shower water spilled upon the tile, or the automatic dispenser for toothpaste, mouthwash, and soap. All you had to do was press the correct button and the fluid the device expelled would change.

Don't ask me how it kept itself clean, but I'd never in all my years as captain tasted soap when I was expecting mouthwash.

Huu-goh was fascinated with everything, he pushed every button, he celebrated the steady stream of toothpaste with obvious delight—stuck his finger in it—and licked it with his tiny pink tongue just to test.

"Toothpaasteh!" he had crowed in triumph, waggling his damp finger at me. "Wut the fuhk."

I'd grinned, and he hadn't been frightened of my teeth. He never had.

The memory faded as swiftly as it had come.

And my worries came back as my gaze met my own reflection. I tried to make sense of what was going on inside my head so that I could get proper advice. Foam coated my lips as I scrubbed and scrubbed, thoughts spinning.

I was and had always been a traditional Sarhk. Many had teased me for my behaviors in the past, though I'd never let it bother me as their jabs had been good-natured. In all my four decades, I had never been interested in looking at one of the creatures so freely offered on the planets along my route. Never glanced at the pleasure houses. Never entered one.

Sex was for mates.

And I'd never been interested in mating.

Until I'd met Huu-goh.

Huu-goh who was as intriguing as he was delightful. Huu-goh who was not afraid to get angry with me when he was upset despite our size disparity. Huu-goh who was clever and quick on his feet. Huu-goh with his dark eyes, and his pretty orange fur. Huu-goh whose eyes were full of wonder despite the horrors he'd survived.

Huu-goh who was not afraid of me, even though he had every right to be.

He slept just as peacefully now as when I'd left to get ready for the day. As I passed by him on the bed, warmth burst inside my hearts. My mate was a tiny man-shaped ball, the blankets we'd shared bunched around him like a cocoon. The most adorable droning snore escaped him as he slumbered. It was a noise that I'd quickly found I liked. It allowed me to know that he was resting, even when he had been in his bed across the room. It was reassuring.

With a sigh, I left him to continue to sleep, careful to shut the door gently so the sound would not wake him.

I liked to think I was self-sufficient. That I could take care of my own feelings and needs and that I did not need anyone. But that was a lie.

My surface felt icy as I made my way down the hall toward the sparring rooms. I knew Mala would already be there. By the time I arrived most mornings he'd already been exercising for a good few hours. I had no doubt that he'd be surprised to see me so early—but I needed him.

I needed a *friend.*

And it was early enough we wouldn't have to worry about the others that occupied the ship interrupting our discussion.

I had a lot of thoughts to work through.

Like the fact that now that I'd touched him once, when Huu-goh was around all I wanted to do was shove my tentacles all over him and watch him hump my leg again. Breathing in through my nose to calm myself, I did my best to force away the tantalizing thoughts.

At first, I'd thought my mate innocent, but I could see now how wrong I'd been.

And how grateful I was that he'd made a move when he did.

I had begun to lose hope that a creature as brilliant as he was would be interested in a beast like me. I was his senior by…too many years. I was jaded in a way that he was not—despite all that had been done to him. And though I'd seen many things during my time traveling the stars, I had never seen anyone as tantalizing as Huu-goh.

He was *resilient.*

Petulant at times, yes, but I did not begrudge him this. He'd had much taken from him. Everything. Now that he was free it would take many moons for him to feel in control of his life once again—if he ever actually did.

The fact he'd chosen me meant more than he would ever know.

I didn't want to mess this up.

My gut squirmed as I entered the sparring room, searching for a familiar blue fin. Mala was where I expected him to be, his tentacles twisted around one of the punching bags, squeezing it till powder popped from the seams.

"Someone's up early," Mala teased, turning to look at me, his spots pink with affection. Mine shifted to match as I settled into the spot beside him, claiming a bag of my own to warm up.

"I…" It was difficult to admit what was going on inside my head. But I didn't have much time—and I was nothing if not efficient. "Huu-goh has decided to take me as a mate." My fist connected with the punching bag, tendrils exploding out before I retreated and repeated the motion. "I am happy."

Mala made a sound beside me, slamming into his bag one more time before he grabbed it with one hand to stop it from swinging. "You do not sound happy."

"I am happy," I repeated, slamming into the bag again. And again. The harder I hit it, the better I felt. The ache in my limbs was familiar and comforting—as was Mala's presence. Above us, the lights gleamed as bright as they always did. They bleached the corners of darkness, casting the room in a sterile glow.

"That's why you're abusing that poor punching bag?" Mala snarked, as though we didn't do this every morning—with the same brutal exuberance. "Because you're happy."

"Yes." I sucked in a breath, hitting the bag one last time, before I caught it the same way he had. My limbs felt molten, the iciness of my own fears having faded as I twisted to face him. His eyes flickered, head tilting to the side as his spots turned yellow.

"Tell me what's really on your mind," Mala said, stepping away from the bag and beckoning me after him. I trailed after him, for once content to let him call the shots as we headed toward the sparring ring in the center of the room. Back home, many Sahrks wrestled for sport, and out in space was no different. It kept our reflexes quick. And at times like this, when I was indecisive and shaky-footed, it was a comfort to have access to something so familiar.

Mala didn't push again.

And for twenty minutes I worked my feelings out by throwing him to the mat. Over and over. Thump, thump, thump. He laughed every time I did, but even I could tell he was cutting me slack. Normally he'd be annoyed that I was stronger. He'd be insulting me, trying to get a rise out of me. But today, he was silent.

"I don't know if I can be what he needs," I finally admitted. Mala was pinned beneath me, pink and blue melted together as I forced him into the ground. The words hurt to admit as they spilled free. Immediately, my tendrils retreated until our colors were our own again. I offered Mala a hand up. He grunted as he rose to his feet.

"Why would you say that?" he asked, voice quiet and patient.

"I'm..." My own chest was heaving as I scrubbed a hand over my face. I could feel my spots shifting. Probably too fast for him to read them. "I don't want to fail him."

"Roark." Mala's tentacles looped around my wrist and pulled it from my face. "I've known you for a long time."

I nodded, because he had.

"And I've never seen you fail at anything you wanted. Not once."

That was supposed to be reassuring, I knew that. But I just... "This is different," I argued, my hearts beating erratically. Mala and I leaned against the ring that surrounded the sparring mats to keep the occupants inside. "I don't know how to be...what he needs."

"Sure you do." Mala settled beside me. "It's easy."

I scoffed. "How?"

"You listen," Mala shrugged a shoulder. I knew he was speaking from experience. His expression was fond as his eyes took on a faraway sheen. Like he was thinking of his own mate back home. His love—his soulmate. "You care." He twisted to look at me. "And when you mess up, you apologize."

"You make it sound easy."

"It is," Mala replied. "When you love someone—you tend to do those things anyway. Putting in the effort to make them happy is the easiest thing in the world."

"I don't know how to love someone." My hearts thudded. "You know… about my past. I am not like you—I didn't have…examples to learn from."

"I get that," Mala's tone was gentle. "But you're smart, Roark. When you became captain you didn't know how to do that either. And look at you now." He had been with me as I rose through the ranks. We had had many talks just like this one—though all of those felt less important now. "Best fucking captain The Dreamer has ever had."

I scoffed, because that was not true. I had known the best captain. And he had died.

I forced those thoughts aside, focusing instead on Huu-goh. Even the thought of him brought me peace. "Huu-goh has been through…more than I think any of us can comprehend," I added, trying to make sure Mala understood how strong my mate was.

"F'ukYuu is not a…" Mala lowered his voice, glancing around to make sure we were alone so as not to offend the men on board who adored the planet, "very hospitable place. Especially for those of a more gentle nature."

I thought back on Huu-goh's smile, all pearly flat teeth. The way he flipped through his journal, chewing his writing instrument to bits, pages and pages of observations decorating every surface. He didn't seem unhappy. At least…unless he was on the leash. Or when he was…fuck.

When he was left alone in the rooms for too long.

I swallowed the lump in my throat and nodded, grateful he understood.

"I want to make him happy," I admitted. My voice was rough. "But I have no experience. I am blind in a way I've never been before. I don't know if I'm the kind of person who is capable of being…someone's partner."

These were all thoughts I should have had before taking Huu-goh aboard the ship. But there hadn't been time. I'd always been more of an action-man anyway. And in that moment, there had been no choice but to keep him—how could I have done anything different when I'd asked him if he wanted to stay and he'd said no?

Since then, I'd simply been doing my best.

But I'd been flying blind.

"I think you're making excuses because you're scared," Mala accused, always wiser than I gave him credit for. He had a family back home, a mate and three pups. Though I was older, he had more experience.

"I…" My spots lost their color as I clenched my fists and tried to figure out how to tell Mala what I'd done. "You're right," I admitted as visions of Huu-goh's hips pumping against me assaulted my senses. "But—"

Mala rolled his eyes. "You annoy me."

"Fuck you." Despite my own conflicting emotions, I laughed.

"I don't know how else to tell you that the only way you'll fuck this up is by overthinking it." He jabbed me in the chest with a claw and I snorted, batting his hand away. "You said he wanted you? That he made the choice?"

"Yes." My pulse thrummed. "And I want to touch him again. But I haven't even planned the ceremony yet. Isn't that disrespectful? He deserves to be treated with respect. I've never thought about any of this before. It is intimidating. I don't want to get it wrong."

"If you want to touch him then touch him," Mala shrugged.

"It is not so simple."

"It is." He stared at me. I stared back. A few beats passed. "Okay," Mala sighed. "I'm going to tell you something, and you're going to listen." I nodded. "And you're not going to judge me, but you will take this to heart—and to your grave." He narrowed his eyes. "I don't want it getting around or my mate would kill me, but I do think knowing this will bring you some peace."

My hearts thudded. I nodded again.

"Yanet and I…" Mala sighed dreamily, leaning against the counter with a grin as he spoke of his mate. "We had a lot of…fun before our ceremony."

I blinked, shocked.

"*Yanet?*" Yanet was older than me by several years, and far more uptight than anyone I'd ever met. It was nearly impossible to imagine him doing anything of a sexual nature at all. Ugh. That thought was not—no. Just, no.

"He did not let me fuck him with my cocks till the night of our wedding, but…" Mala grinned wickedly. "I had other ways of getting inside him."

I gagged, and Mala chuckled, amused by my pain.

"Spare me the details, please." I was not interested in imagining two of my closest friends in such a setting before their mating.

"The point is," Mala continued. "We were fine. We *are* fine." He met my gaze, trying to get his point across. "You were at the wedding. Was it any less special? Did Yanet look like he felt disrespected?"

He wanted a real answer, so I thought seriously before speaking. The truth tasted light on my tongue. "No."

"Do you think less of Yanet and I now?"

"No."

"See?" He grinned, slapping me on the shoulder, his tendrils splitting out to give me a playful squeeze. "Everyone moves at their own pace. Whatever feels natural to you both is the right course to take."

"Right."

My head was spinning. My hearts were in my throat.

"But…" This was embarrassing. More than a little mortifying to admit. "I don't know…how to do anything. I mean—" I dropped my tone, grateful once again that we were alone. "How does it even work?"

Of course I knew *how* it worked. The fundamentals at least.

"He's not a Sahrk," I added, spots fuschia in embarrassment when I caught a glimpse of myself in the mirrors that lined the rooms. Mala nodded, as if he realized that this was where my true insecurity came from. "What if I can't please him? What if we're not…compatible."

"Were you compatible last night?"

I blinked, head swimming as I thought about Huu-goh again for what felt like the hundredth time that day. I nodded, mouth suddenly dry.

"He's small, so I'd be careful with his ass," Mala spoke clinically, and I had to bite back my growl. He was helping me—but it still made me uncomfortable that he was thinking about my mate this way. "Start with a little tendril. Work your way up." Mala hummed thoughtfully, and I memorized everything he was saying, grateful that I hadn't had to ask for this even though it was mortifying to get such details from someone I considered a dear friend. "Lubrication will be your best friend."

I nodded, wishing I had my HoverPad to take notes.

"Try your tongue first. You can lick his cocks—"

"Cock," I corrected, then immediately wished I hadn't.

"Cock," Mala laughed, shaking his head at me. He sounded vaguely curious, but because he was a good person, did not push. "Lick his cock. Test things out. Go slow—give him plenty of time to tell you when he likes something and when he doesn't. Pay attention to him. And have fun."

I nodded again, head swimming.

"You can communicate a little, right? I've seen it."

Again, I nodded.

"Use that to your advantage."

In a daze, I headed back to our shared room, a plate of breakfast in each hand as I imagined what would await me there. As I'd prepared the food, I'd let my mind wander. I'd replayed my conversation with Mala over and over. And been more than a little distracted when Ushuu had greeted me in the hallway on my way out the door of the mess hall. His slightly weathered face had crinkled in curiosity, head tilted to the side—but I didn't have the extra bandwidth to speak to him after I'd been ignoring him all month.

I felt bad about that, I truly did.

But so much had been going on that I just…didn't know how to tell him about it.

As I hit the code into the keypad, all thoughts of my mentor and my inadequacies fled. Instead, excitement buzzed beneath my surface. The door swung open a few inches, and I paused, eyes drifting shut as pleasant thoughts plagued me all over again.

Tonight, when Huu-goh got up to his mischief…yes.

*Tonight.*

I would play with him again.

I would be gentle as Mala suggested. It didn't matter that I'd never done this before. Or that I'd never wanted to. Because I wanted this with Huu-goh. And clearly, he wanted it too. It was easier to feel relieved now that I'd spoken to Mala candidly about sex.

Apparently all I'd needed was support.

Now my fantasies ran rampant.

My pulse thrummed and I forced back the growl that threatened to erupt at the thought of mounting Huu-goh. I was certain he'd be warmer inside and I couldn't wait to test that theory. I wanted to see his cock without the pesky cloth hiding it. I wanted to watch his eyes roll back and his tongue curl again.

I wanted to taste the secret skin between his ass cheeks, and lick the succulent sweat from his balls and groin. Inhale him like the treasure he was, till he became my little beast again and took what he wanted from me.

I had never been this aroused in all my life.

My red spots betrayed me, and I couldn't even bring myself to care as I pushed open the door the rest of the way and my—no, our—bedroom came into focus. I was unsurprised to find Huu-goh awake and waiting patiently in the center of our bed for my return. His skin was flushed, his eyes darker than normal. There was a bulge in his sleep pants, his sweet—singular—dick pressing insistently against the fabric, full and thick, but so much smaller than my own.

"Fuuhd?" he asked, perking up, his tongue flickering out to wet his lower lip.

I nodded in agreement, biting back a groan as Huu-goh shifted to his knees. My cocks pulsed as he crawled across the surface of the mattress toward the edge so he could climb off. I wished I could see the view from behind. See the way his lithe thighs flexed and his ass jiggled.

It was like something ravenous had awoken inside me.

Saliva filled my mouth, a desperate need to fuck making my hands shake as I crossed the distance between us at a glacial pace and handed him his plate.

*Don't scare him,* I reprimanded myself.

*Tonight you can have him.*

*If he wants you again.*

"Thank yuu," Huu-goh said. Those were words he repeated a lot. Enough so that I'd managed to figure out what they meant. I nodded, my cocks writhing toward him despite being safely tucked away inside my trousers.

I couldn't blame them.

I wanted to touch him too.

So badly.

More than I'd ever wanted anything.

I stroked a hand through Huu-goh's fur as he smiled down at the food. He dug in with gusto. He groaned when he took the first bite, not minding the fact it'd been crushed to a pulp where my bambuu stalk was still whole and crunchy. Thankfully, Huu-goh didn't complain about the petting or the texture of his food. Lately he'd been snapping a lot more— and I'd been hesitant to touch.

It seemed that barrier was gone too.

Maybe he'd been anxious to admit his feelings for me? And the petting had set him off. It'd been close to what he wanted, but not enough. But then last night had happened—and we'd...yes. We were different now. Close in a way I didn't think either of us ever had been before.

Things were different.

When we reached Sha'hPihn I would make the necessary calls home for the ceremony. And when we reached my home planet we would become official. I would keep him safe, for all his life. There was no need for distance anymore.

Not now that we were mates.

"Taastehs like cuucumbehr." Huu-goh took his last bite with a happy sigh. I sat down on the bed, weak-kneed as I watched him, my own plate forgotten in my grip. He had such long, long legs for such a small thing. And such a lovely, tiny waist. And his shoulders! Shoulders that were broad despite the lack of meat on his bones.

My cocks twisted together and I willed them to behave, the heady lust fogging my senses making me light-headed.

*Tonight,* I told myself.

*Tonight,* after my duties are complete, I'll take him.

*Tonight* his body would be mine.

# EIGHT

## HUGO

**AS I WAS GOING THROUGH** puberty I'd still managed to be a model student. I'd bitten back the mood swings. I'd hidden every part of me that wasn't palatable. I'd let my true feelings wither and die with a smile on my face. All because I knew that along with the hormones, acne, and frustration I'd be gifted with my parents' ire if I didn't.

I barely had their attention as it was.

Mom was too preoccupied with her own life to worry about how mine was going. And Dad spent more time with a bottle in his hand, or alone with his secretary, than he did with me. On the few rare occasions we were all together, the only thing either of them talked about were my academic accomplishments. I was a talking report card to them, but even that felt better than the icy silence of our usually empty home.

Realistically, deep down, I'd known the way they treated me wasn't fair.

But it was the only life I'd ever known. I spent so much time invisible that the last thing I wanted was to lose what little love and pride they felt for me.

I'd been everything they wanted me to be and I'd still ended up here. Abducted by aliens, rescued by more aliens, sitting in the darkness as my new owner lay peacefully beside me in bed.

You'd think I'd be mad about that last part but I wasn't.

Because there was no denying Roark was…yeah.

Roark was unlike anyone I'd ever met.

After we'd eaten dinner together and Roark and I took our separate showers, we'd retired to bed. Since Roark had come home for the evening I'd been trying to psych myself up to hit on him again.

But I just…didn't know how to cross that line.

It wasn't like I'd been a Casanova back home. I'd been a loser and that was the honest truth. Even after working on F'ukYuu it was difficult to wrap my head around the idea that someone might want to actually touch me.

Roark had said no to me the first time we'd met, and I'd internalized that probably more than I should've. The last thing I wanted was to pressure him into something he didn't want, just because I did.

Did he like what we'd done the previous day? Had I twisted it around in my head and imagined he was happier about it than he'd actually been? It hadn't helped that he'd been gone earlier than usual that morning. And that he'd been downright *respectful* over breakfast. I'd half-expected him to…you know—yank my pants off or something. Especially after we'd fallen asleep in the same bed the night before. But that hadn't happened.

In fact…*nothing* seemed to be different at all.

Maybe I'd imagined grinding on him?

*Way to gaslight yourself, Hugo.*

No.

*No.*

*It was real.*

*And he liked it.*

I'd *seen* his eyes. The way they flashed black with heat. I'd felt his touch. Felt the way he desired me. There had been a bulge in his pants, far thicker than anything I would've encountered on Earth—I hadn't made that up. I wasn't sure how to feel about that bit, honestly, only that the curious part of me really wanted to pull his pants down and peek.

The nanobots and technology in Roark's living quarters had been a solid enough distraction while he'd been gone for work—but even they hadn't been able to claim all of my attention. I hadn't thought about escaping the room since the previous night, too preoccupied with thoughts of taking Roark to bed again to think about anything else.

I just…I just wanted to have him one more time.

Was that…

Was that bad?

I hoped not.

Maybe it would lead somewhere serious, maybe it wouldn't. Maybe Roark would decide he didn't want to keep me around anymore after he found out I was a sex fiend who was after his space-dick.

But maybe…maybe he wouldn't?

There was only one way to find out.

Like with any good science experiment, trial and error were the only way to get an answer.

Roark was relaxed—and I figured now was as good of a time as any to ogle. If he wanted to stop me, he could. And if he didn't…we could see where this led.

I twisted inside his arms, wiggling as covertly as possible to get a better look at him. Roark's chest rose and fell with steady breaths. Up and down, whoosh, whoosh. His thick belly looked particularly delicious from this angle. Comfortable. The perfect size for me to fuck against till my dick spilled.

There wasn't a single thing about him that wasn't sexy as fuck.

Why the hell would he want *me*?

Roark made an inquisitive sound and I froze. A beat passed. Then two. Nothing bad happened and he didn't admonish me for staring. He didn't even open his eyes. I relaxed, studying his shirtless form with hunger.

He was just so…*different*.

His pink skin, soft to the touch, more gelatinous than solid—was nothing like mine. He may be human-shaped but the way his limbs could shapeshift made that similarity feel moot.

And his teeth. Goddamn. *Hundreds* of them. Teeth I'd discovered were meant not for ripping flesh—like I'd hypothesized—but for crunching through bark and other hard plants. *That's right.* The shark-like man was a fucking *vegetarian*.

His size was another notable difference between us.

I'd never in all my life seen someone as large as Roark. He was easily double my mass. A single one of his hands could nearly wrap around my entire waist. I could admit I'd spent an unhealthy amount of time imagining just that.

By all rights, I shouldn't be attracted to him.

I shouldn't *want* him the way I did.

Shouldn't want to explore him, or learn what he liked, or ogle the cock I'd thought I'd get to touch all those weeks ago. But now that I'd decided what I wanted there was no stopping myself.

The only path I had led forward.

Reaching for the hem of his sleep pants as slowly as I possibly could, my heart climbed into my throat. *He'll say no if he doesn't want this,* I reminded myself. Wasn't like I was going to do anything untoward without his permission—I just wanted a peek at what kinda monster cock he was packing in there. I needed to prepare.

Besides, I'd seen worse in locker rooms.

*Our dicks had to be different, right?*

The biologist in me needed to know.

The elastic gave easily beneath my fingers as I pulled it back, peeking inside the dark depths beneath it to sate my curiosity. I barely got a glimpse of the shadowy shape of Roark's cock before he made a primal, grunt-y sort of noise and the world spun. Suddenly I was on my back, my breath escaping in a quiet whoosh.

I blinked away the daze as Roark purred, his chest vibrating with the force of it as he bracketed me on the bed with his massive arms, his soft belly rubbing against my crotch. I wasn't hard, but I would be soon if he kept that up.

His eyes were black.

His spots were red.

His teeth were bared.

His chest *heaved.*

He was powerful and terrifying and god…so fucking hot. If he sneezed wrong he could kill me. Like—that should not be so sexy. But it was. All that strength, and he somehow managed to be more gentle with me than anyone I'd ever met.

"Huu-goh," Roark rasped, and it didn't sound like an admonishment. It sounded *hungry*. His hands shifted around my wrists, squeezing, once, twice, before they changed, the solid form giving way as thousands of tiny little tentacles crept around my wrists. They writhed and squeezed, the warm squishy texture making me instantly hard.

Jesus fuck.

"Roark," I wiggled a little to test the give of my bonds—only to find I was thoroughly stuck. My heart skipped a beat as butterflies exploded inside my belly. *What was going to happen next? Did red spots mean he was mad?* I'd figured out they changed with his mood but I was still getting a handle on what each color meant.

"Huu-goh," Roark murmured, voice hoarse. He ducked his head down, his snout rubbing against the side of my neck slow and easy, and my entire body trembled. *Shit. Ugh.* The rubbery, almost spongy texture of his skin felt so fucking weird but good. His head was less squishy than the rest of him, though I imagined he felt similar to what a beluga whale would feel like. Kinda rubbery? Soft.

I shivered.

"Huu-goh yesh?"

"What?" It took me a second to realize Roark was speaking in English.

His nose rubbed against me again and my toes curled when I felt the steadily growing swell of his cock pressing against mine through the dual layers of our sleep pants. Damn, that thing was massive. I wished I'd gotten a better look at it.

"Yesh?" he repeated, struggling through the S sound because of his teeth.

"Oh." My head spun. Yes. He was saying *yes*. Did that mean he wanted more too? "Yes?" The tiny tentacles around my wrists squeezed, rubbing against me in a way that shouldn't have been as tantalizing as it was. I should be fucking terrified. At least, if I was a sane person. Which I clearly was not. Because instead of shrinking beneath the bulk of this absolute beast of a man—I was running victory laps in my head.

Because serious, stoic, quiet Roark had finally snapped.

Because of *me*.

It felt like a zillion tiny ropes tickling all my nerve endings at once as the tentacles swirled and squished snug around my wrist. They tested the give, squeezing tight enough for a moment it almost hurt—before loosening at the same time I released a broken exhale.

Holy fuck.

"Roark yes?" I replied, my dick becoming fully hard so fast it gave me dick-lash.

"*Yesh*," Roark agreed, his breath huffing in my ear. I hadn't realized I was so sensitive there. Not till his tongue flickered out through the row of razor-sharp fangs, long and dexterous, and he traced my ear with it. His movements were clumsy and imperfect, but I loved them all the same.

I spread my legs and Roark made the most beautiful, pleased little rumble. I didn't need to understand him to know what *that* meant. Like a big cat with a mouse tucked right between his paws. Roark's approval made my blood sing as I tested my bonds, just to feel the tendrils contract enough to hurt again.

I wanted to see his dick *so* bad.

Even more so now that I could feel it, rubbing, rubbing, rubbing against mine. Growing thicker and bigger by the second. Like he was as turned on by this as I was. Like he liked having me pinned beneath him, immobile. Like the fact I trusted him enough to give him this was getting him off without having to take his dick out at all.

"*Please*," I begged, done with the games.

Roark made that same soothing purring sound he always did, his slippery tongue snaking over my jaw and down my neck, leaving a trail of gooseflesh and saliva in its wake. His spit grew cold as it dried, and the dual sensation of that wicked hot tongue laving down my sternum with the brisk chill that accompanied it had my head spinning anew.

"Oh fuck," I gasped when Roark's tongue found my nipples. He paused. I could see why.

His were different than mine. I wasn't really sure why he had them in the first place—because his were just flat little circles with no nub to tease at all.

Careful of his teeth, Roark's tongue rubbed over one of my nipples curiously, back and forth. It felt different than it had when his tentacles had touched me there. Because this was him, plain and simple. And his eagerness was getting me off almost more than the slick twist of his tongue.

That in itself was freaky as fuck though.

And so amazing, oh my god.

When the tip of his tongue twisted around one, giving it a sharp tug, it felt like my body was being electrocuted. My hips jerked upward, my chest pushing toward him begging for more. His tongue was so hot it nearly burned. And the longer he played with my chest, the more puffy my nipples became.

When I glanced down at them, and got a glimpse of his tongue twisting and pulling, I nearly came.

Roark gave my other nipple the same treatment, exploring me. His actions were inquisitive, and his spots were so red they were nearly fluorescent. Roark's eyes were a ravenous black. There was a calculating gleam to them too—like he was memorizing my reactions and saving the information for later.

Creating a whole new list in his head.

*What things make Hugo tick.*

When Roark's mouth moved lower and he stuck his tongue into my belly button, I thrashed.

"Tickles!" I hissed through my teeth, only to be met with the strangest reaction from him yet. He laughed. *Laughed!* My favorite sound ever. Like a dog's bark, rough and sharp, but charming all the same. His eyes squinted into crescent-like shapes that I realized meant he was smiling. A true smile. The kind that warms you from your head to your toes.

I loved it.

I loved it a lot.

I'd seen it before, but it felt different in this situation.

Intimate.

Roark—because he was a sexy shithead—immediately flicked his tongue into my belly button again. I jolted, joining him in his laughter this time as his tongue slithered back between his teeth. My cock was hard. *Super* hard. *Painfully* hard.

There was something about the snap of his fangs that made me feel weak with lust.

Roark shook his head in amusement at me, like I'd done all of this to distract him, even though he'd been the one teasing me, not the other way around.

In retaliation, I kicked the back of his thigh to urge him to keep grinding. Roark's amusement died a swift death, and his eyes darkened again at the same time he made another one of those animalistic noises. Maybe my thrashing made him see me as prey?

Holy fuck.

More tendrils shot from his arms, reaching down to wrap tight around my thighs. Like a fucked-up version of a spiderweb. Trapping me in place. Holding me exactly where he wanted me so I couldn't kick again. They squeezed into the meat of my legs as he tested the give of my muscle with a pleased little purr.

Roark's tongue slithered lower still, toying with the hem of my pajamas before dipping beneath it. The slippery, pointy tip traced the head of my dick beneath the fabric. There was no way to describe just how good it felt to be touched there like that. The texture of his tongue was seriously fucking awesome, all ropey, searing, and slick.

"Nng," I sobbed.

*Oh fuck.*

*Jesus—*

*God—*

Precum squirted out of my dick. My balls drew up tight as Roark twisted the tip of his tongue around the crown of my cock, then flicked it into my slit to taste the mess he'd caused me to make. His eyes flickered, and he *growled.* This was different from his other growls, though. This was *threatening.*

Like I'd broken the part of him that was studiously in control.

Like he wanted me to leak some more so he could taste it again.

More tendrils, these ones larger, pushed past the hem of my pants, their wiggly lengths teasing along the seam of my groin. I hissed out a ragged breath, a little nervous but still excited as Roark paused, the pointed top of one tendril rubbing at the sensitive skin behind my balls.

I'd gone my whole life without being touched, so this was pretty surreal even without the tendrils and teeth.

"Huu-goh, yesh?" he repeated, his voice hoarse. The tendril twitched, like it couldn't help itself. Like it wanted in as badly as he did.

"Yes," I panted. Roark grinned in response, a feral sort of thing. Young. Eager. With a practiced motion, all at once, the tiny tendrils that had wrapped around my thighs released, even the one I'd been certain was going to head right for my ass. I felt naked for all of two seconds without them encasing my body—before Roark dragged my pants down—and the tendrils rushed forward again.

They squeezed my bare thighs, like they'd forgotten how they felt in those few short seconds. The way they stroked over my leg hair was an odd sensation, but not a bad one. I liked it almost as much as being trapped. I was on a journey of self-discovery today and loving every second of it.

Encased in a sticky pink cocoon again, I could do nothing but lay immobile, my bare dick pointing right at Roark.

My cock strained, balls pulled up tight as I took a moment to admire the alien above me. His chest and belly trembled with labored breaths, his black eyes swirling with emotion. Roark's spots were a vibrant, desperate red.

Lust.

My brain connected.

Red spots probably mean lust.

It seemed so obvious now.

A drop of precum slipped from the tip of my cock onto my belly, and as Roark's tentacles twisted tight around my wrists and thighs I ached for more. I'd wanted to see his dick, and I still hadn't gotten the chance to properly do that.

I bucked my hips as best as I could, straining toward him so he'd get the hint.

"Nnngh," I hissed out as one of the tiny tendrils around my thighs separated from the rest and slunk along the length of my dick. It curled just beneath the crown, contracting until I began to tingle all over. The more it constricted, the more I began to leak.

Like it was *milking* me.

Roark made a satisfied sound, wringing me tighter and encouraging more of the pearly white substance to slip free. He murmured something that sounded complimentary, like he was as pleased by this turn of events as I was.

Smug now that he had me entirely at his mercy, Roark ducked lower, his hot breath caressing my belly. My abs tensed. God, he was so fucking close to my dick. He was going to lick it again, wasn't he? I needed him to.

Now that I'd gotten a taste of what that felt like it was all I wanted.

As Roark stuck his tongue out, slow and deliberate, I stared dumbly down at him. My vision was fuzzy with lust as he rubbed his tongue through the mess I was making on my stomach. He was so close. God. Jesus. Just a few inches and he'd—

Roark moaned, a throaty sort of sound, savoring my taste as the tiny tendril continued to wring my cock for more.

"Fuck," I hissed, clenching my jaw as another drop of precum escaped. *How was he doing this?* It didn't even seem possible. I'd never been this hard in my life. Never wanted something more than I wanted that tongue on me.

Sticky, wet—Roark lapped over my belly, making my abs jump over and over as he savored my cum. It was so goddamn filthy I could barely wrap my mind around the fact it was happening—and to me of all people. This belonged on a porn site behind a paywall, not in my very real life. It was too fucking good. My balls drew tight and I squeezed my eyes shut, willing my body not to come too early.

I wanted this to last.

Wanted to feel his tongue on my dick before I orgasmed.

Who knew if it would happen again?

I needed to remember this.

To memorize it.

To memorize the way Roark's scent filled my nose, apple-like and sweet. The way his tendrils held me tight, so all I could do was enjoy what he decided to give me. He was huge. So fucking huge. This massive, gorgeous creature. A perfect combination of the familiar and unfamiliar. So gentle, yet carnal all the same.

I wasn't sure what had changed, why he felt so inclined to touch me now when he'd all but ignored my body for a month. But I didn't complain. It felt so—

"Oh shit fuck, fuck, fuck—" My head tossed back as his tongue finally—oh god, finally—slithered around the length of my dick. It was long and dexterous, and I would've been amused by the way he was testing my texture and shape like he was memorizing it, if I hadn't been gasping like a fish out of water.

Fireworks exploded behind my eyelids as my back bowed and cum shot right into Roark's waiting mouth.

He *growled*, and I was spinning, spinning, spinning. But he didn't stop.

He just kept slurping and pulling, slurping and pulling. The frankly obscene noise echoed through the room as my dick struggled to rise to the occasion. To keep spilling, even though it was empty.

"I can't, I can't—" I chanted, overstimulated and breathless as the wet muscle sucked around me. "I can't, I can't."

And still, he milked me.

Milked me so tight and snug that a few minutes later he'd managed to jerk my cock to hardness again despite the oversensitivity. My chest was shuddering. I could hardly get a coherent thought to form in my head as Roark pulled back. Settling above me, his head framed by the stars on the ceiling, Roark deliberately licked his lips.

Jesus fuck.

I couldn't help but groan.

"Please," I whined, jerking my hips upward, my body a sweaty mess. "I want your dick." No, that wasn't right. "I *need* it." My hips humped up again and Roark chuckled—or whatever his approximation of a chuckle was—it was a dark rumbly sort of sound, like my desperation both pleased and amused him. Apparently he didn't need to understand what I was saying to know that I was begging.

My ass clenched and his tendrils sucked harder around my wrists and thighs, the ones at the  crease of my groin beginning to tap at my balls. *Tap, tap, tap.* My eyes rolled back.

My dick was so hard it hurt, despite having just come.

Roark released one of my wrists, only for his other limb—limbs?—to replace it, tying my two wrists together above my head in a sticky pink knot. Meanwhile, his free hand formed once again and he pushed down the hem of his own pants.

"Fucking finally," I gasped, straining to see what I was sure was a monster cock between his legs.

I…wasn't wrong.

It was monstrous alright.

Just not in the way I'd expected.

And there were two of them.

*Two* cocks.

If you could call them that. Rather than human-esque dicks, two fat, flushed purple tentacles with suckers down their lengths nestled between Roark's legs. They had thick bases and flared, tapered tips that pointed in my direction, almost like they were reaching for me. They writhed and danced, winding together. A filthy slurping sound filled the air as they rubbed their suckers against each other, a slick viscous fluid glistening along their lengths.

I was suddenly breathless all over again.

Shocked and intrigued.

The biologist in me reawakened.

Tentacle dicks.

Two of them.

Roark wrapped his thick fist around them, squeezing them with a sharp inhale as more fluid leaked free, wetting his fingertips. I forgot about his other tendrils immediately. Holding impossibly still, I watched enthralled as his cocks danced and jerked, still reaching for me like they had a mind of their own.

Oh fuck.

*Maybe they did?*

Maybe there was something wrong with me.

Because I wanted those inside me. On me. Around me. Wanted to feel the suckers leave hickeys all over my dick. Wanted to rut between them and let them squeeze and squeeze and squeeze and—

"Uhhhh." All thoughts left my head. Brain officially on vacation. No communicado. Because Roark's tentacle-dicks were *touching* me now. Threading around my cock. Suckers pulling at the skin, just like I'd wanted. "Uhh," I gasped again, throat bobbing as I tossed my head back against the sheets. Roark's cocks threaded tighter around my own.

They felt almost feverish, they were so warm. Far wetter than they appeared as they squelched a *naughty* sound, suckers pulling at my dick in a rhythmic pulse. A steady beat throbbed as they toyed with me. What was better though, was the way Roark rutted against my body, his teeth bared.

All his usual control was gone.

And instead, he was a beast looking to breed.

Fat tentacles overwhelmed my dick, slurping me deep inside their tight, sticky embrace as my brain melted out my ears. It was about that point that I realized why the hell people had been obsessed with sex since the beginning of time.

Pink alien dick was officially the best thing that had ever happened to me.

There was no way in hell this would be the only time we did this.

Nuh-uh.

Our hips slapped together and my toes curled. Roark's smaller tendrils twisted tighter around my groin, creeping into my crease. They wanted to scout out the new territory. For the first time in my life I didn't have the brain power to process what was going on. All my atoms felt spread thin.

I came a second time with a howl the moment one of the tiny fingerlike tendrils circled my hole, clenching down tight as Roark's left cock sucked my cum out through my slit with its suckers.

A few more desperate thrusts later and Roark came too. I could tell because the corded muscles in his neck tensed as he did so, his breath leaving him in a drawn-out hiss as fluid slicked up my twitchy, overstimulated dick. There was so fucking much of it. It soaked my belly and thighs, and clung to my leg hair. It was the first time I'd seen him orgasm. I got the feeling he'd never done this with anyone else, despite his enthusiasm.

The tendrils at my hole retreated to my relief and disappointment.

Even though they were no longer so insistent, Roark's cocks remained hard enough to wiggle, stroking through the fiery hair at the base of my dick, petting over my balls and shaft like they wanted to taste the sweat and feel its texture. His balls were heavy against my own.

There wasn't a hair on Roark's entire body, so I could understand their curiosity.

Damn.

Cocks with their own motivation.

Holy shit.

This was amazing.

This was all so amazing.

Everything about this.

Roark purred, that happy pleased rumble he only used when he knew he'd done something I liked.

Then he flopped down beside me, careful not to squash me with his bulk as his tendrils untwisted from my wrists and began stroking them tenderly, bringing them down my body and rubbing the circulation back into them. Both his hands reformed and he petted over my chest, giving each of my nipples a cursory pinch. They didn't stay there long, however, diving low to cup my messy dick and balls together in his massive hand, claws tapping at my perineum before he withdrew and gently pulled my pants back over my limp dick.

I felt wrung out, exhausted and mind-blown, visions of tentadicks meaty and dexterous flashing behind my lids as I turned to him and sleepily reached out to lay a hand on his giant squishy pec. I groped it and he barked out another soft laugh, though his hand moved to cup the back of mine, and he held me in place. I didn't even care that I was sticky, I was so happy.

*Thump, thump, thump, thump.*

*Thump, thump, thump, thump.*

I could feel twin heartbeats resonating through his body as I flashed him a sleepy sated grin, and he smiled right back. Twin hearts, to match his twin dicks.

Symmetry.

"You're a fucking genius," I told him, even though I knew he wouldn't understand. "A sex wizard."

Roark nuzzled my cheek affectionately.

Maybe I was his pet, but at that moment, I didn't fucking care. I was too fucked out, and too happy. Curiosity may have killed the cat, but it had gotten me alien dick, so maybe it wasn't such a bad thing.

# NINE

## ROARK

**LIFE WAS GOOD. *REALLY* GOOD.** Better than I could've ever expected considering the ever-present threat of pirates hanging over all of our heads. With every shipment we gathered, the weight of the fear of losing our cargo became heavier and heavier.

The crew was more subdued than usual, and I would've been too—if I wasn't so busy being blissfully happy. Sex. Who knew?

It was mind-boggling to me how fun it was to share physical pleasure with someone as exuberant and responsive as my mate.

Several days had passed since Huu-goh and I had officially become mates and though I was still somewhat nervous that I would not be able to give him what he needed, I was also filled with determination.

Because Mala had been right about me.

There wasn't a single thing that I'd wanted in my life that I had not figured out how to achieve. I'd wanted to chase my father's dream and touch the stars, and I'd done that. I'd wanted to climb up the ranks, and I'd done that too. I'd wanted to captain the ship that I had called home since I was a young recruit—and here I was, captaining it.

Making Huu-goh happy was the most important mission I'd ever embarked on, and failure was not an option. Which meant…that it was time to stop avoiding my mentor.

Mala gave solid advice when it came to the heart—he was as trustworthy as he was blue—but Ushuu was many moons older than the both of us. He had knowledge about the galaxy and the species that inhabited it so vast that it made my understanding look paltry in comparison.

Perhaps he would know better how to help Huu-goh adjust to our lifestyle?

Perhaps he could give me insights into huu-mans that the pamphlet from A&R had not.

It was lunchtime when I returned to Huu-goh and my rooms.

He was unsurprised to see me, as I often made time in the middle of the day to visit. Some of the antsy-ness that he'd been exhibiting before was creeping back in, though our time spent in bed had slapped somewhat of a bandage on the situation.

If huu-mans were anything like Sahrk's, sex released chemicals in the brain that oftentimes left people feeling happier, more connected, and settled. After observing Huu-goh for a few blissful days, I inferred—chemicals or not—the intimacy of the act was more than likely the cause of his emotional turnaround, rather than the actual release itself.

If I was being blatantly honest, the idea of allowing Huu-goh outside our rooms terrified me.

Maybe more than it frightened me to take him to the planets we'd visited along our route. There were other resources then. Allies to rely upon. Armies to protect us, should things go sour. Out in space we were on our own entirely—and while I trusted my crew with my life—the only person I trusted with Huu-goh's was me.

The worst atrocities I'd ever seen had happened on board this very ship when pirates had attacked. And while I knew that we were well-equipped to deal with threats now, that didn't change the fact that if Huu-goh was out in the hallways he could get auto-locked out of the rooms on board, should we be attacked.

It was a safety mechanism on all Sahrk ships now. To keep the crew safe away from threats. To enable pirates to take what they wanted from the cargo without casualties. Before, when I'd been a youth, such things had not been created. We were peaceful beings. But that didn't mean we couldn't fight. In fact, one could argue that our bodies were built for fighting. From our teeth, to our tendrils, down to the bare bones of our society and the way we thrived on physical competition.

Too many casualties, however, had altered the way Sahrks dealt with such things.

I knew better than anyone how dire things could become.

I knew I was over-protective.

I knew that.

But it was so difficult to get my body to do the thing that scared me the most. Especially now that Huu-goh had become my mate officially. The idea of losing him the way that Ushuu had lost his love was crippling. Just thinking about it made my chest grow tight, my hearts sluggish, and my limbs too icy to properly transform.

Still, I could recognize that by locking Huu-goh away I was hurting him too.

And though that didn't change how *scared* I was that he could be harmed—by something innocent on board he didn't understand, or pirates, should they attack our vessel—I couldn't stomach the thought that I was the one causing him pain.

He was far too curious to be trapped in these rooms—even if the terrified, paranoid part of me whispered that he would be safe here. And that nothing could injure him within these walls.

He deserved better than being attached to a paranoid fool.

Which was why we were going out today. For the first time. And why I'd invited Ushuu to come to lunch with us, even though my hearts would not stop thumping, and taking this step made me feel as though my legs were about to give out.

Huu-goh glanced over my spots, a little frown on his lips. It was so odd to see someone emote without teeth like I possessed, but I found it cute too. The little flaps looked particularly soft and lick-able when they turned down like that.

Seeing his grouchy expression sent a thrill through me as I shut the door behind me and approached. He glanced at my empty limbs, no food to occupy my arms, and the folds of his frown multiplied. It was a comical expression. Downright adorable. There was a nanobot on the bed beside him. They couldn't climb soft surfaces, so it was obvious that he'd brought it up there. Why? I had no idea.

His little thighs spread, the clothing he wore—Sahrk childrens' clothing, because I'd had nothing else that would fit him on board—was loose. It draped over his frame, somehow making him appear even tinier than he already was.

My sweet little beast abandoned his nanobot on the table beside the bed and rose to his bare feet.

"Fuhd?" he asked, because he was so goddamn clever he'd already figured out something was different, without me even having to open my mouth at all. We were still space-borne after all, and I hadn't let him out of the rooms before while we were mid-flight.

Pride lit me up from the inside out.

I had not known what it meant to be alive until the day I met Huu-goh—I realized that now. All my feelings before had been dull. Looking at the world through his eyes made it seem like a brighter, more wonderful place. I noticed things I never had—I appreciated things I'd always taken for granted. My world had been gray before I met him, and now it was technicolor.

And though Huu-goh's spots were tiny and brown, and the peachy surface of his skin would never be as vivid as my own, he managed to be the most vibrant person in the entire universe.

He made me want to be a better, stronger man.

Because if someone so *tiny* could be as hardy as he was, then perhaps someone of my size could stand to have a little extra courage.

I unclipped his leash from my belt as I approached him and Huu-goh scowled at me. It was an adorable face. So full of ire it made my blood thrum as I attached the leash to his collar, careful not to nick him with my claws.

My limbs felt icy and it took every ounce of control I had not to forgo this plan entirely and keep him locked up where he was safe.

Eventually, when I was certain that he wouldn't touch something that could accidentally hurt him, or get lost—because of his endless curiosity—I'd unclip the lead. Until then, this was as far as my comfort zone would allow me to go.

I knew Huu-goh couldn't understand me, but I tried to soothe him anyway, hoping my tone was enough to get the feeling across. "It is only for now, precious one," I promised him, stroking over the now connected clasp on his collar. "There are dangerous things aboard, and I fear you would touch something that could harm you." That was true, but because it wasn't the whole truth, I added on. "I cannot lose you. I only just found you."

Huu-goh was not soothed.

He glared at the leash in my hand like it had personally attacked him.

It was only when I brought him to the door and reached for the keypad that he relaxed. As I typed in the code, Huu-goh was silent beside me, watching my every move. Like he was processing what was happening—that, or memorizing the password to the door.

The second thought made my eyes crease in amusement.

Who was I kidding?

No doubt my mate was clever enough he already knew it.

It was simply his loyalty that kept him inside these rooms.

When I gestured for him to go first—a sign of trust, because I knew the leash would be a hard pill for him to swallow—Huu-goh wavered. For a beat he stared out at the empty hallway, his bare feet stuck firmly to the floor.

My hearts thumped and thumped and thumped.

"I cann goh outsiide?" he asked. There was something wary about the way he stood, like he was worried he was misunderstanding the situation and didn't want to be punished. I had never raised a hand to him, or even truly admonished him—so I knew the behavior stemmed from before we'd met.

A thought that made my incredibly angry.

I wanted to bite the heads off all of the people who had conditioned him to expect such things.

"Yesh," I agreed in his own language, making sure to keep my own tone soft. I didn't know what "cann" or "outsiide" were, but I could connect the dots. Huu-goh watched me, then the doorway, then me again, debating with himself.

"*Reelly?*" he asked, like he did not believe me.

Again, I filled in the blanks.

"Reelly," I repeated in his tongue, even though I wasn't one-hundred percent sure I knew what he'd just said.

The cloudiness of his expression faded. Huu-goh stood straighter, his brown eyes bright. And then he did the most endearing—wonderful thing. He began to dance.

A wiggly, happy little squirm—right before he ducked out into the hallway, no fear or shame, just unbridled joy at the opportunity to explore.

*This was the right choice.*

I melted, following after him dutifully as some of the heat returned to my limbs and I shut the door behind us.

The leash jerked a little as he skipped down the hall, forced to a stop when he reached the end of its length. Huu-goh waited impatiently for me to lock up, feet tapping, eyes bright. I did not let him rush me, though his excitement was frankly adorable. When I returned my attention to my tiny tyrant, he was still wiggling animatedly.

"Fuhd?" Huu-goh asked. Clever darling had already figured out where we were headed. I nodded, and he beamed at me.

"Fuhd," I agreed in his strange tongue, fumbling with the shape of the word in my mouth. I crossed the distance between us, and Huu-goh trotted along at my side. I did not mind sounding silly if my efforts put that smile on his face. My strides were much longer than his, and he had to jog to keep pace, even though I was going painfully slow.

Huu-goh did not seem to mind. His eyes were wide, taking in the hallway like it was the first time he'd been inside it. We'd been through here countless times on our trips off ship, but I did not begrudge him his newfound wonder.

Slowing down even more, I took a moment to appreciate the hallway as if I was looking through his eyes. Made of slick metal, it was aerodynamic and streamlined. The round doors that lined its walls were spread out further in our wing, as it was where those with higher ranks resided, like myself. The barracks where the majority of the other Sahrks bunked were located near the bottom floors of the ship. They were closer to the indoor pool, Ushuu's lab, the exercise room, and the cargo hold than we were.

By contrast, the location of my chambers on one of the upper floors made the commute to the helm easier, which I appreciated.

Huu-goh's fingers skimmed the wall, and I had half a mind to yank his hand back so he wouldn't accidentally hit some of the hidden buttons along its surface. But none of them were harmful—at least not near my rooms, so I let him have his fun as we made our way through the ship.

I had only ever seen him this happy when I had his tiny dick wrapped in my tongue.

His good mood was contagious.

And pride, unlike anything I'd ever known, made my chest puff up.

I had done this. By pushing through my fears, I had given him this. I was relieved to know that I had managed to make his life better—even if it was such a simple thing. Still, my fears simmered beneath my surface, but they were farther away now as I basked in Huu-goh's happiness.

I don't think I'd ever made someone smile like that before.

Uncaring that we would soon have an audience, I mirrored Huu-goh's joy. My spots were a thrumming, brilliant white as I debated acting on these new feelings—and if such actions would be welcome.

*He's never shied away from your touch.*

*Why would he now?*

Bolstered, I took the leap, swooping an arm around my huu-man and hoisting his lithe body onto my shoulders. Delighted, he giggled the whole way up. His joy chimed like bells as his little feet kicked at my chest. His thighs squeezed my neck, like he was testing its width. I couldn't help but think about the fact his greedy little cock was pressing right against me.

Huu-goh hardly weighed a thing. My tendrils slithered out to hold him of their own accord, as frightened as I was of him falling to the hard metal floor below. Despite his fragile size, his weight soothed the ache in my chest.

It felt right, having him close.

Even more right, was the fact he trusted me to keep him safe—even high above the ground as he was. Huu-goh's trust had been hard-won. I never wanted to betray it.

Hesitantly, Huu-goh's warm hands fanned curiously along my head fin. I nearly missed a step. No one had ever touched me there. It felt…odd. But not bad.

I wasn't used to anyone touching me at all.

At least…other than Mala when we sparred in the mornings, or Ushuu when he looked to comfort me.

Huu-goh's touch was tentative, like he was afraid he'd hurt me. It grew more confident as I rumbled a pleased purr to soothe him. In response, his fingers tightened, and he used my fin for balance as my hearts beat an unsteady staccato in my chest.

*Could he sense how happy he made me?*

*Did he understand what the color of my spots meant?*

*And that they were only white because of him?*

Being touched by him was such a simple pleasure, and it shook me to the core.

Only a few crewmates were present when we reached the mess hall that our residence was assigned to. The tall sloping ceilings were high enough to accommodate Huu-goh and I together, as I made my way toward the cooling units to begin preparing our food.

Atop my shoulders, Huu-goh was quiet. Knowing him, he was cataloging the details of everything he saw so he could jot them down in his journal later. It was nearly full. Maybe all the way full—and I made a mental note to buy him a new one at our final stop before heading home.

We were still far away—this was the longest stretch of continuous space travel we'd embarked on since Huu-goh had moved in with me.

"Captain," Ushuu's familiar scratchy voice echoed from behind me. I paused, twisting around to greet him. It was impossible for the ice to fill my limbs again when Huu-goh was stroking my fin.

"Ushuu," I responded, smiling at him fondly. He crossed the distance between us, his spots pink with affection.

Ushuu smiled at me in the way he had since I was a boy. Like even though I was fully grown now and had been manning this ship for over a decade, I was still the fresh-spotted recruit he'd snuck sweets to under the table.

When he called me 'captain' it almost felt like an inside joke. Like I was playing dress-up. He was the only person other than Mala who knew where I had come from—and how hard I'd worked to be here.

Instead of feeling humiliated, it always made me warm all over.

Because for just a moment, I could let go of who I'd become and be little Roark again.

Ushuu was the only crewmate left from the original team that had manned The Dreamer when I had first been recruited. I'd been fatherless for far longer than I'd known Ushuu. But if I'd had one still, I would've hoped he would be as level-headed and soft-spoken as Ushuu was. His surface was a lovely pale gray, and paired with the white lab coat he insisted on wearing—to set him aside from the crew—it lent him a demure, but odd air.

Most Sahrks did not wear clothing on their upper bodies. In fact, clothing on the lower body was a new invention. It limited our access to our limbs and made transforming difficult if not impossible. Plus, it made our surface struggle to breathe—and that was uncomfortable.

Ushuu somehow managed to defy all logic, however.

"Is this the huu-man?" Ushuu asked in our tongue, clearly delighted as he reached out to grasp Huu-goh's bare toes. "He is wonderful! I have never seen one up close like this. Look how delightful his little feet are. Five toes! Whatever for?!"

Huu-goh jerked his feet back, his delightful toes wriggling away from Ushuu's fingers. I growled in warning, tendrils shooting up to wrap protectively around Huu-goh's legs without conscious thought. He wiggled his toes inside their grasp, and the sensation tickled in a way that had me calming.

"Mine," I snapped, keeping my voice even, though I was sure my spots betrayed me. Immediately, I regretted the action—as Ushuu's eyes widened and he glanced between me and Huu-goh again, like he was seeing something that he hadn't before.

"Apologies," he replied, tone soft. "It won't happen again."

Huu-goh made a soothing sound as he stroked my fin. I purred back at him, taking comfort from his touch. Ushuu was quiet as he began to prepare his own food. Still feeling a bit dazed by my own brash reaction, I turned toward the coolers and began arranging breakfast for Huu-goh and me. My movements were more jerky than normal, but soon enough, his tiny hands on my fin and their gentle stroking accomplished what Huu-goh had set out to do. I was back to my usually unruffled self, pulse no longer thrumming.

I owed Huu-goh an apology.

I should have moved faster.

I should've anticipated Ushuu's curiosity. He and Huu-goh were far more alike than I'd realized before that moment. Maybe Ushuu needed a leash of his own. The thought almost made me laugh, but then I sobered—realizing suddenly what a ridiculous idea that was.

To chain Ushuu?

Even if it was to keep him out of trouble.

The double standard felt like a slap to the face and the weight of Huu-goh's leash around my wrist suddenly felt impossibly heavy. Tomorrow. When I brought him out tomorrow I'd take him without the chain, my own fears be damned.

The thought of that alone made me feel shaky and frightened—but I forced the feeling aside. It would do me no good here. Not now, when we were supposed to be eating. And I was supposed to be showing Huu-goh around the helm, and introducing him to Ushuu for the first time.

When I checked on Huu-goh his eyes were dancing, and the flicker of fear I'd seen inside them had melted away. He observed Ushuu with as much wonder as he'd taken in the hallways and the cafeteria. Dark intelligent eyes flickered with interest as the older Sahrk made his way toward the tables that lined the back hall, his plate of bambuu piled high.

If Huu-goh was not bothered, then I would choose not to be also.

I would follow his lead.

Huu-goh's leash dangled from my wrist as I finished plating our food and made a beeline for the spot beside Ushuu. I kept my distance for the moment, making sure there was one chair between us so that Huu-goh would not feel intimidated.

Taking a deep breath, I placed both plates on the table and retrieved Huu-goh from his perch on my shoulders. With a gentle nudge, I arranged him on the chair to my left, away from Ushuu, charmed all over again when Huu-goh smiled up at me.

Huu-goh was a small reassuring weight against my side as I diced his food into tiny huu-man-sized bites. When I slid him his plate and a fork, he said his precious "thank yew" again. Charmed like always, I admired how tiny but regal he looked dutifully grabbing the Sahrk-sized fork. It looked huge in his grip, but he didn't seem to mind, his brow furrowed in determination as he speared a piece of bambuu and brought it to his lips.

Huu-goh's attention did not remain on the food for long. It was old news. No, his interest was piqued by the space around him. Dark eyes alight with intrigue, he took in his surroundings, gaze flickering from the cooling units that housed the food, to the tall glass cabinets full of snacks and utensils, then to Ushuu.

He wiggled in his seat, feet struggling to tap against the floor as he tested the give of the cushion with obvious delight.

*If I asked him what was on his mind, what would he say?*

I wished I had the words to do so.

*Does he find us as riveting as I find him?*

A small smile tugged at his lips. No longer bouncing, he swallowed his food then promptly stabbed a new piece with a happy hum. So *happy*, and I hadn't even shown him the best parts of the ship yet. I had no doubt if he found this room delightful he was in for the time of his life when I showed him the sparring room, the pool, and the control room.

Huu-goh finished his food in record time, and when he was done, his feet *tap, tap, tapped* against the legs of his chair. He looked lovely. He always did. But today especially so. His peachy skin shone radiant, the muscles in his thighs flexing beneath the long hem of his shirt as he shifted in his seat.

His little cock lay hidden, and I tried not to think about it—but that was nearly impossible.

I was learning him, slowly but surely. And I knew that this particular dance of his either meant he was impatient, excited, or he needed to pee.

I tilted my head, eyes narrowed as I chewed my own mouthful, deciding how best to proceed. I hadn't meant to ignore Ushuu, but was grateful he hadn't pushed as Huu-goh finished his food. The last thing I wanted was for Huu-goh to get so excited about talking to a new Sahrk that he choked.

"Hi!" Huu-goh chirped, shifting forward in his seat as he stared at Ushuu across the table. Ushuu looked delighted, his spots flickering white as he set his fork down and twisted to greet my little love just as enthusiastically.

"Hi!" Ushuu responded.

"You're uhld!" Huu-goh told him—words I didn't understand. His eyes immediately widened, and he smacked a hand over his mouth like he wished he could take the words back.

Before Huu-goh could say something else, Ushuu said, "yesh. I ehm."

My mentor looked amused and his spots remained a pale pinkish white as he barked out a laugh. It took me a solid ten seconds to realize that he'd replied both times in Huu-goh's native tongue. Ushuu glanced at my now-yellow spots, cocking his head to the side.

"You can communicate with him?" I asked, more than a little excited. My hearts thrummed wildly enough in my chest I worried the sound was audible.

"Some," Ushuu nodded, replying in our language, his lavender eyes soft. "I find their planet fascinating." *Of course he did.* Ushuu had always been as explorative as he was intelligent. He retained information unlike anyone I'd ever met. As though every sight he'd ever seen was a photograph and he could revisit it anytime he liked.

It was a skill that had come in handy when he'd had a more active role on board. Nowadays, he was retired for the most part. His linguistic strengths were very rarely utilized—as we all agreed he deserved a chance to focus on the work that most inspired him.

The healing pods and the tech that fueled our flight through space.

I realized belatedly how stupid it had been to avoid him.

It had been an error.

A grievous one.

"Speak to him, please," I commanded, setting my fork down with a quiet clink. "Please," I added a second time, because while I *was* desperate, I didn't want to be rude. "He has been aboard the ship for over a month now, and I am doing my best—" Admitting weakness was difficult, but

I managed for Huu-goh's sake. "But he is surely under-stimulated. I'm certain he has questions. Things I can't answer with my limited knowledge of his language."

"What do you want me to say?" Ushuu asked, his lavender eyes kind, despite the way I'd snapped at him earlier. That was water under the bridge now, and he knew it as well as I did.

I had always been quick to forgive.

*What do I want to say?*

I racked my brain for answers. The problem wasn't that I didn't have any idea what to tell my little huu-man. What plagued me was the fact that I had *many* questions I wanted to ask. So many things I was desperate to know. So many things I was dying to tell him.

I'd always been a quiet person. Words were used for a purpose. I had found that observing others silently was the fastest way to learn the truth—and used that to my advantage whenever possible. It was something I had always been content with. To be the person who stood stoic and unyielding, a beacon of strength, while others chatted around. The fact that I was not the best at picking the correct words when it came to the heart, certainly helped me come to that conclusion.

When I was younger I struggled even more with communication.

However, I found no lack of words now. And it was only my own practical nature that kept me from blurting out every question I'd ever had so quickly that even Ushuu could not catch them all.

After a moment of quiet deliberation I decided what I wanted most was to know how Huu-goh was fairing on board.

"Ask him how he's feeling, please." My pulse fluttered, and my limbs went icy all over again. *What if I had read him wrong?* What if his wiggles, his tinkling laughter meant he was frightened, rather than excited? What if all that I'd learned about him was backwards?

I couldn't stomach the thought.

"How ahre youh feehling?" Ushuu asked Huu-goh, carefully annunciating his words, though they fit just as awkwardly between his teeth as they did between mine. I memorized the sound of them as best as I could so that I could later replicate the question.

Meanwhile, I studied Huu-goh expectantly, rigidly awaiting his response.

I was sure my spots were gray with anxiety, the negative emotion playing close to the surface. I didn't have to wait long. After Huu-goh's initial reaction—his jaw dropping, his eyes popping wide—he burst into speech so fast I had no way of making sense of the words.

Bless Ushuu, because he did.

After listening intently, and asking Huu-goh to repeat a few things, the older Sahrk turned back to me with a gentle smile. "He says he is happy, but wants to know why we keep feeding him bark."

*He is happy.*

*He is happy, he is happy, he is happy.*

Rigidity melting, I twisted to peer at my huu-man fondly—trying to ignore the fact that Ushuu was watching us with affection of his own. A few wayward tendrils slipped free of the surface of my body to give the back of Huu-goh's neck a grateful squeeze. He made a pleased sound and glanced up at me through his lashes with a questioning expression.

Probably waiting for answers, my curious little beast.

His dark gaze stroked over my spots like a caress as Huu-goh opened his sweet mouth and spoke again. His words ended on a higher note, something I was beginning to understand meant he was asking a question.

"Now he wants to know why your spots change color," Ushuu explained after waiting patiently to parse through the foreign words. He blinked and cocked his head at me. "Would you like me to translate?"

I nodded. Distracted by the emotions that danced across Huu-goh's expressive face. "Our spots are mood indicators," I explained directly to him, keeping my voice soft. Ushuu translated for me, though it took quite a while for him to find each word. I didn't mind. It just gave me more time to look at Huu-goh.

Plus, I was grateful this was an option at all. Though part of me felt like an idiot for not seeking it out sooner. I tried not to dwell on that emotion too long. It would only waste my energy when I could be speaking to Huu-goh instead.

We didn't have long before Ushuu needed to return to work.

Huu-goh nodded very seriously when Ushuu finished speaking. When he turned his attention back to me he searched my gaze. I wasn't sure what he was looking for, but I hoped he found it.

"The 'bahrk' is highly nutritious. You are small and I worry that you were not being properly nourished before you came here," I added, making sure to answer both of his questions to the best of my ability. "There are healers better equipped to check on you when we reach home, but even then, I am unsure if they will have enough knowledge of your species to be able to tell me what your dietary needs are. So for now, 'bahrk' it is."

He was important to me, therefore his questions were important.

Ushuu relayed my words, and I waited for Huu-goh's response, unable to take my eyes off of him as he mulled this new information over. His hairy brow furrowed, sweet eyes swirling with emotion like he was remembering something unsavory. The tendril on the back of his neck pulsed to soothe him, and he sighed. The expression cleared, and Huu-goh's smile returned, eyes blazing with what I hoped was affection as his gaze focused on me once again.

"Whaat doo rehd spahts meen?" he asked in his own language, waiting patiently for Ushuu to translate.

Whatever he said made Ushuu bark in amusement, his eyes creased with mirth. "He wants to know what red spots mean," he translated.

Oh no.

*Oh no.*

Mortification burned through my body as I ducked my head, covering my face with one hand in embarrassment. I almost wanted to beg Ushuu not to tell him, because it was more than a little embarrassing to have the man that was practically my *father* talk to my mate about something so deeply intimate. However, like I'd stated earlier, I found being uncomfortable well worth its pain if my answers benefited Huu-goh—and by extension, our relationship—in the long run.

"Explain," I said quietly, burning from the inside out as I waited. I peeked through my fingers at Huu-goh as Ushuu spoke, watching his reaction. I had never been more humiliated.

Huu-goh's grin was wicked as he listened intently. His eyes danced with mischief. It was attractive. So goddamn attractive. Huu-goh glanced over my spots again thoughtfully, before he spoke to Ushuu again. I waited with bated breath to understand what he'd said in response—my dignity be damned.

"He says," Ushuu barked again, "'That's what he thought it meant.'"

I snorted through my nose, unable to help myself, and Ushuu joined in, obviously as delighted by Huu-goh as I was. I made a mental note to ask for his help again later. Perhaps I could learn Huu-goh's language faster if I had a tutor of my own. Additionally, Ushuu might have more resources about huu-mans if his knowledge of their language was any indication. I owed him an apology for avoiding him for so long. Even though a small, immature part of me wasn't sure I'd ever be able to look him in the eye again.

Thoughts raced through my mind, possibilities twitching just out of reach as I mulled over what to ask Huu-goh next. Time was running out. I had Ushuu's schedule memorized, just as I had everyone else's, and I knew his break was coming to an end.

I didn't want to get this wrong.

And while I suddenly found myself overwhelmed with the foreign urge to skip work for the day so that I could quiz Ushuu and Huu-goh, the crew deserved better. I had my own duties to attend to, and a tour to take my mate on.

I stared down at Huu-goh, mind spinning.

The smile he gifted me was the loveliest thing I'd ever seen. Prettier than the green skies back home. Prettier than open space. Prettier than the stars that glimmered just outside the hull of the command room where I spent most of my time. Prettier than the constellations my birth-father had pointed out to me in the inky sky above when I was just a boy.

I swallowed the lump in my throat, eyes stinging as I turned to Ushuu for one final time. His communicator buzzed like clockwork, indicating his break was over. I'd taken too long to think. He flashed me an apologetic frown before rising from his seat.

"Duty calls," Ushuu said in our tongue again. "This was nice. We should do it again now that you're not avoiding me."

I nodded, though he was right—and it was relieving that he'd addressed the awkward situation so that I would not have to. He'd always been good at that, at putting me at ease.

"Maybe you can tell me later *why* exactly that was," Ushuu added. I nodded, because I would. Along with an apology. And a bottle of his favorite juice—bottles I kept in my room for birthdays and celebrations.

My food still sat mostly untouched on the metal table, but I figured there would be time to eat when he was gone. I nodded, spots coloring fuchsia in embarrassment.

"One last thing," I murmured, as Ushuu tucked his communicator into his back pocket.

"Anything for you, Captain." Ushuu's tone was as easy-going as ever.

"Will you tell Huu-goh that he's beautiful?" I asked. "And that I'm happy he's happy." My hearts wobbled. "And that I hope he knows that he's safe with me."

Ushuu nodded. His eyes flickered with affection as he looked at me. "I'll tell him," he promised, turning his attention back to Huu-goh to relay my message. Once again, I found myself waiting anxiously for his response. As he listened, Huu-goh's expression shuttered and grew frighteningly blank for a moment as though he didn't understand what Ushuu had said—even though it had been in his own language.

I didn't know what to do with *that* face.

I didn't know what it meant.

"Bai bai," Ushuu waved goodbye to the both of us.

"Bai bai," Huu-goh replied, echoing the same words.

I watched Ushuu's white-clad back in a daze as he left the cafeteria and headed down the corridor out of sight. Huu-goh's face was still blank when I got over my own fear and looked down at him again. Though his expression was unreadable, his eyes were not. They swirled like storms as his lips wobbled.

"Thank yuu," he said, voice soft. It felt like a century had passed, and my hearts stuttered to life again as I nodded, leaning down to bump our noses together. Surprising me, he moved his hand to cup my jaw. I held still, frightened to even breathe as Huu-goh's soft, soft lips pressed to the rubbery skin on my snout. I wasn't sure what he was doing. A kiss, maybe?

It was different than the way we Sahrks kissed, but no less lovely.

I wanted to melt, but instead, I held still—unwilling to move for fear of breaking the moment, or accidentally catching him with my teeth.

"Yuu ahre…soh-sweet." Huu-goh swallowed, stroking over my jaw as more tendrils slipped free of my surface to cup the back of his hand. They wrapped tight, pulsing rhythmically as they held his hand in place.

I didn't know what "soh-sweet" meant.

But Huu-goh held me for a long, long time.

He kissed my snout again.

His eyes were warm with affection, that terrifying blankness gone. If I didn't know any better, I'd think that no one had ever called him beautiful before. Or maybe—it was the promise of safety that he had a hard time believing.

I could understand that.

But I knew with surety that I would never let him get hurt. I'd protect him. It felt inherently wrong to do anything else.

Huu-goh's leash dangled, forgotten between us. As the last minutes of my afternoon break passed I wished desperately—with both my hearts— that we would be alright. That we could be happy, even though we were different. That all it would take was a little more time, and a lot more patience, but one day, we'd make a home with each other.

A home where Huu-goh would always feel beautiful.

A home where he felt safe.

# TEN

## HUGO

**YOU KNOW WHAT'S WEIRD? ALIENS.** I mean, seriously. One day you're riding around on a guy's shoulders, he's calling you *beautiful* and telling you you're *safe*. Then that same night he's leaving you alone in your room—instead of banging you with his sexy tenta-fingers, like he should be—only to return so early the following morning it feels literally criminal.

I mean, *seriously.*

*What is up with that?*

Talk about mixed signals.

When he'd woken up—after only a few hours of sleep—Roark was affectionate as always. He disappeared to get ready for the day, disappeared again to wherever he came back sweaty and ripped from—and returned for breakfast.

He petted me with those massive, gentle hands. But his behavior was

145

so bizarrely normal I couldn't fully enjoy it. Okay, yeah. That was a lie. I definitely enjoyed it. After lying alone in bed all night I was even more starved for his affection than usual.

He left to work like always, and while he was away, I used the fork I'd fashioned into a makeshift screwdriver to try and pry apart a nanobot. It was tricky, but not impossible. And it took way less time than I'd hoped it would. Which left me with even more time to overthink.

When Roark returned for lunch—and his hands were empty—I knew the day before had not been a fluke. This time, he hesitated as I stood in front of him, head tipped back, waiting for him to clip my leash.

*Huu-goh the dog now had daily walks!*

Sounded fucking sad, but was truly such an improvement.

When Roark didn't clip the lead, I frowned, confused. His hand hovered for a beat longer, but eventually he abandoned the leash entirely, re-clipping it to his leather belt though his gray spots betrayed how conflicted he felt about the motion.

Was I not going out?

I squinted at him, trying to figure out what the fuck was happening.

But then he held a hand out to me, waiting expectantly, and I knew things had just irrevocably changed. Once was an anomaly. Twice was a pattern. And the lack of leash spoke volumes.

My hand slid into his and he squeezed, little tendrils wrapping all the way around me till I was encased in a warm cocoon of pink as Roark pulled me out the door and into the hallway to go eat lunch at the canteen with him for the second day in a row.

We didn't hold hands for long. Only because both of us had enjoyed the way we'd traveled the day before. With Roark's broad shoulders beneath my legs, and the swoop in my belly after he'd swung me high in the air, I was on cloud nine—the lonely night forgotten.

All during lunch, Roark's tentacles felt me up, poking, rubbing, exploring. He'd rumble and nuzzle my hair as I ate, his long slithery tongue tracing the curve of my cheek like he missed me as much as I'd missed him, audience be damned.

I hadn't seen many of the crew since we'd been space-borne. And they kept their distance, though I caught more than a few curious, and amused looks. Sahrks were interesting people. All different shades of pastels, all seemingly friendly despite their plethora of teeth. That remained true, even with me—an outsider—attached to the man in charge of their ship.

I had no doubt they'd never seen their captain like this before.

Hell, I was surprised myself by how he was acting.

Apparently, Roark was touchy-feely when he was tired.

A fact that I found ridiculously cute—even if I was still super confused as to why he hadn't come to bed like usual.

Dutifully, Roark cut my bark for me into itty-bitty pieces. (I didn't complain. How could I? After he'd explained why he fed it to me.) He stroked my hair, and my fingers, his hot breath huffing against the side of my head the whole time I chewed.

When he'd dropped me off at our rooms to return to his duties, he'd paused in the doorway, staring at me for a beat longer than usual. His posture was as rigid as ever, though he didn't cross the distance between us.

"Bye bye," he said in my language. I perked up, chuckling as he raised one, large pink hand and waved.

"Bye bye," I waved back, feeling fizzy and bright as Roark's spots turned a brilliant, lovely shade of white—and then fuchsia immediately after—

and he shut the door behind him with a quiet click.

Nighttime came, we shared dinner like usual, traded a few more words back and forth. I fell asleep against Roark's chest, certain that his odd behavior the night before had been a fluke.

I was wrong.

At some point, after tossing and turning, I woke up to realize that Roark was gone.

For the second night in a row.

He'd been even more exhausted when he returned in the early hours of the morning. But something felt…wrong. It just did. Maybe because I felt neglected, I wasn't at my best as we made our way toward the cafeteria for lunch that afternoon. But that was just an excuse I gave myself, because on the third day out of our rooms I did something truly stupid.

Something *ridiculously* fucking stupid.

In my defense, the buttons on the wall were barely perceptible. I hadn't even truly realized that was what they were, at least until I pushed one and something actually happened. The little circle lit up beneath my finger, and I barely had a second to get excited about the new discovery before the hallway was plunged into darkness.

A lot of things happened all at once.

Roark roared, for one—this terrifying, frightened sound. The wall met my chest, chilly and hard as Roark slammed his bulk into me. A giant mass of sticky pink surrounded my body, encasing me like a rather anxious womb. It pulsed around me as the hot huff of Roark's breath ruffled my hair.

My heart was pounding.

And for a single, terrifying second, I thought I was going to die.

But that line of thought couldn't have been farther from the truth. Roark wheezed above me, like he couldn't get a solid breath in. His tendrils twist-twist-twisted around my body, holding me safe and close. Like we were one giant being with three hearts beating the same panicked rhythm.

Encased inside him like this, I could hear his pulse.

*Thump, thump, thump.* Far too rapid to mean anything good.

Fumbling through the goo, I managed to push the button again. The lights came on, but Roark's fear still clung heavy to my body—literally. He wouldn't stop shaking. And his breathing was so loud I was certain someone all the way down the hallway would be able to hear it.

"It's okay," I urged, fighting with his body to try and turn around so I could hug him. "It's okay, Roark."

Seeming to understand that we were safe, Roark's tendrils released enough to allow me to move. They didn't let me go though, simply holding on—clinging to me like he was terrified I was about to disappear.

One look at his face and the pitch black of his spots made my stomach tangle in knots. His eyes were glassy, far away, like he wasn't here with me at all.

"I'm so so sorry—" I had no idea why he'd freaked out like this. He had never been scared of the dark in our rooms. Though…now that I thought about it, he *did* leave the galaxy ceiling on every night.

Huh.

Roark didn't know what I was saying, but he responded to my tone anyway, melting into me, his head dropping to nuzzle into my hair as he continued to quake. The puff of his breath was even more obvious like this. And I spared only a single thought for the razor-sharp teeth I hoped he had control over right now—before I was wrapping my arms around what I could of his thick middle and comforting him.

"It's okay," I repeated, shushing him softly. I wished I could purr like he did when I was upset. It was kinda the most soothing thing ever. But I couldn't. So I did the next best thing—humming quietly. His reaction to the sound made it obvious that I'd made the right choice. He sighed, melting into me even more as my chest vibrated and the silliest, most basic song in the world buzzed between us.

"Twinkle, Twinkle Little Star" was a little on the nose.

But it was the first thing that popped into my head.

And it seemed to be working, so I continued to hum my way through the notes. Eventually, when the song ended, I started over from the beginning.

I'm not sure how long we stood there.

I'm not sure how long it took to get Roark's breathing under control.

I wasn't sure what he thought was happening, either. Or why he'd reacted the way he had. But I made a vow not to push anymore fucking buttons—curiosity be damned. I'd never seen him so off-kilter. And it hurt to know I was the reason he'd been scared.

His giant body towered over mine, blocking me from view of the rest of the hallway like a giant pink shield.

Several crewmates passed by us, all sharing worried glances, but none paused. A fact I was grateful for, as every time they glanced at their captain, I could literally feel how icy his body became.

"Shhh," I murmured, stroking my hands up and down his sides. "It's okay." I reassured again, and that got him to relax.

Roark trembled for a long time.

Long enough his lunch break was surely over. And when he'd finally peeled himself off me—literally—he'd herded me back into our bedroom with big gentle hands, his eyes still wide, food forgotten entirely.

The big guy still looked *terrified*—of what, I wasn't sure.

"*I'm so sorry,*" I said again in my own language—even though I knew he couldn't understand. The moment we were safe inside our room again, he stopped shaking quite so much. "I'm so sorry, Roark. I didn't mean to scare you. I'll be more careful. I'm sorry." He'd hugged me close again, his tendrils tickling along my body—less invasive this time—but no less enthusiastic.

Roark's voice was hoarse as he murmured against my hair in his strange gravelly language. The words sounded like reassurances. And that…fuck. That hurt even more. To know that I was the one that scared him, and here he was, trying to comfort me. When he'd pulled back to look me in the eye, his spots were pink again.

His eyes were soft.

They said, *I'm sorry.*

They said, *forgive me.*

They said, *I'm not perfect.*

"Thank you," Roark said in words I could understand.

He cradled my face in his massive hands. Comforting and warm, they covered my ears, blocking out the rest of the world so that all I knew was the fathomless baby blue of his gaze. His eyes reminded me of summer days back home, of clear skies, and the oceans I'd never visit.

When he shut them, I missed his eyes immediately. That loss, however, was easily forgotten when Roark began rubbing our noses together. Rubbery and soft, his surface tickled mine. Back and forth, back and forth.

Then he hugged me close again.

For a long.

Long.

Time.

I had never been more relieved in all my life that someone had accepted my apology.

I'd thought that would be the end of it.

But it wasn't.

Because after we'd both settled, Roark didn't take me out again. He didn't take me to the control room like he had the first day he'd brought me outside. He didn't take me to the cafeteria for lunch. And he certainly didn't take me anywhere new.

And I didn't ask. Because we both needed a break, I thought. And I understood that as steady as he was, even Roark needed recovery time after panicking the way he had. We didn't go hungry, but neither of us spoke the rest of the day. Not at lunch—when Roark buzzed someone using his tablet to bring us food like they had the first days I'd been on board—and not later, when he'd returned for dinner with plates balanced on his limbs.

That night was when the nightmares started with a vengeance. Like I'd triggered something in him. He was shaky and sweaty, droplets forming on his surface in beads—his chest shuddering with fear. When I petted his head fin to soothe him, he jerked awake, and that same faraway look remained in his gaze.

Humming softly, I gathered his head in my lap, trying to undo the damage I'd done—and failing.

Roark's eyes, when they cleared, searched for mine. It was only when our gazes met that he relaxed. Still quaking, he reached up with one hand and stroked over my cheek.

"Huu-goh safe," he said in my language. Words I hadn't known he recognized. Maybe he'd learned them from Ushuu when we'd gone to lunch with him? I wasn't sure. "Roark no hurt Huu-goh," Roark reassured, his first, real, solid sentence. "Roark sorry."

I shook my head, because he didn't need to be.

Later, I'd get excited about how many words he'd apparently been picking up. But for now…for now…I focused on him.

"No, *Hugo* is sorry," I said right back, squeezing his head close, my fingers bumping his teeth. They pricked, and I was lucky as hell that none sliced me. "Hugo hurt Roark."

I doubted he knew the word "scared," so "hurt" was close enough.

Roark huffed back at me, spots shifting colors too fast to track, before they settled on solid, calming blue. "No," he said simply. "No," he repeated stronger, caressing my cheek. "Roark okay."

I nodded.

Then I nodded again.

And my eyes burned as I curled into him, my own chest shuddering as a hot tear spilled down my cheek. I was so fucking glad I hadn't frightened him too much. That he forgave me. Because that was what this was. Forgiveness.

Roark purred to soothe me, and as always it worked. My tears slowed, and we clung to one another, the difficult day drifting away as the stars above us danced.

Roark held me like I was precious.

No one had ever done that before.

I was slowly but surely going insane.

It'd been a week since the Hallway-Terror-Incident and Roark had been missing most of every night since. Nightmares plagued him during the few short hours we spent in bed together. Demons I couldn't even ask him about. I was really, truly doing my best to be patient. Or I *had* been. Until Roark returned with red spots one night and I saw motherfucking red myself.

I vowed—that if the big pink softie was cheating on me I would find out. I would find out and I would chop off his balls with his own monstrously huge dental floss and my dullest, bluntest molars, so help me god.

I didn't actually think he would do that.

I didn't.

Roark wasn't that kind of guy.

But I also knew I was little more than a pet to him. And my own insecurity came rearing up like a slap to the face. I'd never been loved before. Never been appreciated. And I guess…my brain wanted to come up with any possible reason not to believe that Roark would pick me, of all people.

It was easier to believe that he would choose someone else—especially after I'd scared him. I knew he'd forgiven me. But…forgiving myself was another matter entirely. I hated this part of me. I really did.

Sitting alone all day made the thoughts spin and spin.

Small worries became monumental, and without anything to distract my mind, all I could do was stew. My brain had always worked quickly. It was why I'd been considered intelligent back home. But it also meant that without stimulation, it turned on itself.

Tearing me apart piece by piece, bit by bit, the doubt creeping in with every lonely night that passed.

I knew the code to the door. And after scaring Roark, I truly hadn't planned on doing anything that could bring that sort of reaction out again. But…desperate times called for desperate measures.

And I *needed* to know what was going on.

I needed to understand. So I could plan accordingly. So I could stop falling in love with him, if Roark didn't want me anymore. So that my brain would shut the fuck up and leave me alone.

The next night, I feigned sleep.

Roark disturbed the warm cocoon of our blankets, murmured something against my temple with one of his rubbery nose kisses, then rose to his feet. I watched through my lashes as he pulled on what I had privately dubbed his "day pants." His thick ass tested the seam, bare back rippling as he stretched from side to side. He glanced at me, and I shut my eyes, pretending still, careful so that my breathing wouldn't pick up.

He was observant.

Way fucking observant.

I wasn't even sure I'd get away with this at all.

But I did. Because when I next opened my eyes it was because I could hear the beep of Roark's fingers tapping the password into the keypad at the door. It swung open with a quiet hiss, a beam of light from the hallway creeping into the darkened room. Golden, it spread across the floor, Roark's shadow cutting through it.

The nanobots I'd been training while Roark had been away beeped unhappily where they rested in stasis underneath the bed, not at all pleased by the disruption to their programmed slumber.

Behind Roark, the door slid shut with finality.

My heart was pounding as I waited with what felt like an expert level of patience for all of thirty seconds. *Patient, patient. But not too patient—I* reminded myself, before I bolted to the keypad, tapped the password in, and slipped into the hall after my wayward owner.

It wasn't hard to find him, the dude had elephant feet.

All I had to do was follow the thunking.

The hallway chilled my bare feet, but I barely noticed. I only had to duck behind a corner to hide a handful of times from other crew members—which was a relief. Even if every time made me feel like I was James Bond or some shit—and not a nosy bastard, who needed reassurance he couldn't get with words.

Because Roark didn't know the words I needed.

I wasn't sure why I was so angry at the prospect of Roark getting some nookie on the side. I knew I wasn't a shark-dude myself. I hadn't seen a single cross-species pair on the ship, and it didn't take a genius to infer that wasn't a thing these creatures did. How would they procreate, after all? This was a question I'd asked myself about a thousand times—since I hadn't seen a female shark-person even once.

Could male sharks get pregnant?

No. That didn't seem likely. Roark was see-through enough I could somewhat see his organs at the right angle. And I'd never spotted a womb or ovaries.

Besides, he was made of *Jell-O*.

The idea of Roark making hypothetical shark babies with anyone but me made me want to scream, though. So I put that train of speculation to rest. I didn't need another thing to angst about. Not when I was already annoyed at myself for acting out like this. Not when there was no point working myself up before I got solid answers.

I heard quiet barking when I rounded a corner in the hallway, and my hackles rose. It wasn't *Roark's* laugh. I'd recognize that sound anywhere. I seriously doubted he was off laughing in a dark corner alone, so that confirmed that he was with someone else.

Fuck.

I could see more light spilling from the open doorway I'd followed him to. Always aware of the buttons that could be there, I slipped along the surface of the cool metal wall as silently as I could, ready to catch my owner in action.

Except, when I peeked around the lip of the doorway what I saw was… *yeah*.

Not at all what I expected.

*What the hell are they doing?*

I frowned, trying to make sense of the sight in front of me.

Roark sat on a hover-chair in the back corner of the unfamiliar room. Along the walls were all sorts of tools and implements, and in the center was a row of identical tables covered in machines I had no hope of understanding. It looked like a lab.

A science lab.

Similar to the ones I'd worked tirelessly at during high school, but bigger—and brighter—with glowy objects and instruments I'd never imagined in my wildest dreams. Ushuu was beside him. Which again, had not been what I expected. He had a chair of his own, and his sleeves were rolled up, his body turned toward me, where Roark's was tipped away.

And they were—yeah. I didn't really get what I was seeing. I mean, I *did*. Obviously. I was a straight-A student, *hello*! I would've been doing exactly what they were doing right about now if I'd never been abducted.

Except I'd be at Harvard surrounded by trust-fund brats who didn't know what Oscar Mayer hotdogs tasted like.

Which was to say…the two sharks were…

Yeah.

They were *studying*.

Actually—more accurately—*Roark* was studying.

He had about forty images hovering in the air surrounding him, holograms blown up in a myriad of colors. Various illustrations and photographs were splashed across each open window. I was unfortunately too far away to tell exactly what any of them were. The shapes, however, looked somewhat familiar?

Which was weird, because since I'd been abducted three years ago I hadn't really had that thought often, about *anything*. Space was a strange place full of a variety of oddly shaped things. Nothing had the color you expected. Nothing tasted the way you thought it would taste. Nothing smelled the way you thought it should smell.

So, tell me why…*why*—if I squinted—it looked like there were images of Earth hovering in the air? The Eiffel Tower. The Statue of Liberty. The pyramids. *Sushi?*

"Thank yew fuhr comming," Roark said in English, slow and annunciated. The words were clunky on his tongue, but recognizable all the same.

"Thank you," Ushuu corrected him.

"Thank you," Roark repeated, much more slowly, but smoother all the same.

"For."

"For."

"Coming."

"Co…ming." Roark blinked. "Thank you for coming."

My heart thundered and I gawped, slack-jawed as Ushuu trilled happily and clapped his hands. His gaze slid over to me, a knowing look in his eyes as he turned his attention back to Roark.

"Better!"

Ushuu did not betray my presence.

They murmured back and forth in their native tongue for a few minutes. I was *entranced* at the sight of Roark flipping through the slides, making a few larger—large enough I could see them, even from this distance.

Reading glasses were settled over his snout—and he looked so ridiculous and gorgeous it made me ache. He squinted, said something in sharkish, and then waited.

"How are you?" Ushuu sounded out in answer to his question, far slower than any normal person would ever talk.

"How ahre yuu?" Roark repeated in butchered English.

"How are you?" Ushuu corrected.

"How…are…you?" Roark sounded unsure, but Ushuu's applause made his spots flicker white, with what I could only assume was happiness. They murmured back and forth once again, and Roark snorted through his nose at something Ushuu said before he shook his head and gestured toward one of the images in the air with his large, clawed hands.

"I am good," Ushuu said, just as deliberately as the first two times.

"I…um…" Roark shook his head at himself in frustration. "Am," he corrected himself, "*good.*"

Again, Ushuu clapped.

Again, I stared.

Was he learning English? *For me?*

*Is that what he'd been doing this whole time?*

Suddenly things started to make sense.

It seemed after our run-in with Ushuu and what had happened in the hallway Roark had decided he'd had enough with our limited communication. This was…a gift I never would've expected. The amount of effort it took was astounding. Add on the amount of sleep he'd been losing, somehow fitting English lessons into his already hectic schedule—and I just…

God.

I was floored.

My heart was racing, my eyes damp as I watched the two of them for a few more wonderful minutes before I decided I'd seen enough. I still didn't understand why Roark's spots had been red the other night, but it was becoming obvious that I'd made a terrible mistake thinking the worst of him.

Here I was, assuming he was a cheater-cheater pumpkin-eater, when he was *actually* the hugest fucking sweetheart in the entire galaxy. Pun intended. For so long I'd prided myself on my optimism, and yet…I'd given up on Roark so quickly.

*What was wrong with me?*

Dazed, I made my way back to our room. The door slid open with a quiet hiss but I barely noticed as I made a beeline for the bed and collapsed on the mattress. The stars on the ceiling sparkled above me. My lashes were cold and wet as I squeezed my eyes tightly shut and took a shuddering, steadying breath.

One of the nanobots beneath the bed turned on, a little buzzing sound echoing through the metal room as it spun around in an attempt to get comfortable and before going back into stasis.

On the days and nights I'd been alone, I'd been slowly but surely programming them into pets.

Assistants.

Assistant-pets.

I figured if I could prove to Roark I was useful, he'd want to keep me around, even after we reached wherever it was that we were going.

Not that I could tell him that.

But…maybe soon?

Maybe we could have a real conversation—if he kept attending lessons.

With a sigh I scrubbed my hands over my eyes as I tried to make sense of my messy feelings. One thing was certain. I was an asshole. I had jumped to conclusions, chased Roark down like an absolute dick, and worst of all—I'd shat all over his trust.

He deserved better.

He really did.

He was *trying*. He was trying harder than anyone in my life had ever tried for me before. And it made me feel weirdly squirmy and warm all over when I thought about how seriously adorable he'd just been. So stoic, so careful as he repeated words back to Ushuu, his blue eyes full of frustration—like he wanted to learn *faster* so he could talk to me, and he was angry at himself for not catching on more quickly.

A memory surfaced, uninvited.

A memory I hadn't revisited in a long, long time.

It'd been my sixteenth birthday. I'd thrown a party for myself—because I wasn't stupid enough to expect my parents to throw one for me. Sixteen was a *big* number, right? It was the one you celebrated with friends and family. The biggest birthday aside from eighteen and twenty-one.

I was still hopeful then.

Which was why I'd told my mom six months in advance about my party plans, just to make sure she cleared her schedule.

I even went as far as to ask my dad's secretary to remind him. He liked to think he was important because he had a secretary, even though he was one of the lowest performing lawyers at his firm. Probably because he kept alcohol in his water bottle, and didn't know what day it was most of the time. He'd inherited the job because it was his father's company, not on any merit of his own—but that didn't mean he wasn't arrogant.

Every time I'd asked him to come to something when I was little his reply had been "tell my secretary" and he'd said it like he was the goddamn president. I'd never minded humoring him, not when it made him happy. Even though asking his secretary usually didn't do any good, either.

Dad had come to my science fair *once*.

And he'd left before he'd even seen my project.

His work had always been more important to him than I was.

So I wasn't sure why I was surprised when my birthday arrived, and neither of my parents were home. I spent all morning preparing the dining room to host guests, still hoping.

I'd been reminding both my parents about this for *weeks*.

When I thought about how much hope I'd placed in them, it seemed silly. Like any good scientist, I should've hypothesized based on evidence previously gathered. But at the time I was sixteen. And it was my birthday—and I just...

I let all my doubts fly out the window, one final time.

For the first few hours I'd naively figured both my parents were running late.

That *this* was part of an elaborate surprise.

That they'd appear with a dinosaur cake to match my "coming of age" theme—the one I'd spent weeks crafting prehistoric decorations for. That they'd yell "surprise!" And we'd laugh and *laugh*, and it'd be like one of the sitcoms I watched when I was alone after school. Except better. Because it was *real*. And they really cared. And they'd show me that—

They'd see me—and I'd feel *loved*.

But when the party was supposed to start and no one showed up, not even Donald from chess club, or Ned from League For Battery Fueled Assassins, it felt like something inside me withered and died. All the other teens I'd invited had colorful excuses: the football game that night, a math test tomorrow, they forgot they had to do something, blah, blah, blah.

And I hadn't cared.

I honestly *hadn't*.

Because my parents were the guests of honor. And I knew they would come. I *knew* they would. Because they'd *promised*. And even though they weren't the most attentive parents in the world, they weren't cruel.

So I continued to wait, and my excitement never died.

For three hours.

Three hours.

The clock ticked and ticked and ticked.

I called my mom's cell sixteen times. I called my dad's work fifteen times. My dad's secretary told me he was out when she answered on the sixteenth ring. I figured he was getting the cake. You know. To *surprise* me. Because I was naive, and young—and I'd wanted…well.

You can guess what I wanted.

The house was empty.

The clock kept ticking.

It was eleven-thirty when the front door finally pushed open.

When Dad entered, he wobbled on his feet. It didn't take a genius to figure out he was drunk. He had red lipstick on the collar of his shirt. He smelled like menthols and stale beer. I followed after him, legs numb from sitting so long. With every step I hoped and hoped and hoped.

He wobbled up the stairs without acknowledging me, gripping the railing tight. When he tripped, he chuckled to himself, white-knuckled and tipsy. His briefcase spilled across the steps, and I chased after him, picking up the papers and stacking them into a neat little pile. When we reached the top of the stairs I handed them over, my heart in my throat.

He looked me in the eye for the first time since he'd come home, and his gaze was blurry. Like I wasn't even there. Like he couldn't see me at all.

*Say it,* I'd pleaded in my head.

*Say it, please.*

*"Happy birthday, Hugo."*

*That's all I need to hear and I'll forgive you.*

*Say it, say it, say it, say it—*

"Thanks, buddy," he said instead, slapping me on the shoulder twice before taking the papers from my grip and stumbling into his office. He returned after a few seconds, sans briefcase, and my hopes soared a second time. He squinted at me, his copper-colored hair sticking up in a sweaty mess. He smiled, and I waited.

And waited.

And waited.

"Did you need something?" he asked, leaning heavily against the doorframe.

I stared at him for a long time, and as the clock on the wall ticked, my heart shattered in two. I shook my head, and when I smiled I closed myself off, locking away my heart where he couldn't break it again.

"Just wanted to say goodnight," I managed, drowning from the inside out.

"Night," Dad replied.

"And that I love you," I added, my hands clenching so hard into fists I could practically smell the bloody smears my fingernails left behind.

"You too, bud."

Mom didn't come home.

I retreated downstairs to take the decorations down. I put the board games away. The clock kept ticking. When the house was back to being the mausoleum it had been before, I retreated to my room. I lay in bed and zoned out, head tipped toward the glow-in-the-dark stars on my ceiling. Numb. When the tears finally came I willed them away, but stubbornly, they kept coming.

I closed my eyes and slept.

I never planned a party again.

It wasn't a pleasant memory.

And it never managed to hurt any less every time I thought of it. Like having my heart broken by both of my parents on the same night had rearranged something fundamental inside me. Here I was, a galaxy away, and their actions still affected me. My parents taught me that love meant distance. It meant effort when it was necessary for your reputation but not when it was needed.

I wasn't sure why Roark's earnestness had brought this memory to the surface.

Except…maybe I *did* know.

Because Roark wasn't like that.

Roark was the antithesis of what my parents were. He was warm where they were cold. Serious and kind. Gentle. Attentive.

I had the feeling, if I had invited Roark to my birthday party he would've been the first to arrive. He would've brought me flowers, and pizza, and cake. He would've played my dumb games, even though he probably wouldn't have understood what they were talking about, or even liked them. He would've told me happy birthday.

He was just that kinda guy.

An *effort* kinda guy, with a capital E.

I swallowed the lump in my throat and vowed to make this up to him.

I vowed to be better.

To trust him more.

To put in the effort he was, and see what could happen.

To allow the boundless optimism I'd always had to extend to him the way it should've all along.

My parents were shitty parents. I knew that. And it wasn't fair to judge Roark based on their broken relationship with each other and with me. He wasn't them, just like I wasn't.

And maybe I was his pet, but I was quickly coming to realize I didn't care. The way he treated me spoke volumes. And I was grateful now more than ever that he'd decided to take me in.

When Roark returned a few hours later something between us had shifted, only he didn't know it yet. His movements were silent as he shut the door behind him—careful not to "wake" me. When he shucked off his "day pants" and donned his "night pants" (they looked the same, honestly), every movement was careful. Sneakily, he climbed into bed with me for the second time that night, careful not to jostle me too hard—though the effort was wasted because his size made that super fucking impossible.

The whole bed jiggled, but I pretended to sleep through it so he wouldn't feel bad for waking me. Roark was *warm* as he settled behind me. All my earlier thoughts drifted away, his heat scaring them off as a sense of safety settled over me. He pulled the blankets over us both. And when he tucked his nose against the nape of my neck, and immediately started purring like a giant squishy panther, I felt peace.

Roark held still—probably to make sure I was still asleep—before he gave in to his own desires and began tentatively nuzzling my hair. His deliciously hot breath blew against it as he rumbled, very obviously pleased to be back in bed with me. Roark relaxed with a weighty sigh, like holding me in his arms had been what he'd been waiting for all day.

And then, because he was wonderful, he did the one thing I never would've expected.

But maybe I *should've*.

"Good…night," Roark said—in perfect English—his voice heavily accented and thick with sleep, "little…beast."

*Little beast?*

The words were so sweet I burned from the inside out. Throwing caution to the wind, I curled my arms around his and squeezed. *Fuck pretending to sleep.* Hugging Roark back was more important. Roark chuckled softly, holding me just as tight.

A few friendly tendrils wrapped around my limbs, wiggling till our bodies were smooshed so perfectly together I couldn't tell where one of us began and the other ended. Roark's purring eventually evolved into a quiet, sleepy snore.

His hearts thumped.

*Thump, thump, thump.*

When I was sure he was asleep, I gave one of his tendrils a kiss as a hot tear leaked down my cheek. I wasn't sure how he was doing this. How he was healing my childhood, years later, with gentle words and gentle hands.

But he was.

Because the truth was, he may be an alien, but he was far more human than anyone I'd ever met before. And I may be his pet, but Roark was teaching me what it felt like to be loved.

"Goodnight," I whispered, voice hoarse. "Sweet dreams."

# ELEVEN

## ROARK

**THE MORE I LEARNED ABOUT** huu-mans the more fascinating they became as a species. There were many things that intrigued me—too many to keep track of. For example, the fact some of them chose to go to expensive specialized schools called "caw-lege." At home on Osheania, we had our own schools, but attendance was required and cost nothing. It was our society's way of ensuring people could get into whatever career they desired. The most similar thing I'd discovered in huu-man culture was something Ushuu had called an "internship."

They had seasons on Earth, and every area on the planet had different temperatures and weather. And yet—instead of evolving in the north so they had more fur to keep themselves warm, huu-mans came up with *inventions* and *clothing* to combat the chill.

Ushuu showed me pictures of many things.

Many things that helped me understand my own little huu-man better. Things that helped me appreciate him in entirely new, unexpected ways.

Huu-mans displayed their personalities through their choices of clothing. A lot of them relied solely on accessories and colors to project what sort of mate they desired. They hung out in flocks, with huu-mans who wore similar clothing, who liked similar things, who listened to similar music.

Most fascinating of all, however, was the custom huu-mans called "pets."

We had animals on my home planet. The Fruhg for example. Large amphibious creatures that lived in the country and made this awful *ribbit* sound when you got too close. Their webbed feet and flippers had never struck me as anything other than necessary for their survival. I'd certainly never found them cute. I couldn't imagine taking one inside my home and keeping it as a companion.

And yet, huu-mans did that very thing.

With a whole variety of creatures.

So many I couldn't recall all of their names, though visions of furry four-legged beasts had haunted me all week.

Did Huu-goh miss "beanies," "coffee," and "phones"?

I wondered if he'd even *had* any of those things.

What about his family? Did he have one? As an orphan, the thought had simply not occurred to me until Ushuu brought it up. Did he miss the holidays widely celebrated across his planet? Did he miss "autumn" and "summer" and "TV"?

The idea of seeing Huu-goh dressed in one of the fluffy marshmallow-looking outfits Ushuu had shown me made me ache something fierce. He had called them "puffer coats" and I'd been *enamored*.

Did he wish he had a dawg?

Or a kaat?

As I finished packing up work for the day, these thoughts plagued me. All week, as I'd worked throughout the day, Huu-goh occupied my thoughts.

My mind would drift from reality, and I would imagine what his life had been like before he'd been taken. It was easy to forget the threats outside the ship, and even the course we were on, when Huu-goh filled my head.

I despaired for him on more than one occasion. Because learning about his culture only made it more obvious that I could not give him even a fraction of what he'd lost from his home planet. There were some things, however, that I could.

I made a detour to the lab where I'd been spending my nights, determined to give Huu-goh something he could keep. A hobby—or…I don't know. Things to occupy his time while we remained space-borne. I'd been half-tempted to bring him with me all day, but I knew while that would be fun—for both of us—it didn't give him any sort of autonomy to be forced to follow me around.

He needed his own things.

When Huu-goh had hit the light switch it had frightened me. But I'd tried to put those thoughts behind me. Moving forward was the only way to outrun the shadows in my head—and I had goals that were more important than the fear that lived beneath my skin.

That didn't erase its existence, but acknowledging it was there, and that I was choosing to move past it, helped.

The second we'd been plunged into darkness together, memories of my teenage years on this very ship burned through my retinas. For a moment all I'd smelled was blood. I could hear the wheeze of Captain's chest. Could feel the wet-damp blood on my hands, the weak tug of his tendrils trying to soothe me, even though he was dying.

When the lights came back on, and I'd processed that I was not there—but here, with Huu-goh, I was reminded once again of the fear I'd felt when I'd taken him onboard. When I'd locked him in our rooms, terrified he'd be hurt the same way I'd seen others hurt before.

I hated losing control, and for a moment I had.

I'd been just a boy again.

Terrified.

But then he'd comforted me. He'd comforted me—and I'd let him. And for the first time in my life it hadn't felt like I was dealing with those memories alone. I'd always found him fascinating. Always admired his tenacity and his bravery. But that feeling had only exploded when I had my thoughts back in order and I'd realized that not once—during that entire encounter—had Huu-goh shied from me.

There was trust there.

Affection too—that I didn't need him to have spots to read—all over his face. And I'd vowed to myself that I would do everything in my power to make him happy. It wasn't the first time I'd made that promise, but it did strengthen my resolve. Enough so that while I was exhausted—operating on next to no rest at all—I had never been more determined in all my life to see something through.

I was learning Huu-goh's language as swiftly as I could, but the process was a slow one. Some rules in the language made absolutely no sense, and some words were almost impossible for me to pronounce. Ushuu ended up laughing at me more often than not, and while I appreciated his help and enjoyed his amusement, I never let it take time away from my lessons.

I wanted to know how to speak fluently *now*, not later.

At this rate, by the time I learned, we would already be back on Osheania where temporary translators were readily available, and I could contact A&R to purchase the permanent alternative. I refused to think the process was pointless, however, because—like we'd already discovered—removable translators were not a foolproof system. And for all I knew, it could take months to get implants delivered to our planet.

"Captain," Ushuu, greeted me as I paused in the doorway. I huffed, amused as always by our little game.

"I was wondering if you could help me?" I inquired, more than a little giddy.

"Anything you need."

After I explained Huu-goh's cleverness to him, and the nanobots I'd seen him fiddling with using a doctored fork, Ushuu made a thoughtful sound.

"He'd be better off in here with me if you're wanting to give him a purpose." His eyes turned to crescents. "But you're right. Maybe some things of his own would make him happy." He spent the next twenty or so minutes putting together a box of items for me.

Some things I understood, and others I didn't.

"I bet he'll find this interesting," Ushuu beckoned me closer. I hadn't noticed lately—I'd been so busy learning—but the surface of his gray skin was fading with age, and his spots were paler than they'd been a few years ago. "It's not functional, but if he's anything like I was when I was young, he'll enjoy picking these apart."

Inside the box was a set of old translators. They were out of commission now, I was certain. Based on the dust alone, and the broken pieces, I figured it'd been a long time since they'd been useful. I was surprised Ushuu had them at all, considering the fact that they didn't work out in space.

"Thank you," I replied, excited—but still a little stuck on his fading spots. *How had I never noticed before? Had I really been so distracted lately that I hadn't paid attention?*

I feared we were nearing the last of our flights together.

Ushuu stroked a hand over my shoulder, gave my bicep a squeeze, and then wandered off to grab what I'd requested. With his back turned, I let my smile fall as my hearts ached. *Huu-goh would like it here with Ushuu. There isn't a single thing that Ushuu cannot teach him.* "Think about sending him over," he said as he set the box down on the table in front of me. "I promise I'll take good care of him."

"I know," I said—because I did know. I moved to pick up the box, but he held a hand out to stop me. It shook a little, not from nerves but from age.

"I'll ask him if he wants to," I responded, already knowing that Huu-goh would. "If he does, I'll bring him by after lunch in the afternoon if that works for you."

"I've always wanted an apprentice." Ushuu's gaze met mine.

He had always been small for a Sahrk, though his intelligence made up for whatever he lacked in size. A formidable foe. Even as old as he was.

"Your mate," Ushuu made a thoughtful sound, tapping the box with one claw, before removing his hand so I could pick it up. It was heavier than it looked, rattling in my arms. "He is a clever one."

"Too clever," I puffed up with pride.

"There is nothing of harm in that box," Ushuu reassured me. "But there are dangerous things in this room. Dangerous things, I am certain with his level of intelligence, he will be smart enough to work around."

I nodded, appreciating how candid he was with that information. He was giving me an out. He knew me better than anyone. Knew how hard the captain's death had hit me. Knew that even before that, I'd always spent far too much time with the worries of the future clouding my thoughts.

A lot had changed.

My worries were not gone. In fact—they were worse—the more I grew to care for Huu-goh. But my love for him was stronger. And I refused to keep him prisoner. I wanted to see him thrive. To see the things he could create. To give him every opportunity I could. And sometimes that meant he might touch or be around dangerous objects, and I would have to be at peace with that.

And there was no better gift I could give the person I loved than time with Ushuu.

"We would be honored," I said softly. "And I trust you."

Ushuu's spots were a pale, beautiful pink, shining with affection as he leaned in close to bump our snouts together.

"Thank you," he said. "I am proud of you, Roark," Ushuu added. "It is one thing to jump into water without knowing the dangers that lie beneath the surface. It is another to be afraid of such things, but to dive in anyway."

I nodded.

"You cannot stop bad things from happening," Ushuu murmured, his eyes still meeting mine. "And it is incredibly brave of you to choose to love even after what you've seen can happen."

I pressed into the embrace, tendrils slipping free to melt with Ushuu's as his words washed warm over my body.

"You'll be alright," Ushuu promised before stepping back, his tendrils untangling from mine. "And so will he."

"I know," I nodded. Swallowing the lump in my throat, I did my best to control my spots. "I'll be back tonight?" I offered, eager to learn more. "Maybe you can help me come up with more ideas to please him."

Sighing in amusement, Ushuu shook his head fondly. "Take a break tonight. Besides, if you want to please him, why not accept one of the invitations? You could speak to him then. Get a reprieve from the stress on board. Hell, you could let it be a 'date'."

Human mates went on things called "dates" when they were courting. It was something Huu-goh would understand, and might even appreciate.

It was a lovely idea. I blinked, thoughts whirring.

Every time we stopped at Sha'hPihn to collect our cargo and refuel we received an influx of invitations to galas, balls, and parties. Many had a steep price to attend, and I had no doubt the interest in us Sahrks coming had to do with the exorbitant ticket fees and donations that were expected at the events.

I was not unused to being treated as a giant pink wallet—it was exactly what had happened when I'd bought back Huu-goh's rights. Many species looked at Sahrk and saw money signs dangling over our heads. I had been invited to hundreds, maybe thousands of events but *this* was the first time I'd ever been tempted to attend, for one simple reason.

There were *translators* at those parties.

And for one night...

For *one perfect night* Huu-goh and I would be able to speak to one another.

Excitement bubbled up inside me as I leaned down to give Ushuu another happy nuzzle, giddy now that I had a plan. "You are brilliant as always, old man," I grinned.

He snorted, slapping me on the back. "That's why you pay me," he shrugged, downplaying his own brilliance with a grin of his own. The smack was lighter than it should've been, and once again, I was reminded of his age.

I'd have to talk to Naideen when I got home to make sure there was room for Ushuu at the manor. It was the least I could do after all he'd done for me over the years.

"*Brilliant!*" I repeated as I gathered Huu-goh's box against my chest, headed toward the door, and tapped the buttons on the access panel with my tentacles. With a *woosh* I was free, striding down the hallway with purpose as Ushuu's idea settled in the back of my mind.

"Captain," one of the two subordinates I passed in the hallway greeted. Bahrn. A young recruit.

"Evening, Bahrn," I replied on autopilot, my head in the clouds. He stiffened, saluted, and beamed at me.

"He knows my name!" he said to Giren, the recruit who stood beside him.

"Of course he knows your name, idiot. He knows everyone's name."

I hid my smile, though I was amused as I continued down the winding halls toward our rooms.

There was a reason I'd followed in Captain Strongfoot's footsteps and hired half my crew young and scrappy. He had taught me, in many ways, that a person's worth was not determined by their lineage, but by the opportunities they were given, and the people who believed in them.

Plus, the young were endlessly entertaining. Full of life in a way I hadn't been in years. Until Huu-goh became mine, anyway.

However, even my adorable subordinates could not hold my attention for long. No. As always, my mind flitted back to my mate and the plan I was piecing together. Ideas slipped like puzzle pieces into place.

There were many moving parts to it, of course.

His safety would need to be my number one priority. Sha'hPihn wasn't like the rural planets we'd visited before. It was full of as many unsavory people as F'ukYuu was. Though they liked to hide their depravity behind gemstones and storefronts—it was dangerous in its own way.

But…Huu-goh would adore it.

I already knew that.

And there were things we could get him there—that I couldn't get him back home.

Perhaps I could buy him a new journal so that he could fill it with more of his findings? The thought made me giddy. He could have a HoverPad of his own too. A communicator. Clothing he'd chosen himself. His pick of any hobby he desired.

And I could get the damn collar off of him.

We'd need to go to a jeweler to do it—but—

Oh.

Suddenly, memories of how he'd lit up when he'd seen the gems on our first off-planet visit came to mind. *Yes.* I could replace it with something he'd love. Something that was a symbol of his freedom—and not his sacrifice.

Something Huu-goh thought was pretty.

Something that made his pearly teeth smile.

That made his dark eyes dance.

Something that made him feel valued, the way he deserved to feel.

Covered in his colorful clothes—clothes he'd picked on his own—Huugoh would find solid footing in a way he hadn't before. He'd get to choose for himself. Autonomy that I hoped would make his life brighter—and maybe, just maybe, at the ball I could tell him what he meant to me. We could speak candidly like we should've the day we met.

I would get to know him on an entirely new level.

And maybe then, I could summon the courage to tell him how glad I was that he'd picked me. That he'd crossed the line that I'd been scared to. I could tell him how I admired him. I could hold him. Could touch him, the way we both craved—and speak to him at the same time.

# TWELVE

## HUGO

**"NO WAY!" I SCREECHED IN** excitement as I tore through the box of goodies Roark had brought me. I'd never seen anything like the contents it carried, the alien technology glistening and glowing as I pulled it out piece by piece with the help of the nanobots I'd programmed. The most exciting item of all, however, were the sets of old translators that I couldn't wait to pick apart.

Maybe I could figure out how they worked?

And if that was the case, maybe I could alter them so that we could use them onboard the ship? It was an optimistic thought, but I clung to it—and them—as I turned to Roark to thank him.

"Yesh?" Roark looked confused.

It took me a second to realize that the last thing I'd just said had included the word 'no.'

"Oh sorry! I forget you take things so literally," I blinked up at him, setting the things I held down. "I didn't mean 'no way' as in *no*. I meant 'no way' as in 'oh my god, this is awesome!'" He wouldn't understand any of that, but I gushed anyway. I hadn't breathed since he'd shyly handed me my gift, and my lungs wheezed while I beamed at him as fondly as I could. "*Thank you.*" He knew that one, and melted immediately.

He stiffened up again, however, silent for a moment like he was processing something, before he spoke. "You…are…welcome." Roark sounded out the words slowly with a heavy accent, but there was no doubt that he'd been practicing. He looked proud of himself when the words came out correctly. I wanted to kiss him. To smooch his big pink head. But he was too far away—and also—presents!

I had *presents*.

I could totally build something with the rest of this, even if I couldn't salvage the translators. I *knew* I could. I'd taken robotics in my senior year of high school, and also had been captain of its robot fight club, the League For Battery Fueled Assassins. I knew feedback devices, end effectors, and controllers like I knew the back of my hand. It was why, despite the technology being new and—for lack of a better word—alien, I'd been able to manipulate the nanobots so easily. With the set of tools Roark had also given me, there was nothing I couldn't do. No more janky fork for me, yay!

"Happy?" Roark asked. This was one of his newest words. He said it in a funny way, more like "hoppy," but I knew what he meant. He was *really* trying, and with every passing day we were able to communicate better and better. Every time he said a new word, he'd get the most serious, kinda constipated look on his face while he waited to see if he'd used it right way.

It was so fucking cute.

*He* was so fucking cute.

Which was not an impression I ever thought I'd have about the stoic Captain. With every passing day, I liked him more and more.

Roark let me play with the "Box of Awesome," as I privately dubbed it in my head, for a good few hours. He even gave me a snack so I wouldn't get hungry while I worked.

I arranged the items first by size, then by metal type, then by what I thought the devices must've been used for before they'd been broken. Knowing Roark, there was nothing dangerous in the box, so I didn't need to worry.

He always had my best interests at heart.

I appreciated his protectiveness in a way I hadn't before. It made me feel safe to know I had him watching my back. I'd never had that before. Ever.

Now that I understood him better, I could see how difficult it was for him to let go of the reins he'd held so tightly for so long. I could appreciate him for that too. Roark's protectiveness came from a good place. I still didn't understand why he was this way, but for the first time in my life, my burning questions were content to wait.

A quiet snore startled me out of my wandering thoughts. When I lifted my head, tools still in hand and a pile of nanobot bits scattered on the floor between my legs, I saw Roark passed out in bed. It wasn't late. Definitely wasn't bedtime. I'd memorized the squiggles on the clock, and these squiggles usually meant we'd be fucking right about now.

Damn.

That was a distracting thought.

Roark lay propped up against the shell-like edge of the mattress. His tablet was on his belly and his glasses were perched askew on his nose. Poor dude was *exhausted*. It'd been go, go, go for him for a while now, and I wasn't surprised he'd crashed.

It had to happen sometime, right?

I felt guilty, because I wanted to help lift some of the weight he carried, but I didn't know how.

Abandoning the corner of the room that I'd commandeered, I rose to my feet and padded barefoot across the room. My knees bumped the edge of the bed when I arrived.

As if he sensed my presence, Roark woke, blinking pretty blue eyes open, a quiet sigh escaping his lips. "Little…beast," he murmured in English, reaching out with a huge hand to hover inches from my ribs. I leaned into the touch and he sighed again, content, stroking over my flank as tentacles split from his squishy pink forearm and looped around my hip, holding me comfortingly in place.

I didn't know why he called me that. But I liked it.

"Tired?" I asked him. He knew that word too.

"Yesh," Roark agreed, reaching for the tablet laying on his abdomen with sleepy, sluggish movements. I halted him, fingers wrapped around his wrist—how much of it I *could* wrap around, anyway, considering our size difference.

"Let me," I said, not sure if those were words he'd understand or not. He nodded and I grinned at him, picking up the device, before setting it on the nightstand. I removed his glasses next, carefully folding them up and setting them down, unsure how the hell they stayed on his head when it was so large and he didn't have ears.

I wished I could ask him.

Roark was watching me.

His gaze was hot and shivers tickled up my body as I swallowed the lump in my throat.

"Hungry?" I asked, more than willing to get some food for him. We'd been to the cafeteria together enough times I was sure that I could find my way there, especially after my little impromptu adventure when I'd been spying on him.

"Yesh," Roark agreed with a sigh, continuing to stroke my side as he moved to sit up.

"Roark?" I gave his wrist another squeeze and he paused, observing me. It wasn't often I addressed him so plainly. He could sense something was up.

"Yesh?" His entire body was tense, but I held his gaze anyway, unafraid of the teeth and claws—and the predator that I had frozen with one simple touch.

"Let me." It was a simple request, and one I wasn't entirely sure he'd understand.

Apparently he did, because he responded by blinking in confusion. His spots changed color so fast it was hard to pinpoint how he was feeling. Eventually, they settled on a pale gray. I wasn't one hundred percent sure what it meant, but I had to guess it was somewhere close to confusion or anxiety, judging by the alarmed rumble he was emitting.

"Please?" I wanted him to trust me. I needed to prove to him that I could be useful.

Roark grew scarily quiet as he thought. I knew without a doubt that he was going to give in. He was a softie like that.

"Please?" I repeated, squeezing his squishy wrist. "Please, please, please?"

He frowned, shifting a little on the bed before he sighed, dropped his head, closed his eyes—and nodded.

After releasing his wrist, I launched myself at him. Exuberantly, I threw my arms around his thick neck and squashed him tight as I fluttered kisses all over his rubbery cheeks, careful to avoid his teeth. "Thank you, thank you, thank you!"

Roark barked out a laugh and the palm that had petted my side stroked down my back, then up, then down, then up again. His fingers gave my nape a gentle squeeze, and I pulled back to beam at him some more.

*I get to go out on my own!*

*He trusts me!*

"Safe," he commanded, the word a bit garbled. I wasn't surprised he'd made Ushuu teach him that one straight away. "Huu-goh safe." I studied him, warmth tingling all over as I caught the very real fear in his eyes. "Huu-goh safe or I come."

*Another full sentence!*

"Okay," I agreed eagerly. "Safe," I cupped his cheeks in my hands, never more aware of the difference in our size than I was when we were pressed close like this. "I'll be safe, I promise."

His spots stayed that same worried gray shade as I planted a kiss on his snout, backed off his lap, and launched myself at the door. Because I rarely thought things through all the way, I typed in the code to the door while he watched, and eagerly bounced on my heels as it opened with a faint hiss.

It took me a second to realize what I'd done, and when I did, I turned around slowly, ready to be reprimanded for memorizing his password without permission. However, all I saw on Roark's face was affection and amusement as he shook his head and closed his eyes again.

"Huu-goh safe!" he reminded me sternly, eyes still shut.

"Yes, sir!" I called back, bursting out the door and practically skipping all the way to the cafeteria.

It was fairly quiet, but there were enough Sahrks present that I didn't feel alone. It took me a second to figure out how to get the fridge open on my own, but I managed, only to remember belatedly that I kinda needed to get plates first.

Everything here was so unnecessarily…complicated. Cupboards didn't have handles, and the buttons that opened the drawers in the kitchen were as invisible as the ones in the hall. I quite literally had to molest the cabinetry just to get them open. Unfortunately for me, no plates were located on the bottom half of the shelves, which meant I'd have to get the ones up top that Roark usually grabbed.

I'd hoped they wouldn't *all* be up there.

I'd hoped in vain.

So I hiked a knee up onto the counter and struggled onto it. Safe. I'd promised to be safe, so I'd move nice and slow and easy.

There was an anxious murmur behind me, and as suddenly as I'd climbed up, I was yanked back to the floor with gentle hands. When I glanced over my shoulder I realized the person who had cupboard-blocked me was the same blue shark I'd met the day Roark had taken me aboard—his friend, Mala. Roark had said his name enough times I'd caught it, even without a formal introduction.

Mala emitted a short barking sound of amusement—like an asshole— as he shook his head, opened up the cupboard I'd been trying to get into, and pulled down two plates.

When I snatched them from him, he just laughed some more.

To my annoyance, Mala watched over me as I piled our plates high with the same bark stuff we always ate, grabbed utensils—located in the bottom drawer, thank goodness—and headed toward the doorway.

"Huu-goh," Mala called my name before I could leave. I turned around and he beckoned me closer. It made me a bit nervous, but only because I didn't know him as well as I knew Roark, and we'd never been alone together.

Mala pulled the fridge open while I watched. He rustled around for a moment, gesturing for me to hold still. When he was done, he had a bunch of drinks and what looked like a box full of donuts. My stomach rumbled and I gaped at him, before he jerked his head toward the door and led the way down the hall, his arms full.

When we made it back to the room, Roark looked alarmed when he saw his friend enter first. However, he relaxed the moment Mala stepped aside to reveal me standing behind him.

"Mala," Roark greeted the other shark with a grin. He sat up straight, and with remorse I watched as my plan for a lazy night in bed went up in smoke. I huffed at the blue shark who barked out another laugh and gestured at me with one drink-laden hand. He said something to Roark in sharkish that had him laughing as well.

Okay.

So they were actually friends, then.

And if the way Mala collapsed onto the bed beside Roark and passed him a drink was any indication, they were close. I didn't know what to do, since I'd never really had friends like that before. And also because Mala was kinda in *my* spot. And my hands were full. And he'd never been in our room before. So I kinda wanted him out.

Maybe it was a primal thing.

I had no idea.

He and Roark spoke for a few more seconds as I wobbled, trying to decide if this meant I should go back to my doggy bed or sit on Roark's other side. It was a big bed, but the sharks were big too. And even though Mala's body language screamed casual, I still floundered.

Roark, bless him, noticed.

His gaze snapped to me and he said something quietly to his friend before he held a hand out for me. I wasn't sure what he wanted. The food maybe? Cheeks burning, I handed him his plate and bit my lip.

He frowned down at the plate for a moment before placing it gingerly on the nightstand and held his hand out again.

Okay, now I was confused.

"Huu-goh, come," he commanded gently. I did what he said, though I still felt off-kilter. However, that feeling quickly died when he pulled me snug onto his lap.

This was new for us.

He'd never done this before.

But it was…nice.

It was *super* nice.

He was solid and squishy and huge. And honestly super fucking comfortable.

Once settled, I swallowed the lump in my throat as Roark wrapped one arm around me and reached to retrieve his plate from the nightstand with the other. His breath ruffled the hair at my ears as he leaned down and flicked what I assumed were 'kisses' with his tongue along my cheek.

"Thank you," his voice rumbled quietly, and I shivered all over, suddenly lightheaded.

Mala observed us with a fond expression on his face. For what felt like a million years, but was probably only an hour or so, he and Roark chatted. Roark tried to include me, but he didn't know enough English to translate what was happening. I appreciated the effort all the same.

It was nice to see him interact with a friend. Like I was getting to know another side of him. The way we sat snuggled together was even nicer though. He fed me some food and I chewed while he took a bite of his own. When our plates were empty, he set them to the side and Mala passed around donuts from the box.

They were different than the ones we'd eaten on F'ukYuu, but looked delicious all the same. Roark grabbed two and held one out to me. The powder on the outside was sweeter than sugar, and lighter, too. With a happy sigh, I lapped at it before sinking my teeth inside.

Gooey, creamy goodness exploded on my tongue, and Roark barked his amusement when I moaned happily around the treat. Uncaring of the audience I had, I shoved another bite in my mouth immediately, making a mess. Damn, I loved these things.

"Careful, Huu-goh." he reminded me in his carefully annunciated tone.

I got the message loud and clear. Slow down. He didn't want me to choke. I made my bites smaller but couldn't help the way I devoured the treat with quick efficiency. Mala echoed Roark's mirth, eyes crinkling into crescents when Roark handed me the donut that was supposed to be his own.

"Are you sure?" I asked him, biting my lip. I didn't want to take advantage of his kindness. I got the feeling he rarely indulged. He was kinda a robot. But I also really fucking wanted his donut.

"Huu-goh, eat." Roark commanded.

I didn't need to be told twice.

I devoured Roark's donut with just as much enthusiasm as I'd eaten my own. Mala watched us both with a fascination I didn't understand. It was nice, kinda. Like he'd never seen Roark this way before, and was…proud of him, or something. It was the same way Ushuu had looked at us when we'd had lunch together.

When the blue shark finished his last drink, he rose from the bed to his full impressive height, and gathered up our dishes and the empty bottles. He wasn't as large as Roark was, and his colors weren't nearly as striking. But I supposed he was alright looking.

His vibes were not nearly as serious as what Roark gave off.

More…friendly.

Mala and Roark exchanged goodbyes. When Mala paused in the doorway, Roark made a quiet inquisitive sound. Mala said something teasing, cocking his head toward the mess of parts I'd made in the corner of the room, before he smiled, even softer this time.

No doubt he was teasing Roark for the gift.

Roark's spots turned fuchsia and I fanned my fingers along his forearm to soothe him as Mala finally left.

When I wiggled around to face him properly, he looked just as exhausted as he had before, though some of the tension he'd carried was gone.

"Thank you," Roark repeated, cupping my cheek in one massive hand and leaning down till our breaths mingled. His tongue slithered out to skirt along the curve of my jaw, and my lashes fluttered as I smiled, tingling all over.

This had been a big step for him.

He had chosen to trust me.

And that meant…everything to me.

"Thank you," I echoed. We both knew I wasn't talking about the donut. I mean, I was, but…I was talking about everything else, too. The way he always seemed to know what I needed. The way he pulled me close when I felt my most scattered. The way he didn't mind our differences. The way he was teaching me day by day what it meant to belong somewhere.

To be *wanted* by someone else.

I'd never been wanted before.

If only he knew I wanted him back just as fiercely.

We brushed our teeth together in tandem. It was the first time I'd joined Roark, rather than insisting on taking the time for myself. He'd been obviously pleased, his spots turning a lovely shade of pale pink, as he'd stepped back to allow me room to reach the sink in front of him.

My head barely came to his rib cage when I stared at our reflections in the mirror. Roark always took longer than I did, considering the amount of teeth he had—I'd timed him once, and it'd taken him a solid 630 seconds from start to finish. Which translated to ten and a half minutes of active brushing. The *shush, shush* of his motions had grown comforting over the last couple months. I looked forward to it, lying in bed, listening to Roark get ready. He was incredibly thorough.

An alien with *excellent* dental hygiene.

For the first time since I'd boarded the ship I didn't leave the bathroom as he prepared to shower. He didn't ask me to either. He simply shucked his pants off and I gulped as I came face-to-face with his massive pink ass and thighs. Roark checked the shower, making a grumpy sound when he realized he was out of soap.

I didn't know where he kept it, so I hadn't replaced it when we'd run out the night before.

Completely naked, it was easier to see Roark's organs and bones. Which shouldn't have been pretty—but it was. And nope, there definitely was not a womb. I'd been right. I could, however, see the hint of bones inside the squishy pink of his upper thighs, and the thought that I was seeing something he never showed his shipmates made me feel incredibly special.

In all the time I'd known him he'd stayed at least partially clothed. Even at night when we were in bed together, he barely shucked his pants off to play with me, then he pulled them back on. The only exception to that rule was when he was changing clothes.

This was…*intimate*.

Also…his ass was *juicy* as hell.

I'd never really looked at someone's ass and thought—god*damn*, that thing is yummy—before. This was a first for me—just like so many things we'd shared together. Meaty and thick, bouncy and soft. Roark bent over, his shoulder brushing mine as he reached beneath the sink into the cabinet below to grab a bottle of soap to replace the one we'd used up.

There was something weird sitting beside the soap, and when he tried to shut the cupboard, I stuck my leg out to stop him.

"Huu-goh?" Roark's voice rumbled beside my ear as he stood up, soap in hand, his breath ruffling my hair for the second time that night. There was no denying that that was a warning.

I'd never been good at heeding those.

Instead of listening, I pulled the contraption out of the cupboard. It was surprisingly heavy. Pulse thrumming, I placed it on the counter to get a better look. *Why was he hiding this?* When I glanced at Roark, he was watching me, and his spots were a dark fuchsia pink. It was a good look on him when he was naked.

Turning my attention back to the object, I hummed thoughtfully.

The device was block shaped with suction cups on the bottom and back, presumably to hold it in place. The shape wasn't all that interesting, but the squishy black hole in the middle of the block certainly was. As I stared at it I tried to make sense of what exactly its function could be. And why Roark would have it in here—hidden in the bathroom. And *why* he was deathly quiet beside me as I fingered the squishy center, pressing inside incrementally, curious what it would feel like.

The thing was recently cleaned. I could tell because it smelled like Roark's soap, and the surface was slightly damp.

So it was something he must've used recently.

Maybe when he showered?

What the hell *was* it?

As I squished a second finger alongside the first, Roark released a wounded sort of noise. It was then that it hit me like a sledgehammer.

Oh.

*Oh.*

Oh *my* god.

This was a *sex* toy. This was *Roark's* sex toy. *Oh* my god. Oh-my-*god*. I mean, I knew before this moment that he had a sex drive. Because obviously he'd clearly enjoyed playing with me—not that we'd done much in the days since he'd started training with Ushuu.

But…still.

To think of him and those big meaty thighs driving his cocks into this thing was just—Fuck. To imagine him pounding into it while he grunted and growled—like he did when he was on top of me—while that big ass flexed—while his tentadicks twisted together and he—oh shit.

Had he been getting himself off this week? Quick and perfunctory. Because we hadn't had time for sex together?

Fuck.

That was *so* incredibly hot.

"What is this?" I asked him, certain he knew the words. I already knew what it was. But the mischievous part of me needed him to acknowledge what I'd found. How often had he used this thing? Often, if the scratches on its surface were any indicator. Looked like he'd really sunk his claws in a few times when he was fucking it.

Goddamn.

Roark whined and I turned to look at him, my fingers still squishing inside the fuck hole as he stared down at me. His spots were red now. Practically phosphorus. His eyes were black, flooded dark and *hungry*. I had only a second to think, *oh shit, what have I done?* before he was caging me against the counter and his tongue was twining around my neck like a noose.

Slick and hot, it squeezed tight enough stars swam for a moment.

"Huu-goh," Roark groaned, low. "Huu-goh, *bad.*" The words were a bit garbled with his tongue out like that, but the sentiment remained the same.

The responding mewl I released was pitiful at best.

He was *so* big. So fucking big. Looming over me with his muscles straining and that slick as hell tongue twisting just tight enough pleasure zinged down my spine. And he hadn't touched me in days—and I needed him. God, did I need him. So fucking bad.

Roark's tongue slithered back inside his mouth. He bared his teeth at me, fangs glinting. *Tell me why I never once worried he'd hurt me? Even now.*

"Huu-goh, *bad*," Roark repeated. I licked my lips and nodded. Because he was right. I had been bad. I'd been nosy. I'd gone through his personal things, and I'd discovered something he maybe didn't want me to see.

I shivered.

*Dear god, please punish me with your cocks, Roark.*

*I'll never be a nosy bitch again.*

"Roark—" I murmured, because I was a masochist. "Show me?"

He groaned again, his eyes drifting shut like he was praying for patience—the same way I'd just prayed for his dicks. Before I could blink, he'd made his decision. Roark yanked the fucktoy from the counter with one hand, and grabbed my waist with the other. I only had a second to process what was happening before he was steering me toward the shower. There were several gaps in the wall I'd always assumed were for soap, but—as he shoved the toy into one of them to anchor it, I realized they had a much sexier purpose.

I still wanted him to show me how it worked, so I stayed quiet as he gently twisted my body around to face the toy. He arranged me in the back corner of the shower, my dick hard as a rock, so that I would have a good view of the show he was going to put on.

Roark gestured at the toy, his bulk shivery and warm beside mine.

"Yesh?"

I took him in with hunger, mouth dry. Roark's cocks were serpentine as they laced together, writhing and slurping at each other, their suckers catching and pulling in a way that I knew firsthand felt amazing as fuck.

My dick flexed, a sticky patch forming in my pants against it.

They reached toward me and I bit my lip *hard* to stop myself from moaning. I wanted to play with them as badly as they wanted to play with me.

I could still vividly remember how good it had felt to press my cock between them. How they'd toyed with me, throbbing against my dick—*around* it. They leaked a lot. Slippery and hot. I remembered *that* too.

They were flushed purple with arousal, betraying how much Roark was getting off on this too. I nearly passed out when Roark reached down to fist the base of one, panting a little. "Yesh?" he repeated, always a gentleman.

I yanked my shirt off, my pants too. I chucked them outside the shower stall with my heart in my throat. Self-conscious of my scrawny chest, but pushing the ugly thoughts aside, I let Roark see just how much he was affecting me.

My dick was fully hard now, flushed red to match the purple of his. It listed to the left, throbbing with the beat of my heart as a bead of precum slipped down the shaft.

"Yes," I told him, in case my dick wasn't enough to convince him. I gestured at the toy the same way he had, eager to see him step up to it and give it a good fucking. "Show me."

He seemed to debate with himself for a few seconds, gathering courage, before he nodded. That big chest heaved and my eyes traced down his thick belly to where he stroked his cocks one at a time, tight from base to tip to get them wet.

How many times had he done this while I'd been waiting for him in bed?

I'd always just thought he liked to take a long shower.

Fuuuuck, the idea of him in here touching himself while I was twenty feet away was enough to make my head spin. I knew I meant something to him or I wouldn't be here. But the fact that he was showing me something this vulnerable was humbling.

He was important here.

A captain.

He had a purpose and a life. People depended on him. Beyond that, Roark had to be the most uptight guy this side of the galaxy. I don't think he'd ever opened up for anyone the way he was for me right now.

Roark was a saint, he truly was. A saint with two massive needy cocks, and pillowy balls that begged to be sucked. I had never been as glad as I was right then that I hadn't been born with no mouth—like some of the species I'd danced for on F'ukYuu.

I was going to put my mouth to good use, godddammit. Maybe not today—because fucktoy, hello—but sometime in the future. I was gonna smash my face in all that pink skin and rub my lips all over it.

Roark moved.

I inhaled sharply, watching enraptured as he twisted his body, widened his stance, and pressed the tip of one of the flushed tentacles into the hole of the fucktoy in the wall. A quiet groan left his lips as he flexed forward, fucking in an inch or so before pulling out and feeding the other dick in alongside the first.

There was a slick squelching noise I was sure came from his natural lubricant, and I squeezed the base of my own dick so I wouldn't come right then and there as I watched him snap his hips hard into the toy, his big ass flexing.

The thump of his pelvis meeting the toy made me weak-kneed.

It was such a filthy sound.

Seriously fucking filthy.

Made my nipples tingle, and my hole clench tight—like I was imagining my ass in place of that toy—and Roark's hips were pumping so deep inside me I saw stars. I wasn't sure how he would fit, if I was being honest. It didn't seem possible. But I wanted it to be.

I wanted to be stretched so wide my ass couldn't close after.

I wanted to be sore and limping.

I wanted to feel that big, grunting body on top of mine.

Wanted to give Roark all my firsts.

Roark was a *beast*. He pumped in and out of the toy at an almost brutal pace as I watched, shivering and wishing we'd thought to turn the shower on. The only thing that would make this better was if he was glistening and wet.

God.

I was jealous of that damn thing.

I wanted that to be me.

Too soon, Roark pulled back, his cocks still hard and writhing as they dripped slick all over the floor. His nostrils flared as he turned to me, long sharp tongue flickering out—like he could taste my arousal.

"Huu-goh," he demanded, "*come.*"

I very nearly came right then and there—before I realized he had no idea that word had a double meaning.

There was no arguing with *that* voice.

That was his Captain voice. The one I'd heard on occasion, but was never directed at me.

I snapped to attention, swiftly crossing the distance between us as my dick *acheeeed*. Roark grabbed my shoulder and hip, gentle but firm, and arranged my body in front of his like we'd been at the sink.

When the fucktoy was too high for what he wanted, he made a frustrated sound. Before I could speak, I was being hoisted into the air by a thousand tiny tendrils. They spread my legs wide enough that my hole spasmed. I gasped, muscles straining as Roark rumbled against the back of my neck.

This position was obscene, and wrong—and lord. Fuck. So fucking *hot*.

I was so exposed.

While I hovered in the air, Roark put his free hand to good use. Slowly, deliberately, one thick finger flicked the tip of my cock. Hissing, I only had a second to recover, before Roark experimentally pinched it. That was somehow even better—and only became more delicious when he began toying with my slit curiously. He was acting like he'd never touched me before—even though that was far from the truth.

Roark was just as fascinated with my body as I was with his.

Which was as confusing as it was flattering.

I squirmed as he gave my crown another pinch between his massive thumb and forefinger.

"F-fuck," I whimpered as Roark stopped his teasing and aimed my tip at the slick black hole he'd just been fucking.

I held my breath, sure I was dreaming.

That there was no way this was real. It was too fucking good. Too amazing—too—

I couldn't move.

Couldn't fight back.

Couldn't protest, even if I wanted to, as I felt his tentadicks bump against my ass cheeks, their slippery hot surfaces tracing the curves, suckers tugging at my skin.

And then he humped me. Hard. And the movement forced my dick inside the slick-wet-squelchy-good-tightness of the fucktoy so fast I nearly came on the spot. The tendrils surrounding my body writhed, squeezing, squeezing, squeezing as my cock was sucked inside the toy and Roark purred behind me, his hips still flexed against my ass.

One of his dicks tickled down my crack and I clenched my cheeks automatically to force it out—even though I'd just been thinking about wanting it inside me. I'd never had anything actually up there, and even though I was fascinated, the sensation was shocking.

"Huu-goh?" Roark's voice was deeper than I'd ever heard it. Throaty. Like forcing me to fuck the wall turned him on just as much as it turned me on.

"Yes," I told him, already knowing what he wanted. "Yes, yes, yes—" The tendrils tightened all at once, pulling me away from the wall, my dick slipping out of the hole with a wet pop. "No, no, no—" I chanted, shuddering. "Please, please—"

And then he rutted into me again, sending my cock back inside as his dicks fought for dominance, both trying to slip between my cheeks even though they'd have to get along to fit. What if they got in?

That thought was enough to make me whimper.

God, that was amazing.

All of this was.

"Oh, thank you—" I hissed, tossing my head back as my dick pinched inside the toy and my hips flexed, attempting to rut into it. Only I couldn't move. Still. And that realization only made me even harder. I was as immobile now as I'd been when he'd had me on the bed what felt like an eon ago.

"Little beast," Roark repeated his nickname for me, affection in his tone as he pulled back just to fuck forward again. Slick, wet, fuck. Pull, squeeze, hump. In and out of the toy my dick went at the same pace he took pleasure from my body. I could feel his cum smeared along my ass, between my cheeks making them sticky and slippery. There was so much of it that it began to slip down my thighs too, making a mess everywhere, and leaving me thoroughly claimed.

Roark made these delicious little grunts every time he fucked forward, like he couldn't help himself. His hot breath caressed the back of my neck, his tongue slurping over the center of my spine as I melted into bliss and forgot everything but what it felt like to be held, and loved, and pleasured.

The fat tip of one of his cocks rubbed my hole. I howled, shuddering anew as my muscles strained, and I was rocketed out of the foggy headspace I'd been sucked into. For a while there, I'd had no thoughts at all—hypnotized by the rhythm.

The cock's tip rubbed and rubbed and *rubbed*, triumphant that it had gotten past the other dick and found where I was squishy and hot and ready to be taken.

Did I want that?

Did I want him inside me?

I'd fantasized about it, yeah. But this was real life.

I imagined it again. His hips pumping. His tentadicks winding together so they could fill me entirely. I bet it would hurt in the beginning, but I kinda liked that thought. I liked the idea that he'd be the first up there. I'd never even dared to stick a finger inside myself, but the idea of Roark doing it?

Ugh.

Yes.

He'd get me ready. I knew he would. Maybe he'd slick one of his thick pink fingers and go to town. Maybe he'd stick his long dexterous tongue inside me. Or maybe it'd be his tendrils, tiny and strong, wickedly talented as they grew thicker and thicker the deeper they moved. They'd already shown interest in my ass—it wasn't that big of a leap.

He'd tease and tease, stretch me open, and make me come till I was relaxed and ready to take his monster cocks. Every part of Roark's body was making it clear how ready he was to claim me. To own me. No leash or collar necessary.

"Oh fuck, shit," I swore as Roark picked up the pace, huffing against the back of my neck, the tentacle at my ass slipping away as the other one fought to take its place. This one was needier, smarter too. It wiggled till it was wedged between my cheeks, spreading them. Roark growled. His cock shifted again, rubbing like it was…like it was *looking* for something.

The hair on my arms stood on end.

And then it happened.

His cock got what it was searching for.

His suckers aligned, one of the largest settling directly over my hole. I howled, my dick spilling over and over and over inside the fucktoy as Roark shoved hard against my body and the sucker on his cock gave a second greedy pull.

It was heaven and hell all at once. Heaven because I'd never known pleasure like this before. Pleasure that went on and on, that exploded like fireworks behind my eyes, that felt all encompassing and never-ending. Hell, because I knew it would end. I knew I couldn't sit on his cocks one at a time all day every day for the rest of all eternity.

Roark crooned against my ear to soothe me as I shuddered and sobbed, emptying my load inside his fucktoy as he forced my hips to remain flush against it. "Good little beast," Roark purred against the shell of my ear, his tongue flickering out to kiss it.

I could feel his eyes on me, fascinated and aroused as he watched my balls empty.

"Good Huu-goh," Roark murmured.

I hiccuped a whine, head fuzzy and soft as he gave my hips a few last pumps, emptying every last drop, before he carefully tugged me out of the toy. My limp dick glistened with the mess we'd made together and Roark emitted a pleased sound as he reached down with his hand to cup my dick and balls the moment I was free.

It was something he liked to do, not that I was complaining.

His hand was warm. It made me feel a weird combination of safety and arousal as he held my crotch inside it like it was his right to do so.

The tendrils holding me up never wavered, and I never expected them to. It felt second nature to relax against his chest as his cock continued to suck at my entrance. And every time it did, electric shocks zapped through my body.

He was still hard.

Both his dicks were.

But my head was too foggy to do anything but lay limp in his arms as he gathered me in close and fluttered affectionate nuzzles over my cheeks and neck. He held me for a long time. And during that time, he stroked over my body, massaged the feeling back into my limbs, and cradled me inside his arms.

Roark probably knew less about sex than I did—which made the fact he touched me like this even sweeter. Because it was all instinct. And he *wanted* to.

When he turned the shower on he was careful to never get water in my eyes, even when he had to retrace his steps to get the new bottle of soap we'd left behind.

Roark was gentle as he scrubbed me clean, stroking my hair and my back, treating me with such kindness I didn't know how to believe it was real. Here he was—this successful, massive giant. But he wanted *me*, for some reason. Wanted me enough to clutch me close to his chest and wait for my head to come back online.

Wanted me enough that he ignored his own dicks to bring me pleasure.

Eventually, I stroked his chest and without words he understood what I wanted, setting me back on my feet. He didn't move far. Honestly, he looked a bit silly with tendrils shooting out of his body, hovering over and around me like he expected me to fall. Sexy too though.

My sexy pink protector.

I grinned at him and he relaxed, though it didn't escape my notice that his dicks hadn't gone down at all.

"Roark," I murmured, biting my lip.

"Huu-goh," he rumbled back, amused.

"I want to…" I wasn't sure if he'd understand my words, but I knew he'd understand my actions. So I sank to my knees at his feet and peered up at him through my damp lashes. His cocks jerked toward me and his nostrils flared.

"Huu-goh…?" This time it was a question. One I answered by pressing my face against one of his massive supple thighs, my gaze never leaving his.

"Roark, yes?" I teased, asking him for permission the same way he always asked me. Even when it was obvious I wanted this. He barked out a laugh and his eyes twisted into the pleasant little crescent shapes they only formed when he was happy.

"Yesh," he agreed with an indulgent huff, though his eyes told a different story as his spots turned red again, and blue flooded black.

If I was being honest, I didn't know what to do with one dick, let alone two. But I'd always been a quick learner, and nothing about Roark scared me. Not even his monster cocks. I was more than a little glad that the first time I was sucking them hadn't been the day we'd met. I might've run screaming back then if these sexy bad boys had started reaching for me, my own curiosity be damned. As it was now, most of what I felt was genuine excitement.

If I took it slow, and one at a time, I was sure I'd figure it out. Besides, this was exactly what I'd wanted. My mouth watered just looking at him.

I got the feeling Roark didn't care how experienced I was either. Not if the look he was giving me was any indication. His big hand cupped my cheek, practically encompassing half of my head as he pet me encouragingly and I took a steadying breath.

*I could do this.*

I could *totally* do this.

His tentadicks slapped against my cheeks the moment I pressed close enough for them to reach, the first one—the bossier one—pushing at my lips like it knew exactly what I was going for. I gave it a chaste kiss and it shivered—pressed against my lips again, and waited.

When I glanced up again, Roark was staring down at me like I was the fucking messiah. He was shaking all over. I was clearly not horrible at this, if his reaction was anything to go by. Was this weird for him? He'd sucked on me but he hadn't taken me into his mouth. He literally couldn't for fear of his teeth.

Which meant…chances were no one had ever gone down on him either, even if he had banged other shark people—which I doubted.

Roark gaped at me like I was the hottest thing he'd ever seen.

Like all he had to do was look at me to get off.

And god…

God, I'd never felt more desirable in all of my life.

His second cock pushed the first away—it was slightly thinner than the other one, but no less insistent as I gave it a matching kiss, and debated how best to go about this. I wanted it to be fair. But I was new to this. So one at a time it would have to be while I got used to it.

Lick-lick, suck-suck, done-done.

I had this in the bag already.

Reaching up with both hands, I grabbed a cock in each, gently nudging the first toward my lips as I gave the second a long, languorous stroke. It was so odd. The texture was not at all like my own. Slippery and strong—like a tail—but dexterous and malleable as well. The squelching noise that filled the air as Roark's precum coated my hand would live inside my fantasies for the rest of my life. The substance was thicker than cum, and retained its slickness for longer. I wondered what it was made of—but quickly forced the thought away, focusing on the task at hand.

*I can do this.*

*Sure, it's a bit weird.*

*But so am I.*

I pressed cock one against my lips, parted them, and gave it a long leisurely lick. Roark groaned above me and I could literally feel his cocks start to leak even more furiously as the tip wriggled in my mouth, trying to sink deeper.

"Be nice," I reprimanded it, holding the base tighter and giving the second an empathetic squeeze before I opened my mouth and tried again. The flavor wasn't bad. Slightly salty. Almost fruity. Like pineapple? I didn't mind it whatsoever. Relieved, I sucked a little further, the strange bumps of the suckers finally entering my mouth. They got bigger the farther down his cock they went, and the little one wasn't so scary.

It sucked at my tongue a little, and the sensation was nice enough I paused for a moment just to enjoy it. Deeper I went. Inch by inch. There was no way I was getting the whole thing inside, but I sure as hell was going to try.

I gagged a couple times, but that only seemed to make me more determined to get this right. Roark kept making these wounded noises above me. He'd dropped my face early on. Probably because he was worried about losing control and crushing me.

The tentacle was surprisingly polite now that it was down my throat, holding still and patient as I adjusted to its girth and Roark wiped the tears on my cheeks away. This was…yeah. This was nice. As I swallowed around his length and the almost sweet flood of new cum wet my tongue, I let myself drift.

I liked this.

I liked this a lot.

Just like I'd liked everything we'd done together.

When I looked up to check his reaction, Roark was still ogling me. He looked just as enraptured as he had earlier, though there was a distinct primal twist to his lips as he bared his teeth and his chest heaved with each erratic breath. It made me feel powerful to be regarded with such desire.

Poor baby. He was holding back so much right now, trying not to hurt me—to fuck me. With newfound determination, I swallowed around his dick.

"Urhhhhgggg," Roark made a sound like he was dying, his head jerking back as he spurted down my throat. It was a weird feeling because though the liquid was focused at the tip it also leaked everywhere else too. I swallowed what I could, but there was too much to take it all.

I whimpered as his tentacle began to wriggle, still leaking and spurting as it pulled inch by inch out of my throat. I felt empty and desperate for more by the time it was free, coughing a little as it bumped against my lips, feeding me the last few drops of its pleasure before settling against Roark's thigh.

The second cock wriggled as I tried to catch my breath, somehow even hotter in my grip. I twisted my head to look at it, shocked to find it just as hard as it had been when I started.

Two orgasms.

Huh.

Each dick needed their own.

I hadn't realized last time because they'd cum at the same time.

God, I could have so much fun with this.

Without overthinking, I sunk down on the second cock as well. Roark's fists thumped against the wall and he hissed out what sounded like a prayer in his native tongue as I sucked and slurped, far more confident the second time around.

This tentacle was easier to go down on, though longer, and I ended up gagging twice as much as it twisted around inside me. While the other one had been bossy, this one was needy. It wiggled a little, desperate to get deeper. By the time it came too, Roark was a mess above me. He'd been emitting this menacing growl for the last five minutes, his upper body tense, tendons in his neck flexing as I let his tentacle fuck my throat.

I was exhausted but proud.

I pulled off with a slick pop. Tentacle two tried to get back in even though it had come, rubbing against my lips in question, but I gently pushed it away. I had barely enough time to recover before Roark was yanking me high into the air and shoving his tongue down my throat. It took me a second to realize he was tasting himself—god that was so fucking amazing. I surrendered to the kiss immediately, no longer alarmed when his tongue pushed back my gag reflex and it felt like it had quite literally entered my throat.

Roark swirled it around inside the tight orifice and I whined, my entire body floaty and soft all over again. When he eventually pulled out, his pace was agonizingly slow. His tongue traced my lips, almost like a thank you, before he was cradling me close and beginning to wash us off again.

"Thank you," Roark's hoarse murmur against my ear was worth any soreness I felt. "Pretty, pretty, little beast." He sounded as wowed as I felt. And as he stroked me, petted me, cleaned me, and pampered me for the second time that night, I couldn't help but realize three very important things.

Number one: I needed to stop insisting on private showers if *this* is what I could look forward to.

Number two: Roark trusted me. He really actually did!

And number three: *Tentadicks*.

Who knew?

# THIRTEEN

## ROARK

**"GOOD," I MURMURED, MORE THAN** a little pleased as I blinked up at the sparring room's ceiling. Huu-goh had just toppled me over. It was the first time he'd done so, and though it hadn't been a bad fall, I took a moment to gather myself so that he would feel as though it was.

I wanted his chest to fill with pride, like mine did.

Huu-goh had surprise on his side. No one would look at a being his size and assume that he was a capable fighter. Which was exactly *why* I found it imperative to train him.

Mala thought the whole thing was amusing. He had gathered much of the off-duty crewmates as well as Ushuu to watch. And they all placed bets—on Huu-goh, not me—no matter how many times he lost.

A fact that made him more than a little excited. He was pleasantly surprised that all of them actually wanted him to win. And I was equally as pleased, because there was nothing I wanted more in this world than for Huu-goh to feel appreciated and like he belonged here beside me.

Because he did.

It felt odd to fight him. To push him to the ground in this way. But it was fun too. It felt right to share something so central to my culture and childhood with him. Huu-goh was as fast of a learner—even if he lacked the physical strength and stamina needed for battle.

I wasn't looking to turn him into a warrior.

Simply to make sure he could defend himself should the need arise.

He'd been more than a little excited when I'd told him we were nearing planet Sha'hPihn. And he'd been even *more* excited when I told him—in stilted human-speak—that I had something planned for him when we arrived.

Though I still spent time with Ushuu tutoring me, I'd backed off a little. The pace I'd been working that first week had been unsustainable, as shown by my rather major crash. And I couldn't afford to be off my game as we approached the last stop on our way home.

There was too much at risk.

Startled out of my thoughts, I decided enough time had passed that I could stop pretending like the fall had hurt.

"Good?" Huu-goh gasped out from above me. His whole body heaved with each winded breath. He'd gone for the back of my knees—a weakness most creatures shared, so it had been the first I'd shown him.

It was, however, the first time he'd tricked me quickly enough he'd been able to actually send me to the ground. Huu-goh offered me a hand up. There was no way he could lift me, but I thought the gesture was cute, if misguided. Now standing, I could feel a purr building inside my chest. I had never been this playful with another person. I had been a serious child, a serious teenager, and an even more serious adult.

But this was…nice.

"Again," I teased, only for Huu-goh to rebel.

"No!" he whined petulantly. "Tired. Huu-goh is tired. No more."

I suppose we *had* been at it for a good forty minutes. My morning exercise hour was nearly over. I hadn't realized how much time had passed. In light of this, it appeared my plan to bring him to the lower depths of the ship to the pool to recover would need to be postponed.

I sighed, but didn't argue with him as we exited the sparring ring and a few Sahrks barked their laughter on our way past where the colorful crowd had gathered. The curiosity they'd all had for Huu-goh had faded by this point. Now, they saw him as one of their own, and the respect they showed him as my mate made me feel at peace.

It was nice to know that my unorthodox choice of partner was as widely accepted as Mala had promised me he would be. Even if he hadn't been, I wouldn't have changed my choice. Huu-goh was worth too much for me to worry about silly things like fitting in.

My little huu-man continued to huff and puff beside me. "I feel stupid," Huu-goh muttered under his breath, assuming I couldn't hear or understand.

"Huu-goh is no stupid," I grunted back in his language, stopping at the end of the room and twisting to catch his attention. He stumbled a little, glancing up at me in astonishment. Affection softened his expression. "No say that."

He was sweaty.

His hair stuck up in all directions, and his skin was a ruddy, painful looking red.

Still wheezing, my Huu-goh was lovelier than any other being in the entire galaxy.

"Sorry," he apologized, reaching out to lace our fingers together. I smiled, pleased, and gave his hand a squeeze back.

"Training needed," I reminded him. "For *safety*."

"Yeah, yeah, I know." Huu-goh rasped. "I hate it. I hate sports. I hate exercise. I hate all of this."

Those words I didn't know, so I just grunted in commiseration. He was all talk, truly.

We'd be back again the next morning. Huu-goh would be vibrating with glee the second we climbed inside the sparring arena, ready to tussle with me. And just like today—when his physical limits became apparent— he'd get angry and irritable all over again.

He just liked to grumble.

And I didn't blame him.

My little love wasn't built for physical conflict. I couldn't fault him for disliking it. Not when I was sure he would be perfectly content to stay fiddling with his tools and toys, and never exercise—aside from sex—for the rest of his life.

He was always game to try something new, however. And always ready to latch on to any excuse to touch or spend time with me. It was heady, to be the center of someone else's world. To have that sentiment returned. Intoxicating, really. And so…wonderful.

I hadn't known love could be like this.

Father had been a lonely man. He had no mate. He'd used the pods to conceive me, as all modern Sahrks did. But he'd done it alone. I was made in his spitting image. At the orphanage after his passing I'd thought I had learned what love was. When I'd taken care of the other children during

The Great Calamity. When my heart had been full as I provided for them, and I realized that was who and what I wanted to be.

But even that paled in comparison to the joy I felt now, in Huu-goh's presence.

He saw me as a person.

He saw behind my teeth and claws. Behind my rank. Behind the icy exterior I'd maintained to keep my heart safe. He made me smile.

He was brighter than the stars on our ceiling. Brighter than the stars outside the control room. Brighter than the stars that had taught me to chase adventures in the sky.

"Roark?" Huu-goh's voice broke me from my reverie. "You okay?"

"I am good," I replied in his language, giving his tiny hand another squeeze. I yanked him up onto my shoulders as we headed out into the hallway, deciding that today we would bypass the rooms and go straight to the mess hall for breakfast.

Huu-goh was a welcome sweaty weight atop my shoulders, his sweet fingers stroking along my head fin as we moved.

"Captain!" A few cadets greeted me in our tongue, saluting and standing to attention as we passed. Before I could move, Huu-goh saluted back. Their eyes widened, and they glanced at me, and then at the huu-man before murmurs of delight escaped them.

I barked out a laugh, and the two Sahrk's barked along with me.

"Have a good morning, Nim. Netreit," I greeted them both.

"See you up top, sir!"

I nodded, amused as they waited until Huu-goh and I walked off before continuing on their own way.

"*Captain*," Huu-goh repeated—only it was in my language and not his own. He butchered the syllables, but the word was recognizable. I stiffened, and Huu-goh snickered in delight. "Captain!" He teased, sweet little feet kicking with glee.

Oh dear.

My spots betrayed me and Huu-goh's cackle turned into a thoughtful hum.

"Red spots," he purred, back in humanspeak, his soft lips brushing along my fin and making me shiver. "That's good to know."

When we returned to our rooms after breakfast Huu-goh used his newfound knowledge for evil. He slurped my cocks down one at a time, sucked and suckled on my sac, and all the while called me "Captain."

The cool water soothed my body as I sank to the bottom of the pool. It'd been a long time since I'd been down here. Though truthfully I'd been too busy to really miss it. The reason for my absence was swimming directly above my head after all, sweet pale legs kicking. Ripples danced across the sloped sides of the pool as I settled on my back, staring up at Huu-goh, my hearts thumping a peaceful beat.

Before Huu-goh had joined us aboard I'd spent what free time I had working overtime or down here, just as I was now, at the bottom of the large pool on the lowest level of the ship.

Beside what most on board referred to as the "lake", to our left and right were the ship's cargo holds. Their chambers were nearly twice the size of the pool itself, which was an incredible feat, considering just how large it was. It had always brought me peace to soak while I protected our cargo.

On days when the ship was quiet and I needed some extra alone time I'd find myself here. Some years I frequented the lake more than others, swimming laps and soaking as I was now—letting the weight of who and what I was disappear for the precious moments the water caressed my surface.

While I enjoyed sparring with Mala—and now, Huu-goh too—swimming brought forth a different kind of comfort. Exercise yes, but therapy in a way too.

I lingered for a moment, bubbles erupting from my snout, as I observed Huu-goh treading water with delight. It was a simple pleasure, sharing something so inherently ingrained in my culture with the person I adored. It brought me immense joy to know that he liked this too. When I had surprised him, leading him into the room for the first time, his eyes had lit up. He viewed the room like it was something marvelous.

I wondered if he'd be as grouchy by the end as he always was about training. But somehow, I knew he wouldn't.

Swimming at a leisurely pace, I cut through the water, my limbs shifting into something more aerodynamic. Webbing connected my fingers and toes, tendrils trailing like fins as I slunk beneath my little love, stalking him with delight.

He seemed to notice I'd moved, because his treading slowed as he spun in a circle, sweet blurry face rippling as he tried to see me beneath him. I latched on to his wonderful little legs, yanking him down with me.

A stream of bubbles exploded behind him as Huu-goh collided with my body just below the surface of the water. His eyes were wide, but his lips were amused. He shoved at my chest playfully, and I let him go, drifting after him as he popped back up with a squawking guffaw.

"Aasshole!" he spluttered in his language.

I didn't know what that word was, but I liked it. Because he was still smiling, even as he coughed.

I had never played with anyone like this. Not even when I was a boy. I'd been the Sahrk on the sidelines, making sure everyone was safe. Not…not this. Uninhibited and free, my worries no longer shackling me at the moment.

Huu-goh melted when I pulled him close again, nuzzling at his wet cheeks and his soggy orange fur with pleasure. My hands smoothed down his flank and over his pleasantly soft rump, gripping him tight.

"Figuhres you can breethe underwater." I only recognized a few of the words, "can" and "you" and "underwater" but it was easy enough to fill in the gaps. I found pleasure in that too. Like our language was a puzzle, and I was learning it piece by piece. I held up a hand, giving him the up thumb as I huffed in amusement. "Jee-sus, you're cute."

Huu-goh pressed his mouth to my nose and I sighed through my nostrils, eyes drifting shut. His lips were so very soft as he dragged them over mine. I wasn't sure what he was doing. But I liked it, my tongue slithering out to flick along his pillowy soft mouth.

My little huu-man snorted out a laugh, but gamely took my tongue inside his mouth. He suckled, and I groaned low, pulling him in tighter by the hips, my cocks pushing insistently against him through the layers of fabric we both wore.

When Huu-goh released my tongue his cheeks were flushed.

"What was that?" I asked him, because I was certain there was significance to the action.

"A kiss."

"Kissh?" I repeated, logging the word away for later. This was a new kind of kissing. Much less chaste than anything we'd tried before. Now that I knew the word in his language, I could request more of them. The thought made me hungry. This sort of kiss was as close as we had gotten to the kind of kissing my people enjoyed.

"Mhmm," Huu-goh hummed. It was different than the one he used to soothe me. It wasn't a song. A simple few notes he often repeated. "M—hmm" meant yes, somehow. Music that had meaning, just like his songs meant comfort.

Huu-mans were such magical creatures.

And my Huu-goh was the best of them all.

We raced each other. I won. Every time. And every time Huu-goh simply snickered and claimed another filthy kiss. When we returned to our rooms I felt lighter than I ever had before. Things were looking up. They truly were. And even the ever-present threat of space pirates could not dampen my mood as Huu-goh and I showered off and retreated to bed for the night.

Soon we'd speak to each other candidly.

Soon I'd get that damn collar off him.

Soon we'd go home.

# FOURTEEN

### ROARK

**"YOU'LL KEEP AN EYE ON** him." It was a statement, not a question.

Mala rolled his eyes and Ushuu coughed out a laugh. They both thought I was being ridiculous, and maybe I was. This was not my first, second, or even fifth time confirming that both of them would take care of Huu-goh in my absence.

There were negotiations to be made, shipments to be dropped off, and schedules to be updated. Those were all tasks required of Captain, which meant now that we'd landed on planet Sha'hPihn I wouldn't get the opportunity to take Huu-goh out myself until I'd had a chance to finish my duties.

On top of that, landing on Sha'hPihn meant that we were close enough to our home planet that I could send home communications. I would be spending the next few days rather busy planning Huu-goh and my ceremony for when we arrived on Osheania.

It was a momentous occasion. There were many people to invite—all my "siblings" from the orphanage, for one. The caretaker who had taken care of me after my father had passed. All the retired Sahrks that I had served under before I'd become captain—and more.

It was a giddy feeling, knowing what was to come.

Even more than that, however, I was excited to give Huu-goh the autonomy he needed. Which was why...though I wanted to take him shopping—and I would, eventually—I didn't think it was a bad thing to send him out on his own first.

With guards, of course.

Huu-goh needed friends.

And he needed to make choices on his own.

That was important.

"You won't let him out of your sight," I confirmed again.

"We won't let him out of our sight," Mala repeated, obviously making fun of me. Asshole. I glared at him, but it had been a long time since I'd been able to intimidate him, so it did nothing but make him laugh outright.

"If you run into trouble—" I continued.

"We'll call you on your communicator—we know, Roark." Mala slapped my back playfully. Then his snout was bumping against mine. He grabbed my fin to keep me in place, giving it a tight squeeze. "I would *die* before I allowed something to happen to your mate."

I shut my eyes and centered myself as I nodded. "I know," my voice was unusually hoarse.

"He is my heart," I told him, trying to explain why I was acting so irrationally. "It isn't that I don't trust you both."

"I know," Mala gave my fin another squeeze, his breath puffing against my lips. He was slightly smaller than me, but not by much. We were easily the largest Sahrks on the ship. I had only known two larger than us in my life, and both had died before I'd met Mala. It was a sobering thought to have, and one I pushed aside.

When Mala pulled back, I felt settled in a way I hadn't before.

I'd come a long way. Pushed my own limits to the point they'd been forced to expand. There were no more leashes in our future, and I hoped—if given enough time—I would only continue to grow.

I cleared my throat, ducked my head, and sighed.

"Off you go," Mala shooed me, knowing I wouldn't leave without a kick to the ass. "We can handle the huu-man for a few hours."

I nodded again, stalling for a moment. "You have my—"

"We have access to your credits, your number, and your blessing." Mala laughed at me, shaking his head. "Go be our captain, Captain."

I rolled my eyes, but grinned back at him.

Ushuu gave me a hug of his own, squeezing me tight on my way out the door, before I headed down the hallway toward the helm. I'd need to gather a few things prior to entering the city and starting the first meeting of the day. I liked giving the crew a pep talk before we disembarked. Their smiling faces and enthusiasm motivated me to do better every time we made this trip.

So close to home, they were in high spirits. Far higher spirits than they had been when we'd left Osheania all those months ago.

I double-tasked, composing a pep talk in my head, while half my thoughts were full of a certain tiny someone—who was about to go out on his very first shopping trip without me.

Rather than stress about that, I recalled the rather lovely morning Huu-goh and I had shared.

After we'd stirred in bed, he'd yawned, wide and sleepy, his pearly teeth flashing. He'd smiled when he caught sight of me already watching him, and my hearts had rioted. Because he was insatiable, Huu-goh had tried to sneak his hands inside my sleep pants—and I'd let him.

I'd let him coax and lick and toy with my cocks.

This form of pleasure was foreign to me.

All pleasure was.

But this especially.

But unlike penetrative sex—which was commonly spoken about—I had never even *heard* rumors of a Sahrk attemptting to *swallow* someone else's cock.

Such an action would be far too dangerous when you factored in our teeth. To my never-ending embarrassment, Mala often joked that was the reason we'd all been born with such long, dexterous tongues.

Huu-goh did not have the same issue. While his flat teeth were useless when it came to fibrous plants, they were excellent for cock sucking. Even on the rare occasion they grazed my lengths, all it did was make me shudder.

And Huu-goh had made it clear that he preferred to spend a portion of every day with his mouth between my legs.

The entire time Huu-goh had swallowed me that morning he had emitted *sweet* noises. All "hmms" and "nnnnghs." Pretty humming that made my skin buzz. His throat vibrated around me like he truly enjoyed my flavor. Deeper and deeper he went, rubbing his tongue inside my suckers till they clutched back. Toying with each dick one by one, eager to be stuffed full of me.

He could barely get half of my cocks inside his mouth, but I did not mind. His obvious inexperience lit me up from the inside out because it meant he had waited, just like I had. We were each other's firsts, and while I would've loved him regardless, it still felt clandestine.

Like he'd known somehow, a galaxy away, that I was waiting for him.

Only him.

I just hadn't known it yet.

I enjoyed the sounds Huu-goh made more than I should. It was *that*, paired with the tightness of his throat that finally did me in.

As I lay on my back, half-asleep and trembling with pleasure, I was once again delighted by how utterly *brilliant* my little love was. He sucked my other cock with as much enthusiasm as the first—until the stimulation grew too strong—and I burst on his tongue for a second time.

I expected to see his flushed, embarrassed expression looking up at me when I glanced down. Instead, Huu-goh caught me by surprise. Though pink-cheeked, just as I predicted, there was no shyness on my tiny troublemaker's face. His smirk was positively *wicked* as he licked his lips and met my gaze through the gap in my thighs.

Immediately, both of my dicks bumped at his lips like they wanted a second go. He chuckled and pressed a parting kiss on their tips in farewell, even though he was shaky with need of his own.

I'd returned the favor, no longer surprised by my own enthusiasm. In the past, I masturbated because my cocks would not go down, not because I necessarily wanted to. For so long I had dreaded sex. I had thought it would be a chore, something to get through before I could attend to my real duties.

I had never been more wrong in all my life.

Sex was fun, when it was with the right person. It made you learn things about yourself you never would've known. And when there was trust between you, there was nothing better.

Determined to make Huu-goh spill quicker than he'd made me, I reveled in the pitiful cries my little beast made when I wrapped my tongue around his dick. Deliberately, I twisted. Tighter, tighter, till his eyes crossed and his perky balls emptied all over his belly.

His seed was saltier than mine, but I enjoyed the flavor.

If I was being honest, there wasn't *anything* I didn't enjoy about Huu-goh.

I loved the way he looked at the world, his dark eyes always full of wonder.

He saw potential in the ugliest of things.

Scraps of metal, most would consider junk, when placed in his capable hands could be transformed into something new and beautiful. As evidenced by the creations he'd been working on when he wasn't spending his afternoons in Ushuu's lab.

His brain was a wondrous thing.

So brilliant, and so full of mischief.

It was a wonder to me that A&R, or anyone, could've ever found him lacking.

I loved Huu-goh's smile, his laugh, his funny, itty-bitty nose. So small it could hardly be useful—and yet it miraculously managed to work just fine despite its size and odd shape.

I loved his toes. All ten of them.

I loved the tiny scattered spots that covered his body.

I loved his ears. I'd seen ears on other species before, but never had they struck me as adorable. Huu-goh's ears were though. They stuck out a bit to the sides and they flushed the loveliest shade of pink when he was aroused. Like their color was tied directly to his sweet cock.

I loved his kisses. Loved his intelligence. Loved when he was cross with me. Loved when he was happy with me even more. I loved surprising him. Loved playing with him. Loved doting on him.

He kept me on my toes.

And despite his size, Huu-goh never had any trouble keeping up with me. It was hard to believe that a creature so different could be my perfect counterpart. But he was. He didn't seem to mind my control issues. Didn't seem to mind the way I always kept him close, protective to a fault. I was older than he was—and he didn't seem to mind that either.

We were so different, but different had never felt more perfect.

And though he was full of mischief, he had proven to me he could be trusted.

My tight leash on him—sometimes literally—only came from care, but I could see now he was capable of fending for himself. And I was going to do my best moving forward to give him every opportunity to thrive— even though my fear for him never abated.

"Captain," Sahla's quiet voice interrupted my reverie. There was a knowing smirk on his face. Everyone kept looking at me like that. Like I was just a pup, and they were watching me take my first steps—despite the fact it had been months since Huu-goh had become mine.

"Lieutenant." I kept my tone neutral, though I arched my brow bone at him till he stopped smirking. I couldn't blame him, not when I'd arrived to the control room with my head in the clouds.

Daydream time was over.

I needed to get to work.

I had shipments to deliver and a crew that depended on me. A mating ceremony to plan. There was no room for error now, and I couldn't afford doubt among my crew. I took a breath, puffed out my chest, and roared to get their attention. The silence that echoed afterward made my heart sing.

*This* was my calling, my purpose.

This was what Captain Strongfoot had trained me for.

I ended my speech like I always did with a heavy heap of praise and the weight of their duty to their families back home. The recruits, the younger ones in particular, stared at me with wonder in their eyes as they waited patiently for their assignments.

As I handed out orders, wrote down our schedule on the HoverPad that floated in the center of the command deck, and delegated tasks to each crew member, half of my mind remained in the clouds.

I hoped Huu-goh enjoyed today.

I hoped, and hoped, and hoped.

# FIFTEEN

## HUGO

**THE STARS LOOKED LIKE THEY** were barely a hundred feet away, floating in the sky like fairy lights as Ushuu and Mala led me from the ship and through the rows of spaceships that lined the dock. I'd been silent, taking everything in, wishing like hell I had a new journal to take notes.

In the back of my mind, I logged the details for later.

Sha'hPihn, as Ushuu had called it was a consumer hub for this side of the galaxy. Larger than F'ukYuu, and full of high-end buildings that resembled the larger cities of Earth. It was one of the more developed planets when it came to technology—as evidenced by the floating neon signs that pointed down the walkway, and the shuttles that flew overhead.

I'd never seen anything like this.

It was…god. So fucking *cool!*

I'd often wondered what Roark's planet was like—where we were headed.

And when I'd asked Ushuu the other day he'd told me it was similar in infrastructure to Sha'hPihn, but friendlier. I wasn't sure what he meant by "friendlier" but I couldn't wait to find out.

There were so many different species of aliens here. They went about their days, barely sparing us a single glance as they anchored their ships and hauled cargo down ramps to the pier below. The variety of species present were more varied than what I'd seen on F'ukYuu. Which was quite an amazing feat. I could've sworn in my three years enslaved, I'd seen every alien on this side of the galaxy.

I'd been wrong.

I had to move fast to match Mala's pace and he slowed when he noticed, smiling in a way I guessed was apologetic. His spots were blue—calm and confident—and when I glanced at Ushuu, he was grinning down at me like he knew something that I didn't.

He was a crafty bastard.

I'd become quite fond of him over the last few weeks, especially when he'd regale me with tales of Roark's youth, and what a stalwart little soldier he'd been. I'd thought I was a goody two-shoes till I learned about what Roark had been like as a kid.

When I saw a tall man with three heads I stumbled to a stop to get a better look. Hands, hands—let me see his—

"Four thumbs!" I cheered under my breath, stoked to see another of the strange aliens I'd encountered previously. I wondered if this guy was an accountant too, like the one I'd serviced before.

Seeing a familiar organism was soothing in a way.

All the new species and the foreign-looking sky had put me on edge— even if I didn't like to admit it. I was a scientist at heart, but I was also only twenty-one. And some of these creatures reminded me a little too much of how ignorant I actually was when it came to what was out here in the galaxy. Plus, Roark wasn't here to protect me from getting snatched up again, which I thought made it fair for me to be a little on edge—even considering how badass this planet was.

*Stop being a little bitch, Hugo. You have Mala and Ushuu with you. You're fine. If Roark didn't think you were safe, he wouldn't have let you leave.*

*Sure there're tons of aliens, but who gives a fuck?*

*You don't have to dance for any of them.*

*No one is going to take you away.*

*Your only job is to take it all in.*

I wished Roark was here, but Ushuu had explained he would be busy for the next few days with preparations for the last leg of the journey home. I knew that meant a lot more alone time with him later, so I was happy he'd planned this outing for me.

I'd started to feel like I was going crazy we'd been stuck on board so long.

Exploring his cocks and their very different personalities had helped. In my head I liked to call the first one "PushyPush" and the second "PoliteyPants," though I'd never admit that to Roark's face. He was a fascinating creature for certain, and I knew I could spend the rest of my life observing him and never grow bored.

Even after he'd shown me the sparring room and the pool—and all the other cool little nooks and crannies on board The Dreamer—bless you Ushuu for telling me the ship's name—it was still only a matter of time before I needed solid ground to reset.

Not that I was sure the moving sidewalk beneath our feet counted as solid ground. Below us, I could see another docking bay through the glass. And below that there was another. An almost infinite number of them going low, low, low.

*Stop looking down.*

*Or you'll throw up.*

"Four thumbs," I repeated again, amazed as the alien I was staring at passed by our little group, his three heads swiveling. He barked out what I could only assume was a reprimand to one of his crewmates, and I flinched.

"What?" Ushuu blinked down at me, looking amused. I just shook my head, because I didn't know how to explain. It was weird acknowledging where I'd been before Roark had given me a home—and I wasn't sure I was ready to talk to anyone but Roark about it.

"Where are we heading?" I asked instead.

"You'll see," Ushuu replied. Both he and Mala had been acting secretive. I wasn't worried. How could I be when Roark had very carefully reiterated this morning that he had a surprise for me?

He'd *promised* that they'd keep me safe, the best that he could in stilted English.

"Huu-goh safe with Mala, Ushuu. Soo-Prise." Surprise was a new word for him, and the fact he'd disappeared the night before for several hours told me he'd made Ushuu teach it to him just so he could use it this morning.

The sentence had been a bit garbled, but I'd understood what he was trying to say. We'd been talking enough lately that I'd grown better and better at filling in the blanks for him. His pronunciation was getting better too—as was his vocabulary. Ushuu was teaching me to write—because I wasn't capable of saying more than a handful of words in sharkish, but even then, it was frustrating sometimes not to be able to say what I wanted to Roark.

I shook away the morose thoughts and instead took in my surroundings.

The massive buildings that dotted the skyline ahead were even taller the closer we got to them. Small aircrafts that basically looked like floating silver golfballs sped through the air so quickly all you could hear was the quiet *swoosh* of them. I hadn't noticed them at first, as they zoomed high above the usual space shuttles.

I made a mental note about them, too, watching them dance above with fascination.

There was a giant winding staircase ahead—though as we got closer, I realized that "staircase" wasn't the most accurate descriptor to give it. Escalator on crack would be more truthful, because it moved with a blur of bodies, sending them up, up, up what looked like over a thousand feet to a platform so high I couldn't see what was on it.

A bulbous alien with a single eye the size of a dinner plate waited at the exit to the port. He spoke to Mala with a series of clicks and whirrs, swiped something on what looked like a giant tablet with a hologram floating above it, then gestured for us to move past him toward the moving stairs.

As we took our place on the steps, I felt a little giddy.

I still had no idea *where* we were going—or why we were going there—but at this point, that hardly mattered. We were going *out*! And that was a bigger gift than I'd dared hope for since the day I was abducted. The only thing that would've made this better was if Roark was here.

Did he find the city as fascinating as I did?

Or not? Because his planet was similar?

As I gawked at the rising metropolis above, it struck me for the first time how absolutely shitty F'ukYuu had been.

Since it had been the only planet I'd visited, besides my own, it hadn't occurred to me how seedy and dirty it truly was. Sure, the pleasure house

I'd come from was clean and well-kept, but the streets of the planet had been crawling with discarded trash.

It wasn't fair that the wealth there remained in the pockets of the owners of the houses, and that the rest of us were forced to suffer. I was glad I was out now, but that didn't mean my heart didn't hurt for the people I'd left behind.

Sure, I'd never really made any friends—despite trying—but still.

I felt bad.

None of them had been adopted by a giant pink shark daddy.

None of them would ever see a planet like the one I currently occupied.

I truly was the lucky one.

I missed Roark then, fiercely, as our little group reached the top of the winding staircase to discover it led to what I could only describe as a… mall? An *alien* mall.

The structure was made of glass, just like the dock had been, shops stacked on top of one another as high as the eye could see. There was no end to them from left to right—vendors that carried every kind of ware, out haggling on the street or standing in their almost box-like store fronts, waiting for customers to ride the elevators beside each section to meet them.

A mall in space.

Huh.

*Why did Roark send me here?*

Mala stepped off the stairs to lead the way, and as I followed, I couldn't hide my astonishment. Ushuu stayed close behind me, protective of my back, as we shuffled off to join Mala. When we were on solid ground, off to the side and out of the line of traffic, both Sahrks paused to let me take it all in.

The big buildings I'd seen from the pier climbed the sky like giants. But they barely held my attention. No, that was reserved for the stores that lined both sides of the walkway. Hundreds of them. Thousands maybe. All brightly lit and beautiful, looking inviting, clean, and fancier than anything I'd ever seen in all my life. I could see what they sold more clearly up close, and my eyes danced over the glittering gems, lacy corsets, and dresses that were for sale at the shop nearest where we stood.

Swallowing the lump in my throat, I let myself imagine what the fabric must feel like.

Silky probably.

Soft?

It looked comfortable.

My hands clenched into fists and I tore my gaze away—trying not to be floored by how goddamn pretty that dress was. And how much I wanted it.

I came from an average-sized city. It wasn't big enough for true crime, but wasn't small enough to avoid it. Our home had sat between the train tracks and a drug store that got robbed at least four times a year. There were cops that patrolled the block. And the gate that guarded our community—that my father claimed was a symbol of wealth—had only been in place because they wanted to avoid break-ins.

We'd had a nice house, but that had hardly mattered.

For fuck's sake, my high school had only had one working water fountain. They'd claimed they would fix the others—but they'd sat with "out of order" signs the entire time I'd been in school.

Harvard was supposed to be my way out of that life.

And yet here I was…somewhere far more extraordinary.

Somewhere that shouldn't be *real*, but somehow was.

As I stood there, staring at the wonders around me, I felt something inside me settle.

Was it awful of me to be grateful I'd been taken? I know, *I know*. I shouldn't thank A&R for their abduction. Shouldn't thank them for dropping me off on F'ukYuu when they decided I wasn't smart enough for my original purpose.

But I kinda wanted to anyway.

I'd never seen anything more spectacular in all of my life.

And without their interference I never would've been here. Never would've met Roark—or Ushuu, or Mala, or seen the things I was about to see.

There were so many options, I couldn't possibly guess what Roark had had in mind for this little outing, so I didn't stress myself out trying. Instead, I people-watched for a few minutes longer. *Alien-watched?*

If I'd thought the population down at the docks was eclectic, this was a goddamn zoo.

So many shops. So many creatures. All going about their day with their arms laden with shopping bags and the titter of a multitude of languages clogging the air like tinkling bells.

"Do you like it?" Ushuu asked. To his credit, he and Mala had been more than patient as I processed our surroundings.

There was a white flash and I blinked away spots as I turned to look at the older shark-man only to discover his communicator was pointed straight at me. Like he had just taken a *picture*. The device was round rather than rectangular, but it didn't take a genius to recognize it for what it was. It was funny, back on Earth we'd called them cellphones but here they functioned on an intergalactic level, so I guess it made sense they had a different name.

The Manager had one of those too, not that I'd ever gotten close enough to admire it.

For a second, I had the oddest intrusive thought—of me with a rock, smashing The Manager's communicator like a monkey shelling a nut so that I could get at the tech inside.

I bit back a smile, watching Ushuu curiously to figure out why he'd just photographed me.

Ushuu tapped something on his screen, and I practically salivated as I observed the device up close. I hadn't seen Roark use one the entire time we'd been together, though I figured he had to have one for work somewhere, didn't he? He had a tablet. That was similar—though it didn't do phone calls.

I wanted both.

Badly.

So I could pick them apart and see how they worked.

Also, maybe then I could send Roark pictures myself. It took me a second, but I figured out what Ushuu must be doing. He was nosy and sweet, and I had a feeling my own big pink monster would get a kick out of the stunned expression I'd been making since he couldn't be here to see it himself.

Roark was sweet like that.

And for some reason, he seemed to like me. A lot.

Liked to see me giggle and smile.

Liked me enough he'd made it clear he was keeping me.

Ushuu pocketed his phone when Mala made an impatient but indulgent grunt to his left. He didn't speak much when Roark wasn't around, and for some reason that made me like him even more. They'd been regular ole chatty-Kathys whenever I saw them together on the ship, and it was funny—now that I realized both men were the silent stoic type when they weren't ribbing each other.

Mala was more cheerful than Roark was, though. He had this air about him like he wanted to laugh at everything he saw. Whereas Roark viewed the world like it could burst into flames at any moment, so he needed to be prepared with a fire extinguisher.

"Why are we here?" I asked Ushuu, grateful to be spending time with someone I could have a full conversation with. Not that I didn't appreciate Roark and all his grunts, growls, and garbled English. Because I did. And I was *so* grateful for the effort he'd put into communicating with me that it made me breathless sometimes.

But…it had been lonely not having anyone to talk to.

Things were better now that I was apprenticing under Ushuu—and I could only thank Roark for that too.

"I bet you can guess," Ushuu's eyes gleamed, and I giggled, glancing around and squinting in an attempt to read his mind.

"Shopping?" I offered, arching a brow.

"Very good." Ushuu sounded way too amused about all of this. The more he worked with Roark and I, the better his English became. Which was something I found incredibly impressive.

"But for what?" I blinked. "Does Roark need something?" That would make sense. I was delighted he'd trust me to run his errands for him. "Oh! Toothpaste. He was saying something about toothpaste I think…yesterday?"

The dispenser had broken and I'd been fiddling with it only to discover it'd gotten jammed with the last dregs of what was left. We needed more to fix it.

"Oh. Or his glasses!" I added. He'd stepped on them when he'd returned to our rooms after his most recent late-night session with Ushuu. The distressed sound he'd made when he realized he'd snapped them in half with his big elephant feet had made me scurry to fix them for him.

I'd used one of the soldering irons in Ushuu's lab to mend them, and when I'd returned them to him later that night, Roark had placed them on his nose and rubbed his snout against my cheek with a huff of hot breath in thanks.

I bet he was still wearing them right now—even though they looked janky as hell.

*Why did that make me happy?*

"Wrong," Ushuu's grin gentled as he observed me. There was a weird look in his eyes, like he was *seeing* me for the first time. "We're not here for the captain."

"Then what are we here for?"

"You, Huu-goh." He grinned. When I stared at him in disbelief he pulled his communicator out and snapped another picture of me. I waved him off, blinking away the spots.

"Why?" I was dumbfounded. "I have everything I need."

Roark took care of all my stuff. I had my own toothbrush. My own clothes—even if they were all the same outfit.

I mean…shoes would be nice. Real shoes. Not the weird bootie things that I'd been given on F'ukYuu, but still.

"Little one, you're wearing baby clothes." Ushuu kept his voice gentle. But the shame that coursed through my body must've been apparent, because he swore softly in his native tongue and reached out with one massive hand to settle me. "It is not a *bad* thing. You are small, and it was the only thing we had on board that would fit."

I shrank in on myself and Mala made an alarmed sound, glancing between the two of us. They had a whispered conversation—one that sounded reprimanding on Mala's end as Ushuu's spots turned a dark indigo blue.

"Huu-goh," he said gently, hands still hovering like he wasn't sure it was okay to touch. "I'm sorry. I didn't mean to hurt your heart." It was a weird translation, but I made sense of it.

"I'm not hurt," I said, "just surprised."

"There is no shame in your clothing, Huu-goh," Ushuu made an alarmed sound, ignoring Mala's answering growl. "That isn't why Roark wanted us to take you here." He closed the last few inches between us and rubbed his palm up and down my back. It was nice. Soothing. It wasn't as nice as when Roark did it, but I appreciated the touch all the same.

I hadn't had much of that, even when I was living on Earth.

"The captain…" Ushuu kept rubbing as he frowned, spots still indigo with what I assumed was remorse. He was quiet for a moment as he came up with what I assumed were the right words in a tongue that wasn't his. "The captain wants to…" Ushuu frowned, struggling. "Give you many gifts," he finally settled on.

*Give me gifts?*

*Why?*

"He does?" My cheeks flushed for an entirely different reason.

"Yes!" Ushuu perked up, and Mala stopped growling the second he pulled his hand from my back. "Yes. He does."

"So we're here, not because he's embarrassed I'm walking around in baby clothes—" I reiterated as Ushuu shook his head, "but because he wants to buy me *gifts?*"

The older shark nodded. "Exactly."

"What kind of gifts?" I peered out at the stores with new eyes, my heart pounding a little. I'd always loved presents. Roark knew that. After seeing my reaction to the box he'd put together for me he'd started bringing me something new at least a few times a week just to make me smile.

Before that though…

*Man.*

It had been three, four, maybe even *five* years since the last time my parents had done anything for Christmas. We usually didn't do gifts for birthdays—their presence was the gift, or so my mother teased. That had become all too true over the years, even if it had first been said as a joke.

How pitiful was that?

But…

I bit my lip, eyes catching on that same shop I'd been admiring before. This time, I glanced toward the back, struck with fascination when I spotted a row of mannequins of all shapes and sizes wearing fancy, glittery, lacy underthings.

I swallowed thickly, unable to stop ogling when I noticed a mannequin my size dressed in a lacy pink garter belt, panties, and thigh highs.

*Pretty.*

Everything was so pretty.

Fuck.

I wanted to touch *all* of it.

"Anything you want," Ushuu answered, more careful with what he said now. I didn't fault him. As jarring as his words had been, at least I knew the truth. And now that I knew I was wearing baby shark clothes I was itching to get the hell out of them and into something a little more age appropriate.

"Within reason," I added to myself.

"No." Ushuu laughed at me, but it wasn't mean. "Roark specifically told me to tell you that there is no limit."

"No…limit?" I squinted at him.

"No."

I frowned, trying to figure out where the trick was.

I knew Roark was wealthy.

It was obvious.

His ship was a luxury cargo carrier—far nicer and larger than any of the others on the dock. The Manager had made sure I was aware that his pockets were lined in gold before I'd even met him—but it had never occurred to me that he would offer for me to spend any of his wealth.

My head was swimming.

"I need a limit," I told Ushuu, because I did.

I didn't want to mess up today.

I didn't want to cross the line when I was being given the greatest gift that anyone had ever given me. No one, in all my life, had offered me something like this. Ever. It was hard to wrap my mind around it.

Ushuu's spots were yellow.

Confused then.

I'd figured that color out too.

He turned to Mala and they spoke in soft tones again for a few minutes before they came to a decision and Ushuu tapped several buttons on his communicator. I wasn't sure what was about to happen, but my eyes were full of diamonds and panties—and my ears were ringing.

It chimed twice before the dial cut off and Roark's deep rumble filled the air. I'd gotten so used to listening to his scattered English it was odd hearing him talk so fluently in his native tongue with someone else.

He sounded like a captain.

Which I knew he was—but still.

In control. Smart. Serious.

My belly flipped as Ushuu responded to him, before handing the device to me.

I blinked down in surprise when I realized he'd tapped the hologram option and the tiny see-through shape of Roark's head popped up. Holograms. Holy shit. So fucking cool. I'd never get over the fact that they were real.

Or maybe that was because Roark was purring at me in that same soothing way he always did when I was upset. Like magic, I relaxed, curling my palms around the communicator, and pulling it closer like if I did so I could feel his heat against my body or taste his scent in the air.

"Huu-goh," Roark murmured as I cradled him. I wasn't sure what view of me he had right now—only that it was far from flattering. He didn't seem to mind though. He made another rumbly soft sound that I whined in response to. "Little one." It was the same name Ushuu had called me, but when he'd said it, tingles hadn't danced across my entire body. Not like they did when Roark did.

I bit my lip and nodded to show I was listening.

"It is okay," he urged. I could hear the murmur of voices on the other end of the line—like he wasn't alone. Immediately, I felt ashamed. I'd probably interrupted him while he was doing something important.

Shit.

"He's busy," I tried to hand the communicator back to Ushuu, but my hands refused to let go. "I don't want to bother him—" Roark continued to purr at me, and Ushuu turned to his little holo-head and translated for me. He leaned in close, allowing me to continue to hold it as they talked for a few minutes. A couple words of English were tossed back and forth before Roark turned his attention to me and Ushuu stepped back.

"Listen," he said. There was so much command in that one single word I couldn't stop myself from melting. Because Roark was here, and he was giving me orders, and if I followed them I knew everything would be alright. Whatever he was about to say had to be important.

I nodded and he emitted a pleased noise that made my icy limbs go gooey warm.

"I never too busy for my Huu-goh."

No one had ever said that to me before.

Tears stung my eyes and I inhaled sharply, pulling the communicator close enough it almost felt like a hug. When I smiled, Roark did too. His eyes turned into the happy-crescent shapes again and he purred as I dashed away my tears.

"Money is not problem," Roark told me when I was settled.

"It is," I argued, and he made a frustrated noise. I held him out to Ushuu before he had to ask and they spoke back and forth for a few more minutes in the same garbled English-Sharkish. When he stepped back again, Roark didn't look annoyed.

He was as patient as ever as he waited for me to settle before speaking again.

"You need limit?" he asked.

I nodded.

"*Need?*" he reiterated, asking very seriously. I understood what he meant. Was this a thing I couldn't move forward without? I hesitated to say yes, because I knew it was the wrong answer. The *weird* answer. I should just take the gift and shut the fuck up.

But…

I knew Roark didn't want that, and I'd be ruining his present if I kept my mouth shut. So I nodded.

"Good boy," Roark rumbled. "Proud."

I preened, despite my wet lashes and the way my cheeks were flooded red with humiliation. Mala and Ushuu were politely pretending like they weren't listening, but I knew they were. Not that Mala understood much of what was going on, but Ushuu sure did.

"Thank you," I croaked, wanting nothing more than to climb into the hologram to be with him. I had only been apart from him for a few hours and already I missed him like crazy. Roark held up a single thick finger and I waited patiently as he thought.

Always helpful, Ushuu leaned over to help him translate. Their back and forth this time was obvious, and I knew what Roark was about to say before he spoke. But that didn't mean I wasn't completely floored by his next words.

"Huu-goh limit one million credits." Roark annunciated thoughtfully, staring at me the entire time. I nearly choked on my own tongue. That was *huge*. So fucking huge. The equivalent of buying nights with me at the pleasure house for six months straight.

My head spun.

I couldn't even comprehend that amount of money, and yet here he was—dropping it on me like it was nothing. *Again*. Just like when he'd bought me.

"*Are you sure?*" I blurted out, all messy with tears again.

"Yesh," Roark watched me with affection evident on his handsome face. His teeth flashed as the soothing rumbling started again. "Huu-goh?"

"Yes?"

"Promise?"

"Anything."

"Huu-goh has fun," Roark requested. "*Please.*"

"Okay." The word was choked but I managed. I fluttered a few dozen kisses against the cheek of his hologram as he brayed out a laugh before shaking his head, spots fuschia. "Ushuu," he instructed me.

I handed the communicator back over and Roark spoke with his mentor for what felt like another million years. I didn't mind. I needed the time to wrap my head around what had just happened—and what was about to happen. When he forced Ushuu to return the communicator to me so that he could say goodbye, my belly filled with butterflies.

I hadn't noticed before, but Roark's tone wasn't nearly as soft when he talked to Ushuu, as it was when he talked to me.

My belly squirmed.

"Bye bye, Huu-goh," Roark purred, as serious as ever.

"Bye," I said to Roark's floating head. He barked in amusement again.

"Huu-goh fun," he reminded me sternly.

"I'll have fun," I agreed, my heart pounding.

"Good." He looked proud of himself, and I couldn't help but try to kiss him through the hologram again. Roark ended the call as he was laughing, the sound and his spots full of affection. I missed him the moment he was gone, stroking the now silent device forlornly.

When I glanced up, Ushuu and Mala were staring at me like I was a goddamn unicorn. Mala said something to Ushuu, nudged him, and the elder shark held out a hand for the communicator with a gentle smile.

"Mala would like me to inform you that you are a 'miracle worker.'" I snorted, but I didn't get what he meant. "He would also like me to tell you that he has *never* seen Roark laugh as much as he just did, in all the time he's known him."

I swallowed the lump in my throat, suddenly heartsick.

"I echo that sentiment," Ushuu added. "For a long time I worried that he would never be able to let go of what has happened to him. That it would trap him. That he would never know happiness. I am not worried anymore."

I didn't know what any of that meant, and before I could ask, Ushuu interrupted me again.

"You are a tiny little miracle, aren't you?" Ushuu grinned at me, jerked his head toward the shops in front of us. "Lead the way, little one."

And so I did.

# SIXTEEN

## ROARK

**THE WEEK WE SPENT ON** planet Sha'hPihn went by in a busy blur. I performed my duties. I organized our shipments. I made the phone calls back home for our ceremony arrangements. And I visited with the authorities I'd made friends with over the last fifteen years I'd spent as captain. I'd never liked schmoozing, but it was necessary in my line of work. When people valued you they tended to give better deals—and in my case, higher quality cargo.

I'd made a few genuine friends over the years, but no one I'd consider important enough to choose to spend time with over Huu-goh. I counted down the days to the event I'd bought us tickets to attend, desperate for time with my mate where we could speak freely without language barriers.

Ushuu's lessons were helping, and we'd been communicating more and more as of late, but there was still so much I didn't know. Things I needed to understand if I was going to make him happy, comfortable, and carefree.

Things I wanted to know about him—simply because I cared.

As I rode back and forth across the planet, running errands throughout the week, I spent my free time writing a list. It was the most important document I'd ever written, and I spent more than a few hours fretting over its contents. There was no room for error. On the list I included everything I wanted and needed to know about my little mate. Things I'd been desperate to ask, but never been able to.

That wouldn't be the case anymore.

There was no denying the fact that I was *excited*.

Far more excited than I could ever remember feeling.

Though I still experienced some anxiety as well. What if he didn't feel the same way I did? What if, somehow, I'd misread our interactions? What if Huu-goh did not want a mate? What if his proposition had been an accident? What if I had to let him go? What if, what if, what if?

I had never been one to dwell on unpleasantness, so I quickly pushed the thoughts away.

I was too busy to doubt, even if I wanted to.

After what felt like a century, the week ended and the time for our date arrived.

I was a nervous, gray-spotted mess. Not because I wasn't eager, but because I didn't want to get this wrong. Which meant there was no hiding my very real concern from my current audience. My spots were on display as Ushuu helped me prepare for the night.

He'd offered, delighted by the idea of dressing me for my "date" with Huu-goh.

And I appreciated his support, more than he knew.

It was early yet, but I had a few more errands to run. Fun ones. For Huu-goh, of course. I hadn't had a chance until now, as my schedule had been far too busy. The only reason I'd eaten all week was because Huu-goh had been surprisingly stubborn about it—procuring plates of food from the mess hall that sat untouched on the nightstand till I came home. I'd gobble them stale, but even that made me feel loved.

Loved and cared for.

In a way I hadn't known I could.

Huu-goh had become increasingly worried about me as the week progressed, but I'd waved him off. This was a part of the job, and though it wasn't necessarily pleasant, it was important.

I was content with that.

On one of their shopping trips Ushuu told Huu-goh where we'd be spending our Friday night. Afterward, the elder Sahrk informed me through text that my mate had been so excited he'd walked into a wall.

Just imagining that had made me laugh so hard I'd nearly walked into a wall myself.

I'd been giddy that night, anticipating Huu-goh's reaction the moment he saw me. It was another surprise. Lately I'd been full of those. And as the pile of gifts in the corner of our room grew and Huu-goh's words of thank you grew with it, I knew I'd made the right choice.

I wouldn't have been angry if he'd been asleep when I made it home. It was late. Every night had been late. But when I finally arrived to our room well after dark, Huu-goh was waiting up for me.

I grinned and crossed the distance between us, my hearts in my throat.

The moment I collapsed into bed he climbed on top of me, looped his arms around my neck, and performed a happy dance.

The nanobots he'd reprogrammed zoomed around the room like they were feeding off his excitement, and I'd nuzzled the downy soft fur on his head, soaking up his chatter like a sponge as he told me all about how excited he was, and how lovely his day had been. Huu-goh pressed hundreds of those strange little kisses all over my face as I cradled him against my body, lids already drooping.

He'd been doing that a lot lately.

The kissing.

Not that I minded.

It made me feel fuzzy every time he did.

Almost as fuzzy as when the chaste kisses became slick and he sucked on my tongue.

As I basked in his affection, at peace for the first time that day, my eyes scanned the room.

Huu-goh's box of spare parts was scattered in the back corner like he'd been tinkering with them again. The set of tools I'd given him glinted between pieces of used-up metal. The broken translators sat to the side, shinier than before—but still unusable.

His little pile of toys had taken residence in the corner of the room since the day I'd given them to him. The box had to be nearly full by now, as he collected more and more from Ushuu each day.

The clutter should have bothered me but it didn't.

Maybe once upon a time, it would have.

But it had been a long time since I felt that way.

We'd both had to grow a lot to cohabit the same space.

I had never been a messy person myself, but I found Huu-goh and his piles more than a little endearing. His piles of laundry. His piles of blankets. His piles of tools. Every time I saw them, it reminded me how sterile and bland my life had been before he came into it. It was nice seeing the evidence that someone else lived here.

His disarray was soothing, though admittedly I could tell he tried to keep it neat.

As wonderful and exciting as it was that he'd enjoyed my present, there were other gifts I was more curious about. The ones he'd been purchasing on his shopping trips with Ushuu, specifically. The ones that resided in a pile of their own on top of his old bed.

*What had he picked?*

*Clothing?*

*More tools?*

*Frivolous, wonderful little things he'd never be able to find on F'ukYuu?*

*I hope so.*

Every day a bag or two was added to the procession. Never too much all at once, always very practical. Ushuu found Huu-goh hilarious, and I couldn't help but agree. Huu-goh was more careful with my money than I was, and that was saying something.

I had yet to see any of the items he'd bought out of their shiny bags. Ushuu had told me to be patient, and that Huu-goh had something planned. If there was something I usually never lacked, it was patience, though I was learning where Huu-goh was concerned, that wasn't always true.

He'd said thank you about a hundred times, and I'd had to shush him when it didn't seem the gratitude would ever end. It was flattering, to say the least. A far better use of my money than what it had been doing previously—growing stale in my bank account.

I was a little disappointed he hadn't spent more, if I was being honest. I had wanted to *truly* spoil him—for the sky to be the limit. But my little mate was a practical man, and he'd been dead set on not spending a penny above the amount I'd originally told him.

In hindsight, I should've predicted that.

It was poor planning not to give him a higher number. But when he'd asked me, I'd been blindsided. He'd looked so shaky and small. Unsure of himself. I would've done anything to see his smile again, and I hadn't been thinking clearly enough to anticipate this problem.

I should have.

Huu-goh had come to me with nothing. Slaves on F'ukYuu certainly weren't treated like people. And before that, I had no idea what his life had been like. I had no idea how long he'd been with A&R before his relocation. I couldn't fathom what his life on Earth had been like at all. For all I knew he'd grown up the same way he'd spent his time as a pleasure slave. Penniless, beautiful, and alone.

I wanted to spoil him more, but I didn't want to overwhelm him. I had plans for us on our date, and that would have to be enough for now.

This was the last stop on our journey home, and I could practically taste the salt in the air already. Osheania was *close*. Close enough my hearts throbbed toward it and I daydreamed about what Huu-goh would think the moment he stepped foot on my planet's lovely pink soil.

"You are sure he will like this?" I confirmed, eyes narrowed at Ushuu. He hadn't led me astray, thus far, so I wasn't actually concerned.

I was, however, *uncomfortable*.

The stiff clothing Ushuu had insisted I wear barely let my surface breathe. My tendrils hissed unhappily beneath the fabric. They didn't like being trapped, and I didn't like the vulnerability that came with that either.

This event was a safe space so I knew there was no need to fret. The price tag to attend helped weed out the pirates that frequented the planet. There was no need for paranoia, but still, I struggled to reassure myself.

This particular event was being held in a ritzy hotel at the highest point of the planet. It was an area that was known for being high-end and anti-crime. On top of this, there would be security throughout the hotel at every entrance, and along the walls of the ballroom.

We would be safe.

I'd made sure of that, going so far as to interrogate one of my contacts into admitting which of the events on Sha'hPihn would be most secure. At first, wanting to pad his own wallet, he'd tried to convince me to attend one of his own, but I had refused. Huu-goh's safety was of utmost importance and he hadn't been able to promise me his security would be nearly as satisfactory as the event I'd ended up buying us tickets to.

I wasn't above using my size and status to intimidate, though I didn't do it often. However, nothing in my life had been more important than this "date" with Huu-goh. My contact had quaked in fear as I towered over his desk, claws digging into the surface. With my tendrils flailing behind me, I knew there wasn't a being in this galaxy who would not give me what I wanted.

The bulbous alien had immediately told me what I wanted to hear.

We'd finished our business as usual afterward, but he wouldn't stop quaking the entire time. When I'd left, he'd hurried after me to try and mend the bridge he'd burned. It was almost laughable, really, that he thought I cared.

I only had so much time and energy, and all of it belonged to Huu-goh.

I was snapped back to the present by Ushuu's poking and prodding as he carefully adjusted the uncomfortable clothing, making sure the seams lay flat. He'd been kind enough to procure this for me when he'd been out and about, and I was grateful, even though I had already decided that I hated wearing it.

"You look cute," Ushuu teased. I glared at him. His smile softened. "He will love it. It may seem odd to you—" Ushuu's lavender gaze was warm, "because it is not our way. But where Huu-goh is from, what you are wearing right now is…special." Ushuu's voice was reverent as he studied me, pride written all over his face. "If you want to impress him, this is definitely the way to go."

I nodded.

My hearts ached anew.

"Huu-goh will be able to take over for me," Ushuu said. It took me a moment to understand that he was talking about his duties on the ship, and not dressing me in huu-man clothing. "Maybe not this flight, but the next."

"Ushuu," I reached for him, and he came willingly, our snouts rubbing as I closed my eyes.

"All I've ever wanted was to see you happy," Ushuu told me. "I do not have children of my own. After *he* died—" He didn't need to say the name for me to know he was talking about his mate. My first captain. The man who had taught me everything I knew. "I did not want to make a child without him."

I nodded.

"I am glad," Ushuu added. "Because there would've been no better son—pod-made or otherwise—than you, Roark."

We hugged for a long time. The tendrils that could escape around our wrists did so, tangling together as our hearts thumped as one.

When we separated, I was more sure than ever that I had made the right choice.

"I will miss you," I told him, and it was the truth.

"And I will miss you," Ushuu replied.

I wished Huu-goh was here to comfort me with his strange humming song. Because I felt unsteady as I finished dressing and tried to focus on our "date" and not the fact that the only constant in my life would soon be changing.

Maybe it was good, though.

To let things change.

If I had always remained so resistant to it, I never would've met Huu-goh.

The collar of my new shirt was stiff and unyielding, and I tugged at it with a grunt. With purpose, I made my way out of Ushuu's chambers—he'd graciously offered to let me change there so I wouldn't ruin the surprise.

Mala was at the helm of the ship, keeping things running smoothly so I could take time off. Ushuu followed after me, keeping pace with my brisk walk as we headed down the hall.

"I should escort him," I blurted to Ushuu only for him to shake his head.

"It will be more magical if you pick him up from your hotel room like we planned." As we rounded a corner, a few recruits saluted us both. I nodded to them politely, though my mind was far from present. None of them commented on my strange clothing, so I figured it didn't look as off-putting as I'd worried it did.

"I could—"

"No, Captain," Ushuu laughed, obviously amused. I wasn't sure I liked being the butt of a joke, but I let it slide. These were extenuating circumstances. "Don't overthink it."

It was hard not to when I missed Huu-goh, and wanted nothing more than to nuzzle his orange fur and bask in his scent.

Normally I didn't like deviating from the plans I'd made, but standing in my ridiculous getup, after my talk with Ushuu, I felt off-kilter. When Huu-goh was close, things did not seem so dire.

*Would he like what I was wearing?*

I hoped he would.

"*Captain*," Ushuu stressed, catching my attention. His eyes were soft as he sighed. "I may be old, but I am still a capable warrior. Trust that I know what I'm doing."

I knew he was right, but that didn't mean I wasn't nervous.

"You'll take him to the hotel? You won't let him out of—"

"I won't let him out of my sight," Ushuu promised. "Please, Roark. Let me do this for you."

Anxiety flickered at my fingertips and I flexed my hands into fists to stave it off.

"How long?" I asked, gritting my teeth.

"It'll take half an hour to get him to the hotel, and he'll need at least an hour to get ready," Ushuu explained.

"And I'll—"

"And you will arrive to pick him up—" Ushuu stressed, "with *flowers*."

"With flowers." I agreed. I would have brought him a lot more than a single bouquet if it was up to me, but Ushuu had made it clear that flowers were a customary gift for a first date on Earth, and I wanted to do this by the book.

I only had one chance to woo him for the first time.

If all went well, this was the story we'd tell our children.

"Understood," I straightened my collar again, glancing at my dearest friend, before I steeled my nerves and turned away. When I was halfway down the hallway, Ushuu called out to me one last time.

"Captain?"

"Yes?" I twisted to look at him, annoyed but amused when I saw the shit-eating grin on his weathered face.

"Don't wrinkle your tux."

# SEVENTEEN

## HUGO

**NIGHTTIME ON PLANET SHA'HPIHN WAS** magical.

I hadn't been out after the suns had set before, and as Ushuu and I climbed the staircase that took us toward the stars my head stayed tipped toward them. I did my best to memorize the beauty all around me because I wasn't sure I'd ever see anything like it again.

Despite how busy he'd been, Roark had come back earlier that week with a new journal for me. A journal that I had used to sketch the city, expanding across the pages with every passing day.

This was the longest we'd stayed on a planet because it was the last stop before the trip home. Home. To a world I'd never seen, but loved already. Simply because it was the place that Roark came from.

Sha'hPihn was a sparkly blur of neon colors as we crested the top of the stairs. The same people that had populated the shops during the day had morphed into couples dressed in finery. The chitter of laughter rang like bells as shimmery fabric caught the lights above. We kept up with the procession of people moving toward the center of the city, lost in the crowd.

The hotel that held what Ushuu had described as a "ball" was massive. Located smack dab in the middle of the vast sprawl of buildings, it was easily the tallest that lined the sky. As we walked toward it, my hands grew sweaty.

*What if I don't fit in?*

*I've never been somewhere this nice before.*

*Maybe I should've picked a different outfit.*

My skin itched.

"When is Roark coming?" I asked Ushuu for the fourth time. He yipped in amusement, sticking close to my left, careful to walk between me and the bulk of the strangers. He was here to guide as well as guard me.

Sometimes Roark treated me like I was the goddamn president.

I'd never really been important before. It was a new feeling, and one I was still learning how to process. It was nice though. Really nice.

Overwhelming too—but, this wouldn't be the first time I came to terms with something overwhelming. It would, however, maybe be the first time that the overwhelming thing had turned out to be good.

"He's grabbing a few things, then he'll be here to collect you." Ushuu— to his credit—never acted annoyed with my repeated questions. Most of the time he looked *delighted* actually, kinda like I was an overgrown puppy and he thought I was adorable.

It was the way I'd expected Roark to look at me, but he never had.

Which reminded me of a burning question I was dying to ask him.

After all that had happened, I had come to the conclusion that I wasn't Roark's pet.

At first I'd thought so, but to be fair I'd had no frame of reference for the way he had treated me. In my experience dogs were the ones that were petted, given treats, and cherished. Children were for scolding and ignoring. And partners were for cheating and betraying. I hadn't fit into either of the last two categories, so I'd used scientific theory to eliminate them.

Only now the evidence pointed in a different direction entirely.

Hope was a scary, slippery thing. It wasn't something I'd allowed myself to feel often since the day I turned sixteen and realized just how little I mattered. But with every passing day I spent in Roark's company, it became easier and easier to forget why I'd lost it in the first place. Optimism had been the only reason I'd survived as long as I had alone, but behind my smiles, I'd still never let myself dream that I would ever be loved by someone else. That I would ever be valued or cared for or respected.

Until recently.

There was no denying that Roark didn't make me feel inconsequential.

Roark didn't make me feel *invisible*.

I wasn't replaceable, ignorable, or forgettable.

He saw me—he had, from the very first day we'd been together.

He respected me.

He trusted me.

Maybe I was naive and inexperienced when it came to real relationships—but I had eyes. And a heart. I could feel the way he reached for me, even when he wasn't physically at my side. Like his heart called to mine no matter how far apart we were. I could feel that things had evolved between us. Like we shared the same gravitational pull.

When Ushuu had broken the news that Roark planned to take me out on a date, I swear time stopped. The world spun. My axis tilted.

Everything I'd ever known was rewritten in that single, precious moment. Most people didn't take their pets on dates or shopping sprees, right? They didn't sleep wrapped around each other. They didn't shower together. Brush their teeth together. They didn't learn an entire new language just to communicate.

Maybe partners could be treated gently?

Maybe lovers could be cherished?

Maybe my parents had taught me wrong?

Because if Roark was taking me on a "date" it meant we were something special, didn't it? It wasn't confirmation that Roark felt as strongly for me as I felt for him, but it was close enough. Close enough, despite my best efforts, a new seed of hope was planted in my heart.

It was barely a bud, just pushing through the soil, but it was there.

And it grew with every day that had passed since then. It grew as our date approached, and I let myself imagine what forever would be like with the big pink alien by my side. There was so much I didn't know about him. So many things I'd been dying to learn. At first, the questions would've been mostly scientific.

Why his people were pastel, for one.

Why they were gelatinous—?

How it was possible they had tendrils at all.

Two cocks. For what purpose!?

But as time passed the questions changed.

They became softer, sweeter.

More personal.

More important.

*What scares you?*

*What excites you?*

*Where did you grow up?*

*Do you have a family?*

*Do you miss them?*

*What made you so frightened that day in the hallway?*

*Can I help?*

*Why are you nice to me?*

*Why did you save me?*

*Are you happy when I'm around? Because I'm happy when you are.*

*Do you want me forever?*

*Do you really think I'm pretty? No one else has ever called me pretty before.*

*What am I to you?*

*Is it safe to fall in love with you?*

Roark's actions had shown me what he thought of me, but I still desperately wanted to hear his answers to my questions.

And…I figured by the end of tonight I would.

Ushuu had told me earlier that Roark had rented translators for us to use during the event. A fact that was as intimidating as it was exciting. We'd gone so long without being able to fully communicate I worried things would change between us when we could.

It took me a second to remember what Ushuu had just said, I was so lost in my thoughts. He didn't seem to mind though, so I relaxed. I'd been too distracted to realize I'd fallen behind him as we'd been walking. Ushuu slowed, slipping back into place at my side.

As equals.

My head spun.

"It will be a good night." Ushuu bumped reassuringly against my shoulder as we neared the entrance to the hotel. *Shit. I'd spaced out the entire walk.*

"Don't look so worried."

*I hope he's right.*

"I have a lot of questions," I told him.

He nodded, his eyes as kind as ever. "He has answers."

*I hope they're the answers I want.*

What if we weren't compatible?

No. That was a silly thought. And one I pushed aside quickly.

Roark was Roark.

There was no need to worry when he was involved.

We stepped through the large glass doors that led into the hotel lobby with a *whoosh* of chilly AC. My ears started to roar. Overstimulated and overwhelmed, my senses went haywire as I took it all in.

The air tasted like perfume, thick and cloying. Aliens in slinky dresses flitted across the shiny floor. Silken suits and elbow-length party gloves decorated half the sparkly population. Everyone was mingling and interacting—and nothing was familiar. Nothing at all.

There seemed to be no rhyme or reason to who wore what, which settled some of my nerves as I clutched the bag full of my party clothes close. Male aliens dressed in chiffon skirts, and their female counterparts donned pants and jackets. Most clothing resembled what one might expect from a high-end party back on Earth, only without the restricting gender norms. It was odd to see aliens with six, seven, even twelve limbs wearing cocktail dresses and flirting with their shorter, more tentacle-laden companions.

This was basically…an alien version of prom.

My gaze caught on one guest in particular, heart racing. *Huh. He looked…he looked suspiciously human.* His short hair was pale white and slicked back. The dress he wore was too short to be considered a mini skirt and I had no idea how he managed to keep it in place. Long, muscular legs coated in glittering tights peeped from beneath the hem as he was escorted around the room by a massive, almost rhinoceros-looking alien. Said alien kept a possessive taloned grasp on human-looking-guy's lower back at all times.

He had a collar around his neck, just like the one I was wearing.

*He had to be human, right?*

*Or maybe…maybe not?*

From behind, it was impossible to tell for sure, and he disappeared before I could ask Ushuu to help me approach. I could've sworn that I'd seen a second set of ears on his head, as well as wings and a tail, though, so I must've been imagining things. He wasn't a human after all.

While I'd been busy ogling the guests, Ushuu had led us through the line to the reception desk. A friendly alien with dark red skin, six eyes, and artfully styled, long, faded hair greeted us with a chirp.

I couldn't understand what they were saying, so I remained quiet.

All six of the receptionist's yellow eyes were trained on my large companion as though I wasn't here at all. Their lips stretched into a broad grin as they dragged their gaze up and down Ushuu's frame. In response, Ushuu's spots turned fuschia and I had to muffle my laughter.

It didn't take a genius to realize the receptionist was flirting with him. His reactions, however, were adorable.

*He's embarrassed.*

While I'd spent a lot of time with shark-aliens lately, I hadn't seen anything like this before. Ushuu, while flattered, did not look interested in flirting back.

Did Ushuu have a mate waiting back home for him?

Were sharks a monogamous species?

The receptionist's eyes dragged over the older male's form a second time before their clicks turned business-like again. They asked Ushuu a few more questions, before passing him what looked like a gift baggie. *Did that have the translators inside it?* Ushuu immediately clutched it close to his chest protectively, tendrils tangling around the handles to keep it shut like it held something precious inside.

"Upstairs," Ushuu urged me with a serene little grin.

Halfway there, an alien with antlers bumped into Ushuu's shoulder, jostling the both of us. Distracted, I tried to get a better look at him, my head tilted upward. Alien grunted an apology and moved, but my eyes stayed trained on the ceiling as he passed.

Holy shit. *Damn.* I hadn't realized how big the hotel *really* was. The ceiling was impossibly high to accommodate the larger guests. Glittering chandeliers flickered at the apex of it, placed in even rows that spanned the top of the entire monstrous lobby. As my gaze drifted down again, recognition made me pause.

*Huh.*

Security cameras.

A shit-ton of security cameras.

Lining the walls halfway up, like they were trying to be sneaky but failed spectacularly. We'd had the same sort of technology in some of the rooms on F'ukYuu. They were far beyond the technology Earth possessed, almost capable of predicting the future so that problems could be eradicated before they even arose. A quick glance around the room confirmed that there were as many security guards as there were cameras.

*At least if something happens, they're prepared.*

*No wonder why Roark picked this place.*

I wasn't surprised. It was obvious based on how the others were dressed, and the large beefy aliens in suits that stood stoic against the walls, watching the party-goers, that this was no small event. This was a *fancy* party. Like the ones my dad's work used to host. I'd never been invited to those, but he'd bragged about them enough times it felt like I had.

How was I supposed to act here?

*I've never been to something like this.*

*I've never been on a date at all.*

Crossing my arms over my chest protectively, my bag clutched close, I felt more than a little naked. Ushuu frowned at me, but thankfully didn't ask what was wrong as we reached the massive golden elevators. They opened with a tinkling sound that reminded me of the wind chimes I'd hung on our porch back home. A group of drunk aliens stumbled out, leaving it empty.

As the door took its sweet time shutting behind us, I could feel eyes on the back of my neck.

*Shit.*

Apparently, I'd caught the attention of a few nosy guests. One of them sneered at me. Another licked his lips. I shivered, nails digging hard into my arms as I closed my eyes.

*Just ignore it, Hugo.*

*You're fine.*

*They weren't looking at you weird.*

*You're just nervous and you're projecting.*

*It's because of your time on F'ukYuu.*

The moment the doors slid shut, Ushuu exhaled raggedly and relaxed. He slung an arm around my shoulders and gave me a gentle squeeze. It was a nice gesture, and I sunk into it.

"Almost there, little one," Ushuu promised.

I nodded silently.

Truthfully, the hotel was incredible. I had never seen carpets more red, or wealth so opulent. But I was agitated, tiny, and dressed in "baby" clothes. I should've worn one of the outfits I'd bought this week, but I hadn't wanted to get it dirty walking through the city.

I'd miscalculated.

I wouldn't do that again.

Ushuu dug through the baggie he'd been gifted by the receptionist as soon as we reached our room. He pulled what looked like an average hotel keycard from the bag and tapped it against the interface beside the door handle. I was more than a little disappointed it hadn't been translators, like I'd hoped. The door opened with a *whoosh* and we stepped inside the room.

"Stay," Ushuu urged, before he stalked around the space, flipping on light switches and checking for threats. I almost wanted to roll my eyes, but I didn't. I knew Roark had put him up to this, and his protectiveness was sweet, even if it was unnecessary. When Ushuu decided our room was safe, he beckoned me forward.

The moment he did, I allowed myself to stare.

There was a massive bed in the center of the space—even larger than the one Roark and I shared on the ship. It was the first thing that caught my attention as I took in the large pink pillows that sat against the headboard, and the piles of puffy blankets that draped over the edges like icing on a cupcake.

The whole thing looked like a giant marshmallow.

*I want to bury myself in there and never come out.*

*I'll become a marshmallow person.*

*There's enough pillows to make an army.*

The bed wasn't the only magnificent part of the room. There was a huge red chaise lounger resting against what had to be the largest windows I'd ever seen. The view of the city beneath us was breathtaking, lights glimmering just like the stars above.

I was dizzy with amazement as Ushuu led me toward the bathroom where I would be getting ready. Once inside, I released the death hold I had on my bag of clothing, setting it gingerly on the counter. I tried to scrub the sweaty fingerprints off of it, but the action was futile.

"Do you need help figuring out how to turn the shower on?" Ushuu inquired. I shook my head, still dazed. "Okay," he eyed me, amused. "I'll be right outside. If you need me, yell."

"Will do," I said, needing space more than anything—not that I'd be rude enough to tell him that.

Ushuu gave me one last amused-slash-worried look before he left the bathroom—and me, alone. The second I could, I pushed the door shut after him. Locking it with a flick of my wrist, I laid my head against its cool surface and took a ragged breath.

*I want Roark,* the little voice in the back of my head whispered as I sunk to my knees and buried my face inside them.

*I want Roark.*

*I need Roark.*

*Roark, Roark, Roark.*

If he was here, this wouldn't be nearly so scary or overwhelming.

If he was here, maybe I'd be able to breathe.

I was *so* excited for our date, so *incredibly* excited. And that was the problem. The higher the high, the harder the crash. My excitement had turned into fear about the same time I'd stepped onto the elevator and realized how the other guests were looking at me.

I wasn't disillusioned.

I knew *what* I was.

I wasn't sure Roark realized though.

To his credit, Roark had never looked at me and made me feel the way I had on F'ukYuu. I wasn't even sure he knew just how fucked up I was, or how little value I could offer him.

On the ship, Roark and I lived in our own little bubble. It was easy to forget where I'd come from and what I'd been before he found me. But *here*? Here I was just the slave he'd bought. Abducted and discarded. Cheap entertainment.

No amount of opulent clothing could make up for the collar around my neck.

One look and everyone here could already tell what I was. A scared, lonely man with a fucked-up childhood. A virgin—not by choice—but because no one had ever wanted to touch him. A kid even parents couldn't love. And if they hadn't been able to love me, what did that say about me?

What if Roark *saw* all that?

He'd never call me pretty again.

I'd lose him.

It took a decent amount of effort to pull myself together, but I managed. I wasn't sure how long it took, only that by the time I'd showered and dressed in my clothing for the night, I was *exhausted*. Strung out. My hands shook as I attempted to comb my hair into place without looking in the mirror, afraid of what I might find there.

This was my first date.

I should be happy.

I shouldn't be panicking, or crying, or hyperventilating.

I splashed some more water on my face. *Get yourself together, Hugo. You only get one chance to do this right. Stop disappointing him, and yourself. If you want to prove yourself you're gonna need to do better than this.*

My eyes pinched shut. Water droplets dripped from my chin down the drain.

Roark wouldn't have taken me here if it wasn't safe.

It didn't matter how the people downstairs looked at me.

Not when I knew how *he* looked at me.

Just like I'd told myself earlier, Roark was Roark. He was as steady as he was stubborn. His opinion of me wouldn't change based on something as dumb as a crowd of strangers. In fact, I doubted he'd even notice them. He'd be too distracted being adorable and stern, making sure I was having fun, and that we both were safe.

Feeling settled again, I finished styling my hair.

My new clothes were tighter than anything I'd worn on Earth. They were classy though. Tasteful. Maybe a hair slutty, but nothing like I'd had when I worked the sex-pods. Exhaling raggedly, I tugged my garter belt into place beneath the silky fabric of the dress, then hiked the slit on my skirt up so the lace at the top of the thigh-high socks I was wearing was visible.

Ushuu had assured me that it wouldn't be odd for me to wear a dress. After seeing the eclectic mix of androgyny in the lobby, I knew he'd been correct.

I wouldn't stick out.

But that didn't mean I wasn't nervous.

I'd never worn anything like *this* before.

Ever.

Not that I hadn't wanted to—I'd just…yeah.

I'd been raised to be a "good" boy. To never toe the line. And I'd been careful to only stick out in the ways my parents wanted me to. Even though that meant ignoring the ache I felt every time I passed a pretty display in a window—or filling my cart with lace in an incognito tab, and never checking out.

If I was being totally honest, I'd always been more attracted to dresses than suits. I liked the way they swooshed through the air. Loved how soft the fabric looked. Loved the different cuts to the necklines, the sleeves, the skirts.

One time, right after I'd turned eighteen, I'd rode the bus to the mall and spent a whole day inside a lingerie store just staring. When an associate finally noticed me and asked me what I wanted, I hadn't been able to get a single word out. I'd just pointed at a pair of panties, and like the complete angel she was, she'd grabbed them for me and plopped them in a shopping basket.

I'd stood in line, shaking all the way to my toes, positive everyone was judging me—even though they weren't.

By the time it was my turn to pay, I chickened out.

I didn't buy the panties, but I sure thought about them. Thought about them every time I jerked off. Imagined what they would've felt like clinging to my dick. If they would've been as soft on my cock as they'd felt between my fingers.

I'd never gone back to that store again, afraid the employee would remember me.

It was a stupid fear, but my life was full of those.

I couldn't believe I was wearing a dress. An actual, real-life dress. And not a cheap one either—this was one thing I hadn't been frugal about. It was the dress I'd admired from the window. The one I'd wanted desperately. The price had made me gag, but I'd bought it anyway, because the moment I'd seen the mannequin—just my size—dressed in the silky white fabric, I'd fallen in love.

Fanning my hand along the glittery cloth, smooth to the touch despite its sparkle, I released the breath I'd been holding. It was *beautiful.* Absolutely beautiful. I hadn't dared look in the mirror as I'd been pulling it on—I'd felt foolish enough when it got stuck halfway over my shoulders and I'd had to contort to get out—I didn't need to *see* it too.

*I bet it looks awful.*

I swallowed the lump in my throat, afraid to look. I knew I was plain. I'd never been the kind of boy that got second glances. I'd filled out some since training with Roark, but there was no denying how scrawny I was.

I wasn't a stunner like my mother, or classically handsome like my dad. Never had shoulders to write home about. Never had abs, or sculpted biceps, or a big bouncy chest like Roark did. I didn't have the curves to fill out the dress either, no ass, hips, or breasts.

By all rights, I never should've bought the damn thing in the first place. But…

But I'd *wanted* to. And Roark had said to have fun. And I'd promised— but even more than that I'd wanted…

I'd *wanted*…

I'd wanted Roark to think I was…to think I was *pretty*.

I wanted to *feel* pretty.

I'd wanted it so badly I ached.

*You can do this, Hugo.*

*Like ripping off a Band-Aid.*

*If it looks bad you can take the damn thing off before anyone else sees.*

I'd brought a backup outfit, just in case. Though my heart ached anew at the thought of changing once again. It felt like failing a test I'd given myself.

*Look, Hugo.*

*It's just a silly reflection.*

*If you don't you'll never know.*

Sucking in a fortifying breath, I tilted my head up, and met my own reflection.

# EIGHTEEN

## HUGO

**I'D ALWAYS THOUGHT PRETTY WAS** a word reserved for girls, action stars, and botanical gardens. It was a delicate word. Soft. It smelled like fresh-cut fruit and springtime blossoms. If it had a sound, it'd ring like bells. Pretty was the shade of my mother's lipstick. Pretty was the color of Roark's lovely pink skin.

It wasn't for me.

Or at least…I hadn't thought it was.

I'd been wrong.

Because as my gaze flickered over my own reflection, *pretty* was the only word that came to mind.

The white glittery dress clung to my slender frame, highlighting the dip of my waist and clinging to my hip bones. It dipped at the collar, showing a hint of nipples, the skinny straps pulled taut so the fabric kept them

273

covered. When I twisted, I could see the pale skin of my ribs peeking out where the fabric dropped around the back. And for the first time in my life, I embraced my own appearance as I took a hesitant step back from the mirror and really stared.

My legs looked longer than usual.

My ass looked fuller.

The slit in the fabric exposed enough of my leg to tease, but not so much I felt cheap. The collar around my neck glinted in the light, and though I hated it, for a moment it was the only part of my body I recognized.

If I pushed aside what it had meant for so long, I could pretend it was only a necklace. I didn't mind the way it hugged my throat, or the way it brought attention to my collarbones.

I didn't look like a girl. I wasn't sure that was possible. But the femininity of the lovely fabric made me feel complete in a way I never had. Like I'd been a half-empty cup, and never realized it till I was full.

*Huh.*

A startled laugh burst out as I gripped the counter tight so I wouldn't lose my balance, and stared unabashedly. I wasn't sure I knew the man that gaped back at me from the mirror, but I *wanted* to. Exhausted but vibrant, he looked like the kind of guy who knew how to laugh.

"Wow," I murmured. "Not bad." I'd never minded the dark brown shade of my eyes or my cupid's bow the way I'd hated my nose and ears. But as I inspected my face for what felt like the first time in years, the features I'd often disparaged no longer felt quite so ugly.

They suited me.

Maybe I was a bit bird-like, fluffy and soft around the edges, with a too-round face, and too many freckles. But…I must not be too awful to look at, or Roark wouldn't have asked me on a date—or taken me home, for that matter.

It was strange.

So many things were nowadays.

A gentle knock sounded at the door. I spared one last glance to the low swooping neckline of my dress, and the way the fabric made my shoulders appear broader than they normally did before crossing the room toward it.

"Ushuu, I'm almost don—" I yanked the door open and suddenly every thought I'd ever had flew straight out of my head.

All I could think was—

*Roark.*

*Roark, Roark, Roark, Roark.*

*Roark—*

"Woah," I gasped, unable to stop staring at the giant pink shark-man in front of me. He looked as serious as ever, his blue eyes soft, his fangs pearly white. His big hands flexed at his sides, like he was just as startled as I was.

He inhaled sharply.

His gaze burned hot with desire as it trailed over my body.

I didn't even have the energy to be self-conscious.

*How could I be?* When Roark was standing in front of me, all nine feet of delicious, squishy pink stuffed into an honest-to-god *tuxedo.*

It clung to his muscles, highlighting how broad he was all over, making him somehow look both bigger and stronger than he did when he was shirtless. The sweet little bowtie at his thick throat was slightly loose, like he'd been tugging at it, but instead of detracting from his look, the messiness only seemed to add to his overall debonair appearance.

*He looks so sexy.*

"*Roark*," I croaked the same time Roark groaned like he'd been shot.

"*Huu-goh*," Roark's voice was throaty, and full of emotion as he slid down to his knees in front of me, unable to hold himself up. Even kneeling, he was massive, his large body towering over my own as he clenched his hands into tighter fists—the bag he was holding in one of them crinkling.

My heart raced as he leaned forward, our foreheads brushing together. Just that little contact was enough to have electricity zinging through my body. I whined and Roark responded with a soothing rumble that had me settling. His breath was minty sweet as it mingled with my own, making it obvious he'd just brushed his teeth.

*Was he as nervous as I'd been for this?*

It certainly seemed so. It was hard to imagine Roark nervous, he was so put together all the time. That little bit of vulnerability only made my silly crush on him grow. Crush was probably a bad word to describe my feelings for the big beast, but I wasn't sure I was ready to call them love just yet.

At least…until he said it first.

I wasn't sure my heart could take the rejection.

With a gentility a creature as large as he was should never have possessed, Roark reached into the gift bag he was carrying and pulled out a translator just my size. It was almost a carbon copy of the one I'd been able to use sparingly on the pleasure planet. GPS locked, the devices were useful on location only—to stop thieves from selling them on the black market. Realistically, I'd known we'd have them tonight, but that didn't make me any less excited.

My breath hitched, happiness buzzing beneath my skin as Roark delicately tucked it over my ear, his blue eyes warm with affection. He was deliberate with his movements as he turned the tiny device on, waiting for the machine to boot up. I waited anxiously to hear him for the first time since the night he'd called me pretty and decided to take me home.

I don't know why he'd done what he'd done—why he'd looked at a broken man and seen something worth saving, but I was grateful.

"Huu-goh." Roark sounded winded.

"I—"

"I don't have…" He shook his head, overcome with emotion. "I don't have the words." His tone was reverent as one large claw caught the strap that had slipped down my shoulder and tenderly slid it back into place. "You make my knees weak." The translator on his head blinked, signalling it was on. "You always have."

He was so awkwardly earnest that I had to believe him.

Roark's voice was familiar, though odd. I'd gotten so used to his garbled English and the rough grunts and growls of his native language that listening to him through the translator felt off. It was too put-together, and far too easy. *It's only for one night,* I reminded myself. *Enjoy it.*

*You make my knees weak.*

I'd never made anyone's *anything* weak before. I hadn't known I could.

The low rumble of Roark's voice echoed around inside my head as I stared at him. Stared at the tuxedo he had stretched across his massive supple pecs. Stared at the way it hugged his body in all the right places, the black fabric highlighting the striking vivid pink of his skin. Stared at this beautiful, wonderful, monster of a man—floored by his sweetness.

I'd never seen Roark wear anything but his pants and that fancy sash he'd sported when he'd first bought me. Seeing him in a tuxedo was making my heart—and my dick—perform acrobatics.

"T-Thank you," I managed, staring at him with new eyes as excitement buzzed under my skin. "You look—you look so—" I floundered. I wanted to get this right. I *needed* to. "You look so *handsome!*" I blurted, cheeks tingling bright red. It wasn't a sentence I'd ever uttered before, and it was hard to get out, though honest.

Roark made a happy grunt-y little noise, ducking his head, his spots turning fuchsia with embarrassment. "Thank you."

"No, really!" I waved my hands, clutching at his wrist as I tried to gather my wits about me. "You look…I mean. *Wow*. Helloooo, Shark Daddy. Seriously. Like. You should be on a magazine or something—or in movies— Hollywood has nothing on you." None of that had been very coherent. "I never—" I blinked, tried to speak again—and failed. "I've never flirted before—sorry if this is…you know, as painful for you as it is for me."

"I am not in pain," Roark reassured, voice soft. He looked as nervous as I felt. "Well, maybe a bit."

"Yeah?" I chuckled.

"I am not good at flirting."

There were butterflies in my belly. "I think you're doing well."

"I am trying," Roark's nostrils flared as his eyes shut for a moment like he was gathering strength. "I am not…good with words."

"Coulda fooled me."

"I am trying," he repeated, his eyes opening, the vivid blue as striking as ever. "For you, I will do anything. Even *flirt*." He said that like flirting was the worst thing I could've ever asked him to do. Which was…so cute. Jesus.

"You don't normally have an issue when you're being all captain-y," I said, curious.

"That is different. They are my subordinates. You are…*you*. I can't get this wrong. I only have one chance."

I couldn't believe we'd had that exact same thought.

I grinned, unable to help myself. "Your middle name is effort, isn't it?"

"What do you mean?" Roark frowned, and I snickered, though I was too distracted by how good he looked to answer the question.

I gestured at his outfit. "You're in a *tux*." Maybe Roark needed reassurance too?

"I am." Confusion forgotten, Roark was obviously amused. I didn't mind. Behind him the room was empty, Ushuu was long gone. I was glad, even though that might make me an ass. Because having one person witness my total brain melt was enough humiliation for one day, thank you very much.

"I love it!" I choked out. "I don't—I mean." I paused to get my thoughts in order. "You're definitely getting this right. I think you might have broken my brain."

"Impossible. Your brain is too brilliant for that." Roark barked out a laugh, stroking a single claw down my arm with a shake of his head. "The feeling is mutual," he added. "My thoughts are far from coherent." His big-hot-delicious hand latched onto my hip, fingers tickling against the silky fabric as he gazed at me. Roark's eyes flashed black for a moment at the same time his spots grew molten red. There was no doubt in my mind that he liked what he saw.

"A *dress*, Hugo?" Roark murmured, stricken. "That is not *fair*. How am I supposed to let you leave the room without touching you?"

Grinning, I stood taller, my nerves all but forgotten. I never should've worried that things would be awkward between us. They weren't. I reached up to shift the translator he'd put over my ear more comfortably into place. It hadn't occurred to me until now how absolutely *emotional* being able to speak to Roark freely would make me feel. If I didn't get ahold of myself I was going to start blubbering. And while I knew Roark wouldn't judge me, ugly-crying was not hot.

*Pretty one, do not cry.*

*I will make it okay.*

*You make my knees weak.*

*You always have.*

Since we'd met I'd collected each of Roark's sweet words inside my heart. Keeping them close at hand for the days when I felt weak.

My eyes were wet as I fanned my fingers over the back of Roark's hand, still trying not to cry. "You're looking pretty hot yourself, big guy," I managed, voice rough. "I can't believe you found a tux in your size!" Sure, a lot of aliens in the lobby had worn similar clothing. But none of them had been close to Roark's size.

Roark grunted, spots flushed pale pink with pleasure. "Finding one that fit was no easy feat. Ushuu helped. I can't take credit." His voice was still warm, but stiff.

*Did talking to me make him nervous?*

*Is that why he'd been so quiet the day we'd met?*

That was…flattering to say the least.

Roark chose each word carefully and slowly, like if he didn't pick the perfect ones he'd rather not speak at all.

"You are correct, it *is* hotter than I am used to," Roark added, jolting me from my thoughts. He frowned down at his clothing like it had personally offended him, plucking at the mussed collar where it hugged his thick throat.

Hotter than he—

*Oh.*

I snorted, shocked by the sound as I slapped a hand over my mouth. Apparently translators didn't understand slang.

"I can imagine! I mean…you never wear clothing up top—I assume because your skin needs access to the air to be able to function properly. Two layers must feel like a lot." I chewed my lip, buzzing with excitement as the threat of tears faded.

*Get back on track, Hugo.*

"*Seriously,* though."

The look Roark gave me made me tingle, like he thought I was clever—and like he was…god, like he was *pleased* that I understood him. Once again, he was seeing me—in a way that no one else ever had.

"The word 'hot' on Earth can sometimes be used as slang for 'attractive'," I tried to explain.

"Ah," Roark's nodded.

Breathless and flushed, I croaked, "When I said that what I meant was that you're sexy. *Really* sexy." *Stop acting so weird! This is just Roark.*

"I see," Roark's voice was gravelly soft.

His eyes bled from blue to hungry black.

I shivered.

The glance we shared was multi-layered. Hot as a dry summer day, with *longing* simmering underneath the heat. Roark's nostrils flared. He shook his head, the black arousal that had swum over his eyes fading back to pale blue.

Centering himself, like a switch had flipped—my beast became a gentleman once again.

"I have something for you," Roark managed. He reached inside the bag he carried for the second time that night. *What else had he brought?* He'd given me more gifts in the last week than I'd had in my entire life.

My eyes widened when he pulled the object free.

It was a bouquet. A lovely collection of colorful foreign flowers. They were strange-looking, and I was pretty sure they had teeth—but...I *loved* them for their oddity. They were perfect. Interesting in a way red roses never could be.

No one had ever given me flowers before.

"T-Thank you," I took the bundle gingerly in my arms, startled when one of the blossoms snapped at me. It narrowly missed taking a chunk out of my bare shoulder. Before I could react, Roark snatched the bouquet right out of my hands. His eyes were wide with alarm as he looked down at the flowers like they'd personally betrayed him.

Which, I mean, I guess they had.

"They are carnivorous," he choked out, horrified—like he hadn't realized. "Apologies, little one." And then he quite literally chucked the entire bouquet across the room—as far away from me as possible.

I doubled over, snort-laughing. *God, he was cute.*

"I can't believe you just *threw* them like that," I blurted out between giggles.

Roark stared at me, spots a vibrant fuchsia. "I am so sorry—"

"Roark," I cupped his face in my palms, amazed by the way he immediately settled. "I love them."

"They tried to *bite* you."

"They did," I agreed, his giant teeth only centimeters from my face.

"But I love them, still." I gave his head a little shake, smooching his snout with a happy hum.

"Oh," Roark's spots lightened to pink again as his eyes fluttered shut. He made a soft sound like a content cat. "Next time I will do better."

"Why didn't they bite you?" I asked, curious as ever.

Roark blinked. "My coloring," his spots shifted a variety of colors so fast I couldn't keep track. "They must think I'm poisonous. It didn't occur to me until now."

That made sense.

I loved learning new brilliant little things about his species.

"Are you?" I asked.

"W-what?"

"Are you poisonous?"

Roark huffed in offense. "No."

"Good to know." Feeling more confident than I ever had before, I peeked at him through my lashes, dragging my gaze down his heaving pecs to his thick belly, and the lump of his cocks where they nestled between meaty thighs. "Because I really like tasting you."

Roark sputtered like I'd just electrocuted him. Taking pity on him, I returned my attention to his face just in time to catch the red tinge to the spots on his forehead.

"Can I see the flowers again?" I asked, holding his face gingerly in my palms. Roark wavered. He was obviously worried they would try to bite me again. Meanwhile, realistically, I wasn't sure they'd even be alive after the way he'd brutally smashed them into the wall. "Please?"

With a sigh, Roark gave in.

He was careful as he extricated himself from my grip, and rose to his full height. Twisting, he made his way toward the discarded bouquet.

*Damn.* That ass though.

Seriously, he deserved an award.

It flexed, bouncy and full as Roark crossed the room, the tight black pants he wore clinging to every curve and crevice. I bit back a groan when he bent over. Roark was careful as ever, as he gathered up the abused flowers.

It still amazed me how a creature so very large could be so gentle.

When Roark returned to my side, he looked more settled than when he'd left. Like the fact I'd given him a mission to complete had settled him. The flowers were a little worse for wear, but not entirely ruined like I'd worried.

I held my hands out expectantly.

"Huu-goh…" Roark fretted. He obviously did not want me anywhere near the bouquet. But we'd built a lot of trust between us—and I knew, if I gave him a moment to settle, he'd realize that I was more than capable of handling this particular threat myself.

Besides, I was curious.

And he liked that about me.

"*Please,*" I repeated, waiting patiently. "I'll be careful."

It took a few seconds of deliberation, Roark's brow bone furrowed, but eventually he relented. His blue eyes remained narrowed as he *very* carefully handed me the bundle of flowers.

He truly couldn't have given me a better first bouquet.

The blossoms were even lovelier up close. Closer to small, petaled creatures than they were to the plants we had back home. Excited, I examined their tiny, toothy faces, making sure to hold them far away from my body so when they snapped they couldn't reach.

I was so glad he'd given me these—teeth be damned.

We were on an alien planet, in *space* after all, and my date was the toothiest, largest creature I had ever encountered.

It would've been a shame to receive flowers that were anything but extraordinary—and despite the fact they were a little dangerous, and a whole lot weird—that's exactly what this bouquet was.

*Extraordinary.*

Just like the person who'd given it to me.

Roark hovered over me, ready to snatch the flowers away the second it looked like I was in danger. But I never let their teeth get close enough to my body for him to truly worry. Partly because I didn't want to get chomped—but mostly because while they'd been hardy enough to survive the first toss, I wasn't sure they'd survive a second.

"You like them," Roark observed.

He sounded unsurprised. He was used to my curious bullshit by now. A fact that made me feel warm all over.

"I do," I grinned down at the little creatures with wonder. "They're so tiny but so resilient."

"Tiny, resilient things are my favorite," Roark flirted stiffly, clearing his throat afterward like he was still shy. I got the feeling he wasn't talking about the flowers. My cheeks warmed, and I ached to reach out to soothe his nerves.

I retreated into the bathroom for a moment, gently laying the bouquet on the counter for later. When I returned to Roark's side, I held a hand out for him. Roark latched on to it, pulling me against his sturdy chest. A purr started up, the buzzing sensation lulling me into a sense of calm as I buried my face between his pillowy pecs, all my earlier unease forgotten.

Roark was a man of action. And though his communication was somehow even more awkward than my own, I never once doubted his intentions. I could *feel* how earnest he was with every beat of his hearts against my own. Two hearts. Because one wouldn't be big enough for a person as kind as he was.

It was weird being able to talk to him.

Super weird.

But in a nice way.

A *very* nice way.

The weight over my ear from the translator was a reminder that this wouldn't last.

*I need to make every moment count.*

"No one's ever given me flowers before," I blurted against his chest, safe enough there I felt I could admit this. Roark grunted in question. "Back on Earth I was kind of a loser," I admitted, ripping off the Band-Aid early. It was surprisingly easy to get the words out with my face hidden against him. He smelled good. His body was solid against my cheek as I wrapped my arms around his waist and he nuzzled my hair.

"No matter how hard I tried I was…invisible. The only thing I had going for me was the fact that I was the 'brainy' kid, but even that ended up meaning nothing in the end."

"I…" Roark's hearts were beating so incredibly fast as he gathered his words, "don't understand." Roark scoffed, like the idea of me being ignored was ridiculous.

I laughed, because he was sweet—and predictable, and I wasn't surprised he thought so highly of me—not after the way he'd treated me.

"How could someone as vibrant as you ever be invisible?" Roark reiterated.

My eyes burned and I squeezed them shut. "I've always been easily forgotten," I admitted. "That's why it's so…weird that you…"

"That I what?"

"That you *see* me…the way you do. I've spent so long being inconsequential I thought that was my lot in life. But then you came along. And you took me in—and you treated me with such kindness. Which is why I don't know what to do with this—with…*you.*" My heart was pounding. "I mean—this *is* a date, isn't it? Ushuu said it was."

"Yes," Roark confirmed. "I am courting you." He sounded proud of that fact, and wasn't that a mind-fuck of its own. Roark. Being proud to be with *me.*

"Courting me?"

"Yes." Roark murmured—and no words had ever settled my heart faster.

"Why?"

"Because you are mine."

"Yours?"

"Yes." Roark cleared his throat. "From the moment I saw you in that window, you have been mine." His hearts thumped erratically. "Don't you…feel it too? I thought…"

"You thought?" I swallowed the lump in my throat, off-kilter as I decided how I felt about that particular statement.

"I thought you wanted this." Roark sounded so lost for a moment it felt like I was breaking.

"Of course I do," I replied immediately, now fully aware of what I was agreeing to. "Of course I want you."

Roark relaxed with a gusty sigh, melting over me like he'd been terrified I was about to reject him. When he began purring again, I squeezed my eyes shut, inhaling his heavenly scent. Masculine and sweet all at once. Kinda pineapple-y today like his cum.

He was steady, solid, and delicious.

And I'd been right about him.

Right about what we'd become—even if I'd gotten it wrong at first.

Did that mean that the leash had been to…to protect me? Not because he saw me as property, but because I was precious, and he wanted to keep me safe? I belonged with Roark in a way I'd never belonged anywhere else—because that thought made me feel warm.

"Does that mean you're going to keep me when we get to your planet?" My words were muffled, but no less important. "Because I don't—" my voice broke. "I don't want to be without you."

It was something I'd fretted about since the day he'd bought me. I was property, whether I liked to believe it or not. The fact I'd been bought meant I could be sold just as easily.

Roark rumbled softly to soothe me. There was no room for misinterpretation, as his next words echoed in the space between us, a balm over my tattered heart. "If I had my way, Huu-goh, you would never leave my side."

My eyes burned and I shuddered, melting when his hand rubbed steady circles against the center of my back.

"You would never be lonely," Roark added softly. "You would never know hunger, or pain, or fear." *Rub, rub, rub,* I shook beneath his palm. "I'd replace your bitter memories with new happy ones. You would forget how it feels to be unseen. You would have so many choices and opportunities you would lose track of them all. Every day I would be honored that you chose to stay at my side."

My heart felt cracked open.

This was like my sixteenth birthday all over again, except instead of leaving me to gather my brittle pieces alone, Roark was right beside me, picking them up and putting them together. Until I was a newer, better version of what I'd been before. Roark made it clear I would never have to beg for his attention. In fact, the way he spoke made it seem as though he was the one begging for mine.

*God, if you're out there, let me keep him and I'll never ask for anything again.*

"What's wrong, little beast?" Roark murmured, his purr vibrating my cheek.

I hadn't said anything, so I could see why he was concerned. My silence probably made him worry he'd said the wrong thing. Which couldn't be further from the truth. I just didn't know how to process such a frankly beautiful declaration.

Roark was waiting for me to speak, so I said the first thing that popped into my head, because admitting that I'd been praying to keep Roark was too embarrassing.

"I don't know how to dance." I blurted out. And because I was the worst—I just kept going. "I didn't go to prom," I tried to explain.

He made a confused sound.

"It's like…a formal ball, like this one. Except for older teens, and hosted at schools. You get together and it's meant to be this big fancy thing that everyone talks about for the rest of all time." I moved, chin digging into his chest as I looked up at him. I figured that the translator didn't have the word "prom" in its dictionary just like it hadn't had the second definition for "hot", so I continued to explain.

"Boys usually ask the girls—but I was…I mean—I've always been—I just—" *Spit it out, Hugo*, I chided myself. "I've never *liked* girls like that, so I never asked anybody. Even if I had, I honestly don't think they would've said yes." I chewed on my lip. "Plus, I was way too chicken to ask a boy. No fucking way. Uh-uh."

*Get to the point.*

*You're rambling.*

"So my formal dancing experience is in the negatives. And I…don't really know how to act at like…fancy events. We did some parties back on F'ukYuu. I worked them, I mean. But shaking my ass and spinning half-naked on a pole is a way different skill set than what I'm assuming is required of me tonight. And I'm pretty sure you would be shocked if I started twerking out there. And I really, really don't want to disappoint you. Tonight is important."

Roark was silent, obviously trying to process my words—but I still kept going, unable to stop now that I'd started. "I know this is supposed to be super fun and you put so much *work* into it—and we just had an awesome moment!—but I have to admit that I am seriously terrified you're going to realize I'm a loser the second we get out there—because I am—obviously—and I don't know what I'm doing—and I'm just—I'm just trying to manage your expectations."

Wow. Word vomit.

A *lot* of word vomit.

I guess after months of not being able to talk to him—it all just… wanted to come out.

"Huu-goh," Roark murmured, chest rumbling as he stroked a hand down my back. "Slow down."

I sucked in a breath, held it, and released it—nodding. "Yeah, yeah."

I pulled him tighter, continuing to stare up at him though my heart was pounding. "You're right. I should probably let you talk, huh?"

"You are not a 'loser' because you don't know how to dance," Roark's voice was as soothing and solemn as ever. It was so different hearing him like this—fully coherent. He still had a bit of an accent but it was easy enough to tell what he was saying. The translators did a bang-up job, honestly.

"Oh, I know *how* to dance—" I corrected him with a leer. "But only the slutty kind."

Roark snorted in amusement. "A skill that I am sure was necessary for your survival."

"Yeah," I nodded, weirdly touched that he understood that. "It was."

"I remember your dances," Roark rumbled. "*Fondly.*"

My belly flipped.

I seriously had not expected Roark to ever say that. In fact, I'd been under the impression that he'd been kind of offended by my performance. Only…I thought back on it—trying to remember what color his spots had been. Sure, they'd been changing a lot…but I was pretty sure in hindsight I remembered red in there somewhere.

Damn.

Before I could recover from *that*—excuse you Mr. "I am not good at flirting"—Roark gently pulled me from his body, far enough that we could speak better—*wow*. Wow. Roark in a tux was breathtaking. Eye-candy galore. I'd never get over it.

"I have been coming to this planet for over twenty years," Roark explained, "and I have never attended any of these events."

I nodded.

"I was a quiet child. I kept to my studies, always watching over the others at the orphanage rather than indulge in entertainment. There was no time for parties or games when The Great Calamity hit. After we discovered the cure to the illness that had plagued our people, I was even less inclined to play. I joined the military the second I was of age," Roark continued, keeping his voice soft. "What little I know of 'dances' and 'dancing' comes from the handful of mating ceremonies I've attended over the years, and the videos I watched on my HoverPad in preparation for taking you out tonight."

Oh. *Oh.* "So you're saying that you don't know how to fancy dance either?" *I probably shouldn't be giddy about this.* But this was the most information I'd ever learned about him, and I tucked every new tidbit away protectively inside my heart.

"No," Roark said seriously. "I don't." He let that sink in for a second before continuing. "If not knowing how to 'fancy' dance is what makes one a loser, I hope it soothes you to learn we are on equal standing."

"So we'll…"

"Fail together?" He arched his brow bone and I grinned, my belly full of butterflies.

"Fail together," I echoed, no longer feeling quite so unsettled. "I guess that's not so bad."

"No, little one, it's not." Roark huffed out a breath that ruffled my hair, looking so impossibly handsome it made my head spin. "There are far worse things in life than earnestly attempting something and looking silly." He stroked a finger over my cheek, making me shiver all over again.

"How has no one snatched you up?" I asked, unable to help myself. I immediately regretted the question, not sure it was appropriate—but Roark laughed in response, so I figured it was fine.

"I would not allow it, even if they'd tried," he purred again, leaning down so his long slithery tongue could snake out and tickle the place his finger had just traced. "I have no interest in anyone but you. Besides, I prefer to be the one that does the snatching." And then he did just that—yanking me into his arms like I weighed nothing at all. I shivered—trying to hide how aroused I was by his easy manhandling as we headed out the door to our room, down the hallway, and into the same gold elevator I'd rode up.

I didn't think about the unfriendly eyes.

I didn't think about my insecurities, or my past.

I didn't think about the human-like man I'd seen in the lobby.

Or the world I'd left behind.

And now that Roark had made his intentions clear, the labels I'd given myself disappeared. I wasn't a slave. I wasn't a pet. Wasn't a loser.

I was just a dude on my first date, with someone who made my heart race.

And we were just two people who couldn't dance, but wanted to spend the night in each other's arms anyway.

# NINETEEN

## ROARK

**WHEN I WAS A CHILD** I often gazed at the stars. My father and I would sit on our front lawn together, feet angled toward the house, our heads tipped back. Starlight would dance across his pink surface, the same shade as my own, and his stories would fill my mind with fantasies of the future.

I asked him so many questions, I'm sure he lost count. Long before he'd succumbed to the plague, he'd been a dreamer, like I was.

*How could the stars be so large, but look so small?*

*Where do they come from?*

"What do they taste like, do you think?" I once asked. Barely six years old but already able to fully articulate my questions and feelings. Father read to me often. He shared his thoughts and aspirations. He answered my questions whenever he knew the answer. And his tutelage was part of why I'd grown so rapidly and so seriously. People often said I was his spitting image. A fact that had always filled me with pride.

"Stars taste like freedom," Father answered. He'd been to space once. Once was enough.

*Freedom.*

He'd died not many years later. The doctor had tried to keep me at his bedside, but the lack of color in his surface made it obvious what had happened. So I'd run outside, the grass tickling my feet, instead. Staring at his corpse wouldn't bring him back.

I looked at the constellations above, the inky night spread high and wide. And as I mourned, I wondered if he was right. So much had changed in such a small amount of time, and yet the stars remained the same as they'd always been. Father's stories and dreams preserved in the sky he'd left behind and the son he'd left behind with it.

After I was moved to the orphanage, most days I spent my time corralling and protecting my adoptive siblings. I cleaned their messes, trailing behind them and sweeping up their chaos with a broom and dustpan. I was the Sahrk that kept them in line. I was the Sahrk that kept them safe. And when the plague struck, again, and our shared bedroom filled with sickly children—I was the one who was ready at hand for the healer and caretaker, to help wherever I could.

I couldn't stand idly by. Not when those younger and smaller than me were at stake. I went hungry some days, so that those who needed extra provisions had them. And when the great storm cleared, and The Calamity lifted—the cure administered to all that occupied our planet—that drive to see those weaker than me safe, stayed.

I never forgot my father's words, or the promise of the stars.

I never forgot who I was.

"I have never met a teenager more allergic to fun," our caretaker would laugh, years later, when I'd sit on the grass, observing my siblings rather than joining them. When the sky bled violet and the moons peeked out, I ignored the other children's chatter and counted down the days till I was old enough I could taste the stars myself.

I'd been captain for fifteen years now.

I'd been chasing the stars for far longer than that.

And yet—it wasn't until *this* moment that I got a taste of what my father had promised. Huu-goh's lips trembled against my own as I cradled him close.

He was warm.

His heat pressed tight against my body as we swung together to the lilting glide of the music in the air. The live orchestra at the ball was talented, but even their flawless performance didn't hold a candle to the beauty of the small huu-man cradled in my arms.

He didn't seem to mind the fact his feet didn't touch the floor. He didn't mind that I didn't know how to mimic the other dancers surrounding us. He didn't mind the way I cradled him close, tucked in the crook of my arm, his head on my chest.

Huu-goh's lovely dark gaze hadn't left mine once. Not when we'd left the elevator, not when we'd entered the ballroom, and not when we'd joined the group on the dance floor.

His eyes were mine and mine alone.

His lips tasted like freedom, slick from the trail of my tongue. I wished I had lips like he did. Soft, cushiony things I could kiss and nuzzle him with. Unfortunately, my tongue would have to do.

We were horrible at dancing, that much was true. But neither of us cared, or truly even noticed, despite Huu-goh's earlier fears.

"What's this?" Huu-goh asked as his fingers played with the pocket on my suit jacket. It took me a moment to blink away the daze I'd found myself in.

*Oh.*

*I hadn't meant for him to see that yet.*

I recognized the paper he'd found with fuschia-spotted embarrassment.

"Ah." My throat clogged up like it had earlier, the words getting stuck as I shifted his body so it was supported by my right arm alone. Tendrils erupted from my wrist, winding around him to ensure he remained snuggly in place as my attention divided between dancing and the paper in his hand.

I pulled the note from his grip to flip it open.

Huu-goh examined it with sparkling curiosity.

*What had I expected?*

*It was like he could sniff out all my secrets.*

I should've known my clever mate would find my list.

"It's a…" I'd spent an entire week writing the contents of this paper. I'd poured my heart and soul into it. I was *embarrassed*. Far more embarrassed of the list than I was of my lack of rhythm.

My hand trembled a little as I smoothed out its edges, buying myself time. Huu-goh's tiny hand helped me with the worst of the creases. "It's a list," I admitted—painfully awkward.

*Calm yourself, Roark.*

*This is what you wanted.*

*There is no need to fear.*

"A list?" Huu-goh tilted his head inquisitively to the side. I didn't think

I'd ever tire of that particular tone of his voice, especially now that I could understand his questions. I only wished we could take the translators with us and that they'd work on the ship. That I wouldn't have to wait until we reached home to speak freely again.

"It's a list I prepared of all the questions I'd like to ask you," I clarified.

Huu-goh's eyes searched mine, full of something close enough to worship it made my throat close up. "Really?"

*Why was he so surprised?*

"I want to *know* you." It took me a while to find the right words, but when I did, peace settled over me.

"Oh." Huu-goh blinked, taking a moment to process this before he traced the first line on the list with his lovely peach-colored fingers. "What's the first one say?"

He couldn't read Common, so I'd be forced to ask him rather than let him read for himself. It was a blessing and a curse. It forced me out of my comfort zone, to speak when normally I'd stay silent. But it also meant getting to talk to Huu-goh with a list to aid me, and apparently I needed all the help I could get now that I was a nervous, happy wreck.

I took a steadying breath. I hadn't expected to get into this so soon, and not while we were still dancing, but I figured if Huu-goh wanted to start now—who was I to stop him?

"When is your birthday?" I asked, voice gruff.

"April twenty-third," he answered quickly. "I don't know when that actually is, relative to what time it is now. Not anymore." His last comment wasn't sad, or even resigned. He was stating a fact, totally detached from the way it should've made him feel to lose something so important.

"Would you like a new birthday?" I asked, curious.

Huu-goh blinked, his big brown eyes swimming with an emotion I couldn't name. His eyes squeezed shut and he nodded, a single tear slipping down his cheek.

"We'll pick one together when we get back to the ship," I murmured, a tendril slipping from my collar to swipe away the sticky, salty streak. I couldn't believe how odd I'd found his tears at first. And now…*now* I had never seen anything more beautiful than Huu-goh's vulnerability.

"How old are you?" I asked next. This was a lot. I didn't want to overwhelm him.

"Twenty-one."

I barked in amusement. "You are a *baby*," I teased.

"Oh, fuck you," Huu-goh chuckled, then slapped a hand over his mouth like he hadn't meant to say that. He'd been doing that a lot today.

"Later," I promised, unable to help myself, tendrils urging his hand away from his mouth.

"How old are *you*?" Huu-goh asked, his eyes narrowing, cheeks ruddy red.

"Forty-two," I answered. "I do not know what that translates to in huu-man years, but on my planet I am within my prime."

"Oh," Huu-goh bit his lip. "I'm an adult too," he blurted. "In case you literally meant you thought I was a baby. Dunno about being in my 'prime' or whatever, but…" I hadn't worried, but I appreciated the reassurance all the same. It was common knowledge that A&R only abducted adults, so I'd never had cause to fear.

"How long did you work on F'ukYuu?" I asked, working my way down the list.

"Three years as far as I can tell."

"Did you like it?"

This question took Huu-goh a lot longer to answer. His expression was pensive as he twisted his fingers in my suit, chewing on his bottom lip. "I liked…some of it."

"What parts?" That was an easy one, hopefully.

"I liked…" Huu-goh batted his lashes, peeking shyly up at me, his lovely lip still caught between his blunt pearly teeth. "Meeting new people. Seeing different species. Learning new things—" He blinked, flushing a dark luscious pink. "I liked that people *wanted* to look at me. That I was…" he swallowed.

"Desired?"

"Yeah," Huu-goh admitted. He appeared ashamed, and while every emotion looked lovely on him, I hated seeing him feel so unsure. After what he'd told me earlier, this did not surprise me. Nodding, I made a vow to never allow him to feel ignored or unimportant again.

"You deserve to be desired," I told him.

"Thank you." Huu-goh's smile was tentative and shy. "Roark?"

"Yes?"

"That one night…you…" His brow furrowed like he was too embarrassed to ask. "You came back with red spots one time." It seemed my little love had some questions of his own. He didn't need a list to recall them, however—he was far cleverer than I was.

I frowned, confused.

Red spots? What was he talking about?

"Why were you…" Huu-goh looked miserable and scared. "I mean…I know what they mean. And you came back like that. But you were with Ushuu—so I just…"

"When was this?"

"Right after we had lunch with Ushuu?"

I racked my brain, trying to remember what he was talking about. When I did, I couldn't stop a laugh from escaping. "You…" I shook my head. "You were so cute, Huu-goh. Pillow creases on your cheeks. Grumpy." My words were stilted and shy, throat hoarse. "I wanted to fuck you the moment I opened the door."

"Oh." I had never seen him more pleased. "Ha! Okay. I mean. Cool. Cool, cool, cool." He only paused for a moment before he added, "I have more questions."

"I have answers."

He chewed on his lip again, quiet for a few beats as music flooded the air and he very obviously mulled over what to say next. His nose scrunched like he was thinking hard. I loved the way his speckles danced when he did that, like stars on his skin. "Why were you there?" Huu-goh blinked.

*What did he mean?*

I grunted in question.

"At the club," Huu-goh clarified. "You don't seem like the kinda guy who goes to pleasure houses. No offense. Not that you couldn't go, or *shouldn't*—or anything. But you just…yeah. I'm gonna shut up now."

I shook my head, offering him a soft smile that I hoped would convey that I was not offended.

*I do not want to get this wrong.*

I picked my next words carefully before I spoke.

*I will not lie or frighten him.*

There was a fine line between acting protective and treating him like a child. Huu-goh had seen more than I probably would in my entire lifetime. He didn't let the fear of what had happened to him taint his future or the way he looked at the world. He had been through more than I would ever be able to fully comprehend. He had adapted and thrived where most fell and withered. He was not weak or naive, by any stretch.

But he *was* precious.

The most precious thing in my life.

And he could handle the weight of fear that I carried easily.

"There have been an increase in pirate attacks lately. Not on my ship, but others." Just talking about it was enough to cause me to stiffen. "Traveling during this time is stressful. We had been in space for many moons before we reached your planet. The men needed something to distract themselves with so I accompanied them to your place of business out of worry for their safety." For a moment I almost left it at that. But… then I realized what that implied about our species, and I quickly added on. "Sahrk culture is not…" I frowned, trying to find the right words to explain. "We are not as *frivolous* with our physical affection as some other species. Sex is for mates, but *looking* is allowed."

"Sahrk," Huu-goh echoed, rolling the name of my species over his tongue. He shook his head, then blinked, clearing his vision. "So, a strip club is kinda…the best thing ever for you guys then? And you were there because you wanted to protect the others?"

I wasn't so sure about the first thing he'd said, but I nodded, because it seemed he understood.

"What about you?"

My brow furrowed. I made a questioning noise and he clarified. "You just explained why you accompanied them, but not why you went inside." Huu-goh's eyes filled with mischief. "Do *you* like to look, Roark?"

His cheeks were still flushed and the color was so pretty I wanted to taste it.

So I did.

Huu-goh giggled, his nose scrunching up delightfully all over again as my tongue slipped back inside my mouth, freedom dancing across my tastebuds. I loved that face. I loved all his faces, but that one was my favorite.

"I don't," I admitted honestly. He stiffened a little and I was quick to soothe. "Or at least. I hadn't. Not until…I saw you."

"Oh." Huu-goh's cheeks pinked again. "In the window?"

I had mentioned that, hadn't I?

It'd been a slip of the tongue, but one I was glad for now.

Huu-goh cleared his throat, obviously embarrassed but pleased. He poked my list and I nodded, looking at the next item, prepared to read it off. "And…what about…the other part?" His voice got endearingly squeaky. "The sex thing. The touching. You said Sahrks only touch their mates."

"That is correct," I agreed.

"So is that what I am then?" Huu-goh asked, voice soft. "Your…mate?"

I'd had no doubt of my own intentions since the day Huu-goh had expressed his interest in mating with me.

"Yes. I am committed to you," I needed him to know that. "I said no when we met because I did not know you. Mating is…personal. It is not something I had interest in before I met you. Sahrks mate for life."

"Oh," Huu-goh's voice trembled.

"You proposed and I was shocked," I admitted. The huu-man's eyes widened, like it was only now that he was realizing the way his actions had been interpreted.

"Oh shit," Huu-goh gasped out.

"I didn't know if you'd meant what you'd done," I added—now certain that he hadn't. Did that mean…did that mean he hadn't later either? That day when he'd gotten angry with me? The day that had changed my life irrevocably for the better?

The spots on my head must've betrayed my panic, because Huu-goh was quick to soothe. Intelligent enough he'd already figured out most colors.

"Roark," he said softly, cupping my cheek. "I would propose again in a heartbeat, this time knowingly."

Melting, I nodded, bumping my snout against his hair and sucking in his sweet smell.

"When we had sex for the first time, you didn't intend for it to be serious?" I asked, terrified of his answer.

"I thought I was your pet," Huu-goh countered.

"My…pet?" The thought was so absurd it made me laugh. But then I recalled the leash. And the way I'd kept him close—controlling his every move, and I sobered. "I am sorry."

"Don't be."

"In trying to keep you safe I left a terrible impression," I admitted, and it was the truth. "I didn't think you were incapable," I hurried to add, in case he thought I did not see him as my equal when I did. "I have never thought of you as anything but my equal. My respect for you has no bounds. You have to understand that I have seen things…horrible things. And because of that, sometimes it is difficult for me to trust the world around me. It was not about you."

"I'm glad you did," Huu-goh admitted. "I'll admit, it sucked because I didn't understand what was happening. But…I think you were right to be worried I'd get into trouble. I mean—after that time in the hallway when I hit the switch I realized how easy it would've been for me to accidentally fuck something up. I was lucky that time was simply the light."

I was ashamed as that day came back to me. The way I'd reacted. The way Huu-goh had to comfort me.

"I am sorry for the way I treated you," I said.

Huu-goh shook his head, "I'm not." I frowned, and he continued. "You let me comfort you. It was…nice." He didn't ask me why I'd reacted the way I had. And maybe that was why, despite never speaking of this—not once since it had happened—I opened up.

"When I was a new recruit we were invaded."

Huu-goh's eyes widened, but he didn't interrupt.

"The lights went off—as they always do during pirate attacks. A safety measure to alert the ship that we've been breached midair." Huu-goh nodded. "My captain…" I trailed off, jaw clenching tight as the memories assaulted my senses. "He…died."

"Roark," Huu-goh said softly, "I am *so* sorry."

"It was my fault," I admitted, still tense. My thoughts were suddenly very far away.

"It wasn't," Huu-goh reassured, his soft hands curling over my jaw and stroking the tense skin. He hadn't been there, but his reassurance meant more than he'd ever know, even if he was wrong. My eyes drifted shut as he hummed softly, our same, sweet song. Though the orchestra continued to play, my heart only heard the notes on his tongue.

"You are not my pet," I said quietly, because it needed to be said outright.

"I know," Huu-goh replied with confidence.

Spinning in slow, lazy circles, Huu-goh and I didn't speak for a while. I found myself swinging us to the beat of his song, and not the instruments. The other couples surrounding us glanced our way, some going so far as to make a rude gesture or comment, but we ignored them.

When I was ready to speak again, I turned to the list for help, reading off the next question. "What makes you happiest?" My voice was rough and I had to clear my throat multiple times to get the question out.

Huu-goh didn't comment on our earlier silence, eagerly picking up the game right where we'd left off, like I hadn't laid my heart out in the open for him. I was grateful. It was this silence that made me realize just how lucky I'd been to meet such a lovely, perfect man.

"What makes me happy…hmm," Huu-goh frowned, thinking hard. "I guess…" his frown only grew deeper as he thought. "I guess—I like learning?" He blinked, his big brown eyes beseeching.

How delightful! I too, loved learning. It was one of the reasons I enjoyed space-travel so much. There was always something new to discover.

"What else?"

"I like…" Huu-goh toyed with my lapel, his voice quiet enough I had to lean closer to hear him. "Technology. Biology. Physics. Chemistry. *Dogs*." He sucked in a breath. "Donuts."

"Donuts," I echoed, confused.

"Those pastry things. With the stuffing."

"Ah."

"I like pretty things," Huu-goh blurted next, when it became obvious I was waiting for more. He shifted, his dress sparkling as the light caught the fabric. "Like this." He plucked at the swooping neckline to demonstrate. "It makes me feel…" he trailed off.

I arched my brow, waiting.

"It makes me feel…" Huu-goh flushed again. "*Pretty*." The word was so quiet it wasn't even a whisper.

"You *are* pretty," I assured him, this time not stuttering or stumbling at all.

"Thank you," Huu-goh flashed me another shy smile as he picked at my clothing, brown eyes warm. "You know you're the first person who ever told me that?"

My heart ached for him.

"So yeah. *Thank you.* Seriously. I don't think I've ever felt so appreciated? Even my parents were—" Huu-goh continued.

"Your parents?" I perked up. I hadn't wanted to mention his family, knowing that there was nothing I could do to return him to them. Our ships did not have the capacity to travel that far. The only vessels that could were owned by the same company that had abducted him.

"They never saw me," Huu-goh's lips wobbled. "I could be painted rainbow, holding a neon sign, and still be invisible. I used to think it was because I'm ugly. You know? So the fact that you think I'm not means... so much to me."

"You are not ugly," I scoffed.

"I know," Huu-goh's eyes crinkled with affection. "It was a dumb thought I had when I was a kid. Because I wasn't...what either of them wanted. I feel different now. At least—I do right now. Today. Wearing this."

Ah.

Suddenly, so much made sense. His brilliance, and the way he acted nervous every time he exhibited it. The way he searched for praise. The way he melted beneath kind words and touch, like it was his first time experiencing either.

Maybe it was.

"I am sorry your parents did not love you the way you deserve to be loved." No words had ever felt more important. "If they did not see you, it was because they are blind, not because you are not worthy of attention."

Tears spilled down Huu-goh's cheeks as he laughed, a bright, desperate little sound. "You have..." he sucked in a breath, "no idea what that means to me."

My tongue snaked out to kiss him again.

For hours, I learned everything I could about my little love. I learned his favorite food was something called *pee-za*. I learned that he'd been about to attend *caw-lege* when he was abducted. I learned what kind of music he liked, what his hobbies were, the things that kept him up at night. I learned about his father, the late-night meetings, the lipstick on his collar. The way Huu-goh never felt he could truly trust someone because he'd been raised by a liar and knew what it looked like. I learned about pretty things.

The things he'd always wanted, but never knew he could have. The things he'd been certain wouldn't suit someone "plain" like he was.

Huu-goh told me about his sixteenth birthday.

The birthday that changed everything.

The way his heart had broken in half when he'd realized how little he mattered to the people who were supposed to love him most.

He told me about the science fairs he'd won.

About his scholarship to Her-Verd—a highly prestigious school.

About the dog he'd tried to adopt. About his favorite movie, Spai-Der Man.

He told me about how he'd flunked the test A&R had given him on purpose. Because he'd thought they'd send him back home. But then they didn't.

He laughed, and laughed, and laughed when he told me about the man with "too-many-thumbs", and he shook when he spoke of "the red door" that had made him more frightened than anything else he'd experienced.

I asked how to please him when we went back aboard the ship.

Asked what he was missing.

And Huu-goh opened up for me. His vulnerability was far more beautiful than anything I'd ever seen, the stars included. If I'd thought he was brilliant and resilient before—it was nothing compared to how I felt about him now.

I had never respected another being more than I did Huu-goh. And I made sure to tell him as much, the truth to soothe whatever aches the talk of the past had left on his heart.

And when Huu-goh was done answering my questions, he asked me questions of his own.

And I returned the favor.

He had a question to match every one of mine, and despite the way the words felt awkward and too large, I still answered. I told him things I'd never told anyone. Personal things. Stories I'd thought I'd bring to my grave with me.

I spoke of Ushuu. The way he'd taken me under his wing. I regaled him with tales about Captain Strongfoot, the man that had taught me everything I knew.

How I ached when I remembered his last words, spoken with blood spilling from his lips.

I recalled the nightmares that still plagued me when I was most vulnerable.

He learned about my father, and the way I couldn't truly miss him because every time I looked at the stars I felt him looking back. I told

Huu-goh about my siblings, all seventy-three of them. The way I'd watched children get adopted into new families, while I stood in the background, aching.

Happy for them.

Glad to stay, so that I could be of use.

But sad all the same.

I told him he tasted like starlight and freedom.

And he told me he loved how protective I was.

That he could see how much I cared because of it.

My greatest insecurity. The part of me that I knew could be the darkest, and ugliest. And Huu-goh told me he *loved* it.

Most important of all, however, I told Huu-goh that I had never been happier in all my life.

And he fluttered my face with kisses and told me, "Same."

I understood what Huu-goh meant now, about being invisible. Because with every chortle, every smile, every kind word, I felt myself solidify. With every silent story I'd kept to myself, shared, I felt real in a way I never had before.

It was funny how it had taken me this long to realize just how desperately lonely I'd been all this time.

But I wasn't lonely anymore.

I had my mate beside me, and he was remarkable, clever, and vibrant.

When the ballroom emptied and the orchestra packed up their instruments, despite the fact we'd been dancing off beat for hours, Huu-goh and I continued to spin. My hearts thumped and thumped and *thumped.* In the silence, as everyone else left, Huu-goh laid his head on my chest, toying with the collar of my shirt, and I thought…

I thought—

*You are what I've been waiting for.*

All of my life.

# TWENTY

## HUGO

**ROARK AND I TALKED UNTIL** we both went hoarse. It was funny, really. I'd been silent for so long that I hadn't known what it felt like for someone to really listen. I mean, the guys in the chess club listened to me. My teachers listened. My guidance counselor listened. But…it wasn't the same.

They weren't special and pink and squishy.

*They* hadn't looked at me like I meant something.

"Are you hungry?" Roark asked, his voice quiet and sweet as he cradled me against his chest while we finally rode up the elevator, long after the party had ended. My stomach growled, and he huffed in amusement. "I'll order room service."

It was later than late and I was honestly surprised he was still awake considering how busy he'd been this week—and the fact he'd been the one doing all the legwork for our date, literally.

*How was he still standing?*

"Thank you," I nuzzled under Roark's chin. He did that purring thing I loved as the elevator dinged open and he walked us down the hall to our room. Once inside, the blast of cool air soothed my flushed skin as Roark locked the door and led me to the bed.

"I hope you don't mind sharing," he said, his voice all nervous again.

"We always share," I chuckled as he laid me down on the mattress, then adjusted the strap on my dress where it had fallen again. His gaze snapped to my thigh, and the lace stocking that adorned it—visible through the slit in my skirt.

His eyes flickered black for a moment.

"We do," he agreed, blinking back to blue. "And you…like that?"

"I love it," I reached out, catching his hand with mine, my heart pounding as the night and all its intimacy burst inside me all at once. *I love you*, I wanted to say but didn't. "It's my favorite part of the day."

Surprising me, the usually stoic Roark made a joke. "Don't lie. You prefer your time in Ushuu's lab."

"Not true," I laughed incredulously. "Though that *is* a close second."

"A very close second," Roark huffed, still playful.

I licked my lips, spreading my legs a little so he could get a better peep of what was between them, encased in sparkly white fabric. "Thank you for that by the way. He's already taught me more than I could've ever dreamed of learning."

"He is a smart man." Roark said with pride.

"He is," I agreed, gaze tracing over his body. "Why are we talking about your almost-dad again?"

Roark snorted in amusement, flexing his chest at me, his eyes flashing with heat when he saw how affected I was. "Rest," Roark commanded grouchily. He stroked my cheek, and despite his playful grumpiness his spots were white—betraying his true emotions.

Happy.

*Happy, happy, happy.*

I did as I was told, grateful that Roark seemed to enjoy looking after me as much as I enjoyed him doing it. He crossed the room with a few confident strides and pushed a button on the wall. What looked like a menu popped out. The colorful hologram wavered as I watched in fascination while Roark put practically every item listed into his cart, before hitting a button to pay.

"That was a lot of food," I commented from the bed, trying to sound coy and failing. Space food! Shit-tons of space food!

"While we're here I figured you would want to try the planet's cuisine." Roark spots were fuchsia—embarrassed now—and I melted.

He paid attention.

It had only been a few hours since I'd told him how much I wanted to learn and experience new things now that I was in space—and he'd…wow.

He may be a man who "struggled with words" but as always his actions spoke fluently enough.

When the food arrived, Roark had the hotel attendants lay it out for us on a dining table that took up the back corner of the hotel room. Honestly? I hadn't even noticed the table was there—and who could blame me? My focus had been primarily on A. Marshmallow bed or B. My new mate in a tux. The dining table was the least interesting thing I'd seen all night.

At least it *had* been until they'd covered it in food.

I gravitated toward it immediately like a moth to flame, and Roark expertly side-stepped between me and the foreign aliens, protective stance activated till they departed the way they'd come. He pulled my seat out for me with a jerky tug that betrayed his nerves.

"Earthlings do this?" Roark waited, stiff as a board. "For dates. The pulling of chairs is customary."

"They do," I replied, heart wobbling with affection. "Thank you."

He was so damn charming I didn't know what to do with him.

Once seated, Roark dished me up a plate full of alien delicacies. There were pastries and fruits, pies and sandwiches. Nothing looked exactly like it did on Earth, but it was close enough for me to feel comfortable dipping my toes in so to speak.

Roark refused to touch his own meal until I'd started eating, maybe to be polite? Or maybe because he couldn't stop studying my reactions. He watched me like I was his favorite movie and that…wow. That was just… *Wow*.

Despite the fact we were safely inside our room and the night was dwindling to an end, Roark didn't take his tuxedo off. He did, however, undo an obscene amount of buttons. The peek of his lovely pink skin was enough to make my dick perk up and my cheeks flush all over again.

He was *so* tall.

Even while we were seated, he towered over me, sitting ramrod straight, his blue eyes flickering with warmth. Not once did he stop observing me, his eyes narrowing with amusement every time I moaned and slapped the table. It was impossible not to! Especially after I tried a particularly delicious bite of something I could only describe as a spiky-green-fruit-sushi.

When I was full, I felt my flush travel lower as Roark's eyes flickered from amused, to affectionate, to hungry black.

I licked my lips, and he groaned.

I was half-tempted to crawl across the table and sit in his lap—but…

I refrained.

Because I had a surprise for him.

A lacy, pink surprise.

And I was confident now—in a way I'd never been before.

"Do you mind if I go wash up? You know. Freshen up and stuff?" Oh no, that had not been smooth. "Because you know. Dancing. For hours. And food. And like—"

"Go ahead, little one."

Little one. I loved that damn nickname.

I shot to my feet so fast I made myself light-headed, gripping the lip of the table to catch my balance. I flashed him a grateful, nervous smile. Then I bolted across the room, skirt hiked high so I wouldn't trip, and disappeared into the bathroom.

Roark's middle name really should've been Effort.

And I'd vowed to myself that I'd do something to show him my appreciation. Not because it felt transactional—like my parents' affection—but because it didn't. Roark didn't expect anything in return for his kindness.

When I caught my reflection, I barely recognized it. Not because of the dress—I'd come to terms with that earlier. And not because I felt pretty, which I still did, despite being flushed and sweaty, my hair an absolute mess.

No.

I didn't recognize myself because I looked *happy*. The kinda happiness you see in commercials for allergy medication or in Hallmark movies. The carefree kind. The kind that meant white spots, and crescent eyes, and barking laughter. The kind that costs nothing at all.

It didn't take long to strip my dress off, do a quick sponge bath, and try to fix my hair. *This would be so much better if I had makeup,* I thought, even though I had no idea how the hell to use it. But still, I was sure a little makeup would help. Maybe some of that black stuff girls put on their lashes? Or like—lipstick. Lipstick would definitely look nice. Pink, like my mom's.

Hair done, I stepped back to inspect my new duds.

The lingerie I'd selected for tonight fit like a glove. It clung to my hips and thighs, highlighting the curves and dips of my body in a way I hoped was enticing. I'd never worn anything like this before today and it was liberating. Somehow even more liberating than wearing the dress and garter had been.

I was committing to this—and *god*, did that feel good.

Like I finally found something that fit who I was.

*Roark will like it.*

I didn't know how I knew that, but I did.

Roark liked anything that made me happy.

I patted myself down one last time, did a quick pit sniff to make sure I smelled good—fruity, hell yes—and then jumped when one of the flowers on the counter tried to snap at me. I'd hardly noticed them, I'd been so concerned with my attempts to look hot.

"Sorry, buddies." They probably needed water. I filled the sink after pulling down its stopper—some things were apparently the same even if you were a galaxy away—grabbed the bouquet, and carefully laid the stems inside, all the while avoiding the snap, snap, snap of the flowers' teeth.

With that finished, I was ready.

Nervous, but ready.

I was going to blow Roark's mind.

# TWENTY-ONE

## ROARK

**THE MOMENT HUU-GOH STEPPED OUT** of the bathroom, time stuttered to a stop. Heat had been simmering between us all night as we'd laid our truths bare, so I wasn't surprised the date would end in intimacy—however…

I was still shocked.

Awed, enamored.

Obsessed.

Smitten.

*Speechless.*

My little huu-man was a vision in pink. I'd thought he looked glorious in his dress but this was…wow. I was not worthy. Not even a little bit.

Huu-goh's brown eyes shone with confidence, an expression I'd seen appearing more and more recently. He knew he looked good, and that thought made my cocks rapidly harden. I sank to my knees halfway to the bed, eyes trained on the swivel of his hips. I'd just finished cleaning up—and been about to wait for him there, but my legs suddenly no longer worked.

I'd heard of lingerie.

I'd seen it in windows throughout my travels.

I'd observed people in the windows of pleasure houses wearing all sorts of varying styles of it when my crew passed through F'ukYuu.

But nothing in my life had ever prepared me for the sight of my lover dressed in nothing but lace. My hearts were about to beat right out of my chest.

"Surpriiiiise!" Huu-goh did an endearing little spin, arms wide.

The view of his tight little ass in those panties was just…

Stars above.

So *this* was why he'd wanted to "freshen up," the little *minx*.

I didn't think my brain was capable of functioning at the moment—or ever again.

"Are you surprised?" Huu-goh batted his lashes, flirtier now that he was comfortable. I was honored to be the recipient of his attention. My hands were sweaty and I rubbed them on my thighs as I nodded, dazed. "Do you like it?" Another nod. "Speechless again, aren't you, big guy?" Again, I nodded.

Huu-goh beamed at me, a giddy cackle escaping as he took another step closer. Astounded by his beauty, my gaze traced from the tips of his tiny, wonderful toes, up the shapely curve of his stocking-clad leg, to the bare strip of skin above the lace on his socks.

I wanted to lick it.

Wanted to bite it till my teeth left marks.

Huu-goh took another step and my gaze snapped up the fancy little ties that pulled the socks to what I could only describe as a frilly belt around his waist. I knew that wasn't what it was actually called—it more than likely had a far sexier name, but I had never paid enough attention to notice.

His slim waist was only highlighted by the shape of the garment as it draped down his pelvis, connecting to his thigh-high socks, and framing the tiniest, pinkest, most wonderful panties I had ever seen.

Huu-goh's needy cock pushed against them, already half hard, a wet spot forming at the tip. His sweet balls were clutched tight in the silky fabric, and I could only imagine how good that felt when he moved, like being cupped by a waterfall.

"Huu-goh," his name escaped, my jaw officially on the floor.

The moon could explode outside the windows and I would not have noticed, he so entirely commanded my attention.

"I'm going to give you a lap dance," Huu-goh hummed. My brain short-circuited. "Like I should've given you when we met." He took another step and the hunger in his eyes had me spinning. "I'm going to make you go cross-eyed."

I didn't know what that was but I wanted it.

"I'm going to tease you till your spots are red and your cocks are aching."

Please. Fuck. I wanted that.

"And then I'm going to let you touch me however you want, for however long you want—*anywhere* you want."

I nodded, snapping my head up and down as he closed the last few feet between us. "On the couch," he commanded, and I complied. I had never moved faster in my life. One second I was on my knees and the next I was sitting on the couch in the corner of the left side of the room. My dicks were twitching inside my slacks as Huu-goh picked up my communicator from the table and tapped a few buttons on it.

He was so damn clever.

He'd memorized my password there too.

He must've played with it when I brought it into our rooms this week.

And as music started to fill the room Huu-goh's eyes were nearly as black with lust as mine were.

To the beat of the music, Huu-goh crossed the distance between us, a sway to his hips that was enchanting. I couldn't look away, not as he ran his fingers along the outside of his thigh. Not as he trailed them over his pelvis, framing his little dick with his hand. Not when that same dexterous hand slid upward, tickling along the pale flesh of his belly, across his ribcage, and up the center of his chest.

All the while, he danced, moving closer and closer. When he reached the couch, the heat of Huu-goh's body bled against my thighs. Still undulating, the clever huu-man straddled one at the same time that sweet hand pinched one of his own nipples.

"Nnnngh," Huu-goh whined, hips doing a filthy shimmy against my leg. I grunted, shifting so I could feel more of him, his balls tapping against my slacks. "No touching," he reminded me.

I hadn't even realized I'd lifted one of my hands till he said something.

I dropped it just as quickly, my mouth dry as I watched his fingers abuse the poor pebbled nipple before moving on to the other one. They were puffy by the time he released them. My cocks were aching, just like he'd wanted.

"Fuck," the word left without my permission, low and gruff.

Huu-goh shivered. "Yeah, sweetheart. That's exactly what we're going to do," he agreed, both hands framing his flat chest, before sliding up his neck. It was a nice throat, long and slender, as delicate as it was strong. I loved the way it felt under my tongue when I twisted snug around it—and I could feel every breath he took.

My hands flexed in an effort to hold still as Huu-goh continued to gyrate on my lap. My cocks strained toward him, fighting each other to break through my slacks, though the fabric had no give.

"I love when your eyes go black like that," Huu-goh sighed, the praise going straight to my hearts. My claws bit into my palms—a reminder to hold still. Roll, roll, grind. "It's so goddamn sexy, you have no idea."

"You're killing me," I gasped out, twisting to look over his shoulder so I could see his tiny ass flex. He was so small, a simple shift was all I needed to see either view.

"I hope not," Huu-goh giggled and the sound was breathy and dripping with sex. "Are you looking at my ass?" Huu-goh's voice turned incredulous.

"Yes." I didn't think my voice had ever been lower.

"Bad Roark." Huu-goh placed a single finger between my heaving pecs and pushed. I went back willingly, back pressed to the couch, my tongue lolling to see if I could taste the scent of sex in the air. "Fuck, I love that too." Huu-goh's voice grew darker, needier, as he continued to wiggle to the beat, back and forth across my thighs, his plump ass brushing me just enough to drive me crazy.

I grunted in question.

"That—" Huu-goh pointed at me, at my flared nostrils, my heaving chest, then my tongue. "You're this big, serious pink softie—always—" Big, serious *what* now? "And you look like you want to *eat* me."

"Not eat," I groaned, shaking my head, though the idea was tempting.

"Taste? Yes."

"And that voice," Huu-goh continued, on a roll now that he'd found his confidence. "Even when I can't understand you I know what you're saying. All growly. Low. Like you're so turned on even your vocal cords can't help but show it."

He hadn't been joking when he'd said he'd tease me.

"Please."

Huu-goh grinned, this wide, bright, feral thing. It lit me up from the inside out. Made me taste the stars all over again. "Stay still."

And then he slid off my lap and turned around.

"Oh fuck."

Huu-goh bent over, the curve of his ass wrapped in lace as his pretty pink hole flashed beneath the strap of the underwear, and those sweet balls hung between his spread thighs. His hands trailed up his legs, toying with the hem of his socks, snapping the little belts holding the big belt in place.

"Fuck," I repeated, leaning forward to get a better look. Huu-goh slid his hands up to his ass, framed it, and pulled his cheeks wide. At the same time, a clever thumb tucked under the little strap that ran between them, tugging it to the side so that I had a full unobstructed view of his hole.

I'd known he had one.

I'd seen glimpses of it often, but never like this. Never with the light on, with him just holding himself open for me. With him offering himself for perusal. Like a delicacy.

I wanted to eat his little ass till he screamed.

"You haven't fucked me here yet," Huu-goh said, his tone conversational. All thoughts of waiting for our ceremony on Osheania to train his ass immediately flew out of my head. I wanted inside him. Right the fuck now. Especially when he started swiveling his hips again, releasing his cheeks so I couldn't see that sweet little hole anymore.

"Nhhgh," I grunted, because he was right.

"Is it because you're scared?" Huu-goh's ass was doing this shaking thing that had me actively drooling on the floor, pushing close enough I could taste his sweat in the air—could feel the breeze his movements caused. "I don't want you to be scared."

"Don't want to hurt you," I managed, though it was difficult.

*Just a taste. Just a little taste. Just a bit.*

"Then don't." Huu-goh spun around before I could stick my tongue where I wanted to. His own chest was heaving, sweat glistening across his peachy skin. The tip of that sweet, delicious dick was now poking out of the panties, too hard to be contained, and it was aimed right at me.

Flushed, pink, and wet.

Drier than mine, but no less eager.

I licked my lips, retreating back to where he'd pushed me against the couch.

"You know the word no," Huu-goh murmured, sliding into the space between my thighs again as his tiny hands cupped my face. "I promise I'll use it if I don't like something, even when we can't fully communicate." There was a depth of emotion in his eyes I had no idea how to fathom. "I was scared at first too—but I'm not anymore." I got the feeling he wasn't just talking about getting fucked. "You make me feel brave. You make me feel…" The music stopped, shifting to something sweeter as Huu-goh let his weight rest across my lap and his hand burned brands against my cheeks. "You make me feel like I can do and have anything I want. And what I want…is for you to *touch* me. I want *everything* with you.

Especially after tonight." His expressive brown eyes were full of emotion as his lips tipped into a sincere smile. "When you're ready too of course."

I kissed him instead of answering, pouring all of my love and adoration—all my promises—into that single gesture. My tongue slid inside his mouth, tangling with his own, carving out a place for myself inside his body.

When I laid him on the bed he was a writhing, jittery mess. He sucked sweet, nipping little kisses along my neck, tiny nails scratching down my chest as I pulled my shirt free and off my shoulders. The slight sting was welcome as I shoved the rest of my clothing off as hastily as I could. Relief only came when I was bare and the only thing between Huu-goh and my cocks were the silky strips of lace he still wore.

With one hand I traced across his delicate ankles, sliding upward till my fingers bumped the strip of unadorned flesh at the top of his stockings. "You are beautiful," I promised him, guarding him from the world—from the light above—from anything bad that had ever happened to him as I gently sunk my teeth into the flesh, careful not to break it.

Huu-goh shuddered as he spread his legs. It was obvious from this angle just how much his cock had been leaking.

"You are perfect," I told him, leaning over to slide my tongue down his neck, his sternum, across his nipples, and into his belly button. When I reached his dick, he howled. Invigorated, I slipped the tip of my tongue inside his leaking slit. When I'd chased all the salt that gathered there, I dove down, sliding beneath the silk of his panties.

He was muskier beneath them, sweaty and sweet.

Farther back I crept, as Huu-goh grabbed onto my head fin, babbling encouragement. His thighs clamped around my neck and my tongue snuck deeper and deeper into his crease.

Till I found what I wanted.

His hole.

It twitched beneath my tongue, a curious sensation as I rubbed against it. He tasted thicker here, headier. It was wonderful, and I chided myself for not trying this sooner. The more I rubbed his sweet little ass the softer it became. Like playing with it was enough to convince it to let me in further.

"Fuck," Huu-goh mewled, shoving back against my face. It was a *naughty* word, and though I had also said it, it surprised me to hear it on his sweet little tongue. Was he always saying such filthy things when we were in bed? The thought made my cocks harder than ever. "Oh, fuck. *Roark*—"

When the tip of my tongue pushed inside his furled entrance he howled again, hips stuttering, his tiny thighs pinching me tight like he was trying to squeeze me out. He wasn't strong enough to force me off, even if he wanted to. And the moment he realized that his moans only got throatier.

Huu-goh liked being pinned.

He liked that I was bigger than him.

He liked feeling powerless.

He liked the choice being taken away.

Probably because it meant he didn't have to think, or worry, or stress at all. He'd spent so much of his life stressing. He'd had to be strong at all times or he'd break. But here, in our bed, I was the strong one. I was the one holding him together. He could trust this pleasure because I was the one giving it.

He had my full, undivided attention.

The deeper I pressed, the louder Huu-goh became. By the time I had a quarter of my tongue inside the hot clutch of his body, he was a sobbing mess. Compliments, insults, and exaltations left his tongue. He scratched at my fin, a steady litany of "yes, yes, yes" scattered between his other babbled nonsense.

When he spilled he did so silently.

He jerked, and jerked, and *jerked* a third time, all the while squeezing around me, his hips gyrating as he rode my tongue like it was a cock itself.

The scrap of silk slid back into place between his cheeks the moment I pulled out of his hole. Huu-goh's reedy whine was the only other response he gave me as his thighs fell back, no longer pinching me in place. I licked my lips to savor the flavor of him, before crawling up his body to see his face better.

Pleased, I admired the charming pinch of his brow, his bitten red lips, the sweat that beaded at his temple, and the lovely brown spots scattered across the bridge of his nose.

When Huu-goh's eyes opened my hearts lurched.

"Did you like it?" I asked, just to be sure.

"Fuck yes," Huu-goh sighed, sated and soft, his fingers fumbling down my chest and toward my pelvis like he was trying to reach my cocks.

"No, darling," I murmured—feeling foolish the moment the pet name escaped. That feeling quickly died however because instead of condemning me for being cheesy, Huu-goh turned to putty in my grip.

"*Darling*," he whispered, like the angel he was.

"Yes," my pulse stuttered. "That's what you are." I swallowed the lump in my throat. "You're my darling."

"I like that," Huu-goh sighed, looking drunk from his orgasm, his eyes full of stars.

"I like *you*," I said, awkward but sincere.

"Can I touch you?" he asked again, voice sweet. "I want to."

"This was for you, Huu-goh," I murmured, leaning down to nuzzle our noses together. "But if you'd like…maybe after the next round?"

"The next round?" he squeaked, eyes going round—and it was *adorable*.

"Yes," I grinned. "You didn't think I was only going to make you come once tonight, did you?"

"I…"

"Not in *that* outfit," and then I proceeded to taste him.

Every inch.

Thoroughly.

By the time the sky was light and the stars had fled, I had collected four orgasms out of the tiny pink-tinged creature, and he had collected one.

I was more than a little grateful I'd taken the weekend off as I curled around his small defenseless form. There were no thoughts of pirates in my head, or shipments, or tragedy. And no nightmares plagued me as I toyed with the edges of his stained panties and finally drifted to sleep, content.

If only I'd known what was coming.

Then maybe I could've prepared better for it.

# TWENTY-TWO

## HUGO

**ROARK TOOK ME SHOPPING THE** following evening. After a week spent at the space-mall-planet I figured I'd bought more than enough things to last me a lifetime. Roark seemed to think otherwise. In fact, he told me before we left our room that while he appreciated my frugality with his money—he had the means to take care of us for many lifetimes— and refused to miss the opportunity to spoil me.

I'd never been a spoiled kid—and on F'ukYuu I'd had very few belongings, so it was mind-boggling to suddenly find myself the owner of...

Of *everything*.

Everything I'd ever wanted.

Except...well...

Except for the one thing I truly needed.

Both of us had slept like the dead till early afternoon. I'd woken first, enjoying a solid half hour of Roark snoring, his big chest heaving as I slung my body over his and soaked up his warmth. We'd talked again when he'd roused, shared brunch—and jokes—and Roark had nuzzled all of my toes and called them delightful.

He told me he couldn't wait to take me home.

That he couldn't wait to hold me in his bed.

That he couldn't wait to fuck me the way I so clearly wanted.

To show me the planet his heart always longed to return to.

But those sweet promises didn't negate the loss I felt as our last true conversation ended and we'd headed downstairs. Now, standing in the lobby with the alien clerk waiting expectantly, I tried to summon some of the peace I'd felt in Roark's arms.

We had to return the translators to the hotel clerk at check-out.

I knew that.

But it hurt to have the power of conversation taken away from us only a few short hours after we'd gotten it.

Roark looked just as jarred as I felt. When he paid our bill and handed back both of our translators, he wavered—like he wasn't sure he wanted to return them either. His spots went gray and I latched on to his elbow, rubbing the soft skin—he was shirtless, like usual—until his spots turned pink and he flashed me a grateful smile.

It was rough, leaving them behind, for both of us.

Silence weighed us down as we stepped out of the lobby and the sprawl of the city spread at our feet below the steps.

Roark, as always, was quick to reassure.

Exhaling, he leaned down to nuzzle the top of my head. The hot puff of his breath in my hair soothed us both as he guided me down the steps and to the busy street on our way toward the main stretch of shops.

"Huu-goh is go-een shopping with me." Roark spoke carefully in English, the words gruff and stilted like I'd grown to expect from him. We'd already hashed this out, so I knew he was trying to get my mind off things—which I appreciated.

"I've already been shopping." I blinked at him and he huffed in amusement, eyes shifting into happy crescents. His spots were white.

"Huu-goh went shopping with Ushuu," Roark shook his head. "Has not gone with *me*."

My belly flipped.

There was no room for argument in his tone, and I liked that even more now that we'd shared so much the night before.

I knew him in a way I hadn't before.

I didn't think I'd ever been closer to another person.

Scientifically speaking, I'd never contemplated the idea of soulmates. I'd never thought that could be a thing. It was magic—and I didn't believe in that. But…maybe I'd need to rethink my earlier hypothesis. Because I was pretty sure I'd met my soulmate. And he was big, and pink, and his cum tasted like pineapple—and I couldn't imagine my life without him.

I kinda wanted to send A&R a thank-you letter.

"Lead the way, Captain." I made sure to use the word for "Captain" in sharkish. Roark sounded so sure of himself, so proud of his bossiness that I wanted to tease.

He stumbled a little, then barked out a laugh, shaking his head at me.

"Brat," he said in perfect English.

For a second, I didn't know how to respond. Because the fact he knew that word meant that he'd learned it from Ushuu. And that was just—so fucking funny and embarrassing I wasn't sure if I wanted to laugh or scream.

Instead, I just grinned, wide and unrepentant.

And let Roark lead the way.

He'd already done so much for me, I was hesitant to take more. But… there was nothing but pleasure on Roark's face as he brought me to my very first tech store. My eyes went wide, the possibilities endless. I'd never seen Roark more proud of himself than he was at that moment, as I proceeded to spend the next two hours flipping the fuck out over alien electronics.

I couldn't read the price tags, and without Ushuu there to translate I had no idea how much anything cost.

Though, I didn't think Roark really wanted me to know. He'd made that clear. And god…the smarmy little smile on his face as he followed behind me, grabbing one of every item I touched—a steadily growing pile in his arms—was just…fuck. He was gorgeous and wonderful and…*man*—I'd rarely seen him this elated.

Like spoiling me was doing something for *him*.

In light of this, I came to the conclusion that maybe I shouldn't argue.

Maybe I should *let* him spoil me.

If it made him *that* happy—I'd do anything.

Plus…I mean. Tech. *All* the fucking tech.

Jesus Christ on a cracker.

By the time we finished up at the tech store I had a communicator of my own, a tablet, and a plethora of other gadgets I didn't recognize but Roark kept insisting in garbled English that I'd need.

After the first, "Huu-goh need. No argue."

I didn't try to ask any more questions.

Well, I mean, a couple more times.

But that was because I liked listening to him talk, awkward English and all.

We visited a huge variety of stores. Different from the ones I'd gone to with Ushuu. There was a tailor of some sort, more tech stores, what seemed like a swap-meet full of random stuff from all over, including a few human vinyl records, and a shit-ton of candy shops. Roark had figured out early on that I had a sweet tooth—even before he'd asked me about it last night—and as I lapped at what looked like a popsicle but tasted like goddamn pumpkin pie, his fucking smile was brighter than the stars he'd told me he loved.

By that point, Roark's entire left arm was full. Boxes, bags, and parcels stacked in a rainbow tower tall enough they settled against his chin so they wouldn't fall. Tendrils looped to help, keeping them in place. His right arm, however, he left empty just for me.

Any time I tried to help carry something, Roark threw a big fit about it, huffing and growling till I eventually acquiesced.

Now I just enjoyed him, lapping at my popsicle as I curled around his forearm and we exited the section of shops full of food.

"One…more…" Roark spoke, distracted as his head swiveled to scan the shops like he was looking for something in particular.

I had no idea what else we could possibly buy, but I didn't want the day to end, so I didn't argue.

We walked for long enough that I finished my snack. I was lapping the juice from my fingertips as Roark spotted the store we'd been looking for and pushed the door open wide for me to enter. It jingled—just like doors on Earth did—and I was charmed by the similarity as I stepped into the air-conditioned space.

The scent of flowers accosted my senses. Sweet and opulent, like perfume. The carpet was plush beneath my new shoes as I moved to the side to allow Roark enough room to enter after me. He didn't have to squeeze too hard, as the store was definitely one of the larger ones we'd visited.

A chandelier twinkled from high above and I found myself transfixed by the way shooting lights spun around it like magic.

An attendant hurried over, dressed in a spiffy black suit—similar to the style on Earth but with a *lot* more buttons. Maybe his species used buttons as a sign of wealth? Because otherwise, I had no idea why he needed five hundred of them.

The attendant took Roark's bags from him, spouting off rapid-fire alien-speak, his speckled head swiveling. Roark was polite but gruff as he always was, his hand rubbing the small of my back as I took in the rest of the shop with fascination.

Glass floating cabinets lined the room. They hovered at varying levels in the air, full of rich dark velvet, and a variety of glittering jewelry in all sorts of shapes, sizes, and colors. Bracelets, necklaces, earrings, and other oddly shaped objects I had no idea the purpose of. Everything seemed to be catered to the wild variety of clientele that visited this planet.

"Huu-goh," Roark said my name softly to get my attention. "*Come.*"

I followed the order obediently, trailing behind Roark and the employee guy as we moved past the hovering cases full of glittering treasures. He led us through a hallway and into a separate, even larger room than the first. Inside it, near the back wall there was a bed with a hole in it—much like a massage bed.

Beside it was a tall dark cabinet that looked like it housed machinery of some sort, if the outlets on to its left were any indicator. I didn't understand why the hell there was a massage bed in a jewelry store, or why we were here at all.

It didn't take long to figure that out though, when Roark directed me to the bed and helped me up onto it. Sitting there, I tried to make sense of where we were. He tapped the collar that sat around my neck with one gentle claw and suddenly...I got it.

My thoughts spun in circles.

*He's going to take it off.*

*He's going to take it off.*

*He's going to take it off.*

A million emotions flitted through me all at once. Fear, excitement, trepidation.

I'd been wearing this thing for so long I wasn't sure who I was without it.

I guess I was about to find out.

Roark stroked a hand through my hair as I lay on my belly. The bed squeaked beneath me and I inhaled, then exhaled just as slow. *Scratch, scratch,* Roark petted me as he murmured in sweet low tones to the attendant. I was certain he spoke that way for my benefit, as he had to know how scary this was.

These fucking collars were nearly impossible to get off.

Mine had been *literally* welded on.

I imagined there would be some pain when it came free. Heat, more than likely—from a welding iron of some sort—like the one that had been used to secure it in the first place.

I should've been more scared than I was.

But Roark was there.

And when Roark was there I knew things would be okay.

My ears were ringing the entire time I waited for the employee to get set up. And the entire time, Roark purred at me, petting me to keep me from full-on panicking.

"Huu-goh yesh?" he asked, as the heat of whatever tool was going to be used to free me moved in close. I couldn't see him. Could only see the carpet.

"Yes," I agreed, voice a little choked.

All the while, Roark's hand was a heavy, comforting weight on my head.

I barely felt a pinch when the collar finally came off. One second it was sitting heavy around my neck—a symbol of everything I was and wasn't—and the next it was gone. *Gone.* Like it had never been there at all.

Like I hadn't been taken, sold, and bought.

Like for three entire years I hadn't belonged to someone else.

I hadn't expected the sheer force of emotion that hit me as a sob tore free of my chest. Tears spilled, hot and angry as Roark cooed, caressing my hair again.

He understood what was happening. The pain, the relief, the fear.

I hadn't realized how heavy the collar was until I no longer had to carry its weight.

I launched myself off the bench and into his arms before I could think. Roark made a surprised sound as I latched onto him like a barnacle, arms and legs pulled around as much of him as I could. He continued to purr against my ear, holding me safe above the ground.

I didn't look at the collar. Not as the employee picked it up. And not as he took it away—probably to throw it in the trash.

"Huu-goh," Roark said, like a prayer.

My eyes were swimming with tears, ugly and hot, and awful.

When I'd been taken I hadn't cried.

I hadn't let myself.

There was no point mourning a life I'd never have again. That would've been pointless and exhausting. I'd made the best of a shitty situation. I'd tried to be positive. I'd looked for the good—despite all the bad. All because I'd never actually thought I'd be free again, not really.

But here I was.

And I was free—and happy and—and—Roark was right here with me, feeling my pain like it was his own, his body wrapped around mine.

"Is okay," Roark cooed, nuzzling my ears as I blubbered, fingers digging into his chest and poking inside the sticky flesh. Tiny tendrils burst out, wrapping around them—encasing them so they were safe. "Is okay, little beast."

I wanted to tell him it wasn't.

That it wasn't okay.

That none of this was.

But that wasn't true. Not anymore.

Because I may have been abducted, I may have lost my life, my family, and the future I'd been counting on. But I had gained something far more precious. Futures could be rewritten, families could be made. My life wasn't lost, it was just reconstructed.

And now I could build from the ground up—with him.

"I thought…" I sucked in a breath, voice quaking. "I thought I'd wear that thing forever."

Roark rumbled, nuzzling my other cheek with concern. He couldn't understand those words. I could tell by the way he didn't reply. But that didn't matter. His empathy was enough. What he'd just done for me was enough. "Thank you, thank you, thank you." My gratitude spilled out, shaky and wet and needy. "Thank you for saving me. Thank you for picking me. Thank you for giving me my life back."

Roark's tongue flickered out to swipe at my tears and I giggled, overwhelmed and happy and excited now that the weight had begun to finally lift.

We stayed there a long time, in that quiet backroom. I don't know when the attendant left. Some time between my first sob and the moment I'd crawled into Roark's arms. But it didn't matter.

When my shudders calmed to sniffles, Roark carried me back down the hallway to the front room and all its sparkly treasures. He never set me down, just cradled me close, murmuring sweet words in his native tongue against my ear as we perused the collection of jewelry and Roark stroked a big palm over my body.

His tendrils were everywhere, like the need to be close was mutual. They twisted and writhed around me, keeping me safe and warm in their squishy embrace as Roark picked something out and the employee unlocked the cabinet to procure it.

It was my size, so I knew it was for me.

A glittering choker that reminded me of the pearls my mom used to wear.

My neck felt empty and barren—an unsettling sensation despite the freedom it represented.

"Huu-goh want?" Roark asked gently, a few of his tendrils tapping against the hand I'd been using to rub my neck as we looked. I hadn't stopped rubbing my bare neck since the moment we'd stepped out of the hallway.

I had no idea how expensive that damn thing was.

But Roark looked so hopeful I couldn't help but agree. Besides, I *did* want it. I wanted his mark around my neck. I wanted to rewrite the bad memories and make new ones, like he'd said.

I wanted to forget what it meant to be a slave.

But I still wanted to be his.

Roark paid, and it was his tendrils that clipped the clasp into place behind my neck.

The choker settled there, the weight of the necklace not oppressive like my collar had been. But it was heavy enough to make me feel settled. Warm. It didn't carry darkness along with it, only love.

Only new beginnings.

Only hope.

On our way out of the space-mall, things took a turn for the worse. I'd almost convinced myself that the human I'd seen the night before hadn't been a human—he'd had cat ears, wings, and a tail, for god's sake. Besides, I'd only seen him for a split second, and even then, it had been from behind.

I figured I'd made it up.

Apparently, I hadn't been mistaken.

There were humans on Sha'hPihn.

They just weren't free like me.

"Roark," I gave his massive hand an anxious squeeze, unsure if he was seeing what I was. Roark's other arm was full of the packages he'd bought me, and he shifted a little, careful not to drop them as he looked where I was pointing.

A long line of humans were standing on a platform near the spiral escalator that led from the shops to the docks. Every single human was dressed in white shorts and gossamer fabric, their bodies on display, heads hanging.

None of them had a second set of ears like the man from the night before—they were simply…normal.

Like me.

An alien with a long bulbous nose and four arms was waving at them. He wore a white robe, kinda like a medieval priest—and his voice was jarring as he blurted words in his native tongue rapid-fire into a microphone as the humans stayed perfectly still. Beside me, Roark tensed, his entire body going rigid as a low menacing growl buzzed inside his chest.

A large gathering of aliens of all sorts stood between me and the stage. Creatures of all shapes and sizes—smashed close together, as though they were here for this event specifically. I wasn't an idiot. I could guess that what was happening was bad—based on Roark's reaction alone.

I didn't speak Common—the language most at these ports did—but Roark did.

Without thinking, I released Roark's arm.

It was like everything in me broke.

My ears were ringing, my head was swimming.

*What were they doing here?*

*What was going on?*

Before I knew it, I was somewhere in the middle of the crowd, and Roark was lost behind me. I hadn't meant to leave him. For a moment, it had almost felt like I'd blacked out. Like I wasn't in control of my body at all.

My vision swam as I took in the line of human captives from a closer vantage point.

There had to be at least fifteen of them—all with matching collars just like the one I'd just had removed. Despite my emotional exhaustion, I still managed the lurching in my stomach as I stumbled to a stop ten feet away from the stage itself, my eyes wide. A few aliens had jostled me as I'd moved, but I hardly felt their touches.

Like ice had filled my body.

Like I wasn't me at all.

*What was this?*

*Was this…*

"Ah," A low, sultry, masculine voice hummed behind me. "First auction?"

First—

It took me a second to realize I'd been spoken to in English.

I whipped my head around to face the newcomer, only to be distracted when I saw a frantic pink shark-man a dozen or so feet near the back of the crowd. I could hear his thudding elephant feet as he forced his way through the other aliens toward me.

I hadn't realized till that moment what I'd done, leaving him behind. But my head was still swimming. And I couldn't get a full breath in. And in a way, it felt like I was dying.

*Shit.*

*I'm an asshole.*

*I bet he's freaking out.*

I'd seen humans and I'd…fuck. It's like my brain went completely offline.

My mouth was dry as I addressed the person speaking. When my vision focused, I was startled to realize that I'd just come face-to-face with the same white-haired human I'd seen at the ball. *Holy shit. What are the chances of that?* I blinked, surprised.

Acid swam up my throat.

*Don't throw up.*

*Don't throw up.*

"First…auction?" I repeated hoarsely, unable to stop staring at him.

He had snowy white eyelashes and skin as pale as his hair. Paired with the lilac color of his eyes, and the pointy ears on his head, it was difficult to believe he was actually human at all. On his back sat a pair of wings, they were gorgeous and snowy, made of downy feathers that glittered in the light.

It gave him the appearance of an angel.

"They happen every once in a while," the other human shrugged. His wings fluttered behind him, catching my attention for a moment. My stomach churned when I realized they were far too small for him to ever achieve actual flight. So why…did he have them then? "It can be jarring the first time, but you get used to it."

"You live here?" I asked, so distracted by him that I barely registered Roark coming to a halt behind me. He was panting, a stressed little whine escaping him. Though I was still reeling, it felt second nature to lean back against his chest to comfort him. His tendrils shot out, sucking at me almost desperately—like he wanted to pull me inside himself so I couldn't disappear again.

"I'm sorry," I glanced up at Roark apologetically, my fingers tangling with the tendrils that wrapped around my body. They curled around my fingers, almost like a glove. Similar to the way I'd seen his tendrils mesh with Mala's before when they were play-fighting. "I'm okay. I'm sorry. I'm *so* sorry."

"Is he bothering you?" the other human asked curiously. He didn't sound alarmed, his tone scarily neutral. "Your owner?"

"Ah…no." I flushed, feeling the weight of the glittering necklace that sat around my neck settle. "He's my…" I licked my lips. Roark rubbed his cheek against my hair to self-soothe, the protective bastard. "He's kinda my boyfriend?" That seemed wrong. "Space-boyfriend." That also seemed wrong. "Lover-beast. Almost-husband. Mate."

The other human snorted, lips twisting into a serene smile. "I see."

"We're just visiting."

Roark had informed me that this was our last stop before we reached his planet. I'd actually laughed out loud when he taught me its name, "Osheania." Seemed God had jokes, even this far out in the galaxy.

"How did you manage that?" Blondie lifted a pale brow. There was hunger in his eyes—though his expression remained serene.

"How did I manage…getting a space-boyfriend?"

"No. How are you *free*?"

"Oh." I glanced up at Roark, then the platform full of humans, then my new cat-like bird-buddy. "Um." Something moved behind him, and I flinched—before I realized it was the tail I'd seen earlier. Because apparently the wings weren't enough. "I was a slave on F'ukYuu and he bought me. But then…" my eyes stung a little. "But then he *freed* me. So I'm just…"

"How do you *know* you're free?" He cocked his head. I knew he wasn't trying to be mean. Well, actually, I didn't know that. But I hoped. "He could be lying. Did he tell you explicitly?"

"He didn't have to." There were a lot of things I didn't understand anymore. A lot of things that made me shaky and scared—that made me feel like I was stuck in a car with a bad driver at the wheel. But this wasn't one of them. I stood firm, defending Roark to this perfect stranger as he watched me, eyes flickering with emotion. "Roark is a *good* person. Noble."

"You are…fortunate," blondie responded. "Far more fortunate than anyone else I know."

"I am," I agreed, rubbing Roark's tendrils as he watched the two of us interact. I could tell he was two seconds from bolting. From taking us back to the safety of the ship where no one could touch me. Where I couldn't be sold like cattle—or even have to *see* it happen to anyone else.

I knew for a fact that Roark would've preferred I hadn't seen this.

But I was glad I had.

"What's your name?" the human asked.

"Hugo."

"Interesting."

"What's yours?" I wasn't sure he'd give it, but I hoped he would.

"Briar."

Briar. It suited him. As beautiful as he was—and he *was*, Jesus Christ, the most beautiful man I'd ever seen in my entire fucking life—I could tell he had thorns. Something twisted and scared lurked behind his eyes, his serene smile nothing but armor.

What had he lived through that had taught him to hide like that?

I could see the envy bubbling behind his gaze as he watched me and Roark. The longing. The desperation.

"Do you want to stay here, Briar?" I asked, though I got the feeling I already knew the answer. Roark had asked me that same exact question a lifetime ago.

"Why wouldn't I?" He smiled, wide and bright. "It's *wonderful.*"

"I…" Didn't know what to do. He was lying. He was so clearly lying. I peered up at Roark and he rumbled quietly back to me to reassure me. He said something in his native tongue, but I couldn't understand.

"Tell your friend to stop worrying," Briar rolled his eyes. "I'm not going to hurt you—convert you—adopt you, or enlist you."

"You can understand him?" I blinked.

Briar shrugged, tipping his head so I could see the back of his neck. He tapped something behind his ear, a tiny silver disk that looked like it had been inlaid directly into his skin. "I can understand everyone," he replied as if that wasn't the coolest shit in the world.

I stared at him for a moment, doing my best not to be jealous and failing. I knew there would be more headsets on Osheania, but seeing a reminder of the permanent implant I should've received but hadn't, sucked. I'd been alone with Roark so long I'd nearly forgotten about the implants entirely. Swiftly, I shoved those feelings aside. They didn't serve me at the moment, not so far into our travels, and so close to our new home.

There were more important things right now than envy.

I whipped around to face Roark, tipping my head to meet his worried gaze. I knew he didn't understand me a lot of the time, and this was a big ask after all the money he'd dropped today.

But…

I couldn't leave Briar here.

I couldn't leave *any* of the humans here.

Not if I could help it.

I got the feeling he'd understand.

Roark's eyes searched mine. His shoulders relaxed, his spots morphing from gray to white as I reached up and he bent down to place his big head in my hands, meeting me halfway. "Roark," I said carefully. "*Please*."

He blinked, brow furrowed, his spots yellow as he thought.

"*Please*."

I knew he'd understand what I wanted.

Roark's gaze flickered to Briar.

Then to the stage.

He was in captain-mode as he twisted out of my grip, standing to his full impressive height as he observed the dais covered in humans with a calculating glint in his gaze. Probably counting them and calculating how much they cost, and if we had room on board to take them in.

I knew this was a big ask.

Though our ship was large, there was still limited space. Limited food resources. And I was asking him to drop…fuck. I didn't even know how many credits. I didn't even know if he had it. I could only hope.

Roark settled, a look of determination crossing his features as his spots turned from yellow to blue and he gave me a single, solitary nod.

"Do you want to come home with me?" I jerked my attention to Briar the second I had Roark on board. "Do you want to be free?"

He glared at me like I was an idiot. "Don't fuck with me."

"I'm serious," I told him. "Do you want to come? Don't lie this time."

Briar was silent for a moment, a war waging in his eyes. "Me and…the others?" He glanced toward the group of humans. "You're going to buy *all* of us?" He sounded dubious at best.

"We're going to *free* all of you," I countered. Sure it was only fifteen people—sixteen, adding Briar on. But…it was a start, right? Sahrks were gentle. Maybe the humans could come home with us and find mates and occupations too.

"You're the stupidest human I've ever met," Briar sighed, but his tone was almost affectionate when he realized I was truly going to do this. "Taking all of us isn't going to be easy. Humans are a hot commodity on this side of the galaxy. There's a reason they're being sold on that stage."

"Why aren't you…" I flushed, realizing I was being rude. "If you're for sale, why aren't you up *there*?"

Briar's expression barely wavered. His eyes were dark as his lips spread into a brilliant smile—the only sign that he was affected by the question at all was the stiff way he stood. "If *they're* the main course." Briar jerked his shoulder toward the platform and its slaves, decked in gossamer like he was—currently being auctioned off like cattle. "That makes me the sample plate."

The horror of that statement washed through my body.

"For the buyers that aren't certain, I'm offered as incentive. A little taste of what they could have," he continued speaking, tone as acerbic as usual. It hadn't occurred to me that there were worse fates out there than what I'd ended up with on F'ukYuu. My heart hurt for Briar as I sucked in a breath.

"Fucking hell, dude. That's awful."

"Yes, well. It *is* my life." Briar's smile never wavered. "But apparently you want to change that." He eyed the glittering diamonds around my neck, the packages in Roark's arms, and then the big pink man himself. It felt like a test. "Are you sure you're going to do this? I mean—you do realize you're going to be painting a giant neon target on the back of your ship?"

Roark already knew that.

I was certain.

And he'd said yes.

"I'm sure," I reached out to squeeze Roark's palm as he rumbled thoughtfully, probably doing math still—or calculating the logistics of taking home sixteen humans. I knew it wasn't a simple ask, but I just…

I *couldn't* leave them.

Especially after finding out what happened to Briar.

Roark returned my tight grip, before he pulled his communicator out of his pocket and began making calls. My eyes never strayed from the humans for sale. Briar was quiet beside me, as somber as I was despite his dazzling smile.

I didn't know how Roark was going to manage this. Didn't know how that was possible—at all. But I had faith anyway. Roark was a planner, a captain, a leader. If anyone could figure this out, it was him.

He had a bigger heart—hearts—than anyone I'd ever met.

Forty minutes later, Roark showed me exactly why he'd been named Captain.

There was a line-up of humans trailing behind us, all of them varying versions of terrified as they followed us down the escalator and toward our ship. Briar stayed beside me, silent for the most part. His eyes flickered everywhere, like he was searching the crowd for a danger only he could see.

As far as I could tell, he was the only human who had been experimented on. None of the others had tails or wings. Additionally, I was one of the only humans without a permanent translator implant. I could only assume Briar's body modifications had something to do with the statement he'd made earlier about being a sample for customers.

Which was an awful thought that also led me to wonder why he'd been at the ball the night before.

Had he been in the process of being "tasted" then?

*That's so fucking awful.*

The thought made me sick to my stomach, and I was quickly distracted from it as Roark's crew met us at the bottom of the escalator. There were more Sahrk's than humans, and they fanned out around the procession, guarding them silently while Roark and I led them toward the ship that would take us to our new home.

The colorful variety of aliens that wandered the docks shifted to the side, making room for us as they paused what they were doing to observe the steadily moving procession. All of them stared as we passed, their many eyes trained on the humans and their toothy saviors. It wasn't positive attention. And some aliens wore more calculating expressions than others.

The attention was as sobering as it was frightening.

When I glanced up to check on Roark, his expression was grim, his spots were blue, and his eyes were distant. Like he was seeing a tragedy occur before it even happened.

After what he'd told me, I ached to comfort him.

So I tugged on his arm a little. He glanced down at me as we *finally*—ohmygod—reached the ship's boarding ramp. He blinked away the daze with a soft smile, but I could tell he was still worried.

"Huu-goh," he said, a tendril leaking out of his arm to tuck a wayward strand of my hair behind my ear. "Is okay, little beast. Roark will make okay."

It was the second time he'd made that promise.

And this time I was just as worried as the first.

I wasn't sure it was okay.

Not if Roark was scared.

"Is *okay*," he promised. "Roark will keep safe."

I believed him.

Because of course I did.

It wasn't till much later that I realized by trying to save all the humans I'd made Roark's worst nightmare come true.

# TWENTY-THREE

## ROARK

**UNEASE COLORED MY SPOTS GRAY** the moment we left planet Sha'hPihn. Mala and Ushuu were the only other people that understood my true trepidation.

It wasn't the huu-mans themselves that worried me, or even that we now had sixteen extra mouths to feed—though that in itself was a challenge. I was concerned because the *moment* we had publicly boarded the ship with such precious cargo, I knew it was only a matter of time before someone tried to take the huu-mans back.

As a whole, the flock of huu-mans were quiet, sweet, mildly terrified—and not threatening in the slightest. Huu-mans were smaller than most species, their limbs weak and unchangeable. And all of them were so different-looking, it was fascinating. They had more varieties than Sahrks did when it came to coloring, and I knew I was not the only man on board who found that beautiful.

My crew was as enamored with them as I was.

And despite all that they had been through before joining us, there was no dissent amongst the tiny creatures, for which I was glad. I did not fear the huu-mans, but I did worry about their safety and their happiness. I worried for Huu-goh's heart, because he had given it to them the moment he'd seen them at the auction.

Their peace was a relief.

Though my unease never fully faded.

Huu-goh and the prickly huu-man—Briar—had their work cut out for them. Watching my little mate come into himself as a leader was riveting. He spent as much time away from our room as I did now, tending to his people in the section of the ship we'd cleared for them. Less and less time was spent in the labs with Ushuu at first, but the elder Sahrk didn't mind. He'd often be found down with Huu-goh and the huu-mans himself, enjoying their stories, and sharing some of his own.

His presence made a large difference, helping the huu-mans feel more at ease around us.

I always kept extra bunks in the cargo hold for emergencies and it had only taken a few hours on that first day to get an extra storage room set up for their flock. I wished I could offer more to them, but it wasn't safe to linger. The target painted on our back made it imperative we seek the stars immediately.

My nightmares returned.

Every night, the same memory repeated.

Huu-goh tried to comfort me—and I tried to hide, but he saw right through me.

I was certain I wouldn't be able to breathe again till we arrived safely home on Osheania. It was a month-long journey from Sha'hPihn. It would be the longest month of my life. Between my very real fears, and Huu-goh and my mating ceremony, there was a never-ending list of things to worry about.

"Roark," Ushuu was gentle as he latched onto my elbow, pulling me aside. Huu-goh had been tinkering around inside the lab all day today—for the first time since we'd set off three weeks ago—and I'd finished my duties at the helm of the ship in time to catch him in action.

"You are going to worry yourself sick," Ushuu frowned at me, his spots gray with concern.

"I cannot help it."

Huu-goh sat obliviously on a stool across the room, fiddling with a machine on the counter. I had no idea what it was, and wasn't certain I wanted to. My head was too full. Maybe when I felt more like myself, I'd ask.

Part of me wanted to pull him into our rooms and hide with him until all of this passed. But that was the coward's route. And not one I would ever take. I was ashamed of myself for even thinking it.

Briar eyed me suspiciously from his seat beside my mate. He had stuck close to Huu-goh since the moment the huu-mans had come aboard. Almost like he was guarding him, as I did. I did not like the way Briar looked at me. As if he thought I was not what I said I was, and he was waiting for me to show my true colors.

It was a shame that one so small could be so injured.

His heart was battered and bruised, and I hoped time with my Huu-goh would help him realize that not all beasts were monsters.

"You can't control the future," Ushuu said as he gave my arm a gentle rub, his tendrils finding mine and winding us together in a soothing squeeze. "You are exhausting yourself to the point of weakness. Should something happen, do you not think your strength would be your greatest asset?"

He had a point.

I grunted, then sighed, dropping my head in shame. "I don't know if I can survive it a second time." I wished I was being dramatic, but it was the truth. My darkest truth. Gnarled, broken, brittle. "The first time I did not have much, and still, having that taken nearly broke me. Now I have *everything*. I cannot afford to lose my heart so soon after I found it."

Ushuu would understand better than anyone.

He'd lived through my worst nightmare.

Huu-goh must have sensed my distress because he turned, his bright eyes dimming as a worried twist curled his lips. He was off his seat and across the room in seconds, looking between the two of us with concern. "What's wrong?" he asked in his own language.

"Huu-goh is okay," I promised him, so he wouldn't worry that he was in danger. His lovely brown eyes peeked at me through his fluffy orange fur. It was longer now than ever, and hung over his forehead. I enjoyed it, maybe a little too much.

Ushuu rolled his eyes at my hypocrisy.

"Are *you* okay?" Huu-goh scowled, tapping his cute little toes on the ground impatiently. It had been three weeks of this. Of me skirting around his questions, avoiding his concern. Pampering and loving him in the quiet of our room, and pretending like danger hadn't sunk its claws inside our ship. Like I wasn't trying to outrun fate.

"I…" I smiled, hoping my spots didn't betray me. "I am okay."

"Liar," Huu-goh reached up, his tiny hands trying to get to my face.

He didn't care that we had an audience, and truthfully, I didn't either. I released my mentor, tendrils twining around my love's little body so that I could haul him high enough he could reach. "*Roark.*"

"Little beast," I murmured, nuzzling his sweet cheeks. "I am fine," I promised gently.

"*Roark,*" he tried again, obviously concerned.

"*Huu-goh,*" I countered just as seriously. Huu-goh's lips wobbled, and a snicker burst free. My worries melted away. He babbled something I didn't understand, far too fast for me to catch the words despite how many of them I knew now. Then he kissed me, slow and sweet, his little tongue twisting out to meet mine—the way Sahrks mated with their mouths.

I shuddered.

"You guys are dihsguhsting," Briar huffed. He'd walked over while we'd been tongue-kissing. I separated from Huu-goh's mouth, watching Huu-goh's pale friend curiously. I did not need to know the word "dihsguhsting" to know it was not complimentary.

However, I saw the way Briar looked at us with a mixture of jealousy and affection, so I was not offended.

"It will be okay," Huu-goh said softly to me in his own tongue, one of his little hands sinking into my chest. He ignored his friend's comments, his attention mine and mine alone. His fingers tangled with my tendrils as he smiled encouragingly. Apparently it was his turn to comfort me.

*I hate this.*

*I never wanted to show him this side of myself.*

It was my purpose to be strong—to be...big enough, smart enough, capable of protecting him.

I could remember the day that haunted my thoughts as clearly as if it had happened yesterday. I'd been a new recruit and the tragedy had occurred during my first voyage. Captain had been a practical man, his eyes only found the stars when he was looking toward where we were traveling. If he had dreams, he never spoke of them, but he was always warm.

He was everything I'd always wanted to be.

Reliable, tough, no-nonsense.

From the day we'd boarded and he'd caught me jotting down notes, he'd taken a liking to me. I climbed through the ranks rapidly, lucky enough to be chosen as a runner for him and Ushuu early on. After six months traveling through the stars we'd settled into a pattern together. Most of my days I shadowed Captain and Ushuu around the ship—learning all there was to learn, aiding them when they needed errands run or messages relayed. As a nervous, but eager young man, his wealth of knowledge and example had meant the world. Captain was the one that had taught me that I could work through my difficulties talking.

He told me he had struggled as I did when he was young. It was hard to believe, seeing him for what he was now. Grizzled and aged, hard edges, and wrinkled surface. His spots never changed color, always blue.

Everything Captain said was spoken with purpose.

I hung on every word.

Not because he was perfect, but because he spent every moment he could making sure that I understood that there was no shame in strength built from hard work. He wanted me to turn my weaknesses into assets. He said that if I was stubborn, if I never gave up, one day I could man the ship on my own.

I'd always been large—gifted with a stature that turned most heads back home. But I had never had the gift of communication. My thoughts were often hard to articulate, they came out clumsy, especially when I was nervous. There had been many times in my life that I wished I was better. There had been even more occasions that I'd been convinced my struggles communicating would prevent me from achieving my dream of commanding a ship myself.

Captain taught me to work hard.

He taught me so long as you were trying, you were succeeding.

So I took notes. I devoured his words. I followed behind him, his loyal pink shadow. I guarded his room when Ushuu visited, redirecting traffic so that they could have privacy. I tucked him inside my heart in the space beside my father, and I prayed to the stars that one day I could be half the Sahrk he was.

The day that the ship was attacked had been just like any other.

I'd made my bed, taken a shower, dressed in my uniform. With my bag slung over my shoulder, I'd woken my bunk mate, Kael up. He swore at me like he always did, annoyed to be roused so early. Then we'd made our way to the cafeteria. We roughhoused a bit down the halls, and he talked a mile a minute about what he'd do when we reached our first planet.

Kael had as many dreams as I did, but while mine involved chasing responsibility, his revolved around escaping as much of it as possible.

Captain and Ushuu had been at breakfast, like they often were. I was certain the majority of the ship had no idea that they were together, as they'd never officially mated. It was a wonder they hadn't noticed when it was obvious how much they cared for one another.

We'd eaten together and things had been fine.

They'd been fine.

Captain asked me how I slept—I said "good". Ushuu passed me a bottle of water—and then—

And then—

The lights went out.

And the screaming started.

I tried to save them. I tried to fight. When the pirates entered the room, I challenged them—certain my strength, my gift, would be enough. Even rising to my full impressive height, the invaders were not intimidated.

It wasn't enough.

Shots rang out, deafening and loud.

Kael hit the ground first, his dark, nearly black surface growing pale as blood pooled beneath his body. It was hard to see much in the dark, but I managed.

When I jumped in front of Captain, he yanked me out of the way—another bang sounding loud enough my ears rang. I was close enough to him that I could see the wound that blossomed in the center of his forehead spot. Blue blood leaked down either side of his snout as his eyes grew cloudy and his spots paled, colorless and dead, just as Kael's had.

He fell to the floor with a thud.

Before I could scream and attack—before I could so much as breathe, Ushuu yanked me to the ground.

Together we lay in the puddle of blood, as the world spun and spun and spun.

The pirates left to retrieve the cargo they'd been after.

Ushuu's quick thinking had saved our lives.

I learned a lesson that day.

The most valuable lesson I'd ever learn.

Good things don't last, so they need to be cherished. Coveted. Protected.

Because one day they'll disappear.

Death takes no prisoners.

And I needed to be vigilant, if I wanted to keep the people I loved safe.

# TWENTY-FOUR

## HUGO

**AS THE DAYS TICKED DOWN** until our arrival on his—no, *our*—planet, Roark's apprehension only grew. Following him around like the pet I'd used to think I was, helped a little—but it made it difficult for Roark to do his job. And he had eventually put a stop to that. He wanted me to act normal.

So…normal I acted.

I'd spend time with the other humans, telling them stories about the places Roark and I had visited. About him in general, because I knew some of them were still wary of the Sahrks and worried that they had traded one captor for another.

Ushuu's presence helped. He was less threatening than the others, and when I wasn't in the lab with him he was down with the humans, sharing food with them and telling them stories about his life traveling the stars.

There was no stopping my anxiety about the threat of pirates—but I could admit, even that fear was outweighed by my excitement.

Which made me feel guilty.

Don't get me wrong—of course, I was deeply concerned for Roark and his very real fears. This entire situation had to be awful for him. Not that he regretted saving the humans—because I knew he didn't—but because it brought up things from his past he'd had to bury for the sake of his own sanity.

The nightmares were a testament to that.

I was concerned—and empathetic—but the part of me that had never been loved, that had never even left the city he'd grown up in, was elated to visit my new home for the very first time. And with every day that passed, that home grew closer, and the likelihood that we'd be attacked grew slimmer.

Some of the humans asked about returning "home" to Earth. Which had caused me a lot of mixed feelings. Ushuu, thankfully, had explained that wasn't possible. I hadn't wanted to be the one to broach that subject. Truthfully, I didn't know how.

Though I'd become kind of a defacto leader for the small group of Earthlings, I was still just…me. The only leadership positions I'd ever had had been for the chess and robotics clubs back home, and that felt like a lifetime ago. I was doing my best, but there was only so much I could do.

I seemed to be one of a select few who felt no remorse at the discovery that we would not be returning to the place of our origin. I wasn't a good actor, and I didn't think I could believably fake being sad about it for long.

Truthfully, even if I'd *had* the means to return to Earth, I had no interest in doing that. My life there had been like peeking through a pinhole. I couldn't see the possibilities, not with my vision so limited.

Now I could.

My world had expanded. There were endless adventures, endless opportunities. If I'd thought the planet and customers on F'ukYuu were fascinating, the universe and species outside it was infinitely more so.

Even more than that though…it was the little things that enticed me to stay. Not the extraordinary. Not the stars, or the space travel, or the exploration.

But the mornings in bed. Days spent incorporated into the pattern of Roark's life.

I could envision our future as easily as I saw the view from the helm spread inky black and glittery. And it was a beautiful, wonderful thing to be so enchanted by the way a person snored, or the way he held himself stiff and at attention, or the way he was ready to give his life for the people he loved.

I'd learned a lot of things while out in space.

But the most important thing I'd learned was that happiness tasted like Roark's laughter.

It was a precious thing.

And it needed protecting, just like he did.

Even if the person I was protecting him from was himself. I did my best to distract him—using my arsenal of lingerie and new toys to entice and tease. And for a few hours each night, it worked. He'd smile, he'd spend time with me, we'd fuck and fall into bed.

But every night, like clockwork, when I lay curled inside his arms, doing my best to comfort him—it was never enough. The humming *helped*, but that was only at first. Eventually, I'd succumb to sleep, and Roark's nightmares would return with a vengeance.

Several weeks in, Roark had given up resting at all.

And I was out of new lingerie to distract him with.

He'd lay with me, yes, but he'd remain stiff as a board. Blue eyes, unseeing, stared up at the stars on the ceiling, and as far as I knew—they never shut. His demons refused to let him free. Not when he had such precious cargo aboard.

I got the feeling he thought he had to face them alone.

But he didn't.

Not anymore.

I was thinking about that fact, my heart tied in knots as Ushuu spoke softly. I knew what Ushuu was to Roark, but even before that I'd always shown him the utmost respect. As our journey neared its end, I hung on his every word, listening to everything he taught me with rapt attention.

Ushuu was brilliant.

He knew things.

Crazy-ass space-y things.

About tech, and biology, and more recently since the humans had boarded—the fuel he created on the ship to replenish the supply when we were running low between ports. According to Ushuu, it was a volatile substance—highly poisonous—and the most important thing he produced.

Roark had fueled up when we were on Sha'hPihn, but that didn't mean we wouldn't run low. It was better to be prepared than sorry. That was Ushuu's favorite thing to say. He said it all the time. About everything—including how high he piled his plate full of snacks to get him through the day.

There were big empty vats for "Ushuu's special fuel" lining the back of the lab. Briar and I had worn hazmat suits to get them into place—and

Ushuu had activated a holo-shield to act as a guard between them and the rest of the lab, so no one could accidentally knock into them during the period when we were finishing brewing the viscous substance.

Ushuu and I had spent the better part of the current day refilling the barrels with the fluorescent green liquid. We'd gotten to use these giant, frankly amazing, funnels to do it—and my worries had been the last thing on my mind while we worked. One mistake—and I could seriously injure both me and Ushuu. The hazmat suits helped, of course, but accidents still happened.

Meanwhile Briar stood in the corner judging us. He had no interest in actually helping out. He reminded me of a cat, most of the time. Which was apt, considering the fact that I was pretty sure the ears and tail he had were feline. I figured those weren't his only "upgrades" and the one and only time I'd asked him, he'd clammed up so tight I'd made a vow to never bring it up again.

I still couldn't get a read on him.

It was like…he had these *walls*. More walls than I'd ever had, even though we'd come from the same place. I couldn't imagine what he'd been through that would cause him to become an impenetrable fortress—but I hoped with enough time and patience he'd realize he was safe here with us.

"Too much," Briar told me. I jerked the vial I was pouring back, startled. Ushuu made a soothing noise, his wrinkled eyes squinting softly at me with affection.

"Careful, please," he murmured, reaching out with one hand to ruffle my hair.

"Sorry," I smiled back, heart thumping unsteadily, determined now to keep my mind present as we finished our work for the day.

This was one thing I did not want to fuck up.

If I could prove myself useful then maybe…maybe I could earn my place here. Maybe I could actually take over for Ushuu like Roark wanted me to. It was a new dream. Just like I'd hoped I'd one day get. And it was my most brilliant dream yet.

Briar and I were leaving the lab to meet Roark for lunch when I sensed something was wrong. Unease twisted tight as a noose around my throat, cutting off my airways and making it hard to breathe. My gut churned, this swirling, *awful* burn that threatened to climb high enough it spilled free.

I'd experienced something similar to this feeling only once before.

The day I'd been taken.

Three years later and a galaxy away, that day still felt crisp in my mind. Maybe it was the terror I'd felt that memorialized it—or maybe it was simply because nothing like that had ever happened to me before. Either way, even though I didn't often allow myself to recall what had occurred, the memories remained frozen in perfect detail.

It had been a boring day—maybe a little brisk, but nothing memorable. Autumn in my hometown had always been brutal. Colorful leaves littered the ground, my footsteps disjointed as I hopped over cracks—my acceptance letter to Harvard tucked safely in my backpack.

The mailbox was a shared one, positioned at the end of the cul-de-sac. I'd just opened it—just pulled the letter out after arriving home from school, and I was elated.

One moment I was waltzing up the sidewalk toward home—my heart pounding—and the next I was…

I was—

In space.

The only warning I'd received before everything changed was the same exact curl of dread I felt now. Like instinct.

"Ushu—" my words cut off as I twisted back toward the lab, where the elder Sahrk remained, but before I could even finish uttering his name, history repeated itself.

Not my history.

But Roark's.

One moment, the world was illuminated, and the next we were enveloped in sudden darkness. Different than the time I'd accidentally hit the switch, this was the oppressive kind. The kind that suffocated. The kind that tasted like death.

*Fuck.*

*Fuck-fuck-fuck.*

Above us, the door attempted to shut, an awkward beeping sound escaping it when it noticed there was something obstructing its movement. It returned back up, leaving the doorway open, the only indication anything was wrong, the little red light blinking in the dark.

With sweaty palms, I jerked Briar into the lab with me and its relative safety. He made a startled noise.

*If we're quiet enough, maybe they won't know we're here, even without the door.*

Ushuu's worried rumble echoed from behind us as we all slid along the back wall. *Thump, thump, thump.* The beat of my heart felt impossibly loud as we stayed quiet.

"Ushuu—" my voice cut off in the quiet. "Are you okay?"

He'd been handling the chemicals. Chemicals that emitted a soft glow, even in the pitch black. I worried that he'd been hurt—startled by the light going out. Vaguely, I could see the Sahrk-ish shape of his body in the back corner of the room, and I pulled Briar along with me, toward it.

I understood Roark in a new way now. The unknown sunk its icy fingers inside my chest, slicing through my heart as I waited with bated breath to see what would happen next. Pirates were aboard. I knew that. The safety systems wouldn't have been activated if they weren't.

*Roark.*

*Roark has to be so scared—*

"Huu-goh," Ushuu answered, sounding panicked. I'd never heard him like this. And the thought made me ache.

"Are you hurt?" I confirmed, still approaching, but keeping my voice quiet enough I hoped no one would hear.

"N-no." Ushuu was shaking. I hadn't noticed from far away, but as I reached him, laying a hand on his shoulder I could feel him quake.

Roark had told me that he had lost his mate just like this.

The thought made me ache to pull him into a tight embrace. To soothe his fears.

But for a moment my mind…my mind was selfishly on my own mate. On my Roark. Who was on the other side of the ship, currently, and probably freaking the fuck out. With the lights off, there was no way for him to check the security cameras to ensure our safety. The glow from the fuel was enough to illuminate the vague shapes of things, but not nearly bright enough for the cameras to pick up.

With my ears buzzing, I managed to find Ushuu's hand in the dark. It was icy cold, his fingers limp as I pulled him away from the dangerous half of the room and toward the corner least visible from the hallway. He went willingly, and Briar was silent as he helped me lower Ushuu to the floor. When I touched him, even his head fin was icy. Stroking my fingers soothingly over it, I tried to figure out what to do next.

Only…my options became increasingly limited when I heard something out in the hall.

There were footsteps approaching, slow and steady.

*Maybe it's Roark?*

My first thought was hopeful, the steady thud of the feet were as heavy as his, after all.

But…somehow I knew it wasn't him. My gut—the same gut that had told me what was about to go down before it had happened—knew the truth.

The lab was located nearer to the cargo bay than the helm where Roark spent most of his time. I was grateful. So fucking grateful, because if the danger was near me it was far, *far* away from him. I loved him to bits, but I knew his weakness.

If he thought I was out here unprotected—like I was—I knew there was nothing that would stop him from plowing through the pirates without a thought to get to me.

Which…could result in casualty.

Casualties I knew he didn't want to happen.

He was a planner. He always had been. Serious to a fault, and hard to ruffle. But if there was one thing his reaction to me running from him at the auction had taught me, it was that I was his exception. Roark was the most rational person in the world—except when it came to me.

Which meant it was up to me to fix this. To stay safe. And to join him—

I wanted to tell him that things were alright.

But I couldn't.

It was an empty promise.

"It's okay," I whispered quietly to Ushuu as we waited in darkness.

"Shut up," Briar snapped at me, his voice as icy as Ushuu's surface was.

*Thud, thud, thud*—the footsteps in the hallway grew louder the closer they came.

*Please, please, please pass by us.*

*Please, please, please—*

*Thud, thud, thud,* even louder now.

Close.

So close.

Right outside the open door.

My heart was thumping loud enough I feared the intruder would be able to hear it. Briar's breathing was erratic to my left. I could feel the panicked puff of it glancing over my shoulder. I had no doubt the other humans were faring even worse. But in that moment, I couldn't do anything but focus on the people in my immediate vicinity.

Roark would be proud, I told myself, knowing it was true.

*Take care of them.*

Even in the dark, we were close enough that when I glanced at him, I could see that his eyes were pinched tightly shut.

"Found you," an unfamiliar voice grunted.

It wasn't Roark's voice, though it was admittedly similar in cadence.

The newcomer's English was clumsy—much like Roark's was—though there was a confidence to it that made it obvious he knew more of the language than my Sahrk did.

Fear, unlike anything I'd ever known surged through my body.

*Use what Roark taught you*, I reminded myself. Surprise is your best friend.

As the creature approached, his shape became more apparent. If I hadn't been able to guess from his voice alone, the broad shoulders would've betrayed him. There was no denying that whatever creature this was, was a male. His silhouette blocked the door entirely, and as I dragged my gaze upward, with startling clarity I realized I recognized the shape of his head.

A Sahrk?

Was it one of ours?

Maybe someone else had tripped the door mechanism like I had?

Maybe we weren't the only ones running free?

I tried to hope, but that hope was quickly dashed by Briar's immediate response.

"Fuck," Briar swore quietly. "Fuck, fuck, fuck—"

And then he was being yanked around my body like a fucking rag doll. Tendrils snaked inky black around him, yanking him close to the beast in the doorway.

Before I could react, the new Sahrk was speaking again.

"*Safe*," he said, garbled and rough.

"What…is…*happening*?" My words were maybe a bit frantic as the unfamiliar Sahrk hugged Briar to his chest and took a few more steps into the room. "Briar?"

There was a beat of silence as I debated if I could go for this guy's knees with Briar still held aloft.

"He's safe," Briar said, sounding like it pained him to do so. Immediately, I stopped planning my attack.

*What the hell was going on?*

"He's safe?" Was Briar hooking up with someone on board already? Did he know Sahrks mate for life? He *had* to know that. We'd talked about it. Extensively. As the resident Sahrk expert, I'd relayed all the information I'd gathered about the species to every human present to prepare them.

Oh well.

At the moment, it didn't matter whether or not Briar was the next in line for a Sahrk wedding. What mattered was our current predicament—and the fact that Roark was somewhere on the ship more than likely locked inside the helm, terrified.

It was, admittedly, *odd* that the newcomer Sahrk spoke as much English as he did—but then again, so did Ushuu—so I pushed that thought to the back of my mind.

Maybe, like I'd hypothesized, he'd simply been stuck in the doorway when the lights went out. That was why he was free. Briar wouldn't say he was safe if he wasn't. He was a prickly person, but he was loyal. He'd never hurt me, or Ushuu for that matter.

The Sahrk's presence didn't mean he was a *pirate*.

Besides, I doubted Sahrks became pirates. They were peaceful as a species, and Roark had told me as much.

"They've boarded," the newcomer said, his voice growly like he'd been deep-throating a carton of rocks. Or like he never talked. At all. Ever. "They're here for your people."

"They're not *my* people," Briar scoffed, though his voice sounded small and frightened.

That pissed me off a little. "Of course they're your people, Briar."

"They're—ugh. Fuck. Fine." He gave in reluctantly.

"I will take you away—" Growly-guy promised.

"Fuck you," Briar hissed. A sound emitted from between them—kinda like a smack?—and I squinted to try and figure out what the fuck was happening. *Did Briar just hit that dude?* "Set me down."

"This isn't the time to flirt," I admonished, responsibility settling on my shoulders as the situation came into focus. "Roark is out there—and he… fuck. He needs our help. The humans need our help—" I stroked a hand over Ushuu's chilly fin. "Ushuu needs our help."

If we didn't do something the pirates were going to take the humans.

They were going to take the cargo that Roark had just spent months gathering.

They would hurt people.

I couldn't let that happen.

"The helm is safe," Growly informed me, already turning around with Briar in tow, like he was about to make good on his promise to leave with the human, the rest of us be damned. "Humans not so much."

*Where was he going? I didn't understand.*

"What do you mean?" I didn't mean to grab him—except that I did. My nails dug into his forearm, stomach churning with worry. Ushuu rumbled softly to soothe me, but it wasn't the right pitch. It wasn't Roark's pitch. "How do you know where he is?"

"Let me down," Briar made another smacking sound when he hit Growly, and the Sahrk snapped his teeth at him. At least—that's what I assumed that awful sound was. "I'm not going anywhere."

Growly growled—making his nickname apt.

"Please," my fingers jerked in the back of his vest. His *vest.* On board The Dreamer, I hadn't seen a single Sahrk aside from Ushuu wear clothing on their torsos. It was odd. Even odder than the fact he knew English enough to communicate to the both of us.

"Please," I said again, holding still. He could've ripped out of my grip. It would've been easy. He could've hurt me—abandoned Ushuu and I in the dark, and been done with us both. But he didn't. "My mate...Roark is my *mate*. I need to...I need to understand what's happening so I can help him. He's probably so scared—and I...I have to get to him. I have to save the humans on board."

He was quiet for a moment. A moment that felt like a century.

He didn't move, didn't speak, just held Briar aloft, ignoring the increasing frequency of his slapping as he debated with himself. When he turned back around, I dropped my grip on his clothes, sagging a little when it was clear he'd made the choice to help me.

Ushuu was in shock, this...creature was the only person big enough and with enough knowledge to help me save the people I loved.

"It is how it works."

"How what works?"

"Sahrk spacecraft." He sighed, switching Briar to his other side. The blond had stopped hitting Growly about the same time he'd decided to help me. "The helm is the most secure part of the ship. They designed it that way so that no more casualties would befall the craft during invasion."

"Okay."

"Roark is Captain. He is at the helm. He is safe. The invaders will make their way to the cargo hold," he added. "They have no interest in the ship itself. The cargo you carry is worth more."

I nodded, my head swimming with worry.

"How do you...know all of this? Do you work here?"

Briar huffed out a long suffering sigh. It sounded like he hit the dude again. And then again. And then again. "He knows because he's a pirate. It's his job."

"He's a…" my head was spinning. "*What*?"

"Independent space traveler," Growly corrected, obviously not pleased by the term "pirate."

"Yeah, an *independent space* traveler that boards ships and steals shit," Briar snarked. "Which makes you a *pirate*." They had both moved close enough that when Briar's fingers found mine and he gave my hand a tight squeeze, I wasn't surprised.

"So, you're not…"

"With the other pirates? No." Beast huffed in annoyance, syrupy tendrils reached out, wrapping around Briar's wrist and my hand by extension. He growled unhappily, retreating when he realized Briar wasn't about to let go of me. "I am here for one human, and one human only."

"Yeah well, I'm not going with you, dipshit."

"You said these were not your people." Growly sounded adorably confused.

"They're not." Briar's hand tightened around mine. "But *Hugo* is. And I'm not fucking leaving him in a ship full of assholes with no protection."

The raw loyalty in Briar's voice shocked me for a moment. I hadn't realized he cared so much about me. Maybe I should have. As grouchy as he was, he very rarely left my side, always guarding me—even going so far as to try and protect me from my own mate.

"*You* cannot protect," I could literally hear Growly's eyeroll. "You are *small*. Tiny wings. Big temper. No claws. No weapons." I could feel the Sahrk's eyes running over me even in the dark. "Your friend is worse. He is somehow *smaller*. More pathetic. You will both fail. You will die."

He was right.

He was right and it was terrifying.

Except—

Except—shit. Maybe he wasn't right. Maybe we *did* have weapons. Unorthodox ones. But…my gaze slid toward the back wall and the funnel stuck inside the barrel Ushuu had been filling when the lights went out. Briar and I were still halfway inside our hazmat suits, for god's sake.

And that shit could…fuck.

That shit could probably kill someone, couldn't it?

It was the reason Ushuu had been so careful with it—and us.

"We are leaving," Growly reiterated as a plan began to form inside my mind.

Chemicals were dangerous.

I may not be able to incapacitate most of the species I'd met, but I'd taken Roark to his knees. I could do the same. Not many creatures were his size—and if I could get them on the ground, I could pour the fuel on them, couldn't I?

If they didn't see me coming…

Yes.

Roark had said the element of surprise was my greatest strength.

No one would look at me and expect me to be capable of this. Hell, I never would've thought myself capable. But with adrenaline running in my veins—with Roark's voice in my head giving me strength—with the fear I could feel, thick in the air—I…

Yes.

I could do this.

I could.

"No, we aren't," Briar continued to argue, oblivious to my murderous thoughts.

I should feel bad, shouldn't I? Thinking about killing pirates.

But…

I didn't.

How could I? When they didn't feel an ounce of regret for hurting what was mine. For coming after us—like we were objects and not people—for invading Roark's ship. His safe space. For causing him more nightmares.

It didn't occur to me then that I could get hurt.

And just like I had when I'd stepped into the pleasure house on F'ukYuu and they'd welded my collar into place, I accepted my new lot in life. As Roark's protector. As the human's leader. As a man, who wasn't a slave or a pet—but executioner and judge.

"We are leaving," Growly countered again.

"No."

Peace settled warm in my chest as I gave Ushuu's fin another gentle pet, curious to see how this argument played out—though my thoughts were still spinning through scenarios. Ideas about the best way to incapacitate our invaders, one by one, before they could cause lasting damage. I'd start with Growly first. Maybe if I jumped on the counter I could grab the container we'd been using to pour into the funnels? I could splash him with it—startle him enough that I could take him to his knees. If I dumped the rest down his throat I doubted he'd survive. Not when the liquid was acidic enough to eat through flesh.

"I…" Growly lost some of his steam, obviously stumped by Briar's stubbornness. He didn't seem to understand why Briar would choose to stay with me if it meant certain death. Totally unaware that I was currently plotting his demise, he spoke again, "But…"

During this entire exchange I could do nothing but squeeze Briar's hand, trembling a little as Ushuu's limbs reached out, tendrils wrapping around my ankle to comfort me. He was in…what I assumed was shock—and yet, still found a way to make me understand that I was not alone.

It helped steel my resolve even more.

*These* were my people.

The Sahrks, as well as the humans.

This was *my* ship.

If Briar stood beside me, he stood beside *them*.

"I won't go with you," Briar said. "Unless…"

Growly grumbled angrily under his breath, shifting anxiously back and forth as he decided what to do. I could hear his clothing rustle. Which was odd. Sahrk's normally didn't wear enough clothing for it to make sounds like that. "Unless…?" he sighed, defeated.

"Unless you help me save Hugo—and this ship. If you can do that, I'm all yours."

"Briar, no." I tightened my grip on his hand. "No—you can't. We can do it without him—I have a plan."

"Of course you d—" Briar was cut off when Growly spoke, faster than I think either of us had expected.

"Deal."

As Growly set Briar on the ground, he let me go. The Sahrk dipped his head, the shadowy shape of it sliding in close to the pale blur of the other human's body. I reached out blindly to stop him—only to discover Briar and the pirate were already shaking hands.

I was too fucking late.

I couldn't help but feel like he'd just sold his soul to the devil.

"*Stay.*" Growly hissed out, movements surprisingly quiet all of a sudden as he wandered around the room. He never bumped into anything, or tripped. So I could only assume he had some sort of device that was enabling him to see. "Ah." He made a sound, jabbing at something on the counter that emitted a quiet clinking noise when it moved. "This will work."

That was how twenty minutes later, Briar, Growly, and I ended up posed at the corners of a hallway with tiny vials of rocket fuel in our hands. I'd reluctantly explained to him what the fuel was—and what it could do—and while Briar and I had pulled our hazmat suits back into place, Ushuu had filled the vials.

"Do not miss." Growly—whose name was apparently Grimm (a surprisingly accurate name for such a mopey dick)—warned.

"Once again, I am annoyed that my dad and I never played catch," I muttered to myself, the weight of the bottle in my hand a little terrifying—despite the fact that this had been my idea. I didn't trust my aim, especially in the dark, so getting up close and personal would be my only option.

Grimm shoved the gas masks he'd found covered in dust in the back of one of Ushuu's cupboards onto our heads. They had an infrared feature—or what I *assumed* to be an infrared feature, seeing as I'd never used one before—so it was easy to spot both the glowing masses that were Grimm and Briar beside me.

According to Grimm, the pirates would be traveling in groups of three. He had been stalking them for weeks in his own spacecraft, and had hijacked their communications system, so he was privy to all their plans—even if it hadn't been "common sense" as he'd put it.

They were going to work their way down to the lowest levels of the ship to the cargo hold first. As soon as that was secured, they planned to use explosives to begin searching the rooms for the humans.

I was even more glad, then, that we'd decided to act.

Ushuu, who had at some point snapped out of the fog he'd fallen into, was in the lab refilling flasks while we waited in the hallway for our first target.

The Dreamer's emergency protocols were still in place, so we didn't have to worry about accidentally hurting an innocent—which was…relieving to say the least. The last thing I wanted was to hurt one of the crew members who had been so sweet to me over the last few months—or god forbid, Roark.

Unfortunately, because the humans were living in an empty cargo bay there were no doors to protect them from the pirates—and they'd be heading directly for them, even if they didn't know that yet.

Which meant we needed to work quickly and efficiently.

Ruthlessly.

Luck had not been something I'd carried with me for most of my life. It was nice that today of all days, I seemed to have some.

Our plan was to incapacitate the pirates in their clusters. If we were fast enough, they wouldn't even have time to raise the alarm. And we would work systematically through the hallways so that the others wouldn't have a chance to discover the bodies along the way.

Grimm had bullets in his gun, but he'd informed us that it was a last resort—as the sound would attract the exact kind of attention we did not want.

It was a good plan.

Grimm had looked impressed when I'd suggested it.

Truthfully, my thoughts were nothing but selfish. I wanted this *done*. I wanted these fucking assholes somewhere they couldn't hurt the people I loved.

Roark was waiting for me.

Roark was terrified.

His nightmares were coming true.

And I needed to comfort him more than I needed my next breath.

*Thud, thud, thud.* Just like Grimm had said they would, footsteps approached. I tapped my goggles, making sure everything was in place. My pulse was thrumming far faster than the approaching footsteps. *Thud, thud, thud.* Closer they came. Just as Grimm had predicted, there were three sets of footsteps, all with varying gaits.

I tightened my grip on the vial I held.

*You can do this.*

*You can do this, Hugo.*

*It's like a chess game. You just need to plan ahead.*

I'd never been athletic. Never been sporty or physically talented. But when those three pirates rounded the corner I forgot all of that. I forgot my past and the walls I'd erected. I forgot my weaknesses. All of Roark's training kicked in, and I became a man on a mission.

If I hit their abdomen it would incapacitate them long enough Grimm could tie them up. If I went straight for the head, it'd mean death pretty instantly.

My entire body screeched with effort as I launched myself at the smallest of the three glowing blobs and without remorse or hesitation, smashed the jar of fuel right into his face.

He made a gurgling noise as he hit the floor, the hissing sound of rotting flesh filling the air. I was more than a little glad I couldn't smell it—and for a moment, worried that the next pirates would be able to.

Two more thuds sounded from behind me.

My chest was heaving, sticky blood on my gloved hands. I rose from the felled body of the alien I'd just killed and watched as the light he emitted began to dull. What was bright faded with every second that passed.

In the dark, I couldn't see his face, and for that I was glad.

It was easier this way.

"Fuck," Briar hissed out from my left, sounding impressed. "You just *killed* that dude."

I blinked, head spinning.

"Not as weak as I thought," Grimm hummed. I wanted to think I was a good person, but there was no denying how good that had felt. More than good. My blood thrummed as the sticky slick of death coated my gloves. The aliens that Grimm and Briar had knocked out gurgled, and Grimm, following my example, bent low. A snapping sound filled the air as he twisted their necks.

"I guess we're killing all of them now?" Briar confirmed.

*If they were dead they'd never hurt anyone again.*

*Ever.*

It may not have been my original plan to outright murder all of them, but now that I'd done it once, the idea was easier to stomach. It was them or us, after all. It would be naive to think this could go any other way.

"Back into position," I commanded, not responding to Briar or Grimm's approval.

We had a job to do.

I had a pink shark I wanted to see before the day was over.

They both did as they were told without complaint.

I picked up another vial, hefting it in my palm.

And again, my focus narrowed.

If all went well—and Grimm was correct—there were less than thirty aliens to get rid of now. It may seem like a lot. And maybe later I'd feel guilty—but for now…no. No. I didn't think about death or my soul—or how many lives I was about to take.

I thought about *Roark*.

My big squishy pink heartthrob.

My mate.

The beast I *loved*.

I thought about his smile—all toothy and wide. His broken glasses. The way he viewed the world like he was ready for it to betray him. I thought about the way he *looked* at me. *Really* looked. I thought about the future we'd have together. The things we'd share. The home that would be ours, if we could survive today.

And with every pirate I killed, I got one step closer to making that reality.

Since the day we'd met, Roark had been my protector.

But today, it was my turn to return the favor.

# TWENTY-FIVE

## ROARK

**I WAS FRIGHTENED WHEN MY** father died, and I found myself alone. I was frightened when I'd joined the academy and my commanding officer had told me I wouldn't make it far if I couldn't learn to speak up. I was frightened the day our ship had taken off and I'd realized this was it. This was my *chance*. And if I missed it—I'd never get another one.

I was frightened when I picked up Huu-goh. Terrified I wouldn't know how to care for him when I'd never cared for someone else before.

But nothing…nothing in my life compared to the fear I felt the moment the lights went out and the door to the bridge slammed shut, locking me inside. And though in the past I'd always been grateful for their presence, it was only anger I felt as the safety response that had been programmed into my ship cut me off from my mate.

I had never been more desperate to break through metal.

To bend the laws of physics.

To break the things I held dear—just so I could get to him.

I was at the door in less than a second, claws screeching and scraping, tearing at it in an attempt to get through its surface. Tendrils sprang out, enveloping the hinges, looking for gaps and crevices. *Any* weakness that would mean I could get out and get to Huu-goh before they took him. There was no doubt in my mind that the pirates were here for the huu-mans.

And while I was concerned about all the cargo on board, nothing compared to the icy terror I felt when I thought of Huu-goh being stolen from me.

"No, no, no, no." My breathing was erratic, my head spinning. "*No.*"

"Captain!" Mala tried to pull me away but I threw him off.

*What if Huu-goh was with the humans?*

*What if he'd been locked outside the rooms?*

*They'd take him away from me.*

"He's out there—" I slammed my shoulder against the door, pain lancing up my side. "He's out there—he's—"

"*Roark*," Mala pulled at my shoulder again, and I snapped my teeth at him without thinking. He jolted back, fingers slipping away. The emergency lights flickered on, but the room was still far dimmer than normal. A fact that was hard to even notice as I continued to beat the door into submission.

The stars swam outside the windows, unmoving for now while the ship was stalled in space.

"He's—" I panted, claws raking down metal.

"I know."

"He's *out* there—" *Thud, thud.* More pain. More scratching. The damn metal barely gave beneath my fingertips. "He's out there—he's-out-there-he's-out-there-he's-out-there."

"Roark." A second voice. A second set of tendrils crept around my body in an attempt to subdue my frenzy. I fought them as I slammed against the door. By the time a third member of my crew joined in, however, I was lost. They yanked and tugged, their tendrils incapacitating me in a rainbow mass as the three of them dragged me to the cold, metal ground. My chest heaved, limbs icy as I twitched—attempting to get free even though the action was futile.

"He's out there—" I managed, voice brittle.

"I know," Mala said softly from above, his spots indigo with sorrow. "But you're no use to him when you're like *this*."

I didn't know how to *be* anything else.

But I needed to be.

I needed to pull myself together.

Needed to be their captain—even though it felt impossible.

I sucked in a breath, the rage and fear bleeding away as my body relaxed.

Each set of tendrils released me bit by bit, all of their faces tentative and nervous. The two cadets that had intervened, took a step back, averting their eyes out of respect as I lay on the ground, pathetic and sore, and heartsick.

"Come sit down," Mala urged, his tendrils the last to leave as they wrapped around my arms, attempting to pull me up.

"I'm fine," I assured him quietly when I was standing, ignoring the blood on my claws—my own—I shook off his touch as I made a beeline for the control panel. A cold sort of clarity washed over me. "Show me where they're boarding."

It seemed the pirates had managed to latch their ship onto us in such a way that they hadn't broken the gravity seal. Based on the size of the vessel that had docked, there were thirty of them at the most. I switched to the infrared cameras, anxiously awaiting signs of the luminescent blobs that were our invaders.

"Quiet," I instructed.

Immediately, the anxious chatter in the room settled into silence. "Turn up the volume." Thrash, the Sahrk that was sitting at the desk, did as he was told, tapping the button till the buzzing sound of the empty hallways filled the room.

This was torture.

The emergency protocols were meant to make interference impossible. To protect lives over products. But—that only worked when there weren't people outside the rooms. What if Huu-goh had been with the humans when this went down? He often was at this time. I couldn't shake the thought once it had taken root.

What if he was in the cargo hold? Where there were no doors.

What if they found him?

What if they took him from me?

*I will burn the universe down to find him.*

*Think, Roark. Think.*

*All is not lost.*

*This is just speculation.*

*He could be safe in the labs with Ushuu.*

And even if he wasn't, there were bound to be crew members who were still free. Enough of them and they could intercept the attackers. Sahrks were not violent by nature, but we could still fight. And fight well. A handful of us could easily incapacitate a group of pirates this size. Most species could not hold a candle to our strength and mass.

Just because I was trapped did not mean all the Sahrks aboard were.

*Thud, thud.*

That sounded like footsteps. Multiple sets, but it was impossible to tell who they were. Friend or foe, as I stared at the infrared screen and tried to discern how large the creatures approaching the camera were. When they passed by, I still had no idea who or what they were.

Down the hallways they went. We chased them on the cameras.

*Please be ours,* I prayed to the stars above.

To my father, who waited just beyond them.

*Let him be safe.*

*Protect him.*

"Can't believe our luck," one of the blobs grunted in Common. "Fifteen fucking humans." It was not the words I had wanted to hear. My prayers were not answered. He rounded a corner with the other two—who I could now assume were pirates—heading deeper into the ship.

"Seventeen," a smaller, reedier voice corrected.

"You saying I can't count?" the first voice huffed.

"I'm *saying* that there's seventeen," the second voice responded. "Fifteen from the auction. And two others that weren't standing in the line-up."

"What-the-fuck ever, asshole."

My blood boiled, hands curling into fists. Part of me—irrational as it was—wanted to reach out and smash the computer so I wouldn't have to hear them anymore.

"I liked the orange one," a third, whispering tone answered. The sound of it sent a chill racing up my spine, if his words had not. "With the spots."

"The orange one? I didn't see an orange one."

Huu-goh was the only orange-furred human. My stomach churned, and in the reflection on the screen, I could see that my spots were black, black, black.

"He was at the front when they boarded. Do you think his spots change color when he's…you know…aroused?" the third voice added on, as if his first words had not been enough.

"The fuck should I know?" reedy voice huffed.

"No one cares what you like, Brody," the first voice interjected. I had to bite my tongue so I wouldn't growl. If I met Brody, I would force-feed him his own eyeballs and tear his head from his body. He'd deserve it, for having looked at my Huu-goh.

"Boss said we could sample the merchandise if we wanted," Brody complained. "He said that we—"

Suddenly, the three spots became six.

They'd rounded a corner and I watched, stricken as the three pirates made garbled, pained sounds, and in quick succession their bodies hit the floor.

"Ay-hteen dow-n, only twehlve more to go!" a chipper voice said in human-speak.

I'd recognize that voice anywhere.

Huu-goh.

What—

What was he doing in the hallway—

Did Huu-goh just kill three pirates?

"My god, Captain," Mala said from beside me. I hadn't realized he'd been there at all, as focused on the pirates as I'd been. "You sure know how to pick them, don't you?"

"Wha—"

"How are we on few-ehl?" Huu-goh asked the other two blobs. One looked Sahrk-sized, which relieved me. And the other—no doubt, was Briar.

"Ai-vah got six more vai-els," Briar answered.

"Ruh-n back and get more from Ushuu," Huu-goh replied. There was command in his voice I'd never heard before. I didn't understand what they were talking about, but it was clearly something dangerous enough to incapacitate the pirates.

If I hadn't seen it with my own eyes, I wouldn't have believed it.

The large Sahrk at Huu-goh's side abandoned him to accompany Briar to the lab, and I shook as I stared at the single, solitary blob that was my mate. I couldn't blink for fear he'd disappear. He hummed our song under his breath—totally unaware that I could hear him—and yet somehow… soothing me anyway.

When the Sahrk and huu-man returned, Huu-goh directed them down the hall away from the bodies they'd just created.

He'd picked a good spot to fight back, as this hallway was the longest on the ship and the only direct route to the cargo bay and "the lake" at its deepest levels.

For the next hour, I watched as Huu-goh murdered pirate after pirate in cold blood. One by one, section of the hall by section of the hall. When they ran out of what he called "few-ehl" he'd send the others back for more.

The pirates that had not encountered the little group yet were confused. I could hear their chatter through the speakers. Confused as to why their comrades were not answering when they tried to contact them. But none…not a single pirate stood a chance.

Not when they were pitted against Huu-goh's brain.

It was silent for a while as Huu-goh and his entourage waited at the entrance to the corridor they'd worked their way down. They'd just felled what I was certain were the last of the pirates.

"That was thih-rty, I theenk," Huu-goh whispered into the otherwise quiet hallway. "What now?"

My head swam.

"I…cannot believe that just happened," Mala sounded flabbergasted. He'd been enraptured the entire time. "I…feel like I am dreaming."

I couldn't get a single word out, so I didn't try. I simply continued to stare.

"How do we get the lai-ts back on and the dohrs to open?" Huu-goh asked, turning his attention to the Sahrk beside him.

"We wihll need to detaa-ch the shihp that has bore-ded," the Sahrk that was with them responded in the same odd tongue the huu-mans favored.

"Kewl." I didn't understand why Huu-goh was saying his own last name, but I didn't try to. He often did that when he was excited. My thoughts were swimming as it was. "Can you do that?" he asked. "Briar wihll come with me to the he-hlm."

Where was he going?

I could understand most of what he said, but that last word, "he-hlm" was unfamiliar.

"No—" the Sahrk tried to argue. "Briar comes with me—"

"Dohn't tehst mai pay-shins," Huu-goh snapped, and though I did not understand what he'd said, the tone was clear.

The Sahrk did not argue again.

I did not blame him.

Instead, the three blobs separated. The two smallest turning right and heading upward through the hallways as the largest of them turned to the left.

"He's coming here," Mala said, staring at the little blips that were Huu-goh and Briar with fascination.

Mala was correct, Huu-goh was on his way here.

There was no denying that.

Despite the darkness, the little blob that was Huu-goh did not falter.

"Follow him."

Thrash flickered through the cameras as Huu-goh made his way to me. Corridor by corridor. Up, up, up he went.

The lights turned on. The real lights. And as Thrash adjusted the cameras accordingly and I saw my little love hopping down the last corridor, shoving his legs out of a hazmat suit, my hearts beat at what had to be an unhealthy pace.

The door to the helm slid open, and I turned, just in time to see Huu-goh enter the room.

His orange fur was wild all over his head. Puffy and sweaty, there were creases on his face from what—I did not know. Dressed in what he had told me was a "tenk top" with lace around its edges, and the tight pants he'd called "jeens" he was a sight to behold.

"Roark." He paused just inside the doorway, staring at me for a beat as I stared back.

I could hardly breathe, he was so beautiful. In an odd way this moment reminded me of the day we'd met. Though this time it was my turn to showcase vulnerability.

In a blink, I was across the room.

With no hesitation I smashed Huu-goh into the floor, cushioned by a cocoon of tendrils as I sobbed into his lovely, tiny chest. I had no tears, not like he did, but that did not mean I couldn't cry. Even if I'd half convinced myself I was not capable.

"Oh my sweet baybee," Huu-goh stroked over my fin, his tiny hands more soothing than they had any right to be. "I'm okay."

"Huu-goh."

His name was the only word I remembered. The only thing that *mattered* as I held him close. As I shook and shook and shook, and my hearts became whole once again. Right then, I was not a captain. I had no responsibilities. No rules. My discipline was shot.

All I was, was his.

And as I clutched him tight, melting beneath the torrent of tiny huu-man kisses I realized just how lucky that was.

How lucky I was that I had met him.

That he had turned my life around.

That this brilliant, stunning, wonderful man was mine and mine alone.

"I made it okay," Huu-goh whispered, an echo of the first promise I'd ever given him.

"I love you," I said. Three words I'd had Ushuu teach me in English the first lesson we'd had. Three words I hadn't been sure I was equipped to say. Three words that may not have been familiar to me—but I knew would resonate with Huu-goh.

I love you was a promise.

A promise that he would have no more lonely birthdays.

He would never feel invisible again.

He would be blissfully, wonderfully happy.

I love you meant I would rely on him when I could. Because we were equals. Because I trusted him. Because I was grateful that he'd given us another chance to have this. That he'd saved himself—when I could not.

I hadn't known I could love someone. Hadn't known I had it in me. But I did, and I could. Loving Huu-goh made me a better person. It made my world bright and my future full of possibility. And Mala had been right when he'd given me advice. Because loving Huu-goh was the easiest thing I'd ever done.

It was as natural as breathing.

"I love you," Huu-goh confessed, the words choked and wet. He was leaking again, but they were happy tears. At least—I thought they were, based on the smile on his face. "I'm so sorry," he said, smashing a kiss against my jaw. "This was all my fault."

"No," I said, because it hadn't been. "*No*."

"I love you," Huu-goh said again, and I initiated a deeper kiss. Flicked my tongue along those clever, wonderful lips, seeking entrance to the mouth of the man that had just given me the world.

Behind us, the Sahrks in the room applauded. It was embarrassing, and annoying—and wonderful all the same. Confused at first, I thought they were applauding us, and our kiss—and confessions. Though none of them spoke human-speak so that did not make sense.

But when I twisted a little, tongue still inside Huu-goh's mouth I realized they were cheering because of something entirely different.

Shaking, I pulled Huu-goh to his feet.

His human friend stood in the back of the room. I spared him a single glance, noting the glassiness of his gaze, before my attention was on Huu-goh once again.

"Come," I said, slinging him onto my shoulders so that he could see above the bodies that blocked the view.

Huu-goh made a startled sound, like he could not believe his eyes.

"Is that…?"

Which was fair.

The first time I'd seen this sight I, too, had been shocked.

"It is *home*," I told him, my hearts thumping, my tendrils tightly wrapped around his legs. He held my fin in his grip, staring out the giant wall of glass at the front of the helm. Beyond it, the stars glimmered as they always did.

But our planet—our home—stole the show.

Remarkable in its beauty, the pink and green planet swirled between constellations. Far still, a day or so's journey—but visible.

"Mai god," Huu-goh said, leaning his cheek on the top of my head and staring out at the world that would be ours in just a few short hours. "It's beautiful." The applause continued, cheering echoing through the room—for home, for Huu-goh, for Osheania.

"It is," I agreed, wishing I could see his face and the view of our planet all at once.

Huu-goh and I stood there for a long time, tucked together like we were one disjointed being, staring as Osheania grew closer and closer and the stars blurred by.

"Home," Huu-goh echoed, a reverence to his voice that only made me love him even more than I already did.

"*Our* home," I agreed.

Huu-goh and I decided to return to our rooms early. Normally, I'd spend time preparing the ship for landing. And in light of the bodies on board, I should've been up for hours organizing where to store them until we could land.

A primal part of me wanted to see the evidence that my Huu-goh was the little beast I'd always known he was.

But…even more than that, I wanted peace. I wanted to feel him in my arms. I wanted to hold him. Wanted to…be with him—the way I'd feared I never would again.

Mala took over for me, shooing me off as Ushuu wandered into the helm—paler than usual, but chipper. Both of them thanked Huu-goh. Mala in our tongue, Ushuu in his—and Huu-goh's lovely cheeks turned a vibrant, adorable pink as he waved them off, embarrassed, like what he'd done was no big deal at all.

On our way down the hallway, we passed many Sahrks exiting the recently unlocked doorways. It seemed word of Huu-goh's victory had spread already, and all bowed their heads to him, saluting—as they would me.

"Why are they doing that?" Huu-goh asked after the tenth Sahrk we passed offered him the highest respect.

"It is to thank you," I responded, hoping he understood. "You are…" I wasn't sure I knew the right word to describe how they must feel. "You are respect," I told him, grateful when I found one I hoped…fit.

I figured I must have gotten it right because the sound Huu-goh made was positively delightful.

We were halfway to our rooms when Huu-goh seemed to remember something.

"Briar!" he gasped out, holding my fin tight. "Briar. We need to find Briar."

Rather than argue, I let him take the lead.

Hours passed. The entire crew was on high alert.

But no one found Huu-goh's new human friend or the Sahrk that had helped him.

As a last ditch effort, Huu-goh and I returned to the helm to search the cameras. They were a live feed, and did not record more than a few hours, so there wasn't much time to check them. As we sifted through footage with the help of Thrash, Mala sat in my seat and directed the rest of the Sahrks in preparation for landing.

"I thought I told you to go," Mala laughed when he finally acknowledged us. He spoke in our native tongue, but Huu-goh seemed to understand the tone, because he rolled his eyes good-naturedly.

So far all we'd seen was Briar exiting the helm and disappearing down the halls. It was like he knew exactly where to move so that he could not be seen by the cameras.

"Huu-goh's friend is missing," I told Mala. I was unsurprised that he had not heard. Though word had spread, Mala had been focused on the duties I would normally be attending to.

Mala's spots went yellow and then gray with concern. "Missing?"

Thrash made a startled sound, catching all of our attention.

And the sight I saw when I glanced at the cameras made my blood run cold. "What—" I swore softly in my own tongue. Ushuu approached, frowning at all of us in confusion before his own spots paled and his eyes caught on the image playing on the screen.

"Is that…" Ushuu started.

"Kael."

I would not forget his face. I could not. Not when it had haunted me for years. My old roommate. The Sahrk that had died first, that day, all those years ago. Only now…his dark gray surface was littered in scars, and he was far older than the last time I'd seen him. It took a lot to cause scarring like that on a Sahrk. But Kael was no normal Sahrk. He was a hybrid. A pod-child like I was, but mixed with aliens not of our planet. His surface texture was unique. Fuzzier.

The playful man I'd once known was unrecognizable.

"He was the one helping us…and I didn't even notice." Ushuu sounded horrified, and Mala moved to soothe him before I could. "How is he alive?"

"I do not know," I replied, numb as I watched as Kael held the door open to the bay. He must've hacked into the system somehow—knowledge of its inner workings allowing him to dock against us without triggering alarm.

"There!" Huu-goh's sweet words in English startled me out of my thoughts as his pale friend entered the screen. Briar glanced both ways, a bag over his shoulder stuffed full. "No," Huu-goh said softly, wilting at my side as he watched Briar follow the Sahrk through the docking bay and off our vessel. "No," he repeated, sounding defeated.

I squeezed him close, staring at the screen in shock for a few more minutes as the footage continued to play.

"How long ago was that?" I asked Thrash in my own tongue, soothing my sweet mate as he pressed his face to my chest.

"An hour or so, sir," Thrash said.

"I'm sorry," I told Huu-goh, switching back to his native tongue so he could understand. He'd relayed to me most of what had happened but there had been a lot of words I had not understood. Later, I'd ask Ushuu to translate.

Or…

When we reached Osheania—I'd make use of the translators available at the visitor center, though I still planned on surprising Huu-goh with permanent implants as soon as possible. The thought made me giddy— even as it filled me with guilt for being so excited to speak with him again, given the circumstances.

"I'm sorry," I told Huu-goh again, stroking a hand down his back and nuzzling his head. He sighed, defeated.

"It's okay," he said softly, though he pulled away, rising from his seat. He turned to look at me, waiting expectantly. I rose just as quickly as he had, sweeping him into my arms again as we made our way out of the control room and toward the barracks.

Huu-goh and I snuggled for what felt like hours.

We showered together.

We lay in bed, staring at the ceiling, our limbs tangled, our personal stars glimmering above.

And inside, my hearts thumped as one.

One, solid, beautiful beat.

For my mate, for my love, for my little huu-man.

The cleverest being in the entire cosmos. The echo of my own heart.

The man that I couldn't wait to spend the rest of my life with.

The man who had taught me not to be afraid to embrace the unfamiliar. Because sometimes…the things that were most unknown were also the most wonderful.

# EPILOGUE

## HUGO

## THREE YEARS LATER

**THREE BEAUTIFUL YEARS HAD PASSED** since the first day I'd stepped foot on Osheania, and I still couldn't believe my luck. That I could be here—in this place that belonged in a children's story book, and not real life.

The skies were a pale mint green. And the grass was pinker than cotton candy. Somehow, even pinker than my mate's surface was. With a temperate climate, lavender sunsets, and a metropolis full of people so friendly they seemed unreal, this place truly was paradise.

The best part about Osheania had to be how easy it was to find translators. At least—that's what I told Roark when we'd entered the visitor center to register me and the rest of the humans with the government, and the first thing they'd done was hand us all headsets.

I still wanted the permanent one, like Briar had, and I told Roark as much. To which he'd said he'd "take care of it."

It was…humbling honestly, his care and devotion.

Especially when it began to sink in that I wouldn't have to give him up. And that my newfound freedom was mine to keep.

When we'd left the center, it had been with strict orders to visit the Capitol next. The other humans and I needed to turn in our registration so that we could gain the citizenship that would give all of us—the unmated too—access to healthcare and government housing.

Roark and I had been at the head of the procession. And the Sahrks that did not have families of their own on the planet accompanied us. It seemed the crew had become quite attached to the humans during their time on board.

Some had even offered lodgings for a few of them.

It was a long day.

Roark and I hadn't finished the paperwork till well after what I'd assumed was "midnight." And by the time we did, most of the humans in the lobby were fast asleep in their seats. The receptionist had been as fascinated with them as most of the Sahrks I'd met had been, and she'd offered us a pile of blankets that we divied out.

The Capitol building wasn't all that friendly. Which was to be expected. I wasn't sure what the stone it was carved from was called—only that it reminded me of marble back home. Solid and chilly as Roark and I curled up with the others on the floor, too tired to do more than succumb to sleep.

I didn't see our new home until after we'd made sure all the humans had places to stay. Permanent places, that were not the cold floor of the

Capitol. By the time we'd entered the shuttle that would take us to Roark's house, we were both running on fumes.

"Huu-goh," he'd said softly, stroking over my cheek with one, careful claw.

"Mmm," I'd mumbled, leaning against his shoulder as the city below us sped by. It was my third time in a shuttle—and it was no less cool than the first—but I was genuinely so fucking exhausted it was hard to maintain excitement.

Tall, round buildings swam beneath us.

W'aevel, the capital of Osheania, where Roark lived was massive. Easily the size of New York City—or maybe larger, if I guessed based on square footage. The buildings were as tall as the ones on Sha'hPihn, but as Ushuu had promised—much friendlier-looking.

Sahrks were kind.

That was the first thing I'd noticed as I was introduced to the population outside our little bubble. Everyone we'd met had been gentle and curious. We were not met with suspicion, despite being the first "aliens" that most people on the planet had ever seen.

Roark told me they didn't travel often, and that was true.

The reason his vessel was so large was because he was the main—and only—transporter for the tech and birthing pods that were difficult to build on the planet. And those sparkly gems I'd fallen in love with at the mines? Fueled them, among other things. Roark had filled me in with military precision, while we were in the lobby at the Capitol. He'd explained a basic history of the planet, a history of the species as a whole, and why exactly his job was important.

It was all stuff I'd wanted to know—but never had the chance to ask.

And I hung on his every word as he filled out the piles of import and citizenship paperwork. Apparently, to immigrate and find asylum on Osheania you needed a sponsor. Roark had offered to sponsor every last one of the humans, but his crew had stepped forward to help.

That in itself was not boggling.

You know what was?

The fact that the Sahrk species had *females.*

Which was…a shock to discover—as I'd never seen one before. They were far larger than their male counterparts, easily standing at fifteen, maybe even *twenty* feet tall. And they were far less colorful. Most were a beige-y pale shade that made them stand out even more in a city so full of pastels.

The first time I'd seen one, I'd literally tripped.

Roark had informed me that there weren't many of them left after The Great Calamity had struck. There'd been a mural on the wall at the Capitol that showed what had been the saddest depiction of hunger and sickness I'd ever seen. He'd told me that was why the birthing pods had become more and more important as years passed. That once, they had been a viable option—and now they were integral to the planet's survival.

Before we left, Roark had made sure that every last human was vaccinated against the illness—and others—that were common on planet. And I'd finally received the check-up he'd been so desperately wanting me to get.

Apparently, I was no longer malnourished—because of the bambuu Roark had been feeding me. It had been good news. Which I was more than a little glad for. Roark had insisted the doctor be as thorough as he could, and I couldn't be angry.

Not when only a day previously I'd spent a good chunk of the day handling poison.

Only when I was in the clear had Roark relaxed and decided it was time we went home.

I'd been exhausted—my arm sore from being injected—but my head was full of fun new facts as we'd made our way across the city. Below us, I'd sleepily ogled the balconies that decorated all of the residential buildings. Sahrks swam inside the pools that took up the entirety of them. Pool toys, parties, celebrations exploded colorful and bright wherever I looked.

It seemed the whole city was celebrating the safe return of their captain and his crew.

I hadn't realized what a big deal Roark was.

Not until he'd explained the purpose of his supply runs.

And it was with new respect and admiration for him that I'd snuggled into his side and admired the place that I now called home. Creatures that resembled fish and Roark called "Feesh" floated in the air—as high up as we were—fanning their fin-like wings as they flapped along by the windows.

"Tired?" Roark had asked me, still gently stroking my cheek.

"Yes," I'd agreed, melting into him even more. "So tired."

"Excited?"

"So excited!" I'd jerked a little, and the translator I wore nearly fell off. It was a little finicky up in the air like this. But the city was equipped with signal towers that gave most places access to the devices. Roark had told me that fact genuinely surprised him, considering they rarely, if ever had space visitors.

I was too grateful to question it though, glad that my luck was still looking up as the shuttle paused at our stop, and Roark rose to offer me a hand up. I was so tired I swayed, and he'd scooped me into his arms so I wouldn't have to walk.

Down the street we went. A quiet street. So close to the edge of the city that it didn't feel like a part of it at all. Tall drooping lavender trees lined the peaceful cobblestone drive. A few fat frogs—biggest fucking frogs I'd ever seen, omg, the size of bulldogs—hopped across the road. Roark had barked out a laugh when I'd jerked upright, staring at them in fascination.

They were as shiny and as pastel as everything else here. Roark, because he was Roark, had allowed me to watch them hop until they disappeared inside the pink bushes. Everything was opposite here. All the "greenery" seemed to be comprised of a variety of pinks and purples of varying color intensity.

When we'd reached the end of the driveway, Roark's home was not what I'd expected.

It was bigger, for one.

More of a mansion than anything else.

At least—that's what I'd thought as we approached a building that was easily six stories tall, but was clearly not an apartment building like the others we'd passed in the city. It was made of what looked like baby-pink stucco, and there were bulbous purple vines trailing up the front. The structure itself wasn't too dissimilar to what you might see on Earth. It was less round than some of the other buildings I'd observed, and there were doors and windows.

It was more than a little relieving, I'll admit that.

Not that I'd mind a super alien-looking home—I just…I mean…

It was nice not to have to adjust to one more thing.

I'd quickly realized that while this was Roark's house—it would not be where we were staying. At least, when the front door opened and fifteen or more full-grown Sahrk's spilled out. Following after the adults had to be the cutest creatures I'd ever seen. Children—my first Sahrk children—scurried between their legs, thumping across the lawn to greet us.

A lot of the kids were my size, which was embarrassing to say the least, but no less fascinating as the group of people crowded around us.

There were so many of them I'd lost count.

It was a testament to how tired I was that it took me as long as it did to realize that the adults were Roark's siblings. The other children that had been raised at the orphanage. And he...fuck. My big softie had built a house for all of them to raise children of their own.

Roark grunted in greeting, as stoic as ever. He'd shared a few words, but that was it. A simple handful, as he butted snouts with a few of them, before saying his goodbyes and promising to properly introduce me after we'd had some rest.

The children were as curious as Earth kids were. Because a few of them latched onto my toes, their spots green. I didn't fault them, in fact, I chuckled as their snort-y little noses puffed hot air on my legs, teeth far too close for comfort.

Roark rumbled, a low menacing warning, and the children just continued to giggle. They clearly were not afraid of him.

When the fanfare had ended, the crowd watched on as Roark led me around the back of the large home and through what had to be the prettiest garden I'd ever seen. Full of blossoms so large they could've been melons—striped and lovely.

There was a cottage past the garden.

Much smaller than the main house, and with a lovely cobblestone path of its own. It lay tucked between a smattering of large trees. Their leaves were so pale and puffy they looked like cotton candy as they swayed toward us, the twinkling of a little waterfall trickling into the small pond right outside the front door.

One of the frog-like creatures had sat on a lily pad in the center of the pond. It blinked one eye, then the other, its tongue launching out to catch a fat bug, before pulling it into his mouth.

"I love him," I'd told Roark immediately, totally captivated.

He'd laughed. "I knew you would," he'd said softly, adjusting his grip on my body as we climbed the little steps to the front door. The house was far bigger than a cottage on Earth would be to accommodate his size. But it was cozy.

Cozy and perfect—exactly the kind of home I'd always wanted.

When we'd entered it was clear that one of Roark's "siblings" had been maintaining it while he was away. There wasn't a hint of dust in sight. Nor was there any clutter. Just like his room on the ship, however, constellations and posters lined the walls—making it obvious how much of a space-nerd he really was.

I'd taken it all in with astonishment, though my eyes were already drifting.

Roark was simply…comfortable.

He always had been.

"Rest," he'd hummed, leading me through the front room, down a hallway, and to the back where a large, lovely bedroom lay. In the center was a bed—just like the one on the ship—and beside it was a nightstand, again, just like the one on the ship.

Roark was a creature of habit after all.

He'd stripped down and didn't even take us to the shower before we snuggled into the mattress, the long journey behind us. As my eyes had drooped, and Roark's steady breathing lulled me into a sense of calm, I'd gazed at the pool that took up half the room, and melted.

For the first time in my life, I'd found a home.

A real home.

And someone that loved me just as fiercely as I loved them.

Our wedding ceremony had been the stuff of fantasies.

Everyone had come.

And by everyone—I mean literally *everyone*.

And yet Roark only had eyes for me the entire night.

He'd swung me around the dance floor, as awkward as he'd been at the ball we'd attended during our travels. And neither of us had cared what a mess we made of the steps—as we'd mimicked the others and enjoyed the festivities the night had to offer.

Apparently Roark had been preparing our ceremony before we'd even left Sha'hPihn.

Which was…flattering to say the least.

There were a lot of cultural things I was still getting used to at that point. And I'd been pleasantly surprised that the wedding ceremony itself hadn't been all that different than an Earth ceremony. Later, I'd found out that was because Roark had done his research.

Even going so far as to contact A&R to get details, as well as surprise me with permanent translators for the both of us. At that time, he'd also requested more information about Earth customs—though I hadn't learned that for long after our ceremony had passed.

I'd repaired the two broken translators Roark had gifted me on our trip through space as a wedding gift. Neither of us needed them, but I knew he'd appreciate the sentiment all the same. They were a symbol of what we'd been through, a broken communication barrier mended. I intended to give them to him in the morning, after we'd both had adequate rest.

"Huu-goh," Roark had said as the night wound to a close, the guests giggling and drinking, and falling all over the garden in happy, drunken stupors. Humans hung onto their Sahrk counterparts, clusters and pairs of the mix of species dotting the lawn.

"Mmm?" I'd sighed, rubbing my cheek against his bare chest.

Rather than force him into human clothing again, I'd opted to wear what was traditional for his species. Which meant we were both shirtless, wearing gossamer pants and crowns made of flowers picked by hand.

"Huu-goh," Roark had repeated, his voice lower than before. For the first time since I'd met him, he'd also partaken in enough alcohol to get a little buzz going. It'd faded by this point, but the flush was still on his skin. "I want you."

"Oh." My cheeks went hot. "Bed?" I'd urged, wasting no time as I leaned up to place a kiss on the underside of his chin.

Roark had hummed in agreement, already walking us toward the path that would lead us to our home. When he'd shifted me into the other arm to unlock the door, I'd felt his cocks push against my ass.

Ushuu, in preparation for that night, had given me something…useful.

Something I'd made sure to partake in right before Roark and I had hit the dance floor—in case it needed time to work. It was a tonic of some kind. Something he'd been working on with a few others since the humans had arrived on the planet.

He'd called it a wedding gift.

And I couldn't help but feel like he was right when Roark had pushed me onto the bed with a grunt, and my hole clenched—wet—though I hadn't touched it since the last time he'd been up there. Not that that had been all that long ago.

Fuck.

"Roark," I'd murmured softly, staring at him—at his black eyes—and the way his lovely chest heaved. He'd licked his lips, long tongue snaking out and down, to trail over my chest. With a few, pointed flicks, he got my nipples to perk up.

He'd become an expert at that.

He knew exactly how to get my body to react.

And he enjoyed my flush—more than anything.

"I have a surprise for you," I'd told him, because I did. "Courtesy of Ushuu."

"A surprise?" He'd echoed, intrigued.

"Let me just—" I'd pushed at his chest and he went willingly, still bracketing my body with his warm bulk as I shimmied out of my pants, then reached for the hem of his. He'd made an inquisitive sound as I shoved them down, biting my lip when "Pushypush" and "Politeypants" wiggled toward me.

Always so eager.

Jesus.

"What is the surprise?"

Roark was impatient. I couldn't blame him. I'd kinda trained him to be that way. Always surprising him with lingerie and toys—and new ideas when it came to sex. I'd Pavlov's dogged him.

"We've done a lot together…" I'd started, pleased when he grunted in agreement. "But there's one thing…we both want—that you've been too scared to try."

Roark knew what I was talking about immediately. He'd studied me, trepidation and excitement written all over his face. I knew his fear came from not wanting to hurt me. But…that's where Ushuu's present came in.

It was supposed to slick the way. To soften the passage. And to allow something much, much bigger than a human cock to slip inside.

Spreading my legs, I'd placed a hand beneath my knee to pull myself open. Roark had growled, ducking his head to get a better look. The sound that left him was ragged—and high-pitched. A needy whine, as his claws dug into the mattress.

"What is—"

"Ushuu gave me something," I'd told him. "So that you can fit."

It had taken Roark a second to process that. And when he did—it was like a switch had flipped. I was glad. As much as I liked the slow build and the teasing he enjoyed, I'd been wanting this for so long I didn't have the patience to wait any longer.

He'd had me on my knees faster than I could blink.

His tentacle-dicks were slick and wet as they dragged over my thighs, over the curve of my ass, and then fought to get inside my crack. "Do you need stretching?" He'd asked, the heat of his breath at my ear sending my mind spinning.

"No," I'd gasped out—because I didn't.

Still though, because he was Roark—he had to tease.

Tendrils, not his cocks, slid between the slick at my hole and gently pushed inside. He'd been training me, steadily, surely—for this moment. We'd been building up to this. And we would've done it, even without Ushuu's serum.

So it felt second nature to let him slip inside, the slurp-wiggle of a tendril growing thicker and thicker as it stretched me. "You are so wet for me," Roark's voice was reverent.

"I am," I'd agreed, because I was.

"How?"

I'd get into it later. But I just wanted to enjoy this. "Science," I'd said, making a little explosion motion with my hand. Roark had laughed, and his tendril drove deeper. Deep enough it pushed against my prostate and thoughts of science officially fled my head.

It felt so strange. In a good way. But strange all the same. The wriggle, swell of something far more dexterous than a dick spreading me wide. When a second tendril had slipped in with the first, I'd thrashed, arching my back and pressing into it.

"Stars above, you are needy," Roark had said, again, like it was a miracle. "So…beautiful. Look at how pink you are here," he'd purred softly as he stared at where he was fucking me open. "We match."

The squelching noise was filthy. So fucking filthy.

A third tendril had tapped at my stretched rim, rubbing almost politely, like it was requesting entrance.

"F-fuck," I'd whimpered as it began to wiggle its way inside with the other two. On and on, it went. Three became four, then five—and I was stretched so wide I could hardly get a breath in, panting into the mattress as Roark's tongue squeezed so tight around my neck my vision swam.

When his tongue had retreated and his tendrils slid free, I sobbed.

"You are ready now," he'd decided.

I'd left a rather sizable pool of drool on the mattress, but hardly noticed as I nodded. Smearing my cheek into it, I glanced over at him. He'd looked so…serious as he shuffled into place, one massive pink hand grabbing my hip and angling my body up as his other hand aimed his thinner cock tip at my hole.

It was tapered, just like his tentacles were—but that was where the similarities ended.

Roark's cocks were as wet as my hole was. The pointed tentadick poked and prodded, slipping an inch inside as Roark gaped down at my ass like he was seeing God for the first time. He'd been panting, his nostrils flaring, tongue hanging out of his fang-y mouth.

He hadn't seemed capable of doing anything at that moment other than staring at my ass, and what he was putting inside it.

I'd never seen him like this.

Sure, I'd gotten the beast out of him a couple times—but never…never like this.

"You are so tight," his voice was low and brittle. "You are so—"

He'd pressed in a little deeper. And that was when the burn had started. Not in a bad way—in a good way. In a way that had made my lashes feel heavy, and my balls draw up tight. The feeling of Roark entering me was good. So fucking good. Especially when that first sucker popped in. It'd convulsed against my inner walls, sucking at them, pulling the tissue snug enough it had made my eyes roll.

Better than that, however, was the expression on Roark's face when I peeked at him again.

The wonder.

The hunger.

The fact that I was pretty sure for the first time in his life there wasn't a single thought in his head. No worries. Nothing.

Just the need to get this dick—and then the other—inside his mate.

Deeper, deeper, he'd pressed. And with every inch, his reaction had grown stronger. His panting was loud, his big hips beginning to grind, these needy little swivels, like he simply couldn't help himself. "I am…I am…" Roark had managed, voice hoarse. "My cock is inside…of you—"

His second dick had fanned along the curve of my ass, suckers pulling tight, and leaving hickeys in their wake. It'd wriggled, fighting toward my crack like it wanted to sink inside beside the other.

I'd almost told him no.

But when Roark had grabbed it and began feeding its pointed tip alongside the other, I didn't want to.

"Oh—" His head had dropped back, the corded line of his neck flexing as both tentacles pushed an inch inside me. Then two inches. Then three. I had been so full I couldn't do anything but lie still and take it. My dick was leaking—making a mess all over my thighs and stomach, streaks of cum spilling free as Roark pushed and pushed and pushed.

When he was halfway inside, all I could do was breathe. Tears smeared my cheeks, and the pool of drool beneath my mouth was a lake at that point, as my thighs strained and Roark shuddered behind me.

"Oh," he'd managed again, pulling out till only the tapered tips of his cocks remained, before pushing back inside, slow and deliberate. "*Oh.*" Both his hands had squeezed my hips, biting in as he pulled out, only to push back in again, harder this time. "Huu-goh," he'd moaned, undulating. "You feel so good."

Once he'd got going, he couldn't seem to stop.

And I hadn't wanted him to.

I'd wanted to stay speared on his cocks for the rest of all time.

I'd never been happier.

Ever.

In all my life, as I was right then with Roark fucking into me like a beast in heat. His thrusts had grown more erratic as he got closer, and one of his cocks slipped free—so he could pound deeper. He'd grunted, tongue lolling, his eyes empty of anything but lust as he moved his grip from my hips to my back, pushing me flat to the mattress so he could really go to town pounding into my ass. My hole wouldn't stop clutching at him, slick and open any time he pulled free. The ridged texture of his suckers popping in and out as they clung to my inner walls.

"Uh, uh, uh," I'd gasped out with every thrust, my hands lax, my entire body lax—actually. Like I had no muscles or bones at all. "Uh—"

"Take it," Roark had murmured—probably the dirtiest thing he'd ever said. "Take it—" His hand had tightened, pushing harder into me as his pace picked up. Faster, faster. "Please—please—"

When he'd spilled it was with a broken roar. The flood of his cum was leaking out before he'd even finished, sluicing down my thighs and onto the bed. And then he was pulling free—and I was empty, empty, empty— full, full, full, because his second cock was pushing inside now, ready to take its turn.

By the time that one had finished too, I'd cum at least three times myself, entirely untouched. The mattress had been a sticky mess when Roark's tentacle slipped free. He'd keened, the lax appendages tapping my ass, as if to say thank you—before falling limp in a sticky smear right behind my balls.

I couldn't move. Not even a muscle.

Which was why I'd barely done more than twitch when Roark had sunk down between my thighs and proceeded to eat his cum right out of my hole—along with my own natural slick—until it was empty, and I'd cum a fourth time, totally dry.

He was gentle as he cleaned me up—coming back to himself slowly. Long, warm swipes of his tongue cleansed worst of my sweat as he'd stroked over my body. He'd rubbed feeling back into my limbs, whispered sweet nothings into my hair. Petted me, pampered me, and groomed every inch of my body.

"Did you like it?" Roark had asked when the sheets were cleaned and I was snuggled inside a warm pink cocoon of his making. I'd hummed, blissed-out and ready to rest. *Answer him*, I'd reminded myself, *or he'll get worried.*

"I think I'm in heaven," I'd told him, honestly. "My ass won't stop twitching."

He'd snorted out a laugh, bending down to snuffle against my cheek. His tongue flickered out again, long and wet, to "kiss" my lips, before dipping inside them. I'd sucked on it gratefully, lashes still wet from how much I'd cried.

When he pulled free, because he was a sweetheart, he'd checked on me again, "Did you like it? We do not have to do it again if you did not—"

"I loved it," I'd said immediately. "I love you," I'd added, twisting to meet his gaze, because this felt important. "We should do that again," I'd said, my ass still loose and gaping. "Maybe not every day—because holy shit, I don't think I can walk after that—but often."

Roark had barked, his eyes squinting into the sweet crescents I loved so much. "Okay," he'd said, nuzzling my cheek.

"What about you?" I'd asked, surprised when my limbs worked well enough that one of my hands could rise to stroke his big pink cheek. "Did you like it?"

"I would erect a statue in your honor if I could," Roark had promised. "I would build you a chapel with my bare limbs. To show my gratitude to your body."

"Oh jeez," I'd snickered, nuzzling his snout with my nose. "Please don't do that. My ass appreciates a different kind of worship more."

Roark looked pleased with himself. "Noted," he said softly. And then, "I loved it," he'd added. "In case that wasn't clear."

"Good," I'd told him, pecking his snout for good measure.

"I love you," he'd replied, the same way I had just spoken to him.

I'd grinned, unable to help myself. "I'm so happy you're my mate," I'd hummed, because it was true.

Roark's expression had softened even more. "You are the cleverest creature in all the galaxy," he'd murmured with reverence. He'd told me that at least a thousand times since he'd bought us permanent translators, and I didn't think that would ever get old. "The most beautiful being in the cosmos."

"Mhmm, *okay*," I'd snorted, though I didn't tell him he was wrong.

Because even though I knew realistically, there wasn't any way that I was—

When Roark looked at me, I sure felt that way.

Three years had passed since then. Three blissful years. Three years full of laughter, of happiness—of birthdays. Birthdays Roark planned and executed with military precision dedicated to my happiness. I had never been more pampered, more appreciated, more adored in all my life.

He bought me a tamed Fruhg of my own—the same creatures I'd admired that first day. And I often spent mornings with him and our pet, walking it around the property, and playing with the children who came out to talk to us.

They found me fascinating—even after all this time. But everyone was polite. I'd made a few human friends too, over the years. Some of them had mates of their own now, and even children.

Apparently the birth-pods were capable of merging the DNA of multiple species. You'd think Sahrks and humans would make odd looking children, but they didn't. For the most part, a lot of them looked human actually. Just with…quite a bit more teeth, and spots to match. They were as varied in color palette as their parents, but all were fucking adorable.

Roark had reserved a spot for us in the birth-pods after our next trip to space—and I was both excited and nervous for our future.

I wanted to raise children with him. I knew he'd be a fantastic father— and he assured me that he thought I would too. But the idea of taking the child to space with us when we went out supply-gathering made me nervous.

I figured…between the two of us we'd manage to keep them safe, however.

And it was trust, and faith in both Roark and myself that settled any fear I might have.

Together we could do anything we set our minds to.

I'd once thought, years ago when we'd been first courting, that Roark was an "effort" kinda guy, with a capital E. And here I was, a galaxy away, and that had only proven more and more correct the longer he was my husband. My parents had made me think that love was a cold, conditional thing.

But I knew now just how incorrect that had been.

Love wasn't cold.

Love was *soft* and *warm* and *wonderful.*

It was squishy and pink.

It was a safe space when you needed one.

It was gentle, like Roark was.

Protective.

I'd been wrong, all those years ago, when I'd thought Roark would be the first to attend my parties. He wasn't the first to arrive, he was the one that *planned* them. He didn't just buy me flowers, and pizza, and cake—he wrote me love notes too. Awkward, horribly written love notes—that were far from eloquent, but meant the world all the same.

He didn't just play my dumb games—he forced the others to play too.

He was the first to tell me happy birthday at the stroke of midnight.

His love was a silent, protective thing. He didn't ask for anything in return. He didn't ask for praise. Didn't need recognition. He simply loved me…calmly, stoically, seriously. Like loving me was the single greatest mission of his life.

Roark had promised me the day we'd met that he would make things "okay."

But he'd lied.

My life was as far from "okay" as it had ever been.

Because it was full of happiness, in a way I'd never known was possible.

And I had my big, pink, squishy alien to blame for that.

# DEAR READER,

Thank you so much for reading Roark and Hugo's story! Creating this world has been such a joy, and this book is my love letter to anyone who enjoys campy fun, not taking fiction too seriously, and Pretty Woman.

What started as a lighthearted and hilarious journey took a more heartfelt and meaningful turn than I ever anticipated. Roark and Hugo safeguard each other's happiness in such a special way, and giving them the HEA they so deeply deserved was an honor.

This book took longer to create than I expected, but I wouldn't change a thing. It came together exactly as it was meant to, at the perfect time. Thank you for your patience, your sweet comments, and your motivation throughout this process. Your excitement—especially for Roark (Team Shark Daddy 5ever!)—kept me going. I can't wait to explore more stories in this series, especially Briar's and how he met Grimm.

This year has been challenging for all of us, and I want you to know how grateful I am for your support. You've stuck with me, and your love has made my world a brighter, more beautiful place.

Special thanks to Molly for making my books look like magic, to DL for untangling my brain knots, and to my incredible alpha readers for keeping me sane and inspired. I love you all so much.

Thank you to everyone who contributed their time, energy, and love to this project; you are all my dear friends. And most of all, thank you to the reader, because without you, the creation of this story would have been meaningless. I write the words, but you are the ones who bring the story to life. Each and every one of you is priceless. Thank you for falling in love with these characters alongside me. I love all of you so much.

If you'd like to keep in touch with me and get access to exclusive mini-fics, character art, author updates, and more, sign up for my newsletter at **WWW.FAELOVESART.COM**. Or join my Facebook group, **FAE'S FAVES**! You can also find me on Instagram **@FAELOVESART**.

All shares, comments, reviews, and discussion of **I'M NOT YOUR PET!** are encouraged and appreciated!

Happy Holidays, and I'll see you in 2025!

# READ MORE IN THE EXTRA! EXTRATERRESTRIAL SERIES:

# ABOUT THE AUTHOR

**FAE** is obsessed with anything romance. From a young age she realized she had a passion for falling in love over and over again. She loves to tell stories through both her art and writing. With a passion for classical monsters, meet-cutes, and contemporary romance, you can often find her with her nose stuck in a book and her pet corgi, Champa, on her lap.

She currently resides in Utah with her amazing husband and her collection of squishmallows. When you read one of her books you can expect to find love stories between humans, monsters, and loveable assholes that will make you laugh (and cry) as you get lost in their worlds for just a little. Every story comes with a happy ever after guarantee.

*Find her online at:*
**WWW.FAELOVESART.COM**